Wishing on Trains

Michaela collapsed back into her seat.

'If we hurry,' she panted, 'we can catch it at the bridge and if we go under at the same time as it crosses the road, we can wish.'

'I know,' said Antony. 'I know.' He put his foot on the accelerator and pulled out to pass a car towing a caravan with the touch of recklessness Michaela somehow always seemed to inspire. The train had disappeared now behind the hills and the countryside was once more swamped in blackness, only their own headlamps lighting up the grey scrub and bushes at the side of the road.

'There it is!' shrieked Florida, entering into the spirit of things and nearly startling Antony out of his wits for the second time that day. 'Go!'

*Also by Alison Lowry
and available in Mandarin*

Natural Rhythm

Alison Lowry

Wishing
· on Trains ·

Mandarin

A Mandarin Paperback
WISHING ON TRAINS

First published in Great Britain 1994
by William Heinemann Ltd
This edition published 1995
by Mandarin Paperbacks
an imprint of Reed Consumer Books Ltd
Michelin House, 81 Fulham Road, London SW3 6RB
and Auckland, Melbourne, Singapore and Toronto

Copyright © Alison Lowry 1994
The author has asserted her moral rights

A CIP catalogue record for this title
is available from the British Library
ISBN 0 7493 1645 4

Printed and bound in Great Britain by
BPC Paperbacks Ltd
A member of
The British Printing Company Ltd

This book is sold subject to the condition
that it shall not, by way of trade or otherwise,
be lent, resold, hired out, or otherwise circulated
without the publisher's prior consent in any form
of binding or cover other than that in which
it is published and without a similar condition
including this condition being imposed
on the subsequent purchaser.

For Howie

· 1 ·

'The last time I saw Roger he was standing at the side of the road with a plastic bag over his head.'

Michaela was arranging the dozen long-stemmed red roses Simon had sent her by cramming them into the neck of an empty low-fat milk bottle and cursing at the tough brown thorns.

'What sort of plastic bag?' Susan asked.

'There's only eleven,' Janus said. 'I think you should complain.'

Michaela licked a scribble of red blood from her index finger. She put her head on one side, looked at the still tightly folded blooms and felt vague dissatisfaction. 'It was a big one,' she said, not turning. 'The sort you put your garbage out in. With the name of the municipality stencilled on the side.' She had a way of cutting through the many strands of simultaneous conversations that had swung about this kitchen over the years and always responding to Susan's needs first. In the same way as she had perfected the deft lunge with the pacifier in the early days when Susan had been a terrible glaring baby on the kitchen table, sitting bolt upright and imperious in her bouncing chair. Perhaps it had paid off and that was why she had turned into such a placid, unruffled child. Or perhaps she was as much like Mater as everyone said she was.

'Appropriate,' Susan said now, gloomily. 'Roger's head always was full of crap.'

'Suze,' Michaela responded mildly. She looked with irritation at the roses which were standing rigidly to attention as if in shock. 'Oh, I wish people wouldn't send me flowers. I'm no damn good at them. And they only go rotten after a day and make the bottle stink.'

'Very thoughtless,' Janus agreed drily. He wondered whether it was a good moment to mention the milk coupon left at the bottom and decided it probably wasn't. 'How *is* Simon anyway?'

'Fine,' said Michaela.

'Simple,' said Susan.

'Don't children have homework any more?' said Michaela.

Susan was grating cheese onto a wooden board. 'What was he doing with a bag over his head?' she asked.

'It was raining,' Michaela answered absently. 'I was in the car and I happened to draw up next to him. Inadvertently, as it were.'

'You could have given him a lift. Then he wouldn't have needed the bag,' Susan pointed out reasonably, but her mother chose not to debate it.

'I know,' she said. She sat down at the table. 'So let's see this article, J.' She pulled the evening newspaper towards her. Janus had had it open on the table in front of him and he swivelled it round so that Michaela wouldn't have to look at it upside down.

'Why don't you put your glasses on?' he asked, watching his sister narrow her eyes.

Michaela flashed him a look. 'I don't need glasses for Roger,' she said.

'I agree,' said Susan from the sink. 'Better not.'

'Roger the Lodger,' Michaela murmured. 'My God – he has got bald, hasn't he?'

'I wouldn't know,' Janus said tetchily. He was sensitive about his own prematurely receding hairline, and secretive about the extract of placenta he rubbed in hopefully twice a week. 'I never got as close to him as you did, dearest.'

Michaela scooped aside a heavy hank of smooth brown hair that was blocking her vision and stuck it behind an ear. She read the few paragraphs below Roger's picture. Then she sat back and stared at Janus. 'I can't believe they're really going to do this,' she said. 'Bricknell Court is a landmark. It's historic. It's part of, you know – *Cape Town*, for God's sake. The Hottentots used to eat apples from its fruit trees. Roger is —'

'Khoi,' said Susan over her shoulder. She was prodding at something in the oven with a barbecue fork.

'Roger?' Michaela looked up, momentarily distracted. 'Well, I would never have —'

'Khoi. You don't call them Hottentots any more, Mum. Everyone knows that. It's not polite. *And* I doubt they would have been allowed to eat the apples from the orchard either. I'm sure there wasn't even a back entrance in those days.'

Michaela was deep in the paper again. 'Corny copy line,' she said. '"HISTORIC ORCHARD TO GET THE CHOP".' She raised an eyebrow at Janus. Janus was in advertising and he prided himself on a nifty turn of phrase. Below the photograph of the front façade of Bricknell Court and the inset of the balding, pinstriped Roger was a lengthy caption. Michaela read it aloud.

'Bricknell Court, one of Cape Town's most gracious old homes, used as a hospital for convalescing servicemen during the second world war and converted to apartments in the 1950s, is soon to be demolished. Owners of the property, Grosvenor Life Assurance, explained representative Roger Rendell, require the land for Phase 5 of their own head office expansion plans.'

'Well, I can't believe it,' Michaela said again, sitting back in her chair. She pulled a petal off the rosebud closest to her and began to shred it into a perlemoen ashtray. 'I can't believe that Roger would let something like this happen.'

'Oh, come on,' said Janus. 'He's only the personnel manager, Mick, not the head honcho. Roger doesn't have any say. And what would he care anyway? It's just a grim old eyesore really. The old place was practically derelict.'

'That isn't the point.' Michaela wasn't actually sure what the point was, but she felt personally wounded nevertheless by Grosvenor Life's cavalier attitude. She knew it was unreasonable, and she also knew that Janus was right, but she still thought Roger should at least have rung her up about it first. No matter that they'd not been in contact for over two years. Michaela always thought of her old flames as simmering obediently in the background in case she might on occasion need to re-ignite them, never mind that they might have got married and had three children in the meantime.

'I've made supper,' Susan announced. She carried a large Pyrex baking dish to the table, holding it unsteadily between the lips of a pair of camel-faced oven gloves. 'Move your briefcase, please, Mum, and the – oh, fucking hell!'

4

Janus dived for the milk bottle and caught it as it danced absurdly on the edge of the table. 'Do they let you talk like that at school?' he asked as he put the roses on the windowsill. 'All part of free expression, is it?'

'Sorry.' Susan grinned. 'I made pizza with everything on it. Have some, Uncle J.'

Michaela felt morbidly drawn to the newspaper. She reached out for a slice of pizza without looking up, her fingertips passing appraisingly over the topping like a Braille reader. 'Did you make a salad, darling?' she asked, transplanting an olive to an adjoining slice. 'This is good.'

'No,' Susan said. She leaned on the table on her elbows and put her face beside her mother's. 'What's so special about old Roger? I thought he was safely out of our lives. We have Simon the Pieman now, don't we, God help us. And what's all this Hottentot business anyway?'

'It's not about Roger,' Janus explained. 'It's Bricknell Court – here. Your aunt Pauline used to live there before her parents left the country. We spent our holidays there sometimes as kids, me and your mum, mostly when your grandmother was away on tour. Your uncle Antony too. It was a —'

'Special place,' Michaela broke in fiercely. 'A very special place for all of us cousins growing up together, wasn't it, Janus? We had such *good* times there. That garden – well, the whole orchard was our garden – it was like paradise for a city child. When we couldn't go up to Stillwaters it was the next best thing. It was almost like living in the country. We could have had horses there if we'd wanted to, it was that big. I think they actually did have stables at one time.' Michaela looked wistful.

Janus was examining his fingernails, easing back pale strips of cuticle and wincing.

'But you hate horses,' Susan said. 'You always say they try to bite you.'

This time Michaela ignored her. She was beginning to agree with Antony – Susan was becoming precocious. She picked another olive off the top of the pizza and passed it to Janus. Janus took an anchovy off his and put it on her plate.

'Hey,' said Susan. 'What *is* this – swop shop?'

'I think we should call in the others,' Michaela said suddenly. 'Pauline and Antony ought to know what's going on.'

'They read the papers,' said Janus. 'They probably know already.' He was beginning to feel uneasy with his sister in this mood. He looked past her out of the window at a yellow segment of moon coming up eerily over the fence. It looked so like a balloon he half expected to see a piece of string trailing below it. 'They probably know already,' he said again.

'I still think we should call. Where is Pauline, J? At your place or back with Tertius?'

'Tertius,' said Janus. Michaela was unrelenting. She was not to be diverted when she set her mind to something. 'At least as far as I know. I haven't seen her for a while.' He got up to open the fridge. 'Have you got anything to drink, Mick?'

Susan scrambled off her chair. 'Beer, wine or Diet Sprite,' she said. 'Or J & B. I think we've still got some left over from Mum's Christmas loot.'

Susan had long bushy hair, the same brown as Michaela's, shiny as an acorn buffed against a jersey. It was tied back in a loose ponytail that reached almost to her waist. She was twelve years old, and tall and slim as a boy. She had the honey-coloured skin and dark blue eyes of her father Danny. In summer on the beach at Stillwaters she went effortlessly brown, a careless tan, unconscious of the tidemarks of her shorts or the straps of her school swimming costume. Her hair, bleached by the sun, would be as white as sand at the tips, and tangled and wild from the salt on the wind. She was strong, too, handling the dinghy she'd inherited from Danny with a dexterity beyond her years. The waterbaby, Danny had called her, and Susan had never shown a moment's fear in the river or in the sea, crashing into waves that had knocked her over and staggering out drunk with giggles, while bigger children were running for the sanctuary of softer sand beyond the suck and pull of the tide. She was a summer child. She sparkled and flashed in the sun. In winter she was pale and thoughtful and sometimes clumsy.

Michaela got up to find glasses for wine. She put out a hand to Susan as she went and pulled her close, pushing her face against her springy hair. She looked so much like her father, especially now that she was growing so tall and thin. The serious expression, the long brown fingers. There was so much of Danny in his child. They even still wore their hair the same way, she reflected wryly. Michaela felt herself working up to melancholy mode, as Janus would call it. She knew the signs. Antony said it was all part of turning thirty. You started thinking about the past more and wondering about your ancestors. It was also something to do with the continuity of the species and about life-affecting things like death. Michaela thought it was probably just premenstrual but she liked it when Antony got moody and philosophical, especially when it was about her. It gave him a wonderful serenity that made think of fires on the boathouse roof above the river at Stillwaters. She wanted to sit quietly then, her knees up under her chin, and just look at him. She opened a bottle of red wine, working the last section of cork out with her fingers, and poured a glass for Janus and half a glass for herself.

'I'm going to bed now,' said Susan. She sat on Janus's lap and put her arms round his neck. 'Unless you absolutely want me to wash up. Except that I think it's somebody else's turn.'

'I'll do it,' said Michaela. '*And* I'll do your lunch for school if you'll just feed The Dog. Deal?'

'Deal.' Susan sighed. She went to a cupboard, tossed a can of pilchards in tomato sauce and a can opener at Janus and stuck her head out the kitchen window. 'Dog,' she called softly. 'Come on, The Dog – suppertime.'

A cat with long white fur and only one eye jumped almost at once onto the windowsill on the outside. Susan tapped gently on the windowpane. 'Here, twit,' she called fondly. 'This way. Why do you always have to jump up on your blind side?' The cat stepped carefully through the window, lifting its paws up high. It paused at the pizza on the table, licked Janus on the forehead and sprang lightly to the floor.

'Well?' said Michaela.

'Well what?' Janus replied, knowing what was coming.

'Are we going to call Pauline or aren't we?'

Janus looked at his watch. 'It's getting pretty late,' he stalled. 'Look, Mick, all I wanted – I just thought the story would interest you. I didn't think it warranted a whole family meeting, you know. It's not as if —'

'As if what?' Michaela demanded. 'As if what?'

'Oh, all right.' Janus sighed. 'Call her if you want to. I'll do the dishes.'

Michaela hesitated. 'You call, J. Please? I would, but Tertius might pick up the phone and I never know what to say to him after one of their sessions.'

Janus drained his glass and pushed it over for Michaela to refill. He looked resigned. 'In a minute,' he said.

They both heard a car pulling into the driveway outside at the same time and lifted their heads to the sound of hurrying feet.

'Who on earth's that?' Janus said.

Michaela hoped it wasn't Simon come to check on his roses, of which she had now shredded three. They heard a key turn in the lock. 'It's Pauline,' said Michaela. She looked triumphantly at her brother. 'See?'

Pauline had her own key to Michaela's house, as she did to Janus's apartment. It had become necessary over the last months. She came into the kitchen out of breath and swathed in purple scarf, flowing viscose jacket and black bovver boots. 'Did you hear?' she said. 'My parents are coming for Mater's birthday party *and* they're pulling down Bricknell Court.' To the uninitiated this might have sounded confusing, but Michaela and Janus didn't blink. Pauline kissed Michaela and hugged Janus. She looked round. 'I see The Dog's here but where's The Child?' she asked. 'I brought about a ton of coconut-ice that went wrong . . . I thought she might like to flog it off at school.'

'She's gone to bed,' said Michaela. 'But thanks.' She took the plastic ice cream container Pauline held out to her and lifted a corner of the lid.

Pauline was their first cousin, older than Janus and two years younger than Michaela. She was tall and strong as a carthorse and she filled the small room with colour and big gestures. There was a trace of a bruise, a faint yellow smudge, on her cheekbone.

'Where's Tertius?' Michaela asked, trying not to look as if she'd noticed it. 'I thought he didn't like you driving around on your own at night?' They all knew it was best not to do things Tertius didn't like.

Pauline sat down at the table. Janus fetched another glass.

'I've been at the club,' she said, not answering the question, although her hand went halfway up to her face at Michaela's glance. 'They were putting in the fridges today, and then the electrician came to do something to the lights. And when he'd finished it was late so we got a takeaway and sat and had supper on the stage and he told me about his parrot.'

'Just you and the electrician,' said Michaela. Pauline had got herself into trouble this way before.

'Yes, why not? I liked him. He told me he had a way with birds.'

'I'll bet,' said Janus. 'He meant his parrot, of course.'

'Of course,' said Pauline. She looked at Janus, puzzled. 'He's Italian.'

'Did Tertius know where you were?' Michaela couldn't get away from the man. And she was irritated with Pauline for looking so normal and talking about parrots when there were more important things to discuss.

'Ag, Tertius *se voet*.' Pauline smiled at them nervously. Then she paused, bravado visibly withering. 'Actually, I should call him and tell him where I am,' she said. 'May I use the phone?'

When she was out of the room, Michaela and Janus looked at each other.

'I can't stand it,' Michaela said softly. 'I can't stand what that man is doing to her. Remember the time she got talking to the tramp in the lobby of the library? Remember how Tertius reacted?'

Janus smiled. 'One would hardly have imagined a sixty year old meths drinker with a club foot would have posed a threat to their domestic bliss,' he said. 'But hey – Tertius is no hunk of the month, is he? He might do well to feel insecure.' He opened Pauline's container and took out a chunky square of pink and white coconut-ice. It fell apart as he was lifting it to his mouth and thudded softly onto the floor, where The Dog retreated a few steps and sat suspiciously watching white shards of coconut descend like snow.

'I told Tertius I had supper here,' said Pauline, coming into the room and not meeting their eyes. 'I don't think he's really ready for the electrician.' She laughed, and Janus laughed too and looked at his hands.

Michaela thought they'd all forgotten why they were here. 'You know what I remember most of all about Bricknell Court?' she said. 'The club we had in the fig tree our very first summer there. I don't think I'd ever had a fig before then, and not often since, come to think of it.'

Janus's eyes were on the moon again, now a creamy ball at least three streets away and not nearly as comical. Michaela knew he was listening.

'And we'd sit up there on the planks you and Antony nailed across the biggest branches – d'you remember, J? – and gorge ourselves sick. The sticky purple insides that went hard on our chins, and that milky stuff that would leak from the stems. We tried to write secret messages on the branches with it like white ink.'

'I remember the birds,' said Pauline who, after all, had birds on her mind. 'The doves and the *witogies* – the little white eyes. They made such a mess with the fruit at the top, where we couldn't reach. The planks were too sticky to sit on after a while.'

Janus said nothing. He remembered watching a starling one morning when he'd been up the tree before the others. He remembered a black beak, sharp as a piece of glass, dismembering a locust on a fencepost down below, holding it down with its foot and looking hurried and furtive. Guilty almost, as if expecting to be caught out in its blatant greed. Janus couldn't remember which summer holiday that had been – the first one they'd all spent together, or the one after that, the one when —

'Oh, look, we've finished the wine.' Michaela took the neck of the bottle and held it up to the light. 'Shall I open another one, or is it time for coffee?'

'It's time for bed,' Janus said. He had not been prepared for this uncomfortable lurch back into the past.

Michaela laid a hand on his. 'Don't go yet,' she said. Michaela hadn't even changed her clothes since she'd got in from work. Her briefcase on the floor had a pile of submissions in it for the magazine's short fiction competition, a competition which, in a misguided moment, had been her idea. She'd promised herself she'd get through at least half of them this evening and until now she had still intended to do so. But now she couldn't get her head away from that summer at Bricknell Court and she didn't want to be alone. It was probably too late to get even Simon over. When Janus had rung her up to say he was bringing something round to show her, she hadn't expected the flood of feeling which the news had called up inside her. She told herself it was pure nostalgia. She used to think nostalgia was an emotion for old men and has-beens and she would never have predicted that it might attach itself to her in this unattractive way. There was something disreputable about nostalgia. Something weak. Those Nationalist Party MPs had probably got nostalgic about the Whites Only signs they'd auctioned off to raise funds at the Bloemfontein congress which had caused such a stir. Especially when they'd raised almost as much as the previous winter's Blankets for Blankes drive.

There had been many doors Michaela had shut behind her in her life. She had usually managed this with firmness and resolve. There were some where she could have sworn she had turned the key and thrown it away, and never regretted doing so. Regret was another useless emotion, she'd decided after Danny. She had allowed herself to feel regret then: regret that she hadn't been with him the one time she might have made a difference; regret at with what hasty passion she had eradicated all signs of him in her life, a passion which somehow had got her over and through the worst of that time, but which had later left her feeling only bewildered.

The Dog had discovered coconut-ice. She sat neatly behind a damp swirl on the floor below the table, betrayed only by a thread of coconut on her nose, her tail curled against her paws like a mould for a china ornament. With her one golden eye she gazed devotedly up at Janus, the source of this newfound delight.

'I wonder if they'll have pulled the old place down before my parents get here,' said Pauline. 'We lived there for years, you know. They will remember the area before it got so built up. Before Grosvenor Life even bought the property.'

'Their first visit home,' Janus said. His memories of his uncle and aunt were frozen in time: the baggy corduroy trousers that Pauline's father always wore; the noise of her mother's typewriter coming from the study as he drifted off to sleep, a furious clatter of keys punctuated with long pauses and her smoker's cough. 'Do you think they'll find things changed enough to want to stay?'

'I don't know.' Pauline looked thoughtful. 'I know my mother took three library books with her. There's probably a warrant out for her for that. The city has a long memory.'

The Whitehead family had a distinguished history of anti-apartheid campaigning in one way or another. Mater's husband, Josh Whitehead, their grandfather, had been a Supreme Court judge and had also headed several commissions of inquiry into a variety of labour related and civil rights issues. Pauline's mother and Michaela and Janus's mother were sisters and both had in their own way followed in the family tradition, involving themselves and their own subsequent families in protest politics in the most vicious years of apartheid in South Africa. One had gone with satire and cabaret; the other with husband and compass in the dead of night across the border into Botswana, and thence to England and ultimately Australia, leaving Pauline at hotel school learning how not to curdle a sauce and omitting to tell her when they'd be back. Pauline had always maintained she'd understood. She was a child accustomed to coming second to the Struggle and she never appeared to have taken their defection personally, neither at the time nor later. Just as she hadn't expected them to jump at the chance to return when they had been guaranteed safe passage. She knew she wasn't a priority and besides, she was a grown-up now. But the weekend she had arrived home at Bricknell Court for a visit with a soufflé and a walnut salad to find a sinkful of dirty dishes and the beds unmade remained vivid in her memory. She had not seen her parents again for five years.

'We had the most fun at Bricknell Court in the winter,' Pauline said decisively after they'd all lapsed into pensive silence, as if she had been sitting there measuring holidays against each other and selecting a shortlist. Michaela was cleaning out a grim looking espresso machine which appeared not to have been used for some time. She scraped at some elderly black sludge with the point of a knife. 'When we made those huge piles of leaves from the oak and chestnut trees, do you remember? Then we'd take a running jump and land in the middle of them. That was the ultimate fun.'

'The ultimate fun,' Janus echoed, smiling suddenly. 'That's an expression from the past. The ultimate fun. Who used to say that?'

'I don't remember it,' Michaela said abruptly. She turned on the tap at the sink. 'And the only thing I remember about jumping into those leaves was the time dear old Tommy had cleared a nostril into the pile we were so deliriously springing into and *I* happened to land on it and got up with this – *thing* dangling from my fingers.'

'Oh God,' said Pauline. 'Do you have to?'

'Tommy,' said Janus. 'The pinball wizard. He really was amazing on that pinball machine. I remember a score of 950 001 one Saturday morning —'

'Please —' said Michaela. 'Don't. Don't talk about

Tommy. We all agreed . . .' Her voice tailed off into silence.

Pauline looked from one to the other as if she was about to say something, then changed her mind.

Although Janus was the youngest of the four cousins, with Michaela and Antony the oldest and sharing a birthday, Pauline's uncontrived air of innocence made her always seem younger than any of them. They had always felt protective of her. Michaela still thought of her as a kind of charming nuisance. Pauline was so reliable, so willing, such a dedicated hanger-on. Willing was the word that probably best described her as a child and it still did. Pauline had always been the one to offer to go last playing hopscotch, having first been sent off to find suitably flat hopscotch stones for the others. It was Pauline who would march off cheerily to spend her pocket-money at the café, and then give away her share to Tommy anyway. And Pauline it was who would stand patiently behind the ping-pong table to be ball-girl to Janus and Antony's endlessly argumentative tournaments, while Michaela umpired from the top of a stepladder safely out of range. Yet Pauline had grown taller than any of them, and broad and muscular. This had made her a shy, awkward teenager, especially in Michaela's company, and even now she was never very comfortable in a roomful of strangers.

'The electrician was telling me,' she said, changing the subject now that Michaela had neatly ruined her memory, 'that this parrot of his has never said so much as Hello or Pretty Polly, but it can do the whole of Gilbert and Sullivan's *Madame Butterfly* without missing a word.'

'Oh, bullshit,' said Michaela. She was pouring coffee into very small cups. 'What a line.'

'I agree,' said Janus. 'Some men will say anything for a free takeaway.'

'Oh, he paid,' said Pauline, adding apologetically, 'I didn't have any cash on me.'

They had strayed from the point again. 'Listen,' said Michaela, 'I've got an idea. Before you go home, Janus, let's take a quick drive past Bricknell Court. Just to look. We won't go in or anything, just drive past.'

Janus looked appalled.

'Please, J, for me? I don't know what it is tonight, but I feel so restless. Indulge me, just this once.' How many times had Janus heard that, Pauline wondered privately. And delivered without a blush. She was certainly no stranger to the phrase herself. Michaela looked from Janus to Pauline. 'Pauline?'

'It's after eleven,' Pauline answered. 'And I have to get home. I don't see the point myself. Really.' She looked at Michaela and frowned. 'What would there be to see anyway? It probably won't look any different from when you last drove past it.'

'Yes, but I didn't *look* at it then,' Michaela said. She was getting irritable. 'I didn't *know*. You always look at something with new eyes when you *know*.'

'So look at it tomorrow with new eyes,' Janus said, but he knew when he was beaten. He tried one last thing. 'What about Susan? She's asleep.'

'Oh, Suze will understand,' Michaela said airily. 'I'll go wake her up. Thanks, J. You're the best.'

Susan was unimpressed at being woken up and jollied into sweater and slippers. Her hair was tangled and her cheeks flushed from her burrow beneath the duvet. 'It's only for a minute,' Michaela lied, heartlessly stuffing her limp arms through the sleeves of her anorak. 'There's something we have to do and I can't leave you here on your own.'

Susan yawned. 'It couldn't wait till morning?'

Janus met them coming down the passage. He took her hand. 'Apparently not,' he said. 'Your mother is of the opinion that Bricknell Court will have been but a figment of her imagination in the morning. She needs to look at it with new eyes.'

Pauline was waiting at the front door with her basket. She wound her purple scarf twice round Susan's neck. 'Steal a fig for me,' she said.

Janus drove a sports car which had cost about the same as Michaela's house. The lipstick-red bodywork was polished to a high gloss and he drove with the hood down. Susan immediately disappeared into the depths of the back seat, where Janus pulled a black graduation gown over her which the agency had been using in a chocolate commercial. Michaela felt strangely expectant and she moved impatiently in her seat while Janus fussed with his seatbelt and adjusted the driving mirror. She wondered what he'd done with the set of goggles and leather hat with ear flaps she'd given him for Christmas, and which she'd never seen him wear. They'd seemed so apt at the time.

Bricknell Court was a short drive round the side of the mountain, set back against the lower slopes. Once it had been the only building in the area, accessible only from a narrow dirt road, and hidden behind indigenous bush. Now it was in the centre of a built-up suburb, a scruffy neighbour for the yuppies who built and bought here. Grosvenor Life's existing office block stood adjoining the property, impassive as the mountain itself and beautiful too, in a tasteful, cleanly modern way. Michaela had driven past here a hundred times without remarking or even noticing the contrast between old and new. Now it struck her quite forcibly, seeing the white Grosvenor Life walls enhanced with respectable muted spotlights and the ghostly grey chimneys of Bricknell Court thrusting anxiously towards the stars like a poor relation who wouldn't go away. It was not easy to see very much of the apartment block tonight. Corrugated iron hoardings were up already, soon to be splashed with billboards and spray-painted slogans. All that was clearly visible through the trees were the upper level of windows and the rooftops and chimneys. There were no lights in the windows and one could sense the emptiness – desolation, Michaela fancied. She was given to the dramatic at times. They could not see the orchard. That part of the property was to the back of the building and access via the usual route – a side road – was blocked off by large orange and yellow earthmoving equipment. Front-end loaders and cranes stood guard like cumbersome animals in a spooky moonscape.

'All right?' said Janus into the silence. He sounded tired. 'Can we go now?'

A late night bus cruised past in the fast lane and Janus pulled towards the kerb as a gust of diesel swept across them. Michaela put a hand on his arm. 'Just once more, Janus,' she said. 'Go round one more time. Drive slowly.'

'But, Mick, you can't see a thing,' Janus protested. 'It's pitch dark, for crying out loud. What is it you're trying to see here?' He was sorry now he had given in to her. He was usually sorry afterwards.

'Oh, nothing.' Michaela's shoulders slumped into the bucket seat. 'It doesn't matter.' She felt stupidly close to real tears.

Janus put the car into gear and took another turn round the block, driving slowly and close in to the pavement. He took Michaela's fingers in his own. They were cold and she gripped his hand tightly. 'Let go, for Christ's sake Mick,' he said to her, keeping his voice low. 'It's time to let go.'

Susan's head appeared between their shoulders. She had Pauline's scarf over her nose and mouth like a balaclava. Michaela gave a start. She had quite forgotten Susan was there.

'I have a maths test at eight o'clock,' Susan said. Her voice sounded muffled. 'I thought you might like to know in advance that I'll be using this as my excuse.'

Back home, Michaela had left all the lights in the house blazing. And she had forgotten to lock the front door. In the kitchen The Dog was sitting on the lid of the plastic container, licking coconut-ice from her paws.

· 2 ·

Michaela is hiding. She is crouched down in the middle of the thick, stiff stems of the ring of hydrangea bushes round the base of the magnolia tree. They are playing sardines. She holds her breath as she sees Pauline's brown summer legs plod doggedly past. Pauline is singing 'Once in Royal David's City' and she gets a sudden dizzy whiff of Christmas as strong as a smell. There is a shiny-backed rose beetle on the earth at her feet. It is standing listening-still, as if it's in the game too. It has black twiggy legs. Michaela draws her own legs up as it begins to move towards her toes and she hugs her knees. The sun has long since gone down behind the mountain and soon it will be really dark. Then she will hear Pauline's mother calling them: 'Paw-paw! Michaela! Janus! An – to – neee!' And they will trudge up the hill and through the archway and go inside and play Careers until supper.

Big cool leaves flap against her arms and suddenly there is Antony, flushed and tousled, holding up a broken flip-flop and grinning. It's the second pair he's broken this holiday. Snapped off at the base of the rubber thong and quite untreatable. Michaela pulls a face and puts a finger to her lips. Pauline is coming back again. She stops. Stout legs planted squarely in front of them as they hold their breath. And then she's peering through the leaves like the Cheshire Cat, slowly smiling, smug as can be. 'Well, looky here,' she says out loud and Antony is up in a flash and dragging her through, but he's too late – Janus is on top of them, tumbling through to their hideaway and throwing punches at his sister.

'Not fair,' he says. 'I never get to be the sardine.'

'Rough night?' Michaela's relief secretary Roz leaned against the doorframe of her office, cradling a mug of coffee between her hands, rolling it from side to side on flat palms. 'This isn't in my job description but I'll make you a cup for your thoughts.'

'Thanks.' Michaela turned from where she had been standing staring out of the window and smiled a fairly calculated, bleak smile. Roz, she had discovered, was a keen pryer. 'My brother came round last night, and my cousin and – well, I got to bed pretty late.'

If Roz had expected a more thrilling explanation for the dark rings beneath Michaela's eyes, she wasn't going to get it. Michaela wasn't in the mood for confidences. She watched while Roz poured coffee into a mug, shaking her head at the milk jug. 'Black,' she said. 'Thank you.' And then, seeing Roz beginning to compose her features into her concerned helpmate look, she said quickly: 'I need not to be disturbed for an hour or so, Roz. I didn't get to the stories last night after all and if I don't make a start they're going to back up on me.' She opened her briefcase and slapped a wad of papers on her desk to show she meant business. 'Whose dumb idea was this competition anyway?' She'd give Roz that.

Roz pulled a face. Reluctant sympathy. She'd wanted to stay and chat. She planned to be indispensable at the end of her relief period, when Michaela's own secretary was due back from paternity leave. 'I guess that means no calls?' she said.

Michaela walked her to the door. 'No calls,' she said. She felt an absurd impulse to waggle her fingers at Roz's disappointed face.

When she was gone Michaela turned back to the window and threw it wide open. She leaned on the wooden sill and looked three storeys down to the street where the old Coloured flower seller was feeding the pigeons, the sound of her monotonous clucking and whistling drifting up to the windows as it did every day. There was a light breeze off the sea and a damp smell of salt. If she craned her head quite far out, Michaela could see the sea from here and on very clear days like this one Robben Island, a smooth hump off towards the horizon. She'd been out there once, with Antony, who had been taking pictures for an American magazine. They had crossed the water in a noisy boat that stank of diesel and fish. For someone who never felt seasick Michaela had felt decidedly queasy that day, but had put it down to the rank odour of despair and rotting seaweed that seemed to hang over the island like a pall of smoke.

There had been no prisoners left on the island then, of course, but it had also been before easy access could be obtained and the bored policewoman whose chore it had been to take them round was a bad caricature of the fearsome prison wardress with sensible rubber-soled shoes and uncompromising haircut beneath her felt hat. The wind had whipped round them, herding them across the shingle that crunched beneath their feet. Michaela had been struck by a small posse of miniature goats tugging aggressively at the patches of colourless grass and moving in a body from one spot to the next. She saw an ostrich in the distance, looking prehistoric and surprised, and Antony had taken a picture of it. She had the picture still, on the wall of her office. Seen against the sun, the creature had an indistinct halo of hair on its neck and bald grey head like the fuzz on the head a newborn baby, and it had come up to them curiously and stared into the camera with a frank and engaging expression. She'd wondered at the time, and afterwards, how ostriches came to be on the island in the first place – surely they hadn't always been there – but when she'd asked the policewoman she'd been given a terse, noncommittal reply and a sharp look. She probably thought Michaela was making fun of her. Everyone else asked to see Nelson Mandela's cell and this smart alec was only interested in the wildlife. All through their long tour along bare corridors and draughty recreation areas, Michaela worried at the image that wouldn't leave her: of a sort of Nationalist government plot – a Noah's ark with two of everything indigenous crossing the choppy water from Bloubergstrand. Ostriches, goats, two lovesick blue duikers. Petrus and Nomsa Moloi. All of them watching mournfully as Table Mountain retreated and then disappeared into the grey sea mist.

Antony said she had a way of blocking things out in life that were real or otherwise too painful to hold up to scrutiny, and that was why she latched onto absurdities or small, unimportant issues and developed them into intricate three act plays while the rest of the world went up in flames in one. That was why she thought immediately of ostriches when she thought of Robben Island. It was an odd explanation, which Michaela found a little unfair, as she retained other images of the island, less comforting or flippant perhaps, but just as stark. But Antony's astuteness had always been one of the qualities she'd found attractive and disturbing at the same time. She probably wouldn't have admitted it to herself even in her rare moments of self-examination, but Antony was good for her because she knew she couldn't fool him, not ever. And Antony actually liked her. Not for her legs or her smile or her long brown hair. Not because she was family either. Antony just liked her, and that was enough.

Michaela was the fiction editor for a magazine called *Focus* which saw as its target market women who wanted more in their fortnightly glossy than high-priced fashion and how-to-hold-onto-your-man articles. The magazine had built up a sound reputation for quality journalism, food for thought and human interest stories. It was also known, almost by accident, for discovering and nurturing new creative writing talent. This had been achieved by one of Michaela's short story writers getting a historical romance novel accepted by a publisher in America on the strength of a work in progress extract Michaela had run as a filler when someone else had let her down on a deadline. Thanks to this unasked for reputation, she now had to work her way through a large number of unsolicited manuscripts almost daily, although most of the bad stuff was now sifted by Roz before it got as far as her desk.

Michaela looked with a sinking heart at the story on the top of her pile. It had the distinctly suitcase-under-the-bed look of the manuscript doing the rounds in five year cycles. Yellowing paper. Rust stains from the paper clip holding it together. Old-fashioned typewriter keys and single spacing. This one was called *Escape From Hell!*

To keep herself from dropping off whenever she was especially swamped by purple prose, Michaela would play a game with herself, imagining down to the last detail the physical appearance of the authors based on their writing skill. Sometimes they would bring their offerings in personally in the hope that they would be attended to more quickly and their work accepted all the sooner. It had become Roz's job to screen these personal visitations and to let only a select few through to her. Roz had shown a talent for the game too.

'Bottle-bottom glasses on a gold chain?' Michaela would begin, having glanced at the opening line of *City of Sin*.

A nod from Roz and one point.

'Piano legs and Pick 'n Pay tights?'

A point and a half. Woolworths tights with a small run.

'Lipstick on the teeth?'

Bingo — five points and Roz gets to go out for sandwiches at lunchtime.

Escape From Hell! was dead easy. The title gave it away. Ex-RAF, retired. Hout Bay. Flannels and navy blue blazer. Nicotine-stained fingers and a fine dusting of dandruff on the collar. Everyone the man had held glassy-eyed with his prison-of-war yarns had suggested that he might think about channelling his obvious storytelling talent onto the printed page, and the foolish man had tried to do just that, believing sincerely that the world out there would not sleep until it had marched the sands of Tobruk with him, or dropped behind enemy lines in the dead of night from a star-studded sky.

Michaela spent more time on these manuscripts than they ever really warranted. To her own surprise she hated to diminish these old men with standard rejection letters, and she always tried to let them down gently, without encouraging them to submit anything else.

She put *Escape From Hell!* aside for later and slid the next sheaf in front of her. She began to read: 'The rains were late that year as Mpofu Lungile fashioned his little clay ox from the red soil of the dried up river bed, chasing the flies from the sores on his mouth and scratching his distended, rumbling, parched belly . . .' With what, she wondered, his scrawny toe? Michaela sighed. The author was one Poppy McLaren from Table View and she was willing to bet that her experience of distended bellies probably went no further than her husband's beer gut. Not for the first time, Michaela decided the competition was definitely one of her less inspired ideas for the magazine.

She wondered when Joy Beamish's contribution would emerge and whether it already lurked floridly at the bottom of this pile. Mrs Beamish was a regular submitter of short stories and poems. She always addressed her covering letter to Michaela personally on scented notepaper and sometimes she would enclose a small gift – a pressed flower or free sachet of sample handcream, with an appropriate note: 'A little something from my garden.' 'To make you smell good.' A month before she had sent Michaela a giveaway condom – Extra Length – which had rather shaken her and had sent Roz into hysterics. This had come with a stern warning – 'Say NO to AIDS' – and Michaela, alarmed, had been forced to come to the conclusion that Mrs Beamish couldn't have known what it was, but had somehow been receptive enough to AIDS awareness campaigns to want to pass the warning on. She had been sending stories in to the magazine for as long as Michaela had been there and each one of them was as awful as the one before. Michaela sometimes wished for her sake she could have used something now and again, but there wasn't a redeeming phrase in anything she'd seen so far, nor would there ever be, she feared. But Joy Beamish just kept on plugging away, as cheerful and regular as sunrise.

The noonday gun firing from Signal Hill made Michaela sit up and stretch. She took off her glasses and looked at her watch. Nearly lunchtime and she wasn't doing too badly. She buzzed for Roz. Roz was bursting with spiteful excitement when she came through with a collection of telephone messages and the day's mail. 'You'll never guess who was here,' she said without preamble. 'In person.'

'Who, Roz?' Roz was still new enough to find writers and models exciting, and Michaela sometimes humoured her. She flipped through the messages. Blanche. Janus. Simon. The Foreign Minister's wife's press secretary.

'Only La Beamish herself.' Roz grinned slyly as Michaela blinked up at her. 'You said you didn't want to be disturbed.'

'Well,' Michaela said. 'Let me see. Dumpy. Fifty-three. Rouge rather than blusher. Flabby underarms? Did she ask to see me?'

Roz caught herself in mid-response and frowned. 'Actually no, she didn't. In fact she said she didn't want to trouble you. She just wanted to leave her competition entry so as to be sure of catching the deadline.'

'Oh,' said Michaela blankly. 'But the deadline's in two months' time.' She shrugged. 'Oh well. So how close am I?'

Roz had taken careful note, expecting that Michaela would want a full report. And she needed brownie points after the stamped addressed envelope incident. She laid a thick brown envelope on the desk, almost reverently. The looping, backward curving script was distinctive. 'It's hard to tell,' she said reluctantly. 'She was wearing sunglasses, very dark ones. And a hat with one of those sort of old-style veils like the Queen Mother wears, only thicker. You are right about the rouge though, and there was a hint of very puce lipstick.' She thought for another minute. 'She had long sleeves,' she added, 'so I can't tell you about the arms. Sorry.'

'I'm never far out though,' Michaela said with decision, and she put the envelope at the bottom of the pile. She wouldn't give Roz the satisfaction of the first line test.

Blanche was indignant when Michaela finally got back to her. 'Since when don't you take my calls?' she said in peevish tone.

Michaela could hear her exhaling. She could also picture her mother lying smoking on her bed – possibly still in it – her auburn-rinse in a turban, little pastel cottonwool puffs between newly painted toenails. The older Blanche got, the more time she spent on her appearance. She would never have painted her nails in the old days, would indeed have despised the vanity.

'A blanket instruction,' Michaela said. 'I've got a mound of work on my desk. Don't take it personally.'

Blanche had made up her mind to be just a little hurt. 'I was going to suggest lunch,' she told her, 'but

I suppose it's too late now and if you're that busy . . .'

'We can meet somewhere if you like,' said Michaela. Did all mothers contrive to make their children feel guilty on purpose or was it something they did unconsciously and without intentional malice? Did they do it as much to sons as they did daughters? She should ask Antony.

'Well, if you're sure,' Blanche said, although Michaela had been purposely vague. 'I do want to talk to you about this crazy idea of your cousin's.'

Michaela knew what she was referring to and she felt her heart sink. Pauline was soon to open a new supper club in the city's waterfront area down in the harbour. She had worked in a number of restaurants and hotels over the years, gradually making a name for herself as an innovative young chef. There were certain influential food critics who consistently sang her praises and followed her career with interest, and one of them had put up half the capital. The news that Pauline was about to risk all on this new venture had naturally already been leaked to the press. That the legendary Blanche Whitehead was to come out of retirement to sing at the opening had not yet hit the newspapers though, and Michaela was thankful because it looked as if Blanche was getting cold feet and needed more time to think it over. The club, called Pauline's in violent neon, was in yuppie tourist country, amid dozens of bars and restaurants that seemed to shut down almost as quickly as they opened. Pauline was confident, though, and her partner even more so.

Blanche held a forkful of spinach salad poised before her mouth.

'I don't know that I'm up to this,' she said, lowering it for the second time.

30

'Of course you are.' Michaela was conscious of trying to keep weariness out of her voice. They had had this conversation before and doubtless would again. 'Pauline wouldn't have asked you if she didn't think you were.'

'Oh, yes, she would,' Blanche replied, opening and closing her mouth and jabbing the fork at Michaela. 'She doesn't have to pay me.'

Michaela didn't answer. She watched the fork weaving hypnotically in front of her.

'I'm forty-nine,' Blanche said. She narrowed her eyes at the leaves of spinach as if daring them to contradict her. Michaela half expected them to answer back and remind Blanche that she had turned fifty last June and had got seriously drunk to prove it, but she let the inaccuracy slide by without comment.

'Please eat that,' she said instead. 'It's going brown at the edges.'

'I saw Anaïs de Mille at 58 last year and she was dismal.' Blanche put the fork down untouched and picked out a sliver of pink bacon with her long fingernails. 'It was a good try – "Fifty-eight at 58" – but it went off like the proverbial damp squid.'

'Oh, Mother. For a start Anaïs de Mille was never a patch on you, even at her best. She could never pack them in like you did. Secondly, she's got ten years on you, so that's an unfair comparison anyway. You'll be fine. You'll be better than fine.'

'But not great.'

Michaela tried not to lose patience. 'Great enough,' she said. 'And it's only one show after all.'

Blanche waved to someone across the room, flashing an insincere smile and blowing a kiss. 'Who the hell is that?' she murmured without moving her lips.

Michaela looked over her shoulder. 'Don't know,' she said. 'But if it's any consolation I think he was waving at the woman behind you.'

'Christ,' said Blanche. 'Even my sight's going. It'll be my mind next.'

'Oh, that went long ago,' Michaela said briskly, not absolutely sure she was joking. 'I need to get back to the office.'

Driving away from the harbour, Michaela realised that she had forgotten to tell Blanche about Bricknell Court. It was Blanche's singing career that had meant that she and Janus spent their school holidays there. When they were small they had travelled about with her, staying in one-star hotels and playing cards with the waiters on parquet dance floors while Blanche rehearsed with the band. Later it had all got too complicated and it was easier to ship them off to Mater up at Stillwaters or to Bricknell Court.

Michaela knew how much her mother missed the stage, the applause and adulation that had been her due for so long. Pauline's invitation had been eagerly and impulsively grasped, but a conversation in the mirror, Blanche had told Michaela during the first of many subsequent discourses, had revealed that she had perhaps not made an intelligent decision. Too many cigarettes and too little sleep over the years, she reckoned, had damaged her voice. And her legs were too skinny for fishnets.

Michaela had taken the practical line. 'So don't wear fishnets,' she said. 'Wear something more ... flattering.'

'More my age?' Blanche said. 'Come on, you can tell me.'

God. Today Michaela had not been in the mood

for boosting her mother's flagging morale, but she had walked right into it. Just when she needed a bit of boosting of her own, before she knew it Blanche's ego had bounced right up onto the table between them just after they'd ordered their Perriers, and that had put paid to that. Michaela was relieved to get back to the comfortable clutter of her desk and almost grateful to be able to subside into *Birds of Paradise: A Love Story* like the bubbles in a tub of bathwater.

First, though, she looked through her messages. Another appeal to call Simon, and three different numbers where he might be reached through the afternoon. Nothing yet from Antony.

· 3 ·

Antony stood at the side of the swimming pool. He held the strap of his camera loosely twisted round his wrist. Although the sun was already low down in the sky, the afternoon was still warm and the heat off the bricks of the wall behind him was making him drowsy. His denim shirt was damp at the base of his spine and he wished he could strip and dive in to cool off, but with the moustachioed Roosevelt and her police whistle on patrol even he wouldn't have dared. She already disapproved of him being there; he could tell by the way she gritted her teeth when she smiled.

But now Antony's eyes were drawn to the high diving board and the figure standing straight and still at its very end. He lowered himself onto his haunches and slowly raised his camera. A knee in the air, a pointed toe and the board rocked and bounced, the sound coming violently back at him from the high walls all round. He walked over to the edge of the pool where a black swimming cap bobbing aimlessly about on the surface like a large catawba grape skin was the only immediately apparent sign of life. Then a head broke through and Susan gasped and grinned and sent a jet of silver water arcing into the air through the gap in her front teeth. She swam without splashing and plucked the cap off the water. Antony stepped back and caught it with one hand, holding his camera high with the other.

'I hope you didn't get that flop on film,' Susan called. She hooked her toes onto the rail at the side and floated on her back. Her long hair was a dark nest of eels round her shoulders. 'Will you get my towel?'

'This?' Antony held up a long pink and white one with a lurid flamingo design down its centre.

Susan shook her head and disappeared in a slow motion somersault holding her nose underwater. 'That's Florida's,' she said, coming up and shaking water from her hair in a spray of shining drops. 'Mine's that one there – the Windsor Beach Hotel one.'

'Oh,' said Antony. 'Of course.' He'd been with them on that holiday.

'Florida, Christ! Don't *do* that!' Susan had vanished abruptly beneath the surface again and now she shot up, choking, with a dark-skinned, dark-haired girl hanging on her shoulders. 'That's not funny. You'll get into shit if Roosevelt catches you doing that.'

The two girls took Antony's offered hand one by one and climbed out of the pool as the whistle gave out a long, earsplitting blast that had the pool cleared in seconds and the men on a building site three blocks away downing tools for the day. Another, extra sharp blast followed, and as Antony was pretty sure this was meant for him he retreated against the wall and stood watching as twenty-five nubile schoolgirls in black swimming costumes self-consciously scuttled past him, on their way to the changing rooms, some of the bolder ones glancing at him from beneath their lashes.

'See you at the car,' Susan said. She linked arms with Florida, whose humorous black eyes and deep dimples distracted one from the twelve year old puppy fat which might in time prove a problem in social intercourse, and they ran on flat feet to catch up with the others. Antony moved to a concrete bench in the shade and took pictures of Roosevelt in pleated skirt and ankle socks as she tried to balance a tower of polystyrene Kikka-Boards on one hand, and untangle the string of her whistle from the string of her sunglasses with the other. Antony waved and smiled encouragement and she pretended not to see him. Roosevelt always pretended not to see him if she could. Sometimes he wondered if she did.

Antony was taking pictures for a newspaper supplement on integrated schools in the city. 'We want non-racial children,' had been his brief, delivered without apparent irony. 'You know the kind of stuff – happy mixing, racial harmony – all that crap.' He hadn't been able to resist the assignment, even though it paid next to nothing, and he had been sorely tempted to document the wrong kind of scenes in the nursery school section of Susan's progressive school: like the stocky four year old boy, an Aryan angel, blond and blue-eyed, pointing a water pistol at a cowering black kid half his size, or the gang of little black girls he'd watched callously trying to close the door of a Wendyhouse on the fingers of a Chinese boy in a Superman suit. But in the end he had resisted playground normality and concentrated on giving the paper what it wanted, which was easy enough anyway, and he already had some disarming prints on the walls of his darkroom at home. And of course Susan and Florida were perfect candidates when they weren't fighting, as the two of them were not often seen apart. The principal had liked the assignment because it meant publicity for the school at a time when numbers were low and twenty per cent of parents regularly defaulted on their terms' fees. Antony had been allowed free rein at the school for a month, as long as lessons weren't disrupted.

'I didn't know you were coming today,' Susan said in the car. She rubbed at her wet hair with her jersey. Florida opened a wrapper of chewing gum and the sharp smell of spearmint and chlorine filled the car. She held it out to Antony and Susan and they both shook their heads. Antony started the engine.

'Did you take these pictures?' Florida had picked out a contact sheet from a folder she'd found on the back seat.

'Uh-huh. Please put it back.' Antony glanced over his shoulder. Florida was always quick to make herself at home.

'My mother was a model,' she said serenely. 'My birth mother, that is.'

Susan looked at Antony. Florida was in a foster home – her third – and nobody knew who her real mother was. If her foster parents knew, they weren't saying, and it might have been just as well, for Florida had her own, very clear picture of her roots. 'That's where I get my cheekbones from,' she added.

'Does Mum know you're picking us up?' Susan asked. 'She didn't say anything this morning.' She was looking for split ends in her wet hair. 'Mind you, we were so late after last night I'm surprised she remembered to get out of bed.'

'What were you doing last night?'

'Oh, driving.'

'Driving where?'

'Around.'

'*Around*? Jesus, Suze.' Susan could be as exasperating as her mother.

'Janus took us. Mum wanted to look at a crummy old apartment block on the other side of the mountain for some reason. Something to do with Roger.'

Antony looked perplexed. Florida leaned forward and spat a grey ball of gum past his ear into the road.

'Oh, sis,' said Susan. 'Somebody's going to step on that.'

'I was aiming for the bin,' Florida pointed out calmly, 'but Antony's over the speed limit. I'm entirely accurate at sixty.'

'Was it Bricknell Court?' Antony asked. 'Can you remember?'

'Yes, I think so,' Susan replied. 'With an orchard with figs but no horses.'

Antony slowed down to make a turn, then leaned forward to slide a cassette into the tapedeck. In profile his face was thoughtful, one might have said grave. He tapped his fingers on the wheel in time with the music.

'Well, I told your mother last week I'd do the swimming run,' he said after a long silence, during which Florida methodically clicked all the knuckles on her hands from the back seat. 'I hope she remembered.'

'Probably not,' said Susan. 'You know Mum.'

'I've been out on a shoot most of the day,' Antony said, 'or I would have called to confirm. Do I need to drop Florida off or is she coming home with us?'

'Flor?' Susan turned round to look at her. 'It's Friday – stay the night. We'll get videos.'

'OK,' said Florida, 'as long as it's not a yuman drama.'

'Actually, I thought of going up to Stillwaters for the weekend,' Antony said. 'How does that sound?'

'Great,' said Susan. 'Florida?'

Florida shrugged.

'Well, let's see what Michaela says.' Antony pulled up outside the house. Michaela's car was in the driveway. He shifted a schoolbag over each shoulder and looped his camera round his neck. Susan and Florida were already at the door. 'Mum!' Susan shouted. 'Antony's here. He's taking us to Stillies for the weekend. I got three bucks fifty for the coconut-ice The Dog didn't scarf and Florida threw up in assembly.'

Michaela was working in her study. She looked guiltily at her watch as they all trooped in and stood in the doorway. 'I was wondering where you were,' she said. 'Was I supposed to fetch today? I was giving you another fifteen minutes in case you'd caught the late bus.'

'Liar,' Susan said cheerfully. 'Come, Florida, let's call the dreaded custodians and tell them they can have the weekend off.'

'So,' said Michaela when the two girls had gone, leaving their wet swimming towels on a corner of her desk. She began tidying her papers together. Antony let the schoolbags slide down his arms and drop to the carpet. 'You're going up to see Mater?'

'I thought I would. I haven't been up there since Christmas and the party's not far off. I thought I'd go and see what the plan is and if she needs any help with arrangements.' He smiled. 'See if I can land the job of official photographer.'

'I should think that goes without saying,' said Michaela. She could feel tension in her smile and knew that Antony would have noticed.

'Come with me, Mick.'

Michaela looked up at him, then looked away. 'I've got work to do,' she said. She took lunchboxes out of the bags and a nasty smell of garlic polony swam about the room like a genie released from a bottle.

'Bring it with you. You can sit on the veranda in a straw hat and pretend you're Frieda Lawrence.'

Michaela laughed. 'I haven't got a straw hat,' she said.

'Mater has,' Antony countered. 'I saw Frans wearing it driving the tractor on Boxing Day.'

Michaela had a sudden vision of the river, flat and blue, scarcely moving past the old house on the farm, at that undecided moment before the tide turned, when the whole world seemed somehow poised. She could hear the blurt and sputter of a motorboat in the distance and the weird, bereft call of the peacocks on the Barberton sisters' property on the opposite bank. She saw Danny suddenly too, on his knees on a sandbank at low tide, up to his shoulders in grey river mud, digging for bloodworms for bait. And Susan, shivering from the wind on her wet legs, holding the paraffin tin at the ready, where the giant blind worms lay wetly across each other like a squirming live mass of human intestines.

She shook her head to clear it. 'All right,' she said to Antony's back. He had picked up *Escape From Hell!* and appeared to be engrossed. 'I'll get a few things together.'

They were already climbing the pass on the road out of Cape Town and singing 'Yellow Submarine' when Michaela sat up straight and said, 'Oh, sod it – Simon.'

'What about Simon?' Susan said. She had The Dog on her lap and was patting her head rhythmically to make her do aeroplane ears for Florida.

'He's coming over for supper.'

'Oh – oh,' said Florida.

Antony changed gear to begin the climb to the summit of the pass. 'Do you want to turn back?' he asked without enthusiasm. Down below as the road curved they could see the lights of the city left behind softly shining through the evening haze, and the deep purple flanks of Table Mountain as the long shadows fingered their way across its slopes. Soon they would be up and over the pass and heading through forest reserve and the cold grey granite cuttings, with the city forgotten and the wild sharp tang of fynbos filling their nostrils.

'No,' said Michaela. 'I'll call when we get there. Simon will understand.'

Susan expelled the breath she'd been holding. 'Just think, The Dog,' she said, rolling the cat onto her back and massaging her soft belly with her knuckles, 'we might have left you at home to have pilchards with the Pieman.'

'That's enough.' Antony was not as tolerant of Susan's mouth as Janus was and Michaela had never been strong on discipline.

Stillwaters, the Whitehead family home, had been in the family for over a hundred years. It was a meandering three hour drive along the coastline, allowing only occasional, tantalising glimpses of the sea on the way. The farm itself was on the bank of the Stilfontein river a mile or two inland and reached along a treacherous pot-holed road. It had been worked profitably as a farm in the old days, as had other farms in the district, but lean economic times and long periods of drought and political uncertainty over land claims had sent many would-be farmers into the cities to seek alternative means of income, and for Josh Whitehead Stillwaters had in time become more of a tax haven and a place to unwind than a viable living. He and Mater had bought a house in town and another on the Highveld, and they had for a period spent only holidays and Christmases at Stillwaters. But Mater, increasingly, had felt the call of the sea and the tranquillity of country life and she began to spend more and more time there. When their children went off to boarding school she had elected to stay on alone, and with the help of the Coloured farm manager, Frans Swartbooi, and sundry itinerant members of his large family, she had managed to pull the farm together and make of it something that was close to self-sufficient.

Stillwaters, Michaela had decided long ago, was probably her favourite place in the whole world, and Mater was probably her favourite person, too, beside Susan. Her mother had grown up on the farm and had preferred to spend her holidays in boarding school or at schoolfriends' homes and she had left Stillwaters behind just as soon as she possibly could, as had the other Whitehead children, Antony's father and Pauline's mother. But to the next generation of Stillwaters children the farm was nothing like the dead-end prison it had seemed to their parents. Stillwaters meant endless swimming in the river or in the sea. It meant fishing with nets and canoeing in the bristling reeds at low tide. Baked potatoes taken from the soil with Frans in the morning and cooked in the coals at sundown. Paraffin lamps and an outside shower. It meant going to bed with the itch of saltwater on your skin and hearing the energetic revivalist hymns of Frans's relations as they scuffed along the sand road five abreast, on the way to Sunday service in the Stilfontein village Coloured church.

Michaela did not have a clear memory of her grandfather. By the time she was visiting the farm on a regular basis, Josh Whitehead was spending less and less time there. His legal career and anti-apartheid activities meant that not only did he have his permanent base in the city, but that he was travelling abroad too. But for Michaela it was Mater who was the anchor in her life. With her own mother moving from city to city with each new show, Mater seemed as rooted in the soil of Stillwaters as the bluegum trees along its boundary. By this time Mater seldom ventured further than the village for supplies or to the farmstall at the side of the main road where she sold vegetables to passing motorists. Only a serious family crisis or funeral would persuade her to travel to the city. She had refused the offer of electricity when the rest of the village was linked to a main grid – an event which had precipitated a celebration second only to New Year's Eve – preferring the softness of lamplight in her windows and the comforting bulk of her ancient Aga cooker. To Mater this was neither stubborn resistance to progress nor reverse snobbery. She just preferred things this way and when Mater made up her mind about something she was impervious to outside suggestion, no matter how well meant.

Antony stopped for petrol as the last light began to fade from the sky and he bought hamburgers and packets of the cheese and onion crisps The Dog liked. They ate at the side of the road at a dubious looking picnic table. The night was utterly still. The only sound to break the spell was that of a cricket, hidden somewhere in the grass, which chirruped monotonously, stopping only to fox The Dog's confident pouncing from tussock to tussock.

Back on the road they drew parallel with a snake of a train moving smoothly on the railway line against the hillside. It was an old-fashioned goods train with a steam engine, although not an uncommon sight up here. Small squares of yellow light from its carriages measured a strip in the blackness and when Michaela rolled down her window they could hear the faint rattle of its wheels on the track.

'Wave!' yelled Susan, rolling her window down too. 'Hoot, Antony, hoot!'

Judging by his expression of tolerant resignation, Antony was no stranger to this exercise. He pressed his hooter obediently, waving an apology at the only other traffic in evidence, a farm labourer on a bicycle just ahead of them who swerved painfully into the barbed wire fence in surprise. Susan and Michaela were oblivious, hanging halfway out of their windows, laughing wildly and waving their arms. Antony hooted again and they were rewarded with a toot of acknowledgement from the engine driver and a puff of white steam which shot up into the air like a smoke signal. Michaela collapsed back into her seat.

'If we hurry,' she panted, 'we can catch it at the bridge and if we go under at the same time as it crosses the road, we can wish.'

'I know,' said Antony. 'I know.' He put his foot on the accelerator and pulled out to pass a car towing a caravan with the touch of recklessness Michaela somehow always seemed to inspire. The train had disappeared now behind the hills and the countryside was once more swamped in blackness, only their own headlamps lighting up the grey scrub and bushes at the side of the road.

'There it is!' shrieked Florida, entering into the spirit of things and nearly startling Antony out of his wits for the second time that day. 'Go!'

They made the bridge as the engine thundered over it and Antony put the car in neutral and they coasted silently beneath the terrifying racket of the carriages. Michaela had her eyes tightly shut. Susan and Florida were holding hands and screwing up their faces in concentration.

'There,' said Michaela. She opened her eyes and smiled at Antony. 'Now wasn't that a stroke of luck.'

Even before Josh Whitehead's death, Mater had taken a keen interest in the roadside farmstall she'd set up a mile or two from Stillwaters. It had started out as a thatched covering and a counter on the side of the main road before the Stilfontein turnoff and Frans had sold bags of potatoes and some fruit to the passing trade. Then Mater had experimented with homemade ginger beer and it was this perhaps more than anything that had established the farmstall's reputation. In summer it had drawn them and the kick from the ice-cold brew had ensured that they kept coming back for more. Just to make sure no one forgot her, Mater and Frans erected a huge blackboard at the top of the rise before the stall and she chalked up in foot-high letters – HOMEMADE GINGER BEER! STILLWATERS' FAMOUS BREW – just to make quite sure no one would go zooming by without refreshment.

Over the years, although the ginger beer remained the star attraction, Mater had added other irresistibles to her stock: marmalade, lemon curd, chilli relish, and her reputation was ensured. She still used the board to alert motorists, though, but she took to putting up cheery messages, quotations from Oscar Wilde, her own political opinions (brief but always pithy) and personal messages to her family when she knew they were coming. The Stillwaters farmstall bulletin board had made the newspapers and led to a couple of articles on the Whitehead family.

'What'll it be tonight, I wonder,' Michaela murmured as they crested the hill. She had called Mater just before they'd left town.

The headlights lit up the chalked letters as Antony slowed down, but tonight they were disappointed. The message was not new, nor was it for them: SORRY, NO APPLES, it said, VROT CROP. Mater hadn't had time to welcome them.

But she was waiting up for them with whisky and Marmite toast. She held the almost empty Marmite jar out to The Dog, who leapt out of Susan's arms with a friskiness that belied her age and fell immediately to pushing it across the kitchen floor with her nose. They all followed Mater into the front room, discarding bags and jackets as they went. This was the room where everything and nothing happened. It was a long, wooden-floored room running the width of the house. Its windows looked out over the river, at this time of night quite invisible, the only evidence of its presence at all being the light on a small boat out in the middle. This was the deaf postmaster from Stilfontein village and his deaf son skepping for klippies as they did every Friday night, winter and summer. Antony and Janus had been out with them many a time in the wooden dinghy and there were strict rules and duties on these expeditions, all of which were graphically and silently explained. The postmaster's son had charge of the plastic water-filled bucket and the light, while his father, Antony and Janus leant out over the sides and bow with nets, waiting to scoop up the tiddlers which swam to the surface. Only the postman's son was permitted to man the bucket's lid, after Janus had lifted it slightly one night to check on the fish and all six of them had leapt straight back into the water in an impressive display of aquatic aerobics. It was a comfort tonight to Michaela to see that tiny Friday nightlight on the river. She already felt the winding down process beginning to take hold. It had begun when they'd turned onto the gravel road and seen the lights of the farmhouse. Stillwaters always had this restorative effect on her. It was as if someone had put a brake on time, slowing the universe down just a notch or two. Michaela took the tumbler of whisky Mater had poured for her and sank into a deep chair beside the window. She looked around. In a room that never changed from one year to the next, she sensed something out of kilter. Josh Whitehead's billiard table was where it always was. So was the huge wooden table that could seat a comfortable sixteen people. The two double beds were there and the brown velveteen sofas.

'You've moved your chair,' Antony said suddenly. 'And the lamp.'

'And re-covered both mine and your grandfather's – you're observant,' Mater replied. 'Frans's handiwork.'

'Frans is clever with his hands,' Antony said. 'I always said there was more to Frans than met the eye.'

Mater smiled. 'You look tired,' she said to Michaela.

'I've had a busy week.' Michaela was watching

Antony's reflection in the black panes of glass. His dark hair looked singed almost red beside the lamp. Florida and Susan were unrolling their sleeping bags on one of the beds, arguing in low voices about who got to doss down nearest the window and so be closest to the river in the morning.

'So your mother's in a bit of a panic,' said Mater. 'I'm afraid I was forced to disconnect the phone for a day or two.'

'Tell me about it.' Michaela rolled her eyes.

Mater leaned forward suddenly and prised the Marmite jar off The Dog's nose. The Dog, on the brink of her own panic attack, had worked her way backwards through the house and collided with a table leg. 'Blanche will rise to the occasion,' Mater said. 'She always does. She just likes everyone to witness the struggle. We have an unpleasant fungal disease on the potatoes in the bottom field. Frans is at his wits end.' Mater was known for sliding in and out of completely unconnected conversations as if there was a thread of logic only she could see. The family was used to this mild eccentricity and sometimes they fell into the habit themselves when they were here, a habit which could be unsettling to first-time visitors or boyfriends trying to make a good impression in this formidably wealthy old Cape family.

'How is Frans's bad leg?' Antony asked. 'Could it be black spot?'

'That being the only potato blemish he's ever heard of,' said Michaela. 'He wasn't looking too upright at Christmastime.'

'I think that was probably more to do with the festivities,' Mater said drily. 'But he's been getting treatment at the clinic. He walks into town once a month. Actually he's perfectly fit.'

Suddenly they were all startled by the obviously hungry cry of a baby echoing noisily through the house.

'Good Lord,' Michaela exclaimed. 'Was that The Dog?'

Mater smiled serenely. She set her whisky down on the table and got to her feet, brushing toast crumbs from her skirt. 'Frans's sister-in-law had another baby,' she said. 'I'm taking care of her while her mother's looking for work.'

'Where's she looking?' said Antony.

'Cape Town,' Mater replied. 'Last we heard. Excuse me a moment, darlings.'

Susan and Florida jumped out of their bed and ran after Mater. They reappeared a moment later, jostling in the doorway, with Susan holding a very large baby wrapped in Mater's Chinese silk shawl. Swathed in black and gold dragons with sequinned red eyes, like a witch's baby in a children's picture book, the child was yelling its head off. Susan bent over its face and gently put her little finger into its mouth, cutting off the cries in an instant. Pleased with her trick, she looked at Michaela.

'Is your finger clean?' Michaela asked as the baby began to suck vigorously.

'It is now,' said Florida. 'Gimme a turn, Suze.'

Mater came back into the room with a bottle of milk in one hand and an eye dropper in the other. Michaela and Antony watched open-mouthed as Mater plunged the dropper into her whisky glass. Mater had the grace to look a little pink. 'Well it worked for you,' she told Michaela, 'and it sure as hell still works for me.' The baby, now discovering that it had been cheated, twisted its head aside and shrieked wildly in Susan's arms. Mater reached over and took her. 'This is Juanita,' she said, slipping the teat into its mouth. 'Isn't she a poppet?'

Michaela was completely lost for words. Mater was known far and wide for liking children only when they walked on two legs and could carry a bucket of potatoes the length of a field.

'All by yourself?' said Antony. He stood up to peer curiously at the baby. 'What about its father and the rest of Frans's extended family in the village? Why isn't one of them taking responsibility?'

'Oh, men,' Mater said dismissively, as if Antony would know exactly what she meant. 'Do you know what the Barberton sisters have done? Bought themselves a goddamn raucous ski-boat and James McCann the old drunk is teaching them to ski.' Mater shifted the child from one arm to the other. 'I offered to have her,' she went on, misinterpreting Antony's concern. 'They were grateful. And Frans is here every day and Anna helps out on Thursdays. She sees enough of her family, don't worry.' Mater smiled at their blank faces. 'Can you imagine,' she said. 'At their age!'

Mater was seventy this year and every second year she threw a birthday party at Stillwaters. This was an occasion which was the talk of the district for weeks before and weeks afterwards, the latter usually because something had happened to cause a scandal of one degree or another which tended to reverberate up and down the coast. At the last party the waterskiing Barberton sisters from across the river had gone skinny-dipping in full view of the Coloured priest and Jannie Brand and that had been a talking point for weeks – 'Four talking points really,' Mater had chuckled – and Jannie's wife in the bakery would have refused to serve them if things hadn't been so quiet. At that same memorable party Antony's mother Helena, who had multiple sclerosis and was in a wheelchair, started the tradition of the lame ducks race and had beaten Peter Barrett from the hotel with his tin legs in a race to the water's edge and almost tipped herself into the murk in the process.

This year Mater had announced the party was to be her last. It took too much organising and planning, she'd decided. And she was tired of birthdays. Seventy was more than anyone needed in a lifetime. She did concede that this last occasion would be a big one and it was to be open house at Stillwaters. She was even thinking of inviting the mayor.

'Harriet and David are coming from Australia for the party,' said Antony. 'Did you know?'

'Pauline called me,' Mater said. The baby was quiet now, a dribble of white milk on her chin. Mater put her against her shoulder and stroked her back. The knuckles on her hands were swollen and knotted with arthritis. 'It's about time. Pauline has needed them more than I think she knows herself. And is your mother going to behave herself this year?'

Both Antony and Michaela thought they were being addressed and both hesitated. Then they all laughed. Blanche had been known to do outrageous things in her time too, like the year she'd tied a lewd proposal to the leg of Jannie Brand's homing pigeon and he'd invited her fishing with him the very next day.

'I'm going to turn in,' said Mater.

'Where does Juanita sleep?' Michaela asked. She got up and peeped at the baby who was now fast asleep, fat cheeks sagging, on Mater's shoulder.

'Frans has made her a beautiful crib,' Mater replied.

'She sleeps beside my bed. That way I can reach down for her in the night when she cries.'

Susan and Florida were asleep, zipped up to their chins in matching sleeping bags. 'Let's walk down to the river,' said Antony. It was a still, warm night. He put an arm round Michaela's shoulders. 'You want to talk about Bricknell Court, don't you?'

Michaela slipped a sweater over her head. It would be cooler down on the bank, she knew from experience. With the low tide the rocks would also be treacherously slippery, so they took a torch with them to light the way. As they moved away from the house they saw the resident eagle owl on the chimney pot silhouetted against the moon. The tufts on its ears moved slightly in the breeze and it swivelled its head right round to look at them without shifting its body at all. Michaela gave an involuntary shiver and glanced round nervously. The Dog was fairly luminous in the dark.

Antony held the torch and took Michaela's hand to guide her down the rough cut stone steps which led to the rocks and the wooden jetty. Water black as ink lapped at the jetty poles with a greedy sucking sound. The postmaster and his son had long since packed up and gone home, and there was only the starlight and the moon riding high against the clouds to break the night's deep blackness. They walked slowly along the bank in the direction of the sea where they could hear the dull roar and thump of the breakers.

'Look,' Antony began when Michaela volunteered nothing. 'I know what you're thinking and it's not going to do you any good. Years have gone by, more than any of us, I think, want to remember. Maybe it's not so important any more. Have you thought about that?'

'I can't stop thinking about it,' Michaela said in a low voice. 'I haven't thought about Bricknell Court, not really, for years, but all of a sudden it's like I'm a ghost or something hovering about the place, flitting in and out of the trees, just like that wretched Tommy used to do. I know it's crazy but somehow as long as the place was *there*, it was as if the whole thing could still be resolved, put *right*. Now that they're pulling it down, I know I should feel relieved, but I don't. It will be gone. Forever. So why do I feel so horrid, so peculiar? I feel ... I can't explain it ... I don't know what I feel.'

Michaela had walked on while Antony stood tossing small stones into the water, the same ones Mater paid the Coloured children in the village to take out. 'We were children,' he said. 'And even if that doesn't excuse us, the fact remains that we were just kids. We can't be held accountable for ever for being stupid, thoughtless children, no matter how stupid and thoughtless we might have been. Because that's all it was, Mick. You know that as well as I do.' He caught up with her and turned her round to face him. 'It's over now and in the past. There are other memories of Bricknell Court that are more important. To me, anyway.'

'And to me,' Michaela mumbled. She smiled up at him bleakly. Antony put his arms round her and hugged her tightly. He kissed her hair softly. It was clammy and matted from the sea air. Michaela pulled herself gently out of his hold. 'OK, coz,' she said. 'I know when I'm being ridiculous, but thank you for not making me feel foolish.' She kissed his cheek. 'What would I do without you?'

'I hope you never have to find out,' said Antony lightly. 'Hey, The Dog.'

A white shape bounded up to them and The Dog

wound herself round Michaela's legs, purring. Michaela picked her up. 'Great breath,' she said, recoiling. 'Let's go back. I forgot to phone Simon.'

Antony is in charge of the garden rake. It is a particularly long one and has metal rather than rubber tines, which makes it extra heavy and difficult to wield. 'Stand back,' he says officiously. 'Stand back, Janus.'

The cousins are picking loquats in the orchard, but there are no branches low down and the yellow fruit so tantalisingly profuse is high beyond their reach. Right at the top of the trees the doves and starlings and Tommy the pinball wizard have already made short work of the ripest ones and the ground beneath their feet is strewn with hard brown pips.

Pauline has the basket ready and she shades her eyes from the sun. She has a new pudding-bowl haircut, courtesy of Michaela's current career choice, and a fringe which rises raggedly from just beneath her left eyebrow to just above her right. Michaela herself is sitting on the low wall round the sundial with a lapful of loquats which Antony climbed up for earlier. She has already eaten her share and she looks hot and bored.

'Come on, Antony,' she calls. 'Get on with it.'

Antony is planning to join the circus at the end of the holidays and he balances the rake with a flourish. Steady brown arms and muscular legs slightly apart for perfect balance. The rake flies through the dusty green leaves, hooks and holds. 'Way ta go!' Janus shouts, darting forward.

'Look out!' Antony warns. He makes a grab for his cousin and pushes him roughly out of the way as rake and branch wing towards the ground. Pauline snatches at the loquats and holds fast. They are warm from the sun and a little soft.

'My dad says those things are poisonous. They make you shit green.'

They all turn in the direction of the unfamiliar voice. It is coming from a plump boy with glasses and a crewcut. He has brown knee-length socks turned over at the tops and open-toed sandals. He has brown shorts wide as a skirt, and they almost reach to his very white knees.

Antony stares. He shifts the rake from one hand to the other. No one says anything, but Michaela has a look on her face that spells trouble. Her eyes are taking in every feature of this intruder with a calculated and disturbing deliberation. Then Janus steps forward. He spits a loquat pip to one side and it rolls to the feet of the newcomer. In the nine year old piping voice he has taken to affecting because it gets him instant attention from his aunt, if not from his mother, he says: 'And *who*, in the *world*, are *you*?'

The boy takes off his glasses and breathes on them. He polishes one lens at a time on his maroon jersey. Putting his glasses on again and wriggling them into position with his nose, he says, 'My name's Crispian. Crispian Younghusband.'

'What?' says Pauline. She wipes the grey fuzz off a loquat and bites into it.

'We've come to live in Sou'fafrica,' the boy says. 'We just moved in. Can you play French cricket?'

'What?' says Pauline.

'No,' says Michaela, uncurling her legs and slipping softly off the wall. She steps forward until she is standing quite close to the boy. Antony can see him blink uncertainly. He licks his lips. There is a small pulse showing in his neck. 'No,' Michaela says again. 'We can't play French cricket, Crispian Younghusband. We're picking loquats and eating them and then we're going to go inside and see whose shit is the greenest.'

Janus draws his breath in sharply. If their aunt heard Michaela talking like that – and then Michaela is laughing, a toneless, scornful sound, and pointing at the boy's clothes. Despite himself, Antony begins to laugh too, and Janus is showing off, shooting loquat pips perilously close to the boy's left shoulder. The boy stands his ground, his face without expression behind the glasses. Out of the corner of his eye Antony sees Tommy walk by and pause to watch. He is wearing a jersey which Antony recognises as his uncle's.

Michaela walks around Crispian Younghusband in a circle, like a cop with a suspect. She even has her hands behind her back. She is taller than the boy and he looks at her nervously as she stops in front of him again. 'We've got to go now, Crispian Younghusband,' she says, 'but you can have a loquat to remember us by.' Quick as a flash she shoves a loquat into his surprised mouth and runs off shrieking with laughter. Janus gallops after her and so, after a moment, does Antony. Pauline lingers a minute, staring, as the boy splutters and spits. 'They're quite nice really,' Antony hears her say before she turns and runs after them. And he isn't sure whether she means the loquats or the cousins.

· 4 ·

Michaela found the girls in the field nearest to the river, helping Frans lift potatoes from the soil. Juanita was nearby, in Mater's fruit basket in the shade, kicking and rocking with great vigour. Florida had come upon a row of faded green periwinkles on a windowsill, graded in sizes, and she'd threaded them on a length of ribbon and suspended them from the basket's handle just out of the baby's reach. The Dog sat alongside, taking turns with Juanita to bat at the shells with her round white paws.

'Frans,' said Michaela. 'Good morning. How are you? How's the family?'

Frans took off his hat and stood up. 'Number one, Miss Michaela,' he said. He had called her Miss Michaela since she was three years old. He had a band of dirt round his forehead where his hatband had made a greasy dent. He smiled at Michaela and wiped his hands on his trousers. He had strong white teeth and very brown skin, burnt even darker than its natural colour by a life spent working under the sun, and creased by the sharp wind that whistled through the hills in this dry part of the country. He was a short, stocky man in his fifties, but strong and fit, and there was no evidence today of the rheumatism in the legs that plagued him every winter.

'The missus says you've had a problem with the crop this year?'

Although she would instantly have denied it, Michaela rather enjoyed playing the mistress of the manor and wearing dresses in flowing cotton print. She was almost sorry Mater didn't have a houseful of menials to whom she could be gracious on her visits. She had to make do with Frans, who nevertheless did always respond in a gratifying way, respectful but not so deferential as to make her uncomfortable.

'All the farms,' said Frans, throwing out an arm. 'Too much rain last winter.'

'Mmm.' Michaela nodded gravely and they contemplated the undersized spuds together in silence. Then 'Susan,' Michaela called out. 'We must start packing up. Antony wants to get back to town.'

Susan and Florida were in their swimming costumes. Their feet, hands and nails were black with dirt. Florida had a broomstick across her shoulders with a tin bucket slung over each end. She plodded, bent over, down one row and up another while Susan skipped along behind, carefully brushing the soil off the potatoes and flinging them in. 'She's my slave,' she explained. 'I just bought her at the harbour. I saved her from a fate worse than death.'

Michaela observed that the alternative didn't look all that much fun either. 'What was the fate?' she asked.

'Marrying the captain of the pirate ship,' Florida replied, turning round and catching Susan a glancing blow on the head with a bucket. 'And being his sex kitten.'

'Gosh,' said Michaela. She looked at Frans who had put his hat back on and was luckily out of earshot. 'That does sound grim.' She threw a potato into the bucket with a clang. 'I think I'd like to liberate you from the potato field too, if I may. Why don't you both have a last swim while I take Juanita in? Mater's preparing something unmentionable for her supper.'

While the girls ran down to the river, Michaela sat a while on the bank beside the baby, sleeping now and sucking on her thumb. This was the time of day she loved best at Stillwaters, just before the sun went down and the surrounding hills were patched with golden shadows. She watched a johnny duiker sitting on a spike sticking out of the water, drying his seaweed brown wings. She could see a drop of water on his beak as he turned his head this way and that, with his wings spread wide like a cloak.

In the field adjoining this one was the family graveyard. Josh Whitehead was buried there, as were his parents. And so was Danny, beneath the shade of a very old peach tree. She had been across there with Susan earlier in the day and they had cleaned the headstone and put some yellow and blue everlastings in the old glass Ricoffy jar Mater kept there for that purpose. Susan had fashioned a new and intricate triplicate with shells, as she did whenever she came here, entwining the first letters of their names – Danny, Susan, Michaela – in the sandy part on top of the grave.

Susan had only vague memories of her father, whereas Michaela's were vivid and sharply defined. The odd part was that although she hadn't even been there when Danny had bled to death at the mouth of the Stilfontein river, she had relentlessly reconstructed his last moments in her mind, so that to her they were far clearer than any others in their life together. She had not been there to witness the early morning sea mist which blotted out the breakers and dulled the sound of the ocean, when Danny had taken Susan for a swim in the river before breakfast. Susan liked especially to swim in the river and the sea at the same time, as if she wanted to embrace both bodies of water at once, and she loved the way the water churned and foamed at the river mouth when the tide was about to turn. Danny would take her on his back, clinging like a baby dolphin to its mother, her small body pressed flat against his, hands digging into his collarbone. 'Here we go,' Danny would say. 'Hold tight now.' And he would swim breaststroke down the middle of the river, kicking hard against the incoming tide, and make straight for the sea with Susan yelling with delight – 'Are we in the sea yet, Danny? Is this the *sea* or still the *river*?' – until the first waves broke over Danny's head and he would dive through them and turn and catch her beneath her slippery arms before she sank beneath the water.

Everybody knew about the sharks that summer. Everyone had a shark story, particularly after the two great whites had been sighted near the river mouth. They even had lifeguards posted on the main beach, schoolboys from Stilfontein High, sitting up in the tall metal chairs borrowed from the tennis club after the Christmas round robin. There was a demarcated 'safe' area which they would patrol, a few hundred metres up from the rocky beach, the one which had been the Coloured area until not so long ago. All the holidaymakers had been encouraged to stay within this area so that the guards could clear the water in an emergency. There were no shark nets this far down the coast; sharks were uncommon in these waters after all.

The morning Danny died, two days after New Year, when Michaela had gone home to Cape Town for the launching of a new product line, he had taken Susan down to the mouth before breakfast. Instead of using Mater's pick-up and going by road, as they usually did, this time they had walked all the way along the river bank. Danny had probably carried Susan on his shoulders most of the way, for the Barberton sisters said they had seen them passing by their windows like a totem pole at about seven-thirty, singing 'Let's Go Fly a Kite' from Mary Poppins. Michaela had found herself humming it too, for days afterwards, even rather audibly at Danny's funeral until Antony had had to stand on her toe to shock her into silence.

It was quite a long walk to the sea and they would have taken it slowly, stopping to paddle and pick up driftwood and shells. Danny had asked Mater not to keep breakfast for them and she had given them a packet of fruit instead to stay the pangs. It promised to be a blistering hot day. Danny had painted pink and green fluorescent suntan lotion stripes on Susan's nose and cheeks, and she looked like a small Indian brave setting out with her long tangly hair and brocade headband like her father's. It had not been difficult to piece together what had happened. Mater and Frans had eventually gone in search of them and come upon the small crowd huddled on the beach and the deaf postmaster with Susan stiff in his arms. Susan's face was blank with bewilderment and she did not at first recognise Mater stumbling towards her along the sand.

Danny was lying on his back. Someone had put a fisherman's sleeveless jacket over his torso to keep the flies away. There were bits of nylon fishing line and some lead sinkers leaking out of the pockets and a strong smell of fish in the air. It seemed as if every bit of Danny's blood had drained away into the sand. He lay in a wide rusty circle, his normally tanned skin a pale, peculiar, empty colour. Susan's knees and her arms were stained like the sand. The postmaster indicated to Frans that he had found the two of them here, on the sand, as the mist was lifting off the sea, when he had come down for his early morning dip. Susan had wrapped her pink sweater over the place where Danny's leg had been, tying the sleeves together in a bulky knot, in an attempt to stem the gush of blood after Danny had passed out. Then she had simply knelt down beside him and waited for him to wake up. When she was hungry she had eaten a banana from Mater's packet, carefully stowing the peel away. She had put a red apple on a piece of driftwood beside Danny's arm and had smeared suntan lotion on his face. In the circle of blood she had waited and there the postmaster had found them, a bizarre tableau beneath the rising mist.

'Michaela?' It was Antony. 'Mater's waiting for Juanita. She said —'

'I'm just coming.'

'Where are the girls?'

'There.'

They could see Florida and Susan racing each other to the raft anchored in the middle of the river. Antony beckoned to them. 'The car's packed,' he said. 'We should be moving. I've made us sandwiches for the drive.'

Antony picked up the basket with the sleeping baby while Michaela waited for Susan and Florida to reach the bank. A line of grey-backed gulls flew overhead, calling, and she watched their path towards the sea against the crimson sky.

Antony dropped Susan and Michaela off at home and he took Florida home too as it was on his way. It was only when he was pulling into his own garage and about to get out of the car when he heard a sound from beneath the dashboard. 'Oh, Jesus, The Dog,' he muttered. 'Why couldn't you have spoken up sooner?' He was tired and it was a long drive back to Michaela's house. When he got there he found Susan wide-eyed with fright.

'We thought the owl had got her,' she told Antony, snatching The Dog from him. 'Mum wants to show you something. She was about to call.'

Michaela was standing in the kitchen. Without saying anything she unfurled a sheet of newsprint, holding it at the top and bottom edges like a town crier. It didn't take Antony long to read the six huge words, but he stared at the paper for as long as Michaela held it out. Then she let the bottom edge go and it curled itself closed.

'MYSTERY SKELETON FOUND AT BRICKNELL COURT,' Michaela said in capital letters, just in case he'd missed them.

'Where did you get this?' Antony asked carefully.

'I tore it off a pole outside the café.'

'And did you buy the newspaper that normally goes with it?'

'What do you think?' She handed it over to him. She read the piece on the front page over his shoulder. 'A human skeleton was found by demolition workers at Bricknell Court this week. Identity has not yet been established, but it is believed that the skeleton had been in the basement boiler room of the apartment block for some considerable time. Police are investigating.

Anyone with any information which may be helpful is asked to come forward.'

'Yet,' said Michaela, 'is the key word. Identity has not *yet* been established.'

'Mm,' said Antony. 'I brought The Dog back, by the way.'

'Thank you.' Michaela could see he rather wished he hadn't. Right now he could be looking forward to a warm shower and a cold beer and not be staring a potential crisis in the face if it hadn't been for her. A lot of things might not have happened if it hadn't been for her. Antony sat down at the table and sighed heavily. Michaela felt a sudden warm surge of annoyance run through her like an electric current. At least it started her moving. She filled the kettle at the sink and took a teapot down off a shelf. Antony wasn't going to slide off home and leave her to deal with this on her own. She poured brown sugar from a packet into a miniature Toby jug. Not after the unsatisfactory weekend he'd just talked her into. She'd already had to cope with Danny memories, and the unexpectedness of Juanita taking up all of Mater's attention. And Mater hadn't been herself either, and not just because of the baby. She'd seemed distracted and off balance, somehow. It wasn't fair to expect Michaela to digest this all alone. She put two teabags in the pot and stirred in boiling water, moving her face away from the steam. She also had Simon to face and he wasn't a happy person judging by the note that had been tacked to the front door, without concern for the woodwork, when they got home.

When Michaela put a cup in front of him she caught Antony combing through the golf results. She took the newspaper away and folded it so that neither the front page nor the golf was visible, pinching along the creases with her fingertips. Antony began pulling gently at a phantom moustache, a sure sign of inner agitation.

'Now,' Michaela said, walking up and down like a nun at her prayers. 'We have to think.'

'Yes,' said Antony.

'We have to get the others and decide what to do.'

'I know.'

'But we should probably sleep on it tonight so that we can all think more clearly in the morning.'

'Right – hey, those are all my lines, Michaela,' Antony said suddenly, shaking his head as if coming out of a brief trance. 'Isn't this where the strong supportive male calms the hysterical woman and starts to think of a plan? I don't even take sugar in my tea. You know that.'

'Just testing,' Michaela said. She poured tea in a saucer and put it on the floor for The Dog. 'Go ahead then – calm me down. I'm hysterical as you can see.' She laughed, and there was a faint trace of something like panic at the back of her throat. 'I'm sorry about the sugar.'

'Well, you're right about one thing,' Antony said. His voice was firm beneath the weariness. 'There's absolutely nothing we can do about it tonight, and I'm not sure there's really anything we need to do about it at all. But what we *do* need is a night's sleep. Then tomorrow we'll call Pauline and Janus and discuss it with them.' He stood up. 'I'm going home now. Can I take the paper?' He picked it up, still folded in half, without waiting for an answer.

Michaela nodded anyway. She followed him to the front door with a teacup in her hand. Antony touched her cheek and she shivered. 'It might not be him,' he tried feebly and Michaela smiled and nodded.

'Sure,' she said. 'And I'm Ivana Trump.'

When he'd gone she took a long bath. She tried reading a competition story while she soaked – *Country in Chains* – but she found it depressing and could not concentrate. Instead she washed her hair and rubbed a lot of nighttime moisturiser into her skin. She cut her fingernails and her toenails. She made a note on the steamed up mirror to get her legs waxed. Susan and The Dog were listening to a golden oldies request programme on the radio and Michaela sang along with the Kinks and the Hollies under her breath. 'I love. Jennifer Eccles . . .' But no matter what she did, there was no escaping Bricknell Court, which reared up in her head not soft and warm-bricked as she wanted to remember it, but austere and grey and forbidding as a gaol. She could feel the close, dark silence of the boiler room and smell the distinctive odour of unwashed feet and sweat. She could see the threadbare pink blanket Pauline had given to Tommy neatly folded on the floor, and the butts of his hand-rolled cigarettes scattered carelessly about. And at the same time, there was the frightful Crispian Younghusband, pushing into her memories too, the way he had pushed into their lives that summer, with that strand of spiky hair that stood up on his head like a warthog's stiff tail. Somehow his nasal English voice seemed to have holed up in her inner ear: 'Who wants to play French cricket? I can teach you. French cricket is the ultimate fun.'

Michaela never took medication of any sort. When Danny had died the doctor had prescribed sleeping pills to get her through the night waking and the shakes that wouldn't stop. But even then Michaela had put them away in the medicine cupboard and battled it out chemically unaided. Tonight she found herself feeling along the shelves with trembling fingers until she located the small white tablets still in their box. She swallowed two with a glass of water.

Nobody knew Tommy's real name, and exactly when he had first appeared in the Bricknell Court area no one could remember. It seemed as if he had always been there, on the periphery of things, slipping in and out of their lives, appearing and disappearing at any given time. Although his legs were strangely stunted and his head was too large for his thin shoulders, it wasn't pity that he inspired, nor mockery. Perhaps it was his completely self-contained manner, or his noncommittal grunts and mutters that passed for conversation, that made people keep their distance. It was generally believed that Tommy was soft in the head, and although he certainly wasn't blind, he gave a good impression sometimes of being both deaf and dumb. But like the words in the rock opera, and the reason for the name he'd somehow acquired, he sure played a mean pinball, and that was where he was mostly to be found: standing on a tomato box at the pinball machine at the corner café, flicking switches with a concentration that was almost manic. Janus had challenged him to a game once, cocky and confident that he could better a loon, and he had never tried it again.

Tommy was a curious racial mix. He had pale blue eyes in his dark face and a wild, almost aboriginal shock of black woollen hair. His torso was thin but muscular, but from his hips down his legs were thick and heavy and as short as a ten year old's. He was older than Michaela by at least six years, but when she was twelve years old she was already head and shoulders taller than him. Tommy appeared to have no home other than, one suspected, a police cell at regular intervals. When the tomato box stood to one side of the pinball machine, George at the café would shrug his shoulders and say, 'He get picked up again, I think. Last week, this week, who knows.'

It was Pauline who first discovered that he was using the boiler room to sleep in and she had given him the blanket and many smuggled sandwiches before she told the others.

Michaela slept very soundly, but when she woke in the morning she had a residual image from a dream splashed across the inside of her eyelids: there was Tommy, wearing Crispian Younghusband's floppy blue sunhat with the zipper on the side. He was smiling, a sly, sideways, secretive smile and putting his finger to his lips, and when he grinned the pink lips peeled away and the ghastly yellow horse's teeth of a skeleton were swimming towards her, clacking together like someone's old dentures.

Michaela felt sick and even Susan commented on her pallor. She dropped Susan off at school and drove to her office, determined to have a productive day. Work would dispel the nightmare if she went about it methodically. The first thing she did when she got in to the office was write to Joy Beamish. 'Dear Mrs Beamish,' she began. 'I was sorry to miss you the other day. Thank you for your competition entry. This will be evaluated in due course, along with the rest of the entries. Thank you also for the sample of Meltin' Moments Sugarless Chox for diabetics which you enclosed, and which smudged your opening paragraphs just a little. It was thoughtful of you even though I am fortunately not a diabetic.' Michaela looked at the page, then scratched out the last few words and put a fullstop after you. She always wrote her letters out in longhand before giving them to Roz to type. Roz and shorthand were not familiar acquaintances and anyway the act of scribbling was in itself soothing. 'Your last batch of verse was charming,' she went on, 'but sadly not suitable for the magazine's needs at the present time. I am returning them to you under cover of this letter.'

'Why are you being so nice to her today?' Roz asked curiously. 'You're not usually so pleasant.'

'Thanks a lot. I happen to feel sorry for the old bat sometimes. She tries.'

'I'll say.' Roz was grumpy. She had switchboard duty today and she felt it was beneath her talents.

Despite her good night's sleep Michaela still felt brittle round the edges. She put this down to the sleeping pills which, although they had knocked her out as she had intended them to, had left her feeling out of touch with reality ever since she'd woken up. The act of walking, especially, was novel: there was a squashy texture to the ground, as if she were walking on plastic bags filled with air. And everyone had haloes round their heads, a sort of ribbon of light. Roz said she was describing the onset of a migraine, but Michaela never got migraines and her head wasn't sore.

She worked her way steadily through the papers on her desk. She returned phonecalls and pacified Simon, promising him dinner at a restaurant of his choice to make up for her thoughtless behaviour. At ten she chaired an editorial meeting and at one she had lunch with the syndications manager who was triumphant at having made the Worst Dressed list for the third year in a row. By the end of the day everything on her desk was symmetrical and her peace-in-the-home watered.

Antony had made the arrangement: they were to meet up with Janus and Pauline at Pauline's club after work. The electrician was still installing equipment and Pauline was supervising. He wouldn't bother them and as no one else would be around they could talk in private. Driving down to the harbour, Michaela's sense of unreality had all but passed. She felt in control again, satisfied that her life was about to return to normal. It was only when she walked in to the club and saw Pauline, Janus and Antony stop talking and look up at her with anxious faces, that she all of a sudden felt a nudge behind the knees and a cold dampness spreading from her armpits. Perhaps it wasn't going to be so simple after all.

'Well,' she said, sitting down and looking round at them. 'Do we tell or don't we?'

'Meet Ernest,' Pauline said. She waved in the direction of a swarthy man in blue overalls behind her, wearing a nautical cap and a lot of electrical wires about his person.

'Hello, Ernest.' Michaela smiled vaguely at the man who didn't appear to notice.

'No, that's Frank,' said Pauline. '*This* is Ernest.' A large African grey walked sideways along the back of her chair and poked its neck forward.

Michaela grunted. 'It's not going to sing, is it?' she asked. 'I hate Gilbert and Sullivan.'

Antony shifted his chair closer to Michaela's and put his elbows on the table. 'We were just ... did you listen to the news?' he asked.

Michaela shook her head. No news was good news.

'Well, there's nothing further really,' Janus said.

'Nothing that wasn't in the paper yesterday. Except —'

'Except?' Michaela felt her pulse quicken, or thought she did at least.

'Except that it appears they found some ... articles, I think they said, with the ... er ... skeleton, and they're hoping these will provide some clue to its identity.'

'What things?'

'They didn't say,' said Pauline. 'Maybe they're trying to spook someone into coming forward. Also —' She stopped. Ernest was trying to take the gold loop of her earring in his curved beak. She moved away and tapped the bird on its head with her index finger.

'Also,' said Antony slowly, 'some expert from the university has put a date on the thing, a rough date, that is. The skeleton is about twenty years old.'

'It's him all right,' said Michaela. 'The bloody snot-nose. Wouldn't you just know it.' She felt incredibly annoyed. 'Well, he deserved it after all,' she added defiantly but with little conviction.

Outside the window a tug was moving slowly out of the harbour. In its wake some tatty grey seagulls bobbed on the greasy water, amid a flotilla of fruit peels and plastic bags moving up and down on the choppy waves. Two Coloured men were working a huge coil of rope round an iron bollard. The rope was brown and thick as a man's thigh and neither man could get a grip on it. They were laughing and shaking their heads. When Janus had made his brief sortie one summer into the Cubs and had learnt a thing or two about tying knots, the cousins had played hangman with a ferociousness that had frightened them. Tommy had come up with an old car tyre and used their rope to make a swing from the chestnut tree for Pauline. They would take turns to sit in it and twist it round and round and then lift their feet off the ground and spin until they were dizzy.

Pauline handed out flaky pastry pies, wrapped in warm, checked serviettes.

'So what do we do?' she said, holding a piece of pastry out to Ernest who put his head on one side and stared at it blankly. His beak was as black as an old toenail. 'Do we tell the police?'

'Oh, absolutely,' said Janus, with his mouth halfway to his pie. He gave a short laugh. 'Just stroll into Caledon Square in our lunch hour and ask for our things back.'

'We don't know that there's anything of ours there,' said Michaela. Could a pink blanket twenty years old be traced to Pauline's linen closet? 'Why should there be anything to link us to some mouldering old skull and bones? You could hardly call any of us suspects or anything. And besides, has there been any mention of a crime? We don't need to feel like criminals, do we? We were children.' No one said anything. Michaela looked at Antony. 'We were children,' she repeated. 'Children.'

Antony unwrapped his serviette and bent to sniff at the pie. 'It's OK, Michaela,' he said. 'You're not on trial here.'

'Oh, aren't I?' said Michaela. She looked out of the window.

'Ernest all right?' It was the electrician who had padded up quietly, making Michaela jump. He smiled down at her with the liquid-eyed Latin lover look some women (Pauline?) find attractive.

'Ernest's great,' said Pauline. 'But he could do with some handcream and a manicure.' She grinned up at him in a way Michaela might have called flirtatious if she hadn't known Pauline better.

When he was out of earshot again the cousins bent their heads forward like conspirators. 'This is straight out of Enid Blyton, you realise,' Antony whispered. 'Any minute George is going to walk in here with her dyke haircut and her mongrel and say, "I vote we make a pact and never tell a living soul what we know."'

'Well, we never did, did we?' Michaela pointed out, ignoring his attempt at levity. 'And look where it's got us.'

'Where?' Pauline asked, glancing furtively over her shoulder.

'Well, *I* vote,' Antony said, looking firmly at each of them in turn, 'that we do precisely nothing. We carry on with our lives.'

'As if it was nothing to do with us,' Michaela said dully.

'Yes,' said Antony. 'Exactly.' He put his arm round her shoulders and pulled her to him.

Michaela saw that the men had successfully coiled the big rope round the bollard. They were sitting on it now, smoking and looking out to sea. The wind blew the smoke from their cigarettes into their faces and flattened their shirts against their chests.

After Pauline had locked up and they had all walked Michaela to her car, Janus took a stroll round the harbour. It was the time of day before the pubs and restaurants began to fill up and lights were coming on in the buildings in town and beyond. A brisk south-east wind had billowed into a full-scale gale and the boats in the yacht basin moved about restlessly, their masts swaying and creaking.

Janus couldn't remember ever going into the boiler room. He had been nervous of the darkness and the odd hot smell. As a child he hadn't even liked the sound of it. Boiler room. It sounded dangerous.

He stepped out of the wind into the doorway of a women's lingerie shop. He gazed into the window at black lace and flesh-coloured step-ins. A young girl in a miniskirt was draping a chiffon scarf round the flat pink plastic of a model in the window, sticking the bits that were out of sight with Press-Stick and frowning with concentration. The skirt rode up her thighs and she glanced at Janus in the doorway and pulled it down with a self-conscious smile.

'What time do you close?' Janus asked.

The girl looked up. She had long, very white hair and her fingernails were painted in exquisitely curved zebra stripes.

'Nine,' she said. 'In summer.'

Janus walked round the cramped interior. Heaps of soft material lay on a glass-topped table. He picked up a pair of silk stockings and they blew gently in the wind from the doorway, kicking out like an underwater swimmer with a languid, timeless motion.

'That's our sale table,' said the girl, watching him. 'Please don't mess it up. The sale only starts tomorrow.'

Janus held a cool ice-white slip to his cheek. It was as soft as a cloud. He let it slide through his fingers. The girl was still watching him, sitting back on her haunches.

'Are you interested in buying something?' she asked.

'Oh,' said Janus. 'Yes – this.'

The girl looked doubtful. 'That's on sale,' she told him. 'But the sale only starts tomorrow.'

Janus shrugged. 'I won't be here tomorrow,' he said. 'I'm killing myself tonight. This is my last purchase. It's a farewell gift,' he added.

The girl looked at him, half smiling. 'Oh, take it,' she said. 'You can have it at sale price. What the hell.' She took his money, glancing up at him from under her white fringe. 'Someone's lucky,' she said. 'It's a beautiful garment. Something to remember you by.'

Janus took the packet. He walked towards the door.

'Hey,' said the girl. She was leaning with her bottom against the counter. Janus turned. 'So what's it going to be?' she said. 'The highrise or the single gunshot?' She winked at him.

Janus smiled and left, clutching the packet to his side. It was so light it felt empty, and as he got to his car he looked inside just to check that the slip was there at all.

· 5 ·

Pauline put her basket down just inside the front door and switched on the light in the hallway. She could hear the sound of the television coming from the bedroom and see its faint light flickering in the glass of the pictures in the passage. Like a lot of wealthy men, Tertius was always worrying about wasting electricity and he usually sat in the dark when he watched TV. Never have a light on in a room when you're not in it, he told her often, and as a result anyone looking in at their house from the outside for any length of time of an evening, might be forgiven for thinking they were witnessing an elaborate Morse code message, as Pauline and Tertius moved about from room to room, lights winking on and off behind them.

Pauline's basket sighed and creaked. It was one of those wicker baskets you saw in Rupert the Bear books, and she kept it lined with a folded blue and white checked tablecloth in case a sudden picnic was called for. Ever since she had become interested in food, Pauline had carried such a basket about with her filled with snacks for all and sundry. If she wasn't handing out fruit sticks to her friends, she was scattering breadcrumbs for the squirrels or impaling wedges of apple fashioned into rosebuds for mice on fences or thornbushes for the birds. As a child Pauline was never difficult to track down. She left culinary clues all over the place. And like Antony with his camera, which appeared to be permanently attached to his arm, Pauline's basket went everywhere with her.

There was a brass hook behind the front door. Pauline put her red and purple cap on it and went through to the kitchen. Then she turned back quickly and switched off the hall light, cocking an ear for any movement from the bedroom. She took two leftover pies from the basket and put them in the microwave for Tertius. Then she poured herself a glass of iced water and drank it standing up, feeling it run through her body like a cold glass marble. It was hot and close in the kitchen. All the windows were shut fast. There was a dead bee on the windowsill with its legs in the air.

'Good of you to come home.' Tertius was standing in the doorway behind her in his vest and rugby shorts. He looked like a farmer.

'I was just heating up a pie for you,' said Pauline. 'Two pies. Steak and kidney.'

'I already ate,' said Tertius.

Pauline looked at the microwave accusingly, as if it might have said something. 'Oh,' she said. 'Well.' She took off her jacket.

'It would be nice sometimes if we could sit down at a table and have a hot meal together like normal people.' This was not a good sign. When Tertius took normal people as his theme it usually meant trouble.

Pauline moved slowly and steadily across to the microwave like a normal person, not looking in Tertius' direction. She took out the pies. She'd already had two at the club and half of the one Michaela had discarded, but if she had another one Tertius would probably make one of his remarks. He could be startlingly astute sometimes. The pies huddled together on a plate in the centre of the table. She felt embarrassed by their rich, seductive aroma.

'We do eat together Tertius,' Pauline said. 'And we will have more regular meals soon, I promise. It's just the club. You know how it is when you're starting something. I have to be there. I have to supervise just about everything to begin with. You know how important this is to me.'

'*Ja*,' said Tertius, without expression. 'I know.'

Pauline wondered why Tertius didn't appear to have realised that once the club was open he was going to see a lot less of her than he did at present, and home-cooked meals would of necessity have to be put on hold. She would be at the club nearly every night, weekends included. She thought that would have been obvious and had almost hoped that Tertius might have shown signs of enthusiasm or support, at least. But Tertius hadn't ever shown that much interest in the club, and when he couldn't be patronising he usually backed off.

'You sure you won't —' Pauline gestured at the table.

Tertius shook his head. He was frowning to himself and his neck was beginning to turn a blotchy red.

'Coffee?' This was where Tertius' mood could go either way and Pauline told herself that if she could control the tremor in her voice she could avert disaster. She practised her current affirmation statement, a technique she'd read about in a *Reader's Digest* article. *I am calm. I am confident. I am in control. I am calm. I am confident. I am —*

'I called you at the club,' Tertius said, ignoring the

offer of coffee. His voice was a whisper of breath at the back of her neck. Pauline froze with the water jug in her hand. 'And some bloke answered.'

'Ah,' said Pauline, relaxing just a fraction. 'That would have been the electrician. He's been putting in the fridges. I told you.'

'Yes,' Tertius said. 'You told me. But what you didn't tell me was that the two of you were on first name terms.'

Pauline could feel his eyes on her as she filled the jug and put it down on the table. She began to fold silver foil round the pies. It gleamed in the light and set her teeth on edge as she smoothed it. Despite herself, she glanced towards the doorway. Tertius hadn't moved. He had his arms folded across his chest and was rubbing his hands up and down his upper arms in a caressing way that made Pauline's mouth go dry.

'Do you always let people who work for you call you by your first name?' he persisted softly.

'Oh, Tertius, he's —'

'Out of familiarity cometh contempt.' Tertius made the ponderous phrase sound faintly biblical. Pauline had once observed in a dispassionate way that Tertius was given to quoting lines from the Bible just before he let fly with the first backhand. She wondered if proverbs counted.

'Frank isn't being familiar,' she said, picking up the jug and pouring a brave gush of water into the kettle as if nothing was amiss. 'He's just a friendly guy.' *I am calm. I am conf* —

'Friendly, oh yes,' said Tertius. 'Friendly Frankie.' He was rubbing his arms quite fast now.

Pauline took two coffee mugs from a shelf, forgetting that Tertius hadn't said he wanted any. They clattered together as she lifted them down. 'Michaela was there,' she said, knowing that this was about the last thing that would help but unable to think of anything else. 'And Antony and Janus. We talked about Bricknell Court, remember I told you . . . ?'

Tertius was not interested in Bricknell Court.

'The chaperones,' he said. 'How cosy.'

'Tertius, please —'

But tonight Tertius turned abruptly away from her. 'Don't forget the lights when you're finished here,' he said. 'I'm going to bed.'

When he'd gone, Pauline sank onto a kitchen chair. Her legs were trembling violently at the knees and when she put her head in her hands they stuck wetly to her cheeks. Her heart was beating so fast she felt lightheaded. Thank you, she found herself saying in her head, over and over. Thank you. Thank you. Thank you.

Pauline had never had much luck with the men she picked. At least that was Michaela's opinion. Pauline had heard her say so to Antony at one of Mater's birthday parties at Stillwaters, when Pauline was icing the cake and listening to her Walkman. It was a moment between songs and she had heard her quite clearly. But then it was all very well for Michaela to talk. Michaela had everything going for her. She was frankly beautiful, gracefully tall and with a smile that made everyone – men and women – give her their immediate and undivided attention, their hearts, their souls, anything Michaela required, in fact.

And what did she have? Pauline could list her own assets on one hand, well, a couple of fingers really. She was a good listener and she a good cook. Other than these, she really didn't have a lot that was charming. She was overweight and too tall with it, not long and lissome like her cousin, but big and overwhelming, a large baobab to Michaela's poplar. She often felt uncomfortably bulky in small rooms. She did have clear blue eyes and thick auburn hair which shone like copper in the sun, but which she'd cut very short after Tertius had begun using it as a handle when he was beating her. When it was down to her shoulders and glossy as a starling's wing he had watched for the admiring glances and grown morose and withdrawn until they were alone. Then he would make her sit in front of the mirror and brush it with a brush with hard metal teeth – a cat brush, Michaela had one for The Dog – until she could feel blood run down her neck and the tears slid from her eyes.

Pauline was not married to Tertius. She had tried marriage once, just after she'd finished hotel school. Angus was a Scot and an enthusiastic officebearer in the Cape Town Caledonian Society. He it was who carried in the haggis to the skirl of the pipes on Burns Night, and he had pitched up in a kilt without warning on their wedding day. Angus had a bushy moustache and hair in his ears, and the first time he had hit her was when she told him conversationally that the Scots hadn't invented shortbread and certainly hadn't perfected it. Pauline, playful newlywed, had hit him back, imagining that this was no more serious than a pillow fight, if a little rigorous for her liking. She had soon discovered that what Angus really wanted in a wife was a punchbag and Pauline had the makings of the right shape. Seeing her grovel on her hands and knees, begging him to stop, gave him not only intense pleasure but also an instant hard-on. Pauline learnt to be grateful when he stopped assaulting her, put on his Kenneth McKellar records and raped her on the living-room floor. Sometimes, though, she thought the pain of a split lip was preferable.

Where she'd got the courage to leave Angus she never knew – Michaela told Antony it was probably the thirty-fifth rendition of the 'Bonny Bonny Banks of Loch Lomond' that was the clincher – but somehow she did, fleeing up to Stillwaters where she spent six months with Mater, growing brown in the sun and writing long painful letters to her mother in Australia.

After Angus, Pauline had shied away from the company of men and had had a sweet but ultimately unsatisfactory relationship with an art teacher called Sharon, which went some way to restoring her faith in human nature.

She had met Tertius when she was working at a hotel on the beachfront. Tertius owned a string of bottlestores and supplied the hotel chain with liquor. From the first he commanded attention. He was loud and hearty and full of confidence. He told Pauline she needed fresh air and he took her walking on the mountain in springtime. She slogged diligently along the pipetrack behind him with a pack on her back and heavy walking boots from Camp 'n Climb. Pauline would take pains not to tread on the tiny wildflowers and try to make friends with the daisies, while Tertius would stride heavily ahead whistling Afrikaans folk tunes.

The family had never taken to Tertius. Perhaps they had glimpsed lurking in his ruddy features something of the vicious Scot, and they had not done much to disguise their suspicion. Pauline had put their reserve down to nothing but racial snobbery, an accusation which infuriated Mater and caused some ill feeling for a time.

'You'd rather I had a Zulu lover than an Afrikaner, wouldn't you?' Pauline said. 'God forbid I should marry a Dutchman.'

Pauline, Janus and Mater were eating chicken wings with their fingers on the Stillwaters jetty. Antony was fishing further up the bank with Michaela dozing on the rocks behind him.

'Well, not a Dutchman *per se*,' Janus had said carefully. 'Just *this* Dutchman, Pauline. He doesn't even pronounce your name correctly.'

This was true, and Pauline had found this endearing at first, Tertius' emphasis on the first rather than the last syllable. But the stubborn Whitehead genes were deeply embedded. Pauline declared she knew what she was doing and she would not be swayed. Tertius dominated her time and she liked it. She said he made her feel secure. He liked her cooking and he liked to hear her sing when she was baking in the kitchen. He also preferred her not to see too much of her cousins, and for a long time Pauline obediently tried to drop out of their lives, although Michaela phoned her often and Antony frogmarched her to the movies when Tertius was stocktaking.

Tertius wanted to get married, but there were conditions. He wanted Pauline to give up her job and stay home and keep house for him, like his own mother had done for his father. Pauline, however, had not forgotten how Angus had changed once the ring was on her finger and the first batch of cookies had come out of the oven, and she was wary. She agreed to an engagement and, although Tertius was clearly not comfortable with the arrangement, to moving into his house. The other condition to marriage was that Pauline should 'come over' to Tertius's church, the Dutch Reformed Church, and this was another serious obstacle. Pauline's parents had never been big on organised religion and consequently she had not given an awful lot of thought to God over the years. She felt it would be hypocritical of her now, at her age, to start praying all of a sudden, especially in Afrikaans. Michaela had agreed at once.

'You'd have to wear one of those stiff hats and keep it in a hat-box,' she told Pauline. 'And go to *nagmaal* and stuff.'

Pauline looked thoughtful. 'Mater's got a hat-box,' she said.

Living with Tertius had been just fine at first, even though he saw fit to keep her a secret from his parents. And Pauline had given up her job like he wanted. At home on her own she cooked up a storm. She ate up a storm too, and gained twelve pounds in a month. Tertius took to calling her his *vetkoek*, while Michaela tried to enroll her in gym classes. These clashed with meal preparation time, though, and Pauline only went once. She felt self-conscious in her leopardskin leotard beside Michaela. And anyway Tertius didn't like to come home to an empty house.

When Pauline complained that she was lonely Tertius bought her a pair of goldfish in a bowl. She took to watching the soaps with the bowl on her lap every afternoon and talking to Michaela on the telephone until Tertius complained about the bill. When Harry moved in next door and told Pauline he was a nurse who worked nights at the clinic in town, Pauline was thrilled. She and Harry would watch the soaps together and eat crunchies, and Harry would tell her about his love life – which was lurid and promiscuous and involved Taiwanese sailors down at the harbour.

Tertius found out about Harry when he came home early one Friday evening in the middle of *Days of Our Lives*. He threw Pauline from one side of the living room to the other, where she hit her shoulder and hip against the sideboard, and had a bruise the shape of Jamaica for a month. She couldn't remember what her next transgression had been, but it was obviously a bad one, for that time Tertius had broken her nose and pulled a large handful of hair from the crown of her head. She told Michaela she had been in a car accident. 'It was my own fault,' she said. 'I completely ignored the yield sign.'

It was when the accountant was found to have defrauded Tertius's company of a substantial amount of money that he reluctantly agreed that Pauline could go back to work. She saved her money as carefully as any miser, building up an escape fund in a corner of her bank account, and occasionally wondering how she could leave Tertius without him minding.

In the end she had used her escape fund on the club. Mater had put in some money too and Michaela had promised publicity in the magazine. They all felt Pauline's financial independence was a step in the right direction, although they knew better by now than to say so. The opening of the club was only weeks away.

The fridge changing gear and the simultaneous ringing of the telephone brought Pauline back to the present. She had been sitting on the hard kitchen chair with her head in her hands for almost half an hour. Tertius could be heard all over the house snoring like a power drill. She went through to the hallway, automatically turning off the kitchen light, feeling her way in the darkness and putting on the lamp beside the telephone. She picked up the receiver, registering at the same time that the drill had stopped and the extension in the bedroom had been picked up. She was used to censoring her phonecalls when Tertius was at home, although mostly there was no need.

'Pauline darling?'

'Hello, Blanche.'

'I know it's late but I had to call. What do you think about "Fire and Rain"?'

Pauline hesitated. 'One puts out the other?' she said. 'Are you doing a crossword puzzle?'

'To open with,' Blanche said. 'My first set. James Taylor? I always used to open with it, not that anyone will remember. Otherwise I thought of "Wind Beneath My Wings", but it might be too soppy. Maybe that's better for an encore. If there is an encore, that is.'

'Oh,' said Pauline. '*That* "Fire and Rain". It sounds perfect. I love James Taylor. And I'm sure there'll be an encore, Blanche, more than one, if I have anything to do with it, and I'm the boss. Are we getting anywhere with putting the band together yet?' Pauline was conscious of the opening night getting closer and closer.

'Oh, it's all done.' Blanche sounded pleased. 'Those boys playing at Greenbacks have agreed and they're wonderful. Just marvellous. Their bass player and I go way back in fact.'

'Greenbacks,' Pauline said slowly. Greenbacks had been packing them in since the Waterfront area had been developed. And it was right next door to Pauline's, give or take a crane or two. 'Are you sure? Aren't they under contract there? Have you cleared it with their manager?'

'Oh, no need,' said Blanche. 'I promised to jam with them later on. They jumped at it.'

'Well,' Pauline said doubtfully. 'It's just that I wouldn't want to start off on the wrong foot down at the harbour. It's a cut-throat business.'

Blanche laughed gaily. 'You worry too much, darling,' she said. 'I'll take care of it.'

Pauline couldn't help laughing. 'Well, Blanche,' she said, 'I have to say that for someone who wasn't sure just two days ago that one tiny gig wouldn't half kill her, you seem to have your confidence back. But I'm delighted. When do you want to rehearse?'

'Tomorrow. Five o'clock. Can you be there?'

Pauline mentally flicked through her diary. Whose club was this anyway? 'Yes, I think so,' she said. 'But if I'm held up Frank will let you in. He has a key.' The silence from the bedroom extension was poisonous. Pauline could have bitten her tongue off.

'Well, try to make it,' Blanche said, sounding suddenly plaintive. 'Does this Frank, whoever he is, know anything about music?'

'Only if it's Gilbert and Sullivan,' Pauline said recklessly. In for a penny, in for a pounding. 'Frank's my pet electrician.'

Frank was easily dismissed. 'If you say so,' Blanche said. She was about to ring off. 'Oh, Pauline,' she said suddenly. 'You kids don't know anything about this dreadful skeleton person, do you? The one they dug up at —'

'I know the one you mean,' Pauline said quickly. As if there could be several they might have had a hand in. 'No, of course not. Gruesome, though, isn't it?' Did she sound defensive?

'Yes, perfectly,' Blanche said. 'You know, I'm surprised Michaela hasn't mentioned it. She usually likes that sort of thing.'

Tommy is leaning back against the wall. It takes a few minutes for Pauline's eyes to adjust to the gloom. He is sitting on the stone floor, with his strange short legs sticking out in front of him like a child's. He has a squashed looking cigarette cupped in one hand and the space around his head is filled with grey aromatic smoke. The smell is sweet and cloying and it makes Pauline's eyes water.

Tommy shifts his back so that he is sitting more upright. He leans forward. 'Come,' he says. It is half a grunt and Pauline isn't sure she has heard right. She hesitates on the threshold until Tommy crooks a finger and beckons like an old woman in a fairy tale. Perhaps it is this gesture so reminiscent of danger and things untold that makes her pause. Tommy's hair is so matted it looks like a wig. She wonders if he ever washes and if so, where. The boiler room is hot and the mixed smells of cigarette and body odour make her feel dizzy. Tommy is watching her through eyes that are like slits. She is suddenly conscious of her thin cotton dress and the silhouette of her body with the sunlight behind her. Lately she's had a nasty suspicion that she might be getting breasts like Michaela.

Pauline puts the packet of sandwiches she has brought down on the floor just inside the door. Like a zookeeper with a wild animal, she moves slowly and keeps her back to the wall.

'I brought you something to eat,' she says, apologetic. 'Only Marmite, I'm afraid.' She is aware it is a paltry offering, even though she made the sandwiches herself, but if she'd taken the ham her mother might have noticed and asked awkward questions. Tommy remains silent and remote behind his barricade of smoke. Some people say he is deaf and dumb. 'I can't stay,' Pauline adds, as if he's asked her to. 'Not this time, anyway. I'm expected home.'

Still Tommy says nothing. He doesn't look at the packet either. Perhaps she has offended him. Instead he takes a drag from the cigarette and smoke comes out of his nostrils in slow fat curls.

'Well, bye for now.' Pauline lifts a hand, awkwardly. She steps backwards out of the door and pushes it shut behind her. It has a new metal bolt, a sliding one, and it's hot to the touch. Pauline stands outside for a moment, looking around, orientating herself. She can hear Michaela's voice coming from the orchard. She hasn't yet told the others about Tommy using the boiler room as a sleeping place, nor about the blanket she's given him on account of the cement floor. It's not that she's afraid to tell them or anything. They are all used to keeping secrets. But this one, just for once, is her own secret, her personal endeavour, and she wants to keep it that way for just a little longer, before Michaela takes it over.

'What were you doing in there?'

Pauline starts. 'Oh,' she says. 'It's you.'

Crispian Younghusband steps out from behind a tree. He has his cricket ball in his hand and he tosses it up and catches it, turning his fat cheeks to the sun. Everything about him is round; even the knuckles on his hands are rounded and puffy. His knees are dimpled blobs of dough, ready for the oven.

'I saw you go in there,' he says, throwing the ball from one hand to the other and looking directly at her. He isn't afraid of Pauline as he is of Michaela.

'I wasn't doing anything, Crispian Younghusband. Why don't you learn to mind your own beeswax?'

Michaela's favourite expression and one Pauline feels rather pleased with.

But Crispian isn't really interested. He needs to curry favour. 'Where's Michaela?' he asks.

Michaela. Michaela. Always Michaela. 'In the orchard,' she replies, not that it will do him any good. Michaela will have no use for Crispian Younghusband today. She and Antony are rollerskating, working out a routine to show her parents and Blanche when she gets back from Durban.

'C'n I come with you?' Crispian has already started walking beside her. He has sore patches on the insides of his thighs where the skin has chafed.

'If you want,' Pauline says, not very graciously. Better to draw him away from the boiler room. There's no knowing how he might use the information.

Pauline was smiling to herself as she went into the bedroom, thinking of Blanche in her fishnets, belting it out with the boys from Greenbacks. She was very fond of her aunt. Blanche had encouraged her to sing harmonies with her on the occasions when they had all travelled by car up to Stillwaters together in the old days. They would sing 'The Gypsy Rover' and 'California Dreaming', and sometimes, with the right amount of encouragement, Pauline would sing something on her own, in a voice so clear and smooth that the others would stop squabbling over seat space and Blanche would light a cigarette and look out of the car window with a faraway, peaceful expression.

Pauline was unprepared for Tertius standing behind the bedroom door like an intruder, and the simultaneous flooding of the room with light. She felt herself grabbed by the elbow as she walked into the room and the force of it almost lifted her off her feet. Tertius twisted her arm up high behind her back with one hand, and with the other he took hold of her chin between finger and thumb. He forced her face to the light and turned her head this way and that, breathing over her and saying nothing. He had some spittle at the corner of his mouth and a look on his face so dark and mean that Pauline hardly recognised him.

She felt a streak of fire shoot up her arm from the elbow as Tertius gave her a shake and she drew breath sharply. But she did not pull away. She stood absolutely still, willing her muscles to relax, waiting for whatever was coming next. If she had been able to move her head she would probably have let it droop like a patient ox. In her mind, though, she switched to the venison casserole recipe she was developing. She was concerned about the sauce . . .

Then Tertius caught her jaw with the back of his hand, first one way on the knuckles, and then the other with the flat of his palm. Pauline felt the salty burst of blood against her teeth. Instinctively she put a hand to her mouth. Tertius hit her again and then let go of her arm. She fell awkwardly onto the carpet and sat there, trying to catch the blood that dripped from her mouth in a cupped hand before it stained the white flokati and made him angrier.

'Maybe you think I'm stupid,' Tertius said, standing over her like the Colossus of Rhodes. 'You and your snotty family. Just a dumb Dutchman who doesn't know what's going on right before his eyes. But you can't lift your skirt for every Tom, Dick or *Frankie* without getting caught out sooner or later. So I want you to understand that it's sooner. And later you'll be a lot sorrier than you are right now.'

Pauline heard the words but she was still at the kitchen counter. Since Tertius started beating her she had developed her own private defence mechanism to cope with the lecture which inevitably followed. She had discovered that the affirmation statements didn't have much power at these times and they were useless at blotting out the throb of a bruised jaw, but she found if she concentrated her mind on the kitchen, planning menus and improving dishes seemed to take her out of herself, up and away and beyond the pain. It was the juniper berry sauce that was the real problem. It was really far too tart.

When Tertius left her sitting there and went out of the room, he turned the light out behind him. She heard him switch off the hall lamp, open and close the front door and walk down the path. The whole house was in darkness, as if there was no one at home. No one of any consequence, Pauline thought as she ran her tongue along her teeth. Only me. She got painfully to her feet and went into the bathroom. Her face was a vague grey shape in the mirror. She splashed cold water across her mouth and winced. She dabbed at her cheeks with a towel.

There was nothing as sensuous as silk against skin, Janus thought. It was cool, featherlight, transient. Smooth flesh beneath silk was far more erotic than the flesh itself. It promised so much.

Janus had all the windows of his apartment open and Vivaldi threading across the balcony and out towards the silver flanks of Table Mountain, lit up in summer for the tourists. A bottle of Meerlust, half full, caught the light on the table by the window and he got up languidly to fill his glass. He was thinking about Chloë in the apartment downstairs. She seemed lonely. She never went out. And she had a lovely shy smile. Occasionally she came upstairs and had a glass of wine with him and he thought now and then about asking her out, but something always stopped him. If he did, would it mean that they had a relationship? Would Chloë take it to mean they did? Would she expect there to be dinners, movies, a weekend away? Sex? And if none of those things were forthcoming, would she then feel she had to avoid him, and he her? Would she hurry past him in the laundrette downstairs and stop smiling when they accidentally met in the lobby? Janus did not want to be awkward with his neighbours. There was an undeniable attraction between them, he could feel it, but he did not feel compelled yet to explore it.

Janus heard the buzzer on the downstairs security door. He looked with distaste at the device on his own door which was flashing brightly. He hesitated, then pressed the button.

'Who is it?' he said in his world-weary John Gielgud voice.

'Have I pressed the wrong buzzer? Janus, is that you?'

It was Pauline and that could only mean one thing at this time of night.

'No. Yes. Come on up.'

It would take her a couple of minutes in the lift. Janus padded swiftly down the carpeted passage to his bedroom. He paused to look at his reflection in the full-length mirror on the way. The silk slip was very beautiful. It was so white, as white as a diamond, and it clung to his thighs as softly as a whisper.

· 6 ·

Michaela was late getting to the airport because Roz had pencilled the wrong flight arrival time in her diary and she'd got held up by a rent boycott march through the streets round the City Hall. After doing three record-breaking circuits of the jam-packed parking area, she slid defiantly into a bay for disabled persons and then had to effect an awkward limp for the benefit of an airport security guard's frankly sceptical gaze. When she thought she was out of shouting range she broke into a flat-footed run, helped along not a little by the vicious south-easter which whipped at her heels across the unprotected open space to the terminal buildings.

It was one of those hot, late-summer days, perfect beach weather as long as you were on the right side of the mountain. The first pale tumbling wisps of cloud rolling-disappearing over the surface of Table Mountain should have been warning enough, and she cursed the short skirt and sleeveless T-shirt which had seemed such a good idea this morning. The wind was not only gusty, but cold too. It came at her relentlessly, in hard, fierce bursts, buffeting round her legs and lifting her hair in a frenzy.

'Thank you.' Michaela smiled frostily at the man

who held the door open for her and ran his eyes from ankle to hemline. There was a power cut, he told her when she hesitated on the threshold, and the automatic doors weren't working. It was true. There were no lights on inside the airport building. The long concourse filled with people looked like a scene from a black and white movie. Everyone seemed to be in a state of arrested motion and there was a hushed tone to their voices, as if they were all waiting for someone to shout 'Camera – lights – action!' to set them all in motion. Passengers were beginning to come through from Customs, pushing trolleys of precarious luggage before them, their eyes scanning the crowd at the railing, uncertain smiles hovering, ready for that moment of recognition.

Meeting people at airports had a curious effect on Michaela. She found it an enervating experience because she felt herself surreptitiously being drawn into the lives of complete strangers in a way that was almost hypnotic. She watched each traveller come through those bland, blank doors and she would look around helplessly to make the connection, unable to prevent the sudden welling up of tears when eyes locked. She would stare as grandfather embraced son, as mothers dropped to their knees for children's clutching embraces, as lovers moulded bodies hip to hip. Whole family sagas played themselves out in her brain as she stood, keeping one eye on the door for her own connection, whoever it might be. She felt an embarrassing and immediate intimacy that was hard to brush aside.

Today she had her family to distract her. Janus was standing alone in his trendy black suit and white, round-necked granpa vest which had lately come back into fashion yet again.

Michaela sidled up to him. 'All you need is a violin case and two-tone shoes,' she said. 'I gather they haven't come through yet? Where's Pauline?'

'She —'

'Oh, there's Blanche. Right in the thick of things. No — over there. Behind you.'

Janus stared. It was a small reception committee, complete with home-made banner. Most of the party were middle aged — half a dozen men with sparse grey hair and liver spots, and women in flip-flops and jeans which had long since shaped themselves for comfort rather than fashion. There were a few smartly dressed black men and two women in saris who looked more official than the old-style comrades. Blanche was in the middle of the group, standing with her arms folded and cigarette smoke rising in a steady line from somewhere in the vicinity of her elbow. A small man with the biceps of a builder was busy unfurling the banner. He was wearing a T-shirt with some Russian writing on the back and black hair sprouted up from his collar both front and back. Michaela thought he looked like a small exotic plant. When the banner reached the combined width of both his outstretched arms a portly black man in a Swazi shirt stepped forward to help him. He had a camera round his neck.

'Isn't that Gideon Kumalo?' Michaela said.

'So it is,' Janus replied. 'I could have sworn Blanche told me he was dead.'

'That's because he stopped covering her shows when she started to go mainstream.' She caught her mother's eye and waved. 'Old Communists never die.'

The banner went up at the same time as the lights came on to a collective cry of surprise from everyone standing around and the little group moved towards the railing, holding it up high. Like its bearers, it sagged a bit in the middle but the lettering was bold and bright nevertheless.

WELCOME COMRADES, it said. WELCOME HOME.

'David and Harriet will be touched,' Michaela said, misty-eyed. 'It's been so long. They won't be expecting this. Janus – *where* is Pauline? She's cutting it terribly fine.'

'Pauline's not coming.'

'Not coming? What do you mean, not coming? These are her *parents*.' Michaela saw the expression on Janus's face. He ran one finger round the inside of his collar. 'Oh no,' she said. 'Not again.'

Janus nodded distractedly. He was never comfortable discussing his cousin's bruises. 'Here comes the other Whitehead contingent,' he said with relief. 'Later even than you.'

He left Michaela and dodged across to help Antony manoeuvre his mother's wheelchair through the narrow door. Michaela could see her uncle Michael behind them, stretching to hold the door open with his fingers. Antony looked like his father. They had the same floppy hair and gentle eyes.

Helena, who had multiple sclerosis and had written two books on the subject, had a new wheelchair. It was a splendid affair, with spangled scarlet wheelrims, the chrome parts painted an irreverent metallic blue. In honour of David and Harriet, today two helium-filled balloons standing straight up on their strings flew from the back of the chair as proudly as any flag. They were scarlet too, except for the strident hammer and sickle design, which was white.

'Helena,' said Michaela, laughing, 'you are so full of shit.' She bent to kiss her aunt. 'How're you doing?'

'Well, we'd have got here sooner if some inconsiderate idiot hadn't parked in the only disabled bay remotely within wheelie distance of International Arrivals,' she said. 'But we fixed him, didn't we, Antony?'

Antony's eyes smiled innocently over Helena's head. 'Shaving cream,' he said gravely. 'Mother always carries it with her just in case.'

'Now where are they? Push me closer, Michael. If David is wearing one of those hats with the little corks hanging from the brim, I'm not sure that I'll —'

Passengers were coming through faster now. There were walls of luggage moving past. The passenger still delaying the flight to Malawi was wearily requested to present himself at the check-in counter. When Michael and Helena were out of earshot, Michaela turned to Janus.

'How bad?' she asked.

Antony turned back.

'Pauline,' said Janus in response to his look. 'She pitched up at my place a couple of nights ago, not in very good nick.' He pulled a face.

Neither Antony nor Michaela were willing to take up the flippant tone as they were sometimes wont to do when dealing with Pauline's domestic problems. Nobody felt the urge for repartee as they might have done on another occasion.

'She has a bruised jaw and a lacerated tongue,' Janus said. 'And possibly a broken arm.' He paused. 'I sent her off for X-rays today,' he added apologetically, as if he were solely to blame for her non-appearance at the airport. 'I didn't think it should wait.'

'What should we tell Harriet and David?' asked Antony.

'Pauline and I have it worked out,' Janus replied. 'We tell them she's running late. That there's a crisis at the club or something. And that she'll join us at Michaela's house later for dinner.' He looked from one to the other. 'I think they'll buy it.'

'They'll have to, I suppose.' Michaela looked doubtful. 'But if Pauline didn't think she'd be presentable enough for the airport, how will she miraculously look all right by seven o'clock?'

'God, I don't know,' Janus said wearily, 'but she'll be there. She promised.'

Suddenly a small cry went up from the group with the banner. People stopped talking and turned to stare at the fists punching the air and then to listen as Blanche Whitehead began to sing. It was a moving moment. Hesitantly at first, perhaps no longer accustomed to singing freedom songs, the rest of the group joined in until the chorus of harmonising voices drowned out the general underlying noise and the clacking of the Arrivals board turning itself over and over, and filled the space with jubilant, unselfconscious song. The rest of the Whitehead group stood back, waiting their turn. Michaela inched forward and stood behind Helena's wheelchair with her head between the balloon strings. She felt a prickle at the back of her nose as the voices stilled and died. Without turning round, Helena held a handkerchief up to her above the headrest. Michaela took it. 'Thanks,' she whispered. She looked up at Antony beside her.

'They look so . . . so *small*,' she said. 'How could they ever have been dangerous?'

Harriet and David stood with their trolleys, side by side, smiling the bewildered smiles of surprise party victims. Michaela checked the handkerchief for traces of mascara and gazed at her infamous uncle and aunt. David was slightly stooped now, but he still wore his uniform baggy corduroys and loose cardigan with big buttons. Harriet had put on weight and her grey hair was cut as short as Pauline's. Her suit was creased from the hours in the plane. Michaela could see an edge of her petticoat sticking out. They did not look like political exiles. They looked like somebody's parents out for a summer holiday.

Michaela turned in to Antony's chest to blow her nose. 'I'm sorry,' she said to the buttons on his shirt. 'I have no idea what's got into me. You'd think they were leaving, not coming home.'

Antony took her face in his hands and wiped with his thumbs at the tears in the corners of her eyes, which threatened to slide at any moment like raindrops down a windowpane. He didn't say anything. Janus was looking at Michaela anxiously, as if he hoped that for once she wasn't going to steal the limelight. Michaela gave the handkerchief to Antony, who put it in his pocket.

'Oh —' Michaela caught her breath. 'Look!'

A flash of purple skirt and a head hastily withdrawn made her grab at Antony's hand.

'What is it?'

'There. Behind the pillar. I think I saw Pauline.'

'Don't be – *Michaela*.'

But Michaela was off, slipping swiftly through the people behind them without glancing back. Antony followed reluctantly.

'Come on, guys. Let's go and get in the queue.' Janus turned round. 'Hey!' he called. 'Where are you going?'

Michaela took no notice, if she even heard him.

100

She had slowed down and now she walked, softly, steadily, towards the heavy marble pillar opposite the Departures board. She kept her eyes fixed on the pillar, although she could see neither purple skirt now, nor the familiar red head. She stalked the last few paces, taking big strides on her toes, a catnabber poised to strike. When she reached the square bulk she walked around it gingerly. 'Pauline?' she called softly. 'Are you there?' Letters and numbers rolled and clattered above her head. 'Pauline?' She was beginning to attract a few curious glances and she glared at two small boys in matching plastic helmets who walked backwards when they passed her and stuck out their tongues. 'Answer me!' Michaela hissed, darting round the corner one way and then the other. 'Fuck it, Pauline!' But the only person she saw was Antony, peering at her comically from the other side of the pillar as she came round its edge. He waggled his eyebrows.

Michaela tossed her head impatiently. 'I wasn't seeing things,' she said crossly. 'She was right here.'

'Yes, well.' Antony held out his hand as if to a wayward child and together they went back to the others. By now the crowd around Harriet and David had thinned and Antony took some pictures of them and the group of comrades who were standing around lighting fags and chatting. He took a picture of the banner propped up against a metal wastebin full of cigarette ends and Bimbo's polystyrene hamburger containers.

Then Harriet pushed her way across to them, parting people in her way with her hands like a swimmer. Blanche, in green leg warmers, followed behind with her arm round David's waist.

'Oh God,' said Harriet, stopping a few yards away.

She raised her arms and then let them drop to her sides. 'It's so damn good to see you all.'

David was looking round, turning in small circles and frowning. Michaela went up to him and hugged and kissed him. She still had to stand on her toes to do it. 'Pauline's been delayed,' she told him, catching a glance from Janus. 'Some minor crisis at the club. She was hoping to make the airport but said to tell you that if she didn't she would see us all this evening.' Was that too glib, she wondered. Janus was saying the same things to Harriet with a horribly false smile.

Pauline got her height from her father and her weight problem from her mother. David stood well over six feet and although his shoulders had a rounded look to them now and his shoulder blades poked through the back of his cardigan like the beginnings of wings, he was still an imposing man. There was a sharp intelligence in his eyes that had reduced many a cabinet minister to a mumbling idiot when being interviewed by David on television or on radio, and they might perhaps have faded a little, but Michaela detected no loss in their intensity. Those eyes had seen through a few of her own small lies over the years. She had always found his eyebrows disconcerting.

A sudden sharp report made them all jump in fright and three former MK soldiers hit the deck simultaneously.

'What the hell was that!' Michaela spun round, her heart racing.

'Sorry,' said Blanche in a small voice. She was looking at the tip of her cigarette and the shredded remains of one of Helena's brave balloons, which drooped down the back of the wheelchair on the end of its string. There was relieved laughter and the MK soldiers got sheepishly to their feet and brushed their trousers down.

As they moved through the building they were accosted by a trio of news reporters and a small press conference materialised in the coffee shop while Antony went to fetch his car and clean Michaela's windscreen on the way.

What were their first impressions of South Africa after so many years in exile?

Were they intending to come home to stay?

How did they feel today about the man who had betrayed them?

Michaela sat back and watched how Harriet and David fielded questions like they were born to do it. A newsman like David would of course have anticipated everything that could possibly be thrown at them and they would have run through their lines on the plane. Michaela had never known Harriet to be caught off balance and she thought she detected a quiet gleam of enjoyment in Harriet's serene expression now and then. Harriet always did like to have her say and then grumble about being misquoted in the newspapers, especially if it was David's.

They were spending the night with Blanche and travelling up to Stillwaters the next morning. With a week to go before Mater's birthday party, they would relax and rest and help to organise, although Mater and Frans and Frans's friends and relations usually had everything well under control. Michaela had insisted on making them dinner on their first evening home. Blanche voiced no objection. Savoury mince Snackwiches were the only things Blanche could prepare with reasonable expectation of success. She blamed her lack of culinary skill on her years of being on the road and at the mercy of sundry hotel and restaurant food.

Just when Michaela had been about to consult Pauline on a suitable feast, Harriet had written urgently from Australia. 'Please don't go the gourmet route,' she wrote. 'David and I have spent years anticipating this moment and old-fashioned *boerewors* and lamb chops cooked over a wood and charcoal fire, and a big iron pot of *stywepap* we can eat with our fingers are the things that start us salivating. I know these are probably the very things you groan about, but believe me, they can be elevated to mystical proportions when your soul cries out for home. We've made lists of the things we miss the most: the glottal cry of the Argie-boys on the Adderley Street corners selling the evening newspaper; the awful stench of the abattoir wafting across Salt River when the wind is changing and the salt smell of the sea on the mist and the foghorn at Mouille Point. The mangy buck at Rhodes Memorial and Sunday breakfasts at Kirstenbosch Gardens. David misses the toe-curling water at Noordhoek beach and the pong of the seaweed at Kommetjie, and even the grim blast of a black south-easter in the middle of summer which blows your eyelids inside out. I miss Stillwaters most of all . . .'

Well, they'd had the south-easter all right, and a pot of stiff white mealie-meal porridge had been prepared in their honour. Susan and Florida, home from school on their mid-term break, had spent the afternoon on it. Mater had sent up Stillwaters potatoes and Antony had brought the sausages.

By eight o'clock there was still no sign of Pauline. Michaela could see that David was fidgeting and Harriet looked worried.

'What can be keeping her?' Harriet said. She was holding a plate balanced on her knees but had hardly touched her food. Florida sat beside her, teaching The Dog to sit up and beg for a gnarled piece of mutton sausage.

'Did she say what the problem was?' David asked.

'Oh, you know Pauline,' Michaela said vaguely. 'She didn't say exactly.' She was anxious too. During a particularly tense time, Tertius had once threatened to kill Pauline.

'Michaela,' Janus called from the kitchen. 'We're out of red wine. I'm going to dash home and pick up a couple of bottles.'

Susan and Florida went with him, taking The Dog along for the ride. She was a peaceable cat in a car and she liked to lean into the wind with her good eye closed and her whiskers streaming.

Harriet sat crosslegged on the grass beside Helena's wheelchair. Antony and Michaela joined them, Antony leaning gently against his mother's frail legs. They all stared into the coals without speaking. The light was beginning to fade but the cold wind had dropped and the evening was warm and close. In the sudden absence of Florida's enthusiastic chatter Blanche could be heard telling David and Michaela about her show which was coming up soon, and how she thought she might do more than one just to make sure that Pauline's club would get securely on its feet.

'Tell me about Tertius,' Harriet said suddenly, taking Michaela and Antony by surprise. 'Pauline says so little in her letters these days. I don't suppose they've planned the wedding yet?'

'No, thank God,' said Michaela before she could stop herself.

Harriet looked at her.

'Well,' Antony said quickly. 'Pauline is so wrapped up in the club and everything that goes with it – catering, decor, all that – that she hasn't had time to think about anything else. We hardly see her these days and I gather that she and Tertius are rather like ships passing in the night.'

'Colliding's more like it,' Michaela muttered under her breath. 'There's the telephone – excuse me.'

Antony put another log on the fire. A shower of golden sparks skittered into the air.

'He's in liquor, isn't he?' Harriet murmured. She brushed at an ember on her shoe. 'And successful at it. Pauline sent us a photograph of him from a trade magazine – *Liquor Store Monthly*, or some such. I must say, he does look a little like a man who has hair in his ears.' This was a family rule of thumb, the origins of which had been lost and garbled and passed on disconnectedly for years. What it boiled down to, according to old Josh Whitehead, was: never trust a man who has hair in his ears.

Antony laughed uncomfortably. 'Tertius is quite smooth, I think,' he said.

'Tertius, smooth?' said Blanche, coming over. 'Personally I'd have called him very rough around the edges. Pauline is his pumice stone.'

Harriet had fallen silent once again. David sat down next to her and put an arm round her shoulders. She sat with her head back and her arms hugging her knees, staring up at the black points of Devil's Peak as if seeing them for the first time.

Helena gave a sudden, loud guttural snore and sat up abruptly. 'Christ!' she said without opening her eyes. Her chin sagged onto her chest.

'Oh, gosh,' Harriet said, pulling her rug up over her knees. 'The things you miss.'

'Harriet!' Michaela was standing in the kitchen doorway. 'Pauline on the phone for you.'

If Janus had expected to find Pauline in his apartment, he was disappointed. He called her number at home but there was no reply. He phoned the club and Frank said he'd not seen her all day. Janus tried to suppress the knot of worry which he could feel below his ribs. Pauline would be all right. She would turn up. He couldn't linger. Susan and Florida were down by the swimming pool looking for frogs in the filter, an activity which he knew would pall fairly soon. He took two bottles of wine from the rack in the bottom of the wardrobe in the spare room and when he turned there suddenly was Pauline, looking solemn with her arm in a sling.

'Christ!' he said. 'Where were you?'

'Lurking,' said Pauline. 'It's what I'm doing today. I lurk well.'

'No, you don't. You look like shit,' said Janus. 'Your face – the ice-pack didn't help, huh?'

'Thanks,' said Pauline. 'That's all I needed to hear. I have spent the last half hour in your bathroom applying Magi-Stick Blemish Concealer to this fucking jaw (I didn't know you had such stuff, Janus) and I thought I had done a reasonably convincing job. Now I know I haven't.' She sat down on the bed and her eyes filled immediately and brimmed over, as if by the action of sitting she had somehow sent the tears up to the overflow outlet. 'I can't let them see me like this. I just can't. I'd rather die.'

'They won't care,' said Janus, sitting down beside

her. 'They just want to see you. They'll understand.'

'No, they won't,' said Pauline. 'I know I don't amount to very much in their eyes anyway, but just how stupid do you think I will look if I turn up looking like a piece of bruised fruit all over again. They haven't quite coped with Angus yet.'

Janus looked at his hands. 'You don't look like a bruised fruit,' he said. 'Does your arm hurt?'

'I spent all morning at the hospital,' Pauline said. 'It's not broken. Only bruised. The sling makes it a little less uncomfortable.'

'Why don't you call them at Michaela's? They're worried about you. We've covered for you but it does seem odd that you haven't tried to reach them. After all, it's you they've come all this way to see.'

'No, it isn't. It's Mater and her birthday party. Nothing to do with me.'

'Oh, Pauline,' Janus said.

Pauline rolled over on to her stomach. Her purple skirt billowed out like a fat stormcloud. 'How do they seem to you?' she asked. 'Are they OK?'

'They're wonderful. Please pick up the phone, Pauline.' Janus hated being tough with her. He wanted to sit on the end of the bed and rub her feet. Instead he looked anxiously at his watch. Someone was ringing the buzzer – the girls, hopefully frogless, and bored waiting for him to come back down.

'I'm on my way,' Janus yelled into the intercom. He closed the door to the spare bedroom, trying not to be drawn back by Pauline's muffled sobs.

He picked up the phone and dialled Michaela's number.

'What a shame,' Harriet said. 'Pauline's had to rush

off to find parts for a dishwasher at the club. At this time on a Friday night. She sounded exhausted, poor child. I think after David's had a word, we should all turn in. David's getting that gaunt look he always gets when he's tired. His cheeks go hollow.' She turned her face to look for the stars, but the wind seemed to have brushed them all into the Milky Way, which was very faintly the only constellation visible, discernible as an uneven murky strip in the sky.

They were all carrying plates and glasses through to the kitchen when Janus came back with two bottles of red wine.

'I accept that I'm the life and soul,' he said, 'but I've only been gone twenty minutes tops. Couldn't you have talked among yourselves or something?'

'Everyone's tired,' Michaela said. 'Blanche is taking David and Harriet home. Are your bags packed, girls?' It was the school mid-term break and Susan and Florida were spending a week at Stillwaters, travelling up with Blanche, David and Harriet. Florida had had her ears pierced for their arrival, she'd told David coquettishly, which strange little confidence had left him grappling for an appropriate response.

When they were all gone and waved out of sight, Michaela took the glass of wine Janus poured for her and sank down into an armchair in the living room. 'Oh boy,' she said. 'Did we get through that all right?'

Antony came through from the kitchen, unrolling his shirtsleeves. He had just washed all the dishes. 'It was you, wasn't it?' he said to Janus.

Janus shrugged. 'Pauline was in no shape to be coherent on the phone,' he said. 'I had no choice.'

Michaela was admiring. 'You're very good, J,' she said. 'You should do a turn at the club. Impersonations.

Like Shelley Bermann. People don't do impersonations very much any more, do they? I wonder why?' she sat up straight and pulled her skirt to her knees. 'What are we going to do about Tertius? I could cut his balls off, I really could.'

'Oh great idea,' said Janus. 'Subtle.'

'Does she look very bad?' Antony asked.

'She's looked a lot worse. The Tastic Rice incident, for example.'

'She will come to Mater's party, though, won't she?' Michaela asked. 'Mater would be devastated if she didn't, not to mention Harriet. Imagine coming all the way from Australia to see your only daughter and not.'

'She'll be fine by then.' Janus drained his glass and stood up. 'I'm going to suggest she goes up a few days early and spends some time with them.' He shrugged his jacket over his shoulders. 'We can't do anything about Tertius, Mick. Haven't you realised that yet? Only Pauline can sort this dead-end relationship out and only when she's good and ready.'

Michaela saw him to the door and waited while his car blurted into action. We didn't mention Bricknell Court once this evening, she thought to herself. Was that on purpose, I wonder, or am I the only one who can't get it out of my head?

'Antony,' she said as she walked back into the lounge. 'Did you say anything to Harriet and David about the skeleton? Janus didn't. I didn't. Why didn't we? Antony?'

Antony was dozing full-length on the sofa. His mouth was open and he was making soft sighing noises. Michaela stood and looked at him. A button had come off his shirt and she could see the rise and fall of his chest. On impulse she knelt down beside him and slipped a hand beneath the cotton. She could feel his heartbeat beneath her palm, pulsing away like some tiny captured creature.

Without opening his eyes and with barely a change in his breathing, Antony covered Michaela's hand with his own and his fingers traced lightly over her bones.

· 7 ·

Needles of rain stabbing at the oily surface of the Stilfontein river. Like a relentless silver barrage of slanting darts loosed from an impassive grey sky, they came slicing across the reeds on the back of a warm north-west wind. All the windows of the house on the river were thrown wide open under the protection of the roof's overhang, to catch the wild tangled smells of the *fynbos* below. Lemon and vinegar and fresh wet grass filtered through to the rooms inside, mingling with and then quite overpowering the smell of the herbs and spices which filled the kitchen at the back of the house.

Mater, who had been up since dawn, had assembled a team of skilled and not so skilled workers to get things underway for the party. She worked them in carefully planned teams. The afternoon shift consisted of Pauline, Helena, David and Frans's toothless mother who insisted every party year on helping prepare a traditional Stilfontein smorgasbord.

Antony had been on duty all morning. His dishes of smoked salmon pâté gleamed palely on the sideboard, covered with muslin to keep the flies away. Now he was stubbornly fishing from the end of the jetty in a fisherman's mack and transparent plastic rainhat. From the windows of the front room he looked like a disconsolate bag lady, hunched over with one elbow resting on his knee and the slack nylon line invisible behind the shifting sheets of rain. If he knew he was being observed from the house, he seemed oblivious, but as he was the only living thing to be seen outside, he was the focus of idle attention. Michaela could see him from her bedroom window, where she sat reading beneath a Biggie Best quilt, her hair in a ponytail and a creeping depression crowding her concentration. His father was watching him too, from a striped deckchair at the far end of the front room where he was listening to an old Supertramp album on Susan's Walkman.

Susan and Florida were in their customary position on the bed beside the windows, sitting cross-legged and watching for the first sign of the rain easing up. Susan put Antony's binoculars to her eyes and swivelled them up and down, screwing up one eye and then the other. Antony slammed into focus and she adjusted the centrepiece with a careful finger. To be the object of such interest one would have thought he was doing something just a little bit fascinating, instead of sitting motionless in the rain at the edge of the water. Susan ran the binoculars slowly all around him as if she were tracing his outline. There were drops of rain like bubbles all along the length of his fishing line. It made her think of the dew on the fragile spiderweb suspension bridges which linked the stiff stems of the aloes in the early morning, before the sun and squeamish hands swept them aside.

'Seventeen,' she counted. 'Seventeen raindrops, Florida. On Antony's fishing line.'

'So?' said Florida. 'What you gonna do – wish

on each one in turn?' Florida had lately come to the conclusion that there were no normal families and that Susan's in particular was decidedly odd. They all compulsively wished on things – the first strawberry of the season, a sliver of moon, when two people said the exact same word at the exact same moment, even trains ... And Florida was in a grumpy frame of mind today. Her foster mother had made threats with a wire coathanger over the telephone on account of the state in which Florida had left her room before coming away. 'Hear this?' she'd said, rapping briskly with the hanger on the mouthpiece of the phone so that Florida had had to hold it away from her ear. 'Hear this? This is what's waiting for you when you come home on Sunday.' Coming from a woman who had been known to put Florida's dinner in a dog bowl outside the back door as punishment for sloppy table manners, Susan was not surprised at Florida's current gloom.

She put the binoculars down and turned her back to the window. 'Do you want to play chess?' she asked. Florida was the school champion and although Susan could be a mean and canny opponent when she set her mind to it, Florida was currently three games to one ahead in the Stillwaters Rainy Day tournament. They set up the chessboard on the bed between them, but neither of them was in the mood to concentrate. Besides which Antony's father kept bursting loudly into ragged bits of song and beating out a rhythm on the arms of his chair. And outside the windows the rain swept steadily out towards the sea.

The bag lady had moved. Antony was on his haunches on the rocks baiting his hook, struggling to keep his balance with his bare feet on the slimy surface. There was a lot of loose rock and treacherous knotted weed in this part of the river. He had lost track of the number of sinkers and metres of nylon he personally had had to abandon here, and which were undoubtedly responsible for fouling the muddy river bed and buggering up the ecosystem. They watched him prick his finger, curse and shake it, then stick it in his mouth.

'Yeuch,' said Susan. 'Bait slime.'

'It's rai-ning again,' sang Michael. 'Uh-oh it's rai-aining again.'

Florida rolled her eyes. 'Your move,' she said.

At that moment a burst of bawdy laughter came ringing through the house from the direction of the kitchen, where Helena's inexhaustible stock of dirty limericks was the only thing keeping Mater from strangling Frans's mother with her bare hands. The old lady was crotchety and almost completely deaf, and she spoke only an impossible Afrikaans country dialect which no one but Frans could understand. She moved about the kitchen jabbing and pointing and making it clear that everyone was in her way and nobody but her belonged there.

One person who didn't belong there was Blanche. She was hopelessly inept in the kitchen and this was something she cultivated without shame. All the same she had been delegated the task of keeping an eye on the bread in the oven. It was generally felt that this was something she could manage without too much difficulty, but Pauline had set the kitchen timer as a back-up nevertheless. David, who prided himself on being something of a nineties man on the eve of the twenty-first century, was handling the jackets on the scotch eggs and Pauline directed operations from the draining board with her arm in a sling. Helena had reversed her wheelchair into the space between the fridge and the kitchen table. She had been given the lighting portfolio and she sat with a lapful of coloured candles caught in the folds of her skirt.

'These holders,' she said to Mater. 'They're beautiful. Wherever did you get them?' She held up a smooth, slender length of wood. It was pointed at one end and the other end was a carved basket, an intricate criss-cross of almost silver plaits. At the base of the basket was an iron spike and it was Helena's job to insert and secure a candle onto each one.

Mater looked up from the pineapple she was pruning. 'They are beautiful, aren't they?' she said. 'The pineapples are so damn puny this season, why's that, do you think? Frans thought it would be a good idea to line the driveway with them. Instead of candles on my cake.' She lopped off the greenery with a strong flick of her wrist. 'That's why there are seventy.'

David passed Frans's mother a spatula in response to a vicious jab in the ribs.

'You know how people tend to stay rather late at my lunch parties,' Mater went on, 'and that road back along the river is very dark at night.'

'The road will be slippery after this rain,' said Pauline.

David picked up a holder and weighed it on his palm. 'What do you call them,' he asked. 'Candlestakes? God – it's as light as a feather. They are a wonderful find.'

'Where did you buy them?' Blanche asked. She sniffed at the wood. It was fragrant.

'Oh, I didn't *buy* them,' Mater replied. 'Frans made them. From jacaranda branches. They may look and feel fragile, but they're very strong. Frans knows his wood.'

'He does indeed.' David ran his hand down the pale

length. He looked thoughtful. 'Why don't you market these things?' he asked. 'You could sell them at your stall on the main road and supplement Frans's income. People would snap them up, I'm sure of it. Ask Harriet when she comes back from her walk. She's up on the artsy craftsy things. She used to be involved in African Self Help many years ago and she started a lot of small co-operatives that seemed to work quite well.'

'She's been gone ages,' Pauline said. 'She'll get pneumonia.'

Harriet liked to walk in the rain and she was almost never ill. She had very fair skin and stayed out of the sun as much as possible. It was thunderclouds and lightning that she responded to. Even as a child, Mater would say, Harriet would get the weather all wrong, running out to play in a cloudburst, dashing indoors when the sun came out.

'Really,' said David. He gave the stick back to Helena. 'You should.'

Frans's mother had wrested the pineapple from Mater's hands. She elbowed her out of the way and began chopping at it dangerously.

'Oh, yes,' said Mater vaguely. 'I hadn't thought of that.'

Helena leaned forward to prise a candle from Juanita, who was sitting, propped by cushions, in Mater's underwear drawer from the mahogany chest in her bedroom. She had been placed in the centre of the kitchen table like an offering, surrounded by sombre oblongs of wax. If she had been asleep and the candles had been lit, Blanche had observed earlier, she could have been Child in Coffin in a Viresh Singh painting with her perfect cap of black hair and sallow skin. As it was Juanita was wide-eyed and very active, and her small brown fists swung wildly at everything within reach. She was a powerful presence in a house of adults, some of whom were no longer used to babies and all of whom had privately decided in the small hours that child-disturbed sleep was a time in their lives they had either mercifully left behind or never wanted to experience.

But Mater had about her a serenity none of them could recall ever having seen in her before. Her eyes were bright in the morning. She fed Juanita strained peaches from a Whitehead silver spoon.

'Oh God damn it to hell!' Helena clutched uselessly as all the sticks began falling. Like the rattle of hailstones on a tin roof, seventy jacaranda branches banged and rolled about the floor, causing The Dog to perform a sudden and unrehearsed dressage movement and a slowly sagging Juanita to jerk upright and shriek with alarm.

In the middle of the commotion Antony appeared like a spectre at the back door, streams of water sailing down his plastic-covered arms and shoulders. Susan and Florida, having bolted down the passage in response to the noise, ran back to the bathroom to fetch towels and slippers.

'Ooh gross,' Susan said, keeping her distance. 'You pong.'

'I hope you didn't kill any fish,' said Florida uneasily. 'I caught a fish once, in Port Elizabeth, when I was at the children's home there, and the hook went through its *eye*.'

'Thank you for sharing that with us, dear,' said Mater. She looked Antony up and down. He was shivering and stamping his feet. 'Don't come inside,' she said, glancing at Frans's mother who, at eighty-five, had singlehandedly polished the floor on hands and knees at six that morning. 'Take everything off where you are and use the outside shower.'

'I thought I was using the outside shower,' Antony protested. He looked down at his legs. They were olive green from the feet up. He had gobbets of river mud between his toes. Mater closed the door firmly, then opened it a crack to allow Susan to thrust a towel through to him.

'Rain's easing up,' Pauline called after him encouragingly. 'I'll make you a Milo.'

Antony had no option but to slosh round the side of the house and rinse off under the cold showerhead attached to the wall below Michaela's window. The mud slid off him in dirty streaks. He scrubbed at his hands with the oval of soap on the windowsill and watched as the curtain of rain swept past him down the river. The cloud cover was beginning to break up now and a single errant ray of sunshine shot through a gap like a message from God and lit up the sandbank in the middle of the river. Beneath its spotlight, a black-backed gull stood on one leg and preened, opening and closing its beak but making no sound. Over towards the hills further inland, against the grey of the early evening sky, the faint curve of a rainbow bent towards the earth.

Antony stood for a moment, a towel around his waist, buttocks leaning against the wall, and watched as narrow shafts of light pushed their way across the water. Tomorrow it would be hot and crystal clear.

'Did you know that Susan and Florida were studying your private parts through your very own binoculars?' Michaela put her head through the window and looked down at him.

Antony smiled. 'Did you get any work done?' he asked. 'Or have you been sleeping?'

Michaela had dropped off once or twice. She had taken a few days out of the office to come up to Stillwaters, bringing a batch of competition stories with her to ease her conscience. 'Listen to this,' she said, reaching behind her. '"Gavin's eyes locked. He only had them for Letitia since their first meeting at midnight on the beach outside the casino with his winnings burning up his pocket. Letitia's were big and blue with thick grasslike lashes without the hindsight of mascara."'

'The hindsight of mascara?' said Antony. 'You're having me on.'

'I am not. It gets better. Shall I read on?'

'Please don't. Is it Joy Beamish's?'

Michaela sighed. 'No. Poor Joy. I'm saving hers for last.' She pointed. 'Look at the river, Antony. Isn't it enchanted?'

It was hardly raining now. There was only the finest of drizzles, barely strong enough to reach the water. Against the sunlight misty rain danced like glitter and the sun touched the choppy surface of the river with pockets of light. The tide was turning.

'I love a monkey's wedding,' said Antony. 'Don't you?'

Michaela is in the clubhouse. She is supposed to be writing to Blanche, who is doing a revue at an arts and culture festival in Swaziland. Instead she is sitting in dappled sunlight, daydreaming, half asleep. She and Antony have made this clubhouse all by themselves and they are not yet sure whether they will allow Janus and Pauline to be members since Janus told their uncle, and Pauline hadn't denied it, that they had broken branches from the poplar trees to make the roof. They are not allowed to mutilate anything in the orchard. The older the trees, the more fiercely they are protected. It seems a stupid kind of logic to Michaela.

Every holiday they spend at Bricknell Court they make a new clubhouse. They never make one in the same place twice. Last summer it was the storeroom beneath the back stairs, but this year they have discovered that not even Janus can get his wrist through the bars of the protective grille to open the lock from the inside, so they have had to write up a new book of rules and abandon last summer's constitution to the dust of the storeroom. It is one hiding place they have literally grown out of.

The poplar clubhouse is a good one. The storeroom was stuffy and everyone knew they were there because it echoed and they had to keep quiet whenever someone went up or down the stairs above. This one is a really secret place. They have to climb over the fence beside the tennis court to get here and squeeze along a narrow lane next to the property's outer wall. The row of poplars is thick and their trunks are very close together. Michaela and Antony worked together to bend the branches across to form a roof and used thongs of willow to weave the sides. The floor is soft with leaves and blotches of sunlight and the breeze riffles endlessly through the leaves above Michaela's head.

Michaela is wearing shorts and her legs are brown and dusty as sand. She has drawn a heart on her thigh with blue ballpoint. The writing pad lies beside her. The blank white pages lift and sigh in the wind. She listens to the wind in the leaves all around her and thinks about being a writer of detective stories like Agatha Christie.

A sudden puff and a loose page is rising into the

air. She watches it float and spiral and collide with a dirty supermarket packet and then subside, subdued after its brief flirtation, to the ground at her feet. There is a thud and a rustle and the sound of breathing close by. The club has strict rules.

'Passwords,' Michaela barks. 'You're not allowed a *step* closer, Janus, unless you say the passwords.' She knows Janus doesn't know the passwords. Only she and Antony know them because they've only just made them up.

'Monkey's wedding!'

The passwords are right but it's not the right voice, unless Janus is playing the fool. He can sound like anyone when he wants to. Michaela stands up and parts the horizontal branches.

'You've been spying,' she says in a mean, tight voice. 'You sneaky little bastard. You've been spying on us.'

Crispian Younghusband has skinned his shins gasping over the fence. He smells of creosote and the scrapes on his legs are like thick black pencil lines. He stands peering into the sun with his hand shading his eyes. The clubhouse is well camouflaged and he is not quite sure where Michaela is. Then his eyes connect with hers and he can't prevent a sudden smile. She stares back coldly.

'I wasn't spying. I was looking for my cricket ball. I couldn't help hearing you.'

Crispian Younghusband never lets his cricket ball out of his sight.

'Not only are you a spy, but you're a liar too,' Michaela says. She pushes her head out of the low doorway. 'A lying, spying, *crying* little piece of dogshit. Just like the dogshit you've got on your shoe – made you look!'

Crispian Younghusband is still smiling, but he is swallowing hard too and his mouth has a trembly look to it. He flushes a deep red and staggers as he lifts his foot to examine the sole of his shoe. He turns away and begins to go back the way he has come in, scuffing at the loose leaves and sticks in his path. The cricket ball makes a bulge in his pocket like a dislocated hip.

'Wait!' Michaela calls suddenly.

Crispian Younghusband turns. There is hope in his eyes.

'You can stand guard,' Michaela says. 'At the fence. And tell me if anyone comes. Whistle – like this.' She purses her lips and whistles a bar from her school song.

'OK.' Crispian shuffles backwards until he walks into the fence. 'Here?'

'Yes. But turn around. With your back to me. Keep your eyes peeled.'

Crispian Younghusband stands, his saggy bum stained with creosote, looking like a sack of potatoes. Michaela watches him for a moment, but he's been given his orders. He won't risk abandoning his post, nor turning round to incur her wrath. Michaela crawls backwards out of the doorway, her writing pad and pen in her hands. She walks quietly the other way along the pathway beside the tennis court, climbs nimbly onto the coalshed roof, jumps down to the paving stones below and strolls home.

Pauline has promised hotdogs for lunch.

'Bricknell Court,' said David. 'Pauline has been telling us how they are pulling it down in the name of progress.'

'I am surprised it lasted as long as it did,' said Mater. 'I wouldn't have thought it was safe for habitation.'

Antony caught Michaela's eye across the gravy boat. She looked away.

'Well, it has been standing empty for some time,' said Janus. 'There've been any number of petitions over the years every time they threaten to demolish it. But apparently no amount of petitioning this time will save the place. They say the building is unsafe.'

'And Grosvenor Life needs the space, don't forget.' Michaela helped herself to a roast potato from Janus's plate.

Everyone was silent suddenly.

'I think we were happy there by and large,' said Harriet. 'Weren't we, David? Even if it was the scene of our betrayal and the last place we lived before we had to leave. I used to find it so restful. The orchard was a terribly restful place with all those trees. You could sit down under Smuts's plane trees and feel somehow restored, as if something of the spirits of time were all about you, putting your small function on earth into perspective. I used to wonder what those planes would say if they could talk.'

'Actually, they were oaks,' said Janus.

'Don't be pedantic, J.' Blanche blew a smoke ring at him. Blanche was an inconsiderate smoker, lighting up over an unfinished meal without asking. Helena waved a hand at her irritably. 'Oaks, planes, the orchard had everything. Even cypresses, which is strange when you think about it. That row of cypresses on the far wall used to depress me. It was like being in a graveyard sometimes, especially in autumn. It was so quiet down there. Talk about spirits. I bet if you dug a bit round the cypress grove you'd have found some old bones.'

'Oh, Mother –' Michaela got up abruptly and began stacking plates. 'What an imagination you've got.'

'Well, it's not so farfetched,' Blanche replied. 'They *did* dig up a skeleton, didn't they?'

'Yes, but not in the cypress grove,' said Pauline.

'Bones is bones,' said Blanche darkly.

Harriet had been catching up on the papers over the week at Stillwaters. The skeleton in the boiler room intrigued her. 'I wonder if the place is haunted,' she speculated. 'Think about it: the Bricknell Court ghost. It certainly looks the part. The newspapers say that the poor creature had been there for at least twenty years and no one has come forward to shed any light on the case. Twenty years. How can a person not be accounted for for twenty years?'

'That would have made you, what, Pauline – about ten?' asked her father.

'About.' Pauline had taken her arm out of its sling and the bandage flopped round her neck like an unfashionable scarf. 'Who's ready for dessert?'

Pauline herded Michaela in front of her into the kitchen. Then she took her by the arm and gently turned her round to face her. 'It's all right,' she said. 'Try not to look so spooked.'

'Spooked,' echoed Michaela with a laugh. 'Thank you.'

'I mean . . . it's quite natural for them to be curious, Mick. You look as if you're about to blurt the whole story. You're not, are you?'

'Don't be ridiculous.' Michaela took two giant *melkterts* out of the fridge. They were heavy and her hands shook. 'Janus,' she called. 'We need a hand here. Janus has done nothing but drink since he arrived this afternoon,' she said over her shoulder to Pauline. 'I wonder if he has a problem?'

When they got back to the table the conversation

had changed direction. Michaela was relieved, but only for a moment.

'Whatever happened to him, I wonder?' Michael was saying. 'Does anyone know?'

'Who?' asked Michaela.

'Tommy, the pinball wizard,' said Antony. He shrugged. 'I haven't a clue,' he added. 'He'll be looking for trouble somewhere, I guess.'

'You know, I always felt sorry for that boy,' said Harriet. 'But we were so wrapped up in what we were doing, the meetings, the organising, that I just never took much notice of him.' She paused. Nobody said anything. 'Perhaps that was part of his problem, people taking no notice of him. Maybe if we'd made more time for him when he first pitched up at Bricknell Court, made more of an effort to talk to him even, we could have done something for him, prevented him from becoming what he was. Turned him round.'

'He was never around at any one time for long enough, I would have thought,' said Mater. 'At least from what I remember. Didn't he just appear and then disappear again?'

'Just like the Bricknell Court ghost.' David laughed.

Pauline laughed too, after a moment.

Michaela had moved away from the table, leaving her dessert untouched. She sat beside the window looking out at the river and the flickering candlelit reflections of her family behind her. Friday night and there was the light from the postmaster's boat, closer to the far bank than theirs judging by its faintness. The postmaster was as predictable as the tide. All of a sudden she wanted to be out there with him, listening to the lap of the little waves against the hull and the comfortable whinge of the oars in the rowlocks.

'Michaela?' said Blanche. 'What do you think happened to Tommy?'

'I don't know and frankly I don't care,' Michaela said without turning from the window, perhaps more vehemently than she intended.

'Oh.' She could almost hear Blanche raising her eyebrows. She did hear her pull at her cigarette in the surprised silence. 'I'm sorry. I thought you kids were —'

'Let's go out in the boat,' Antony said, standing up and beaming uncharacteristically round at everyone. 'I'll take the old dinghy, J. You take *Christmas Present*. Who wants to come?'

'Not me,' said Blanche. 'It's too damn cold on the river at this time of night, especially after the rain.'

'The postmaster's out there,' Janus pointed out.

'Yes, but he's deaf,' Blanche replied. 'I'll do the dishes with Michael. We'll sing harmonies.'

In the end the four cousins went down to the river together, fleeing down the steps like children. Susan and Florida were fast asleep in their sleeping bags or they would have insisted on going too. Boat rides on black water with the stars overhead were much more thrilling than sorties among the reeds in the heat of the day. *Christmas Present*, the boat they had all clubbed together to buy at the beginning of summer, had been pulled up onto the grassy bank, where it lay overturned to keep out the rain. Janus's creative calligraphy stood out against the white, still-new side. He and Pauline pushed it down to the water, although Pauline wasn't much use with her pulled ligaments. Fortunately, the boat slid easily down the slope of wet grass, squeaking as it went. Antony and Michaela walked over to the boathouse. Antony lit the path with a small pencil torch and Michaela followed a few paces behind, stepping carefully, concentrating on not falling in the mud. Inside the boathouse it was almost pitch dark and they stood still for a minute while their eyes adjusted to the gloom.

'Careful,' Antony said as Michaela trod on an uneven piece of board and grabbed at his arm. An old dinghy bumped gently on the end of its rope, nudging at the planks where they stood.

'Old *Christmas Past*,' said Michaela. 'We've had some good times in her, haven't we?'

It was the dinghy Danny had brought up to Stillwaters years before on the roof of his old Bedford truck. They hadn't given it a name then, but when Janus had christened *Christmas Present*, they had succumbed to the obvious and he had begun the lettering, only to run out of paint and energy at about the same time. At the moment the boat bore the name *Christ*. Suddenly a white shape detached itself from the shadows in the stern and Michaela jumped. It was only The Dog, having made a comfortable nest out of an old beach towel crumpled and forgotten beneath the wooden seat. She stretched and purred.

'What's this?' said Michaela. 'The towel and the pussycat?'

Antony laughed. 'That's the first time you've smiled all evening,' he said. 'I was beginning to despair.'

Michaela bent to untie the rope. 'Well, what do you expect?' she said. 'All this constant harping on Bricknell Court puts me on edge. I feel like a criminal.'

'That's crazy. You're no criminal and there's been no crime,' said Antony. 'There has been no suggestion even of a crime. I've scrutinised every single report on the thing. There's nothing but a puzzle, that's all.'

'Which we could solve.'

'We don't know that for sure. Come on —' Antony leaned down and lifted her to her feet. He put his arms around her and pulled her in close to him. Michaela rested her palms on his chest and looked up at him. His face, partly in shadow, was very close to hers. In the pale light from the torch and the moon outside, he looked so beautiful, so serious and concerned that she reached up impulsively to touch his cheek. Instead she touched his lips, just with the tips of her fingers.

'I may be wrong,' said Antony. 'But I think I'm going to kiss you.'

It was cold on the river. By the time they caught up to the postmaster's boat Pauline was shivering and Janus was complaining rather monotonously about a pain between his shoulder blades.

'But the stars are worth it,' Michaela called to him. 'You have to admit that, little brother. Don't tell me you're getting flabby now.'

Michaela felt reckless and gay. She could have dived off the side of the boat and swum all the way down to the sea. She stood up and flung her arms out, spinning giddily with her head back until the stars were a solid blur of white above her. Antony, laughing, put out a restraining hand. 'Bloody Bricknell Court!' she yelled to the sky. 'Bloody pinball wizard! You can all go to hell, d'you hear me! You can all go to hell!'

Pauline began to laugh. 'Shh,' she hissed, pointing at the postmaster's boat just in front of them, where he and his son were two unmoving indistinct humps in the moonlight. The absurdity of the implication set them all off and next it was Janus who leapt to his feet and began to sing 'John Brown's body lies a-mould'ring in his grave' at the top of his voice, as night turned into day and a blacksmith plover's reproving call signalled them home from the river bank.

Antony had predicted correctly. The day of the party was fine. A light breeze came up off the sea, but the sky was cloudless and the river sparkled and sunbirds hovered and flashed in and out of the bushes with startling rude splashes of blue and gold and crimson. As she usually did, Mater concentrated activities outside the house. The lawn in front was laid out with trestle tables and sundry beach chairs, her own and many borrowed and brought over from neighbours up and down the river bank.

Frans had rallied the usual gang of friends and relatives from the Coloured side of the village, and they had arrived early that morning to begin setting things out and buttering bread and making salads. Florida and Susan had taken charge of digging in the candlestakes and they had set out with a will at dawn, taking a side of the driveway each, a bristle of sticks tucked beneath each arm. Blanche had pointed out that the candles wouldn't be needed till nightfall and that the girls could probably be more usefully employed laying out cutlery or taking a squawking Juanita for a walk, but her words fell on deaf ears. Laying out knives and forks was not as challenging as driving the stakes into the soft, rain-soaked soil and having barefoot slalom races along the dirt road with Frans's nephews. Blanche was obliged to cast around among the Coloured crew to delegate the task.

The first guests began to arrive around noon and Mater emerged fresh from a dip in the river wearing a colourful sarong and her old blue flip-flops with the fishes on them painted silver. A bright blue band held back the dramatic sweep of white hair as regally as any diamond tiara as she came out onto the lawn to be gracious and seventy, handing out sugared fruit balls to all the Coloured children who clustered around her as familiarly as if they belonged there. Although Mater had been adamant about this party being the last, Michaela, watching Antony busy with his camera from the boathouse roof, knew it would take a bit of convincing. Mater's parties were the undisputed high spot on the Stilfontein calendar.

She moved across to Antony and his parents. Antony lowered his camera. 'There's the mayor,' he said. 'Mater says he's out on bail.'

'Well, he's not the mayor any more,' said his father. 'He had to step down. You can't have your fingers in the till and hang on to the gold chains at the same time.'

'Well, he did so quite successfully for a while,' said Helena with a note almost of admiration. 'Or so Mater told me. But he got over-confident. What a pity. He's a very nice man when you get to know him. He and your father were in primary school together.'

'I remember him well,' said Michael. 'He was the one who liberated the tuckshop money in Grade Two.'

Mater had always insisted that no one bring her presents on her birthday and she had a donation box instead, which she usually put in a prominent place, the drinks table or beside the birthday cake. Any money collected went towards funds for the Coloured community across the river behind the hill. So far the generosity of her friends had built the community hall that had burnt down during the '93 riots and a crèche in the village. She was currently working on a second clinic and already had enough for three walls.

By lunchtime there were a hundred people on the lawn in various stages of inebriation. James McCann had been drunk since ten o'clock and Antony took some pictures of him offering drinks to a hydrangea bush.

The surprise of the day so far had been the unexpected arrival of Tertius, who came tearing up the driveway in his Mercedes, flattening three candlestakes and coming to a halt in a cloud of dust. Michaela watched Pauline run over to the car, coughing and choking and tossing her sling into the rain gauge on the way. When the dust cleared they were embracing and Antony was changing the film in his camera.

'How wonderful,' said Harriet when Michaela grudgingly pointed him out. 'I was beginning to think the man didn't exist.'

'No such luck,' Michaela muttered grimly, but Harriet was already walking over to greet her future second son-in-law. They shook hands and Harriet laughed at something Tertius said and he squeezed Pauline's shoulder with a meaty hand. Michaela felt depressed. Tertius was wearing smart fawn pants with the crease down the middle that he insisted Pauline saw to. Pauline was talking and gesturing with her hands. The injury to her elbow from shifting a freezer chest did not seem to bother her at all.

Michaela felt herself losing perspective. She wished she could change places with Mater, be seventy and surrounded by the markers of a steady life and a sureness of directions taken and planned. Mater had reached a tranquil place and all the things that had put her on course had in their way assured this. Michaela had no assurances, only uncertainties. She felt herself going through the motions, smiling, talking, squashing pâté onto strips of warm bread, watching Antony watching her.

As the afternoon drew on she saw Mater slip away inside the house. She seemed to be gone for a long time and just when Michaela thought she would go in search of her, she came out again and went alone to stand on the boathouse roof with her back to the river. She had an empty wineglass in her hand and a soft expression on her face that Michaela found disconcerting. Mater was always in the middle of things at her parties. She had never seen her put herself apart like this as if she were taking stock, as if she were a guest in need of a breather. Michaela needed to know that she was all right.

'Mater? Is something wrong?'

She had not noticed Michaela coming across to her. She held out a hand to her and smiled. 'No, of course not,' she said. 'I'm fine. I've been checking on Juanita. Frans's sister has her on her back. The smoked salmon – it's particularly good this year, don't you think?'

'It's wonderful,' Michaela murmured, frowning. Why were they making small talk? Was that the only safe thing to do these days? Why wouldn't Mater let her in?

They stood side by side, uncomfortably, looking up at the house. Swallows flying low over the water skimmed past their heads to and from the eaves and their crammed, lumpy mud nests.

'I've known most of these people all their lives,' Mater said reflectively, 'and some of their parents too, the brown ones and the white ones, always separately. But I don't feel as if they know me at all. I am close to none of them.' She paused and sighed. 'Tertius is here, I see.'

'Yes,' said Michaela. She was looking at Mater carefully. Mater was gazing speculatively up the lawn to where Frans's nieces were sitting with platefuls of chicken wings. If Michaela hadn't known her better, she would have said that Mater looked immensely sad.

'He and Jannie Brand get along well. They're both fascists.'

Michaela laughed. 'Mater,' she said. 'You've got to get back to your guests. This is your day.'

'You go along,' Mater told her. 'I need to have a word with Frans.'

Frans and his relations played the role of waiters and clearers at these functions and they all had it down to a fine art. Whether his mother had handpicked them for the job, or whether it was because they were most of them in domestic service of one sort or another, their efficiency and unobtrusiveness meant that they were hardly noticed at all. Plates were taken off to the kitchen, glasses spirited away to be washed. Frans smiled and dipped his head behind the bar and answered questions about his rheumatism, his sciatica, his lumbago. Usually he wore a suit which had once belonged to Josh Whitehead, but today he had a new outfit all his own, and one which appeared to fit remarkably well. He was for a change hatless too, and he had a head of surprisingly thick hair, black streaked with grey like an uneven charcoal sketch.

Michaela watched her grandmother talking to him as she made her way back across the lawn. Mater had drawn him away from the bar and they were having what appeared to be almost a heated conversation. Michaela found the scene interesting. So, it seemed, did Antony who, half concealed behind a tree some way off, was taking a rapid succession of photographs. Michaela had never known Mater to raise her voice to a member of her staff, even in the old days when she had had gardeners and labourers and kitchen help.

She had certainly never heard her speak ill of Frans, quite the opposite, but it looked distinctly as if they were having an argument. Mater was doing most of the talking and Frans was shaking his head vigorously and and looking past Mater to the river beyond. Then they moved apart. Mater looked vexed. Just when Michaela became conscious of how she had stopped dead and was staring openly at them, Mater broke into a laugh and left Frans smiling too as she strode back to the throng, head up and silver fishes shining. From inside the house Juanita began to wail.

Suddenly, above the noise of her crying, there came the sound of a motorboat approaching from up the river near the bridge. Everyone turned to look. Although the sound itself was not unusual in holiday time or even on a normal weekend, everyone who was anyone knew that it was Mater's party today and there was no one within a ten mile radius who had not been invited. A white ski-boat came into view, zigzagging slowly back and forth across the water. It appeared to be heading roughly for the jetty at the end of Mater's property. Antony went inside for his binoculars but by the time he came out with them, there was no need, and he picked up his camera instead. Everyone had moved to the edge of the lawn where they stopped, transfixed and speechless, as the second surprise of the day was revealed.

'Christ Almighty,' murmured Blanche, earning a thoughtful look from the dominee, who had never been sure where to position Blanche in the scheme of things. 'Christ Almighty in a bucket.'

It was the Barberton sisters, whose non-arrival had caused some concern earlier in the day before everyone had got drunk. Resplendent in crimson one-piece swimming costumes and balancing confidently on a ski apiece, they sashayed across the chop of the boat's wake like two tarts in a dance hall. At sixty-five and identical twins, they were a vision from another age. One hand gripping the bar of the ski-rope, they held the other aloft, clasping the end of a sheet of white cotton, which fought and struggled to wrench itself free like a creature possessed. HAPPY BIRTHDAY, MATER! it proclaimed to the spellbound watchers on the shore, and they called the message out in unison as the boat turned and slowed and they made their alarming way towards the bank. Flushed with success, at the last minute one of them made the mistake of letting go of the bar and waving. There was a shriek and a groan from the crowd and a splash and a grating of fibreglass on rock and the whole party rushed down to the bank to pick up the pieces. The white sheet took immediate and giddy flight and whirled and danced in a mad, wild flurry across the river before draping itself modestly across a sandbank.

'And I was going to walk on my hands,' said Janus.

After the Barberton sisters had been given drinks and Jannie Brand had handed over the basket of clothes he had hidden away for them, it was time to cut the cake. Blanche, after some persuasion and making a show of uncustomary coyness, sang 'Just the Way You Are' and they all sang 'Happy Birthday' and the little girls from the Coloured Anglican church sang '*Gooi Olie in die Naam van God*' to a spanking beat.

Just as they were recharging their glasses for a series of toasts diversion occurred in the form of Juanita falling out of the open window onto The Dog below, and another latecomer nosing up the driveway in a dust-covered car.

'Oh fuck,' said Michaela, putting down her champagne glass. 'It's Simon. I'd forgotten I'd invited him.'

After the ceremonial cutting of the cake, the usual procedure was the lame ducks race, but although at this stage of the day almost anyone qualified, they decided unanimously to abandon it this year. Peter Barrett had already recounted how, after his ignominious tumble into the water the last time they'd held it, he had had to have a new leg fitted because the old one had rusted at the knee joints and Helena, too, always game in the past, had confided to Mater that she did not feel up to it. Michaela had noticed that Antony was worried about his mother and he had spent much of the day close by her. She had confessed to not feeling well for some time and had lately complained about a creeping numbness in her left hand. In public she was stoic and acerbic; in private she battled constantly with crushing bouts of depression.

As the light faded from the sky and the stars came out one by one, Frans and Janus walked down the driveway lighting the candles in their baskets. Thirty-five down one side and thirty-five down the other, it looked like a small airport runway and Jannie Brand, who owned a Cessna, stood at the gate staring along it and scratching the back of his head.

The party was beginning to break up. Several people were leaving, weaving their way along the river bank to their homes, or driving back along the road which wound along with the river. The mayor was wearing a daisy chain round his neck, Florida's patient handiwork, and he could now be seen, silhouetted against the setting sun, standing at the end of the jetty in his underpants, swinging his arms and taking deep breaths.

'He's going to vomit,' said Susan. 'All that birthday cake. He had three slices, I watched him.'

Everyone was drunk, it seemed, except Michaela, and she suddenly had an overwhelming desire to put herself to bed. Ever since Simon had arrived Antony had got his mingling boots on and had moved briskly among the guests, taking pictures and being so utterly charming that Michaela wanted to kick his kneecaps in. He had been especially pleasant to Simon, throwing a comradely arm about his shoulders and plying him with beer. Now Antony could be seen bringing out a tray laden with coffee cups and bending over to serve first one Barberton sister and then the other.

Just as she was about to turn her back on the whole event, Michaela heard a shout from the jetty and turned back in time to see Simon and David leap back and the mayor execute a graceful swan dive into the muddy shallows, sending up a shower of white spray.

Michaela went wearily into the house. It had been a long day.

· 8 ·

Lying with her back to Simon in the dark, wide awake and aching with exhaustion, Michaela experienced a curious physical numbness in her cheeks and tongue, a sensation not unlike the after-effects of a visit to the dentist. She was sure that her current state of depression, if that was what it was, was the cause. Not normally much given to introspection, this gradual onset of lethargy, laced with a profound feeling of unease, was disturbing.

Everyone had noticed how brittle she was. Blanche had opened her mouth several times to comment. Simon, busy playing the solicitous boyfriend, which apparently put him in something of a privileged position, was pretending that he alone understood what was going on inside her head, that he was privy to some secret information. He had spent the evening affecting a protective air in front of her family, implying a maddening intimacy between them which led to Michaela rudely and childishly ignoring all of his later overtures.

Something else had happened too. Michaela had discovered, disconcertingly, that she had in fact quite gone off Simon. It had happened suddenly, taking her unawares while she was brushing burrs out of The Dog's long fur and Simon was chatting to David on the other side of the room and smoking his pipe. She knew immediately and without a morsel of doubt that any feelings she thought she might have had for Simon had been misguided and misplaced. The fact that he was now patently making himself at home here in the bosom of her family was probably going to make things awkward.

It was Simon's own fault. To begin with he had assumed that he would be sharing her room and that had annoyed her. He had put his overnight bag on her bed and his fishing rod leaning casually at the foot of it. Michaela had eyed them sourly when she went in to light the paraffin lamp, his black and yellow nylon holdall squatting like an overweight bumblebee on the quilt, and the state-of-the-art fishing rod and tackle which all looked suspiciously new. She had the uncomfortable feeling that Simon may have bought these last items especially for this weekend and in anticipation of many future weekends here at Stillwaters. The prospect now gave her a sudden stabbing tension pain at the side of her neck and her cheeks started to prickle unpleasantly. She tried to shift her weight further to the edge of the bed. Simon mumbled something rapid and incoherent, ending with a contemptuous snort. Michaela waited, holding her breath, but he didn't wake. She closed her eyes, but she knew she wasn't going to get to sleep.

Then there was his frightful tobacco. Rum and Maple, cheap stuff. It came off his clothes, and his hair and his fingers, and as she lay beside him listening to the creak and sigh of the old house settling itself after the day's heat, Michaela thought of something she'd read somewhere about aroma association. Years from now she would probably turn her head on a bus somewhere – never mind that she'd never had to catch a bus in her life – at the drift from an old man's pipe and think of Stillwaters and a brand new fishing rod and someone whose name had quite gone out of her head.

The difficult part was that everyone else appeared to like Simon, except Susan probably, but that was par for the course. He was the easygoing type, the kind of person who always fits in. He was a good listener, a good conversationalist (he had quite charmed the Barberton sisters) – a Good Sort. A bonus, too, was that not only was he politically sound, but he had lived in Australia for five years in their very own suburb, so Harriet and David had warmed to him straight away. He was also a keen amateur photographer and could compare cameras with Antony with irritatingly knowledgeable nods of the head. He even liked to cook and had offered to wash the dishes after supper. In the dark closeness of her room, with the small whine of a mosquito somewhere near her right ear, Michaela began to hate Simon with a slow, smouldering certainty. She half expected him to sit up in bed and suggest a game of French cricket on the front lawn.

With cheeks tingling, Michaela got out of bed at two in the morning, picking Simon's arms off her, first one and then the other, and folding them across his chest like a monk on his deathbed. She wandered through the house on bare feet, starting in the kitchen where she took a chicken drumstick from the fridge, and ending up in the front room where the moon, pale as cream, washed against the windows with a soft, cool light. Susan and Florida were asleep on their double bed, too hot for sleeping bags tonight, sprawled on their backs in pastel nightshirts. The Dog had made a nest for herself between them and she looked up at Michaela with one golden eye and chirruped, sniffing the air at the smell of chicken.

Michaela dragged the low-slung deckchair over to the window and sat beside the glass, hugging her knees to her chest like Susan did. She looked over at her daughter. Susan's face was waxen in the moonlight. Her high cheekbones and long aquiline nose were traced with silver. She and Danny had shared this bed whenever they came to Stillwaters, and when Susan was a baby they had had her between them to stop her rolling off onto the floor or, when she could just walk, going for midnight strolls along the back road to the village. She had been a common sight for a while, a miniature local oddity, tripping along in the dark dust with her eyes tightly sealed. Mater was in the habit of leaving doors open in summer so that the night breeze might pass through the house and leave it fresh and cool in the morning, with the curtains smelling of the sea. Danny, always a light sleeper, would wake almost immediately Susan was gone and set off in sleepy pursuit. It was only the sobering prospect of her falling into the black river that had made them all remember to close doors in the end, but by then Susan had given up walking in her sleep and had started singing nursery rhymes instead.

Michaela fell asleep in the deckchair. Someone must have come and covered her up in the night for when the sun's first rays hit the room, she was sweating and unaware beneath a thick tartan blanket.

Sunday was a lazy day. Only Mater was up and about early, feeding Juanita and getting breakfast going. But she looked and admitted to being tired, and she and Juanita took a late morning nap together, declining lunch – which was to be the traditional impromptu picnic Pauline always planned for the day after the party. Antony and a cheerful, well-rested Simon, under Pauline's direction, transformed the party leftovers into picnic fare and tucked them into the wicker basket, together with a chilled bottle of wine and a carry-pack of Cokes for those with hangovers. In the end it was only the cousins and Simon who went to the beach, with Susan and Florida on bicycles behind them. Blanche was sleeping in and everyone else had settled in the front room with newspapers and books.

Antony drove them down to the beach in the pick-up, heading for the shelter of the dunes, quite close to the place where Danny had died. That was the trouble with Stillwaters. Danny was everywhere. It wasn't as if Michaela could ever quite divest herself of bad memories, the memories of Danny's last awful moments, because she could never have simply stayed away. Stillwaters was as much her home as anywhere. It was territory as familiar and as dear to her as Bricknell Court. If she couldn't come back here, then where could she go? Although there were more good memories than bad, she never felt completely peaceful on the beach here any more. She was safer and less vulnerable up the river, closer to home.

It was a blustery morning and the only shelter from the wind was among the dunes, where it was hot and sticky and utterly silent. Foam whipped back off the waves and few people had ventured out into the water this morning. This wind brought the dreaded stinging bluebottles, as the cousins had all learned from experience, and the blue invitation of the water was deceptive.

'Why don't you go for a swim, Simon?' Michaela suggested. She suspected he was responsible for the hot tartan blanket.

Pauline frowned at her and Janus gave a half laugh.

'Too much effort. Later maybe.' Simon was busy stopping his pipe with his middle finger. He had hairy fingers and a hairy back, coarse black hair that Michaela could have sworn hadn't been there the first time she'd seen him without a shirt. He smiled fondly at her and she had the grace to feel a small pang. Sometimes, she knew, she was not a very nice person, and she had after all invited him for the weekend.

'We're going to look for shells,' Susan announced. She looked around. 'What can we put them in? I forgot to bring a bucket.' She turned speculatively to the lunch hamper.

'Take Simon's shirt,' Michaela said, still staring vaguely, before she could help herself. 'You can tie the shells up in the sleeves. If you know what I mean.' She knew she was behaving badly but she just couldn't stop. She was conscious of Antony studying her through the lens of his camera and she wondered for a fleeting instant whether her horns and forked tail would show up on the pictures. 'No – take the plastic bowl,' she said quickly, looking away. 'Here. Rinse it out first.'

'Any requests?' asked Florida. She was wearing David's baseball cap. 'Starfish? Periwinkles? Olly-crocks?'

'Ollycrocks are right here,' said Janus to a general groan. He was lying in the shade with a magazine over his face, having admitted to a very sore head when Susan inquired about the redness of his eyes.

'I'll come with you,' said Pauline suddenly. She got to her feet and brushed sand from her shorts. Pauline had been quiet all morning. Tertius had left before the sun was up and no one had noticed until after breakfast. Michaela wondered if it was that which had brought on her uncharacteristically morose mood or whether they might have had words in the early hours. Pauline herself looked physically intact. Her skin was unbroken and the bruising on her jaw was at least a week old.

Michaela moved away from Simon and watched them walk away down the beach. Antony was taking pictures. She looked at him through her dark glasses. His hair was growing long and it flopped back and forth across his shoulders in the wind. His mouth moved a little in concentration and there were white laugh lines round his eyes, tiny strips in his dark tan. Michaela knew sometimes that she loved her cousin more than she loved her brother and occasionally it bothered her. There was a strong telepathic bond between her and Antony that could be unnerving at times in its intensity. And of course there was the sexual thing. Michaela felt she was in control of this feeling most of the time. Lately, though, when everything was going crazy, she was not so sure, and when Antony took his shirt off, looked over at her and beckoned with a slight movement of his head and a small private smile, she got up to follow him with no hesitation at all. She glanced towards Simon, but he looked as if he was asleep and Janus appeared simply too ill to move.

'We're going for a walk,' she said over her shoulder in a tone that offered no invitation and met with no audible response, and she followed Antony down to the shoreline.

They walked along the edge of the water on the firmer sand, following the hazy curve of the bay towards the Stilfontein harbour. Small fishing boats could be seen heading for home, with clusters of grey gulls bringing them in, calling and diving at each other with their vicious beaks. They passed the Barberton sisters out for a walk with their Kerry blue, who sprang along in front of them bouncing on all fours and slavering after a stout piece of bark they were too engrossed in conversation to throw. Soon they had passed the main bathing beach and had reached the higher sand dunes where the wind tore at the grass and slapped stinging handfuls of white sand into their faces.

Antony took Michaela's hand and pulled her up the beach and into the secret sand passages where the wind couldn't reach them and the sun beat down on their bare arms and heads. Antony held her wrists in his hands. 'I want to talk to you,' he said.

Michaela made as if to sit down, but Antony held her up and looked at her with a serious expression. She felt goosebumps at the back of her neck and a creeping tingling along her jawline. Antony's dark hair was slashed with gold where it had been touched by the sun. He pushed it out of his eyes, sighed and gave a slight shake of the head.

'What?' said Michaela. 'What's the matter?'

'You,' said Antony heavily. He brushed sand off his camera bag with the back of his hand and stowed it carefully beneath a bush in the shade. There were lurid flowers all around them, bright pink with stems thick as a thumb. Flaccid green potato chips crouching, shallow-rooted, in the white sand. Michaela felt apprehensive all of a sudden. This wasn't the scene she had envisaged, nor were Antony's words what she had expected to hear.

'It's Simon,' said Antony. 'I think you need to lighten up on Simon.'

'*What*?' Not the scene at all.

'You're treating him like he was some small, pungent-smelling object you'd found sticking to the sole of your shoe,' Antony pointed out in an even-tempered voice. He paused. 'And we – I – think he deserves better than that. He's a nice person. We all like him and —'

'Why don't you just say dog shit.' Michaela broke free of his hold and walked a few steps away, addressing her next remarks to the leaves of a large bush. 'And?' she said. 'And what? And I'm lucky to have him? Is that it? Frankly, I'm not sure that I really like the idea of you all getting together to discuss my life, especially my private, personal life. What else do you all have to say about me?' The leaves hung silently before the directness of her gaze. They seemed to droop a little, perhaps in the excessive heat of the afternoon.

Behind her Antony chuckled softly and she felt the colour rise to her cheeks. She was beginning to think that she might look foolish.

'Any minute now you're going to toss your head and stamp your foot,' Antony said. 'So watch out for the thorny patch just to the left of your ankle.' He slapped at a horsefly and dropped his voice. 'My God but you're beautiful when you're angry,' he muttered hoarsely.

'Oh, fuck off, Antony.' Despite herself, Michaela was trying not to laugh. At the same time she was genuinely irritated. Antony was supposed to be her ally, not her watchdog. Or not when she had other plans for him.

But Antony was not going to back off either. 'I'm sorry, Mick,' he said, 'but I can't understand why you're behaving like a fourteen year old. And no, we haven't all been discussing your private life. Your attitude towards Simon has not been very private, that's all, and I took it upon myself, fool that I might be, to mention it.' He sat down behind her. Michaela could see a piece of his shadow, an elbow sticking off a knee like a cliff edge. She felt deflated. She scraped her toes childishly through the burning sand and felt sweat run down between her shoulder blades. She wondered why she hadn't noticed whether Simon had hair in his ears or not. Then she sat down and faced her cousin.

'There's no "we",' he repeated steadily. 'No one has been discussing you behind your back – except just now, but then I had no choice.' He smiled at her softly, a slow light across his eyes. 'You know I just want to help, Mick. You know me better than to think otherwise.'

Michaela thought she caught a sudden whiff of Rum and Maple snaking into the dunes and she pulled her hair back off her forehead, winding it round her fingers and holding it up against her head. It was baking hot up here. The sea was a flat blue strip beyond Antony's head. She looked over at him. He gazed back, his eyes amused. She decided not to let herself be humoured.

'Well, thank you, Antony,' she said. 'This was a novel experience. I haven't been lectured by anyone but my mother on a regular basis since I left university, and never before by you of all people. Rest assured, I shall take it to heart.'

'Oh, Michaela.'

But Michaela had made herself cross. She sat very still, tasting a gritty layer of sand and salt on her lips.

She felt that if she stayed there like that with her hair pushed into a bun against the base of her skull, she might turn into a remote sand sculpture up here in the dunes. The sand dune lady. People would come from as far as Dordrecht to gaze at her and marvel. And in time the weather would refine and remould her into some more acceptable shape, someone Antony would be happy to have on a spool of film, to slip into his portfolio with all the other perfect girls he took pictures of. She glanced across at him and knew she had gone too far. Antony was getting to his feet and the smile had disappeared from his face. He looked embarrassed, and not for himself but for her. Michaela despaired of ever getting anything right again.

'Michaela!' It was Janus. Of course it was Janus. How many times had she and Antony heard that voice, that tone. The small, left-out tone of a brother hot on the trail.

'Michaela?' He was close by. Other side of the dune. From habit perhaps, neither of them moved. How long had he been there? It was a voice which would be undeterred by sand sculptures and impenetrable thorn scrub. 'There you are.' Janus sprinted down from the dune above them, landing at their feet in a spray of sand. 'We're packing up,' he said, looking from one to the other. 'Susan's found a porpoise she has to rescue, so you'd better hurry up. She's a little hysterical.' He didn't ask what they were doing way up here in the dunes. How had he guessed they were here and not along the shoreline nearer the harbour?

Antony held out a hand. Michaela allowed herself to be pulled to her feet. She let go of her hair and it fell heavily against her cheeks. 'I'm going into the sea first,' she muttered. 'Bluebottles or no bluebottles.'

Michaela led the way, skidding down the dunes with sand kicking up from her heels like puffs of smoke. She ran into the water, jumping over the little waves and plunging deep into the belly of the first big swell. Janus was next in after her, crashing through the breakers and coming up beside her, laughing and gasping.

'A porpoise?' Michaela called. 'What sort of porpoise?'

'A rapidly expiring one,' Janus called back.

Michaela lay on her back, feeling the gentle push of the tide beneath her and watching Antony walk towards them, stepping over brown lengths of seaweed before diving in and striking out, it appeared from the energy of his strokes, for the distant horizon.

'They were sticking lighted cigarettes into it!' Susan was in outraged tears. 'Lighted cigarettes! And throwing stones. One horrid little shit was getting ready to carve his name on its side with a broken bottle. Jesus Christ, Mum!' She was shaking in her costume, shaking and hugging her arms.

'Is it still alive?' Michaela wasn't sure she had ever seen a porpoise, nor knew anything about them except from Lewis Carroll, and the creature she eyed nervously a few yards away was just a sorry, solid, blackish lump, with no lustre at all. It smelt briny and there was a dainty constellation of shells stuck to the underside of its abdomen. The eyes looked glassy and unfocused.

It was Pauline who had spotted it first. It was surrounded by a group of young men in khaki shorts and what might have been AWB berets. As they drew nearer, they had realised that the object which was the centre of their target practice was this pathetic, clumsy beached porpoise, whose tormented grunts were greeted with jeers and fresh hails of small pebbles and planks of driftwood. She had tried to stop Florida and Susan from looking but Susan had broken into a run and had gone right into the middle of them, kicking and hitting out with her fists and screaming the sort of abuse no one would have expected from a private school education. The boys had retreated in a wider circle, then edged away to safety up the beach, where they regrouped, lighting cigarettes with their heads bent in towards one another, and bursting into loud, uncertain laughter every few moments and glancing back over their shoulders. The porpoise was almost certainly dead by then, or it had looked dead at any rate as far as Pauline was concerned. Susan and Florida wanted to try to get it back into the water to see if there was a chance of reviving it, but Pauline said the task was beyond the three of them. Privately, she told Antony and Michaela, she thought the thing had been there for some time. It had the strong stench of death about it already. Michaela looked at it. One fin stuck uselessly up into the air and moved a little in the wind, as if it were beckoning. If she hadn't wanted to vomit, Michaela might almost have laughed.

Meanwhile, as the adults hovered indecisively, Susan and Florida were taking turns to run down to the water with the plastic shell bowl and pour streams of seawater down its sides. Susan was now quite passionate about getting the creature back to the ocean.

Michaela looked at the flies settling round the porpoise's mouth and eyes and felt distaste wash into her mouth. Neither Antony nor Janus showed much inclination to touch it and Simon was taking the rational view.

'It's dead,' he said. 'There's no point putting it back in the water. The tide will only wash it up again.'

It was not a popular pronouncement with the younger members of the group. Susan stared at him contemptuously. 'How can you be so sure it's dead?' she demanded. 'How many dead porpoises have you seen? Maybe it's unconscious. Look at those burns. Jee-sus.'

Michaela tried to take her arm, but Susan pulled away and walked stubbornly back down to the water for a refill. Florida followed in half-hearted solidarity. Florida was a practical girl. Michaela looked at Antony. 'This is ridiculous,' she said. 'And if you take a picture I'll break your nose.'

Susan pushed through them and poured a careful stream of salt water from the porpoise's head over the curve of its back. The flies rose in a cloud and settled in again.

'Susan —' said Pauline.

'If we all lifted its backside and put a towel underneath it,' Susan said, ignoring everyone and fixing her eyes on Simon again, 'then we could shift it down to the water that way, like Mum and me once lifted a chest of drawers and moved it down the passage at home.' She handed the bowl wordlessly to Florida, who set off for the sea at an obedient trot. 'Sort of slide it down,' Susan added. Simon blinked uncomfortably. There was a spirit of challenge in the air.

'OK,' said Antony suddenly. He put his camera on top of the wicker basket. 'Let's give it a try. What have we got to lose?'

'I don't see the porpoise in this,' Janus murmured,

but he threw aside his shirt and looked speculatively at Simon's towel.

'Use this one,' said Michaela and she unwound her own towel from her waist, conscious of Antony beside her.

The sun blazed from the sky and the porpoise was burning hot and slippery and it stared unmoved up and beyond the toiling group on the beach as they heaved and lifted and tugged, while Susan and Florida, on either side, waited like rugby fly-halves for the right moment to slip the towel beneath its bulk.

'There – go!'

Inch by slow inch they dragged the dead porpoise to the water until small wavelets could dribble over its tail and fins.

'If you pull quickly when I say Pull,' said Susan officiously, looking much better now that she was directing operations and everyone was listening to her, if with a fairly jaundiced collective air, 'you can tumble her over and into the deeper water over there.'

Michaela wondered when 'it' had become 'her' and why not 'him' when it was so much trouble, but she renewed her grip on the edge of the towel and looked away from the fanciful half-smile on its face.

'One, two, three – pull!'

The porpoise flopped into the water with a sigh and lay splayed out in the shallows without moving.

'Right,' Michaela said briskly. 'Let's go.' She washed her hands in a rock pool. Pauline did the same. 'Now don't look back. It's bad luck to look back.'

Florida frowned and bit at a nail on her finger, but she didn't look over her shoulder. They all trailed back up the beach to the car where Janus put the bicycles in the back of the pick-up. Simon tried to take Michaela's hand, but she pulled away, saying, 'Don't – I stink.'

No one spoke very much on the way back. When they reached the house, they saw Mater sitting alone on the front lawn in the lotus position eating green asparagus from a can. The others waved and went inside, but Michaela changed course and strolled across to her.

'It's hot.'

'Michaela, darling, before you sit down.' Mater set the can aside and wiped her mouth on a lime green napkin. 'Call the family out here for me. I have something I want to give you all before you go your separate ways.'

Then Michaela noticed that beside Mater on the grass was a horseshoe of white envelopes. They had single names on them in Mater's bold hand. She saw her own name, and Antony's, before she moved her eyes questioningly to her grandmother's face. Mater smiled a bland smile and held the empty can out to her. 'Please drop this in the bin on your way,' she said.

For once Mater didn't stray from the subject, although she was very brief. She gave the impression almost of having rehearsed her speech. The family sat around her on the grass in the shadow of the overhang of the house. The mood was suddenly sombre. Even Blanche had no desire, it seemed, to interrupt.

'These envelopes,' Mater said, holding them up in her hand like a fan of playing cards, 'will make an impact on each of your lives in one way or another. I have one request which I hope you will honour, and that is that you take them away with you now and open them in private when you get home. Do not open them right away. Wait until you have unpacked your things and are relaxed and settled. Please try – Janus,

Blanche – to resist ripping them open in the car before you reach the end of the driveway. This is, I think, a simple request.' She paused and looked at each of them in turn. Her eyes seemed to linger for a moment longer on Michaela, who shivered suddenly. It was as if a shadow had passed across her face like a cobweb.

'Mater —' she said, but Mater held up a hand. She wasn't finished. There was a secretive gleam in her eyes and Michaela had the distinct sense that she was enjoying making a minor drama of the situation, whatever this odd situation was.

They all knew that Mater was wealthy. The Whitehead fortune had never been a secret and although it didn't impact largely on their lives apart from a trust fund which had been set up for all of them on their sixteenth birthdays, and for which they were all suitably grateful, what happened to Mater's money when she died was not an issue ever debated or which caused tension in the family. Mater was so healthy, so unchanging year after year, that surprising though it suddenly seemed, none of them ever discussed the matter of inheritance. Who, for instance, would get the farm? Presumably Blanche, Harriet and Michael would share it equally and all the cousins would go on having access to it for time immemorial.

'Just to put your minds at ease,' Mater went on gravely, 'this is nothing to do with my will. My will is something I haven't got around to yet and Lodewyck du Preez in the village has been asking me for some time to put my mind to updating it – he was on at me again yesterday over the birthday cake. No, it is something else, but it is something important. I must ask you to treat it as important. Now –' She stood up and moved quickly among them, glancing at the names on the envelopes and handing them out like a spry schoolmistress.

'Is this bad news?' asked Harriet hesitantly. 'Are you sure it's not something we should discuss now, as a family?'

Mater smiled. 'I'm sure,' she said. 'I'm quite sure.'

Michael, too, was looking doubtful. He stuck the envelope in his shirt pocket and smoothed the hair back on Helena's forehead. She was managing with two canes today and had descended the steps from the house by herself. 'When you say this is private,' he said, 'do you mean it's something secret, as in illegal, anything like that?'

'You've done something,' Blanche said suddenly. 'You've done something scandalous and you can't bring yourself to tell us.' She tugged a cigarette from a silver case and snapped it shut. 'It's the farm, isn't it, Mater? You've lost the farm in a wager with the Barberton sisters.'

Michaela looked at her grandmother, but Mater was laughing with her head back. She had some silver fillings in her teeth and her laugh was as infectious as a child's. 'Scandalous,' she repeated breathlessly. 'As scandalous as gambling with the farm. Goodbye, children – go on, shoo. It's getting late and you've all got places to go. Blanche, you should be thinking about your rehearsal at the club tomorrow night. Pauline, you ought to have food on your brain, child. I wish I could be there. Oh, there's Juanita crying, right on cue.'

Mater dashed abruptly inside, taking the side stairs a wobbly two at a time, and they were all left on the grass like figures in an Impressionist painting, holding their white envelopes, bemused and intrigued.

'No,' murmured Antony as he followed Michaela inside. 'Not until you get home.'

Michaela, Susan and Florida went in Simon's car this time, with his fishing rod sticking out of the back window and the wind blowing The Dog's fine white fur into flattened patches on her neck. As they rounded the last bend, the river vanished suddenly from view and the countryside turned all at once into a bare, beige landscape, vegetation sparse and ungenerous. Simon changed gear to begin the climb to the tarred road. They could see the wooden farmstall leaning crookedly at the edge of the gravel. It was all boarded up today, which was unusual for a Sunday. Mater usually employed one of Frans's relations to man the stall for the weekenders returning to town, but Michaela supposed the party had been duty enough. The blackboard had a new message on it though, one which definitely hadn't been there on the way up. OPEN UP IN *PRIVATE*, it urged in foot high chalked letters, IN THE INTERESTS OF FAMILY *LIFE* – *Whitehead*, c 19—. And on the other side as they zoomed past Michaela swivelled her head in time to see WHERE THERE'S A WILL THERE'S A WAY in gay multi-coloured script.

'Good God,' she said. 'How laboured.'

They didn't stop on the way home. Simon tried first to interest them in singing rounds, without any takers, and then in conversation. He chose an unhappy topic right off.

'Pauline was telling me about Bricknell Court,' he began.

'*What* about Bricknell Court?' Michaela turned on him.

He glanced away from the road in surprise. 'About

the games you used to play, the orchard, just – things. It sounded like a beautiful place.'

'It was beautiful,' Michaela said sullenly. Wham – back to reality and a skeleton baring its teeth at her.

Simon decided to concentrate on passing a caravan in front of them which was swaying madly from side to side. Michaela made him nervous lately. Susan was dozing in the back with The Dog on her lap and Florida turning her hair into a myriad miniature plaits. Michaela looked out of the window at the setting sun, trying to wrench her thoughts away from Bricknell Court. Simon had spoilt everything. Also she could tell he was itching to know what was in Mater's envelope and it was probably only his curiosity that had stopped Michaela from opening it in the car. She had put it nonchalantly in her handbag, saying airily, 'Oh, I'm sure it's only money or something' just to irritate him.

The sun had bathed the horizon in a deep pink. Michaela closed her eyes and thought about Danny. She imagined that it was he behind the steering wheel with Susan strapped into her carseat. It was hopeless. Instead she went back to their first meeting which was still as clear as day in her mind. They had met between GARLAP lectures in their first year at university. At least it was Michaela's first year and Danny's third, but he had all but stopped going to any lectures by then and his bursary had dried up. GARLAP was the sort of filler course everyone took because there were no tutorials and no one had ever failed it in living memory. Michaela didn't even know it stood for Greek and Roman Literature and Philosophy until well into the second term.

Michaela was standing looking for her lecture notes when the longhaired boy in front of her in the tea urn queue dropped a Chelsea bun on her foot. They both stared, transfixed, at silver icing painting her toenails. Danny was a god. He could have stepped straight out of one of their set books in toga and sandals. He had the sandals – indeed he made them himself – and if it had been ten years earlier he would probably have had the toga too. As it was he was dressed in jeans and oversized jacket and his long tawny hair reached his shoulders. He was very tall and thin and had long pale fingers. He had a smile that split his face and made his eyes shine. They ended up sharing a table together and drinking tea until the students' union was empty except for a Chinese girl playing Noel Coward melodies on the piano. Michaela could never hear 'The Stately Homes of England' after that day without thinking of Danny.

When they looked back neither of them could remember how it was that they suddenly had a relationship but there it was. Danny and Michaela, as if there had never been anyone else for either of them.

The rest of the family weren't quite as ecstatic as Michaela was. Blanche, on learning that Michaela had moved in with Danny, sent her Janus and angry misspelled letters from all over the country but nothing could stop Michaela from missing lectures and holing up with Danny in his mountain cottage with a view of the bay and the cableway. Danny had given up lectures altogether when he got an export order for his leatherwork from the States. He was an inspired cobbler, spinning out shoes and belts and wallets until the early hours. The cottage smelt like a tannery. On Saturdays he had a stall at a fleamarket in Greenmarket Square and Michaela would sit beside him and catch up on her reading. She made friends with a girl who did miniature paintings of cats and whose model had kittens on the soft suede scrap box beneath the table at their stall. That was where The Dog came from, one-eyed, mewing and naked as a baby mouse. Michaela had overridden Danny's objection to cats by naming the kitten appropriately, and she took it home in a flower basket and kept it by their bed.

They got married after Susan was born, choosing the Coloured chapel at Stilfontein. Blanche couldn't come to the ceremony, but Janus was there representing the immediate family. He gave Michaela away reluctantly and with bad grace. Pauline had sung an old Gaelic wedding song Danny had dug up somewhere and Antony came along at the last minute to take pictures. Michaela was grateful for Mater. Mater was the only one in the family who had not taken her earnestly by the elbow and led her to one side saying 'Now are you *sure* you know ...' And Mater had come up with everything traditional that no one else, not even Michaela herself, had thought of. There was something old: a Belgian lace bedjacket which had come out with the Huguenots and which Michaela wore over her dress. Something new were the white satin shoes which Mater had bought on a whim on a rare shopping spree to town and never worn; something borrowed was her own wedding ring because Danny had forgotten Michaela's, and blue were the still wet bluebells plucked from among the grasses in the family graveyard that morning.

Susan had been taken care of in traditional manner too. Frans's mother had walked her round and round the chapel, burping her on her shoulder and singing loudly as she went, deep mournful Afrikaans hymns which echoed eerily round the empty pews each time she passed the open door. Afterwards they'd all gone back to Stillwaters and had a swim in the river, the pastor too, in a surprising yellow Speedo.

They had all come round eventually to the fact of Danny, but it wasn't an easy ride. Mater was the only one in the family who had accepted it right away, but Blanche said that was because she'd been married too young herself and didn't know any better. Michaela knew she was indebted to Mater and it was Mater who had ensured that she finish her degree by quietly seeing to it that there were sufficient funds in the bank to prevent Michaela from waitressing in the evenings. Michaela studied and Danny took charge of Susan. Susan teethed on keyrings and hanks of soft leather. She was the perfect fleamarket mascot, teetering among the stall owners in her black suede cowboy jerkin and moccasins. Trinkets and castoff ornaments were her early playthings and her father was her whole world.

Danny.

Michaela missed him every day of her life.

· 9 ·

Janus couldn't believe it. It was only as he switched on the big industrial washing machine to begin its lugubrious cycle that he noticed the white envelope in the shirt pocket. Too late he watched the water's sudden noisy gush and churn. Too late he saw underpants and jeans begin to move. Too late. He put a feeble hand to the glass but it was gone, a soggy corner passing the thick pane once, twice and then no more, like a figure waving to the crowd until swallowed up and never seen again. Janus had had this sort of thing happen before with his laundry. Banknotes turned into small bleached pellets, important phone numbers. Once a whole notebook with his Farnboro campaign jottings. He was impossibly careless, everybody told him so.

He sank back onto the seat in the laundrette and cursed out loud. Having resisted opening the thing with every fibre of his being as he drove home from Stillwaters with the hood of his car down and music thumping out into the kloofs and ragged gorges to distract him, was he now destined not to be able to decipher Mater's message, whatever it was, at all? He wondered miserably whether each envelope had contained a different one, whether his message was specific to his needs alone. He would call Michaela as soon as his washing was done, even before he got to grips with the tumbledrier.

'Nothing on TV, huh?'

Janus dragged his eyes from the swirling garments with difficulty, noting as he did so a brave white corner sweeping past. It was Chloë, the girl from downstairs with the smile. She was standing in the doorway with a big red washing basket on her hip. Janus stood up, grinning madly and feeling like a schoolboy. 'I was just going upstairs,' he said illogically. 'To make an urgent phonecall.'

Chloë had put the basket on the floor. There were clothes in it with black and white polka dots. Suddenly Janus couldn't bear to be in the same room as this nice girl and her washing and Mater's useless envelope. He had to call Michaela right away. He couldn't have Chloë watch him claw his way through wet sleeves and bunches of socks. She looked disappointed but he couldn't help it. He edged his way past her and bolted to the lifts. He hoped Michaela was home and that she didn't still have Simon with her.

Michaela answered the phone immediately as if she had been standing beside it. She came directly to the point. 'Have you opened the envelope?' she asked.

'It's in the wash.'

Michaela misunderstood. 'Well, *you* might think it'll all come out in the wash, Janus, but frankly I think this is more serious. I don't think you ought to be treating it lightly.'

'I'm not. I'm treating it with Surf Micro.' Janus felt faintly hysterical. He voice was rising. He explained what he'd done with his envelope, feeling pathetic and unworthy. 'What was in yours?' he asked.

'The same as yours, I imagine, and the same as everybody else's,' Michaela replied. 'A wedding invitation.'

'A what?'

'A wedding invitation. You know – till death us do part?'

Janus was nonplussed. 'Whose wedding?' he asked.

'Mater's.'

'Mater's!'

'Mater and Frans, to be precise. Gilt edged with a double wedding band motif in the top right-hand corner. Courtesy of Every Occasion Printers, Stilfontein.'

There was silence on the telephone. Then Janus laughed. 'She's lost her marbles,' he said flatly. 'She's got slush-brain.'

It was Blanche who always said that all men were deeply damaged and that anyone who contemplated marriage had slush-brain, and she'd repeated this to Michaela and Janus many times over the years. Her invective over Mater's bombshell, though, had burned up the wires between her home and Michaela's for the last twenty minutes. Michaela was already tired of the subject and beginning to be annoyed with Mater for putting her through it this way.

'So have you spoken to Mater?' Janus asked.

'What – to congratulate her?'

'Well —'

'No. Since you ask, I haven't had the courage, and Blanche hasn't given me a minute. Anyway, I wouldn't know what to say at this present moment.'

This was a crisis bigger than Bricknell Court. 'I think this calls for a family meeting,' said Janus. 'Don't you agree? We need to put our heads together and think what to do about it. We can do it at

Pauline's tomorrow night. A family meeting will be best.'

'We seem to have been doing a lot of that lately,' said Michaela. First there was the skeleton in the boiler room, now the skeleton in the cupboard. The Whiteheads were dancing among crises. Michaela felt as if a gunman was shooting at her feet.

Because Harriet and David were about to return to Australia and would not be in town when Pauline's club officially opened, Pauline had planned a grand dress rehearsal for the following night especially for her parents' benefit. The club would be closed to all but a few close friends and the immediate family, and they would do a full run through. It would give Pauline an opportunity to try out the kitchen and Frank to make sure the electrics were operating smoothly. Blanche and the boys from Greenbacks, as they had become known, would perform. They would all be there, guests of honour. Mater's timing couldn't have been better.

Janus went slowly back to the laundrette. His washing cycle had finished its final spin and he lifted the lid and peered cautiously inside. The invitation had parted from its envelope and was soggy, but still decipherable. 'You are invited to celebrate the marriage of Mary May Whitehead and Frans Swartbooi at . . . on . . .' Janus murmured the words aloud.

'Now you're talking to yourself. You're in a bad way.' It was Chloë again, making him start. She smiled tentatively in his direction and began to pull her washing from the tub. 'Hey,' she said, glancing over, 'you've got somebody else's stuff mixed up with yours. That's someone's dress.' Then she blushed. Of course Janus might well have had a visitor.

'Oh. Heavens.' Janus fished a black silk shift from

where it clung fast to the back of his lumberjack shirt. He laid it carelessly aside. 'I can't imagine how that got in there. Last week it was a tablecloth from number 15.' He laughed and cleared his throat. 'Listen, Chloë,' he said. 'Are you doing anything tomorrow night?'

'Pauline's' in neon, flashing intermittent as a motel sign above the door, each letter and swirl still intact, drew the eye in the darker quarter of the wharf. On Monday nights the Waterfront was quieter than during the rest of the week, especially at this end where some clubs and restaurants were even closed. Frank had put a large OPENING SOON sign on the front door, but people still pushed it open and peered round curiously. When they did Frank would call out 'Private function' prissily and they would retreat slowly, unembarrassed.

Inside Pauline had stuck to basic black and it was very dark at first, until one's eyes became accustomed to the gloom. Frank was experimenting still with light fittings and tonight he had a mini laser beam concert directed at the ceiling as Michaela and Susan arrived. It appeared that they were the first guests there. Susan immediately went to inspect Ernest who was crouched, humpbacked, on the edge of the stage, shifting uneasily from foot to foot with all the activity going on. The boys from Greenbacks were setting up behind him. Michaela went through to the kitchen, where she found Pauline at the stove wearing a white chef's cap.

'You need flour on your nose to really look the part,' Michaela told her.

'Frank gave me this as a starting out present,' Pauline said, touching it and smiling. 'Have you spoken to Mater yet?'

They had all been on the phone to each other at

intervals throughout the day. Blanche left half hour spells between her calls to cool down. No one had talked to Mater. Michaela could hardly meet Pauline's eyes. She knew she should have been the one to call Mater and she felt the furtive tug at the net of guilt. Then she noticed that Pauline had a suitcase in the corner of the kitchen and she felt grateful at the prospect of diversion. Pauline saw her looking.

'I wondered if I could come and stay with you for a few days,' she said, stirring at a sauce on the stove with a hand that was firmer than her voice. 'Tertius has been grovelling but I don't think I'm ready to go back home yet. And Janus has been kind as always, but he never has anything to eat in his fridge and I always get the feeling that I might be cramping his style.' She stirred the other way, first taking a swipe at the spoon with a finger and squinting closely at it.

'Of course,' said Michaela. 'Of course you must come. There's always a room for you, you know that.' She was distracted, thinking of Mater, perhaps with Frans right now, at the Stillwaters kitchen table. Frans had made that table, years ago.

Pauline licked her finger. She held the spoon out to Michaela as if she were in her own kitchen at home. For someone about to launch a brand new restaurant, Pauline was very calm, even if it was only her own family and friends she was entertaining tonight. 'Taste,' she instructed. 'Tell me if you think it needs anything. It looks the right consistency but I've been drinking tequila with Frank so I wouldn't know.'

They could hear the boys from Greenbacks beginning to make tuning up noises. A nice intricate little riff on a guitar. A few notes on the keyboards. Then Blanche burst through the swing doors like a cowboy and stood in the doorway, her legs planted firmly in their silver high heels. She had on a fake leopardskin coat which came down to her ankles, and she held a cigarette holder in her hand like a six-shooter.

'I don't know *how* Mater thinks she can do this to me,' she said dramatically, without preamble. 'I don't know how she got up the nerve, and tonight of all nights. God – mothers can ruin their children's lives when they want to, don't you forget it, Michaela.' Blanche was conveniently skipping a generation. Pauline and Michaela looked at each other, but if Blanche was aware of the irony she was letting it go.

'What have you got under that, Mother?' Michaela asked casually but fearing the worst. Blanche in full spate sometimes meant she didn't pay full attention to the more mundane things in life, like clothes, and given the stance, Cowboy Kate was a possibility.

Blanche flung back one side of the coat. Beneath it was a knee-length black skirt and a gold lamé top without sleeves.

'Very nice,' said Pauline quickly. She looked relieved. The cabaret was going to be classy after all. 'You look very nice, Blanche. You're going to knock us dead.'

'I'd like to knock Mater off her feet,' Blanche said. 'Tell me – do you think there's any chance this whole thing might be a joke?' She whipped out the wedding invitation and brandished it in front of them. Michaela blinked. There was no knowing what Blanche might draw forth next from the voluminous folds of her fur.

'No,' Michaela said, turning away from her. 'I don't think it's a joke. I think Mater is getting married to Frans.' She licked her fingers and then rinsed her hands at the sink. 'Salt,' she said to Pauline. 'Maybe a tad more salt.'

'Oh no, she's not,' said Blanche. 'Oh no, not bloody likely. Not on your life. That gold-digging little ... *Hotnot*. I don't know where he found the gall to do this, or how he's managed to get such a disgusting idea into Mater's head, but we've got to put a stop to it before it gets any more involved.'

'Well.' Michaela looked doubtful. 'The gilt-edged wedding invitation and carefully orchestrated plan to announce a marriage seems involved enough to me.'

'Is *this* where the party is?' Antony came strolling into the kitchen and Michaela felt her stomach turn over. Antony was all in black, his dark hair glossy and smoothed back into a ponytail. He was tanned from his weekend away. Behind him in the doorway was a girl. Tall, blonde, beautiful. A complete cliché. Off-the-shoulder black lycra T-shirt and black hotpants. They were the proverbial beautiful couple, and her legs were longer even than Michaela's. Michaela took all of this in without blinking an eye, although she grabbed at the salt cellar and sprinkled a fierce burst into the saucepan before Pauline deftly removed it from her grip and stood with her hand on her shoulder.

'We were just coming out,' Michaela said through clenched teeth. She turned Blanche around. 'You ought to be supervising the boys, oughtn't you,' she told her mother. 'We don't want them to kick off with "Tie a Yellow Ribbon," do we? We'll talk about the other thing later.'

'This is Nancy,' said Antony.

'Oh good,' said Michaela as she swept past. 'Let's all go and sit down. I'm sure we can find another chair.'

As if Antony wasn't annoying enough, Janus had brought a girl too, a serious looking girl with flat brown hair and glasses and nervous fumbling hands. Michaela was furious with both of them. Of all the ill-chosen moments to bring *dates*, for heaven's sake, when they had a major family crisis on their hands. How could they discuss Mater's problem with strangers hovering? She hadn't thought to bring Simon, although he'd hinted. He was feeling far too much part of the family as it was. When were they supposed to thrash this out, when the girls went to the bathroom?

Michaela found her own reaction to Mater's announcement distressing. There were so many conflicting facets ricocheting around her head. The first, of course, was Mater's age. She had just celebrated her seventieth birthday, when most women were already alone or facing the prospect, or only too grateful to have the space to breathe that Mater had already enjoyed for years now. She had been a widow, living alone, for over ten years, and with never the slightest sign that it had bothered her or that she missed a partner. She never seemed lonely. She had the farm, she had all of them coming up to Stillwaters at the drop of a hat. They spent Christmas there, and Easter holidays, and many weekends and holidays in between. Weren't they enough for her? Why on earth would she want to tie herself up in a new marriage at her age? And Frans — Frans couldn't be a day older than sixty. Did anyone even *know* his age? Whatever it was, he was a great deal younger than Mater. And there was the colour issue ... But Michaela wasn't ready to address the colour issue yet. She was too busy digging into all the corners behind it, for the more important things.

Like education. Frans, for all she knew, had never even been to high school, whereas Mater had three degrees, a Masters in sociology and a diploma in home economics. Like most of the children in the

Coloured part of the Stilfontein village, Frans had been to the local village school when he was a boy. It probably wasn't more than a shack and a couple of slates with chalk in those days – it wasn't very much better now – and the quality of the education was abysmal. She knew Frans could read and write, but whether he actually ever *read* anything other than the newspapers' racing pages, or wrote anything more than Mater's notices on the farmstall blackboard was questionable. Michaela could picture him only in his greasy black hat and black jacket, sunshine or rain. There was no other possible image of Frans in her mind.

Michaela tried, but she could not see Frans by lamplight paring away at a length of wood with delicate, strong fingers. Or sitting in shirt-sleeves in the cool of an evening drinking beer from frosted glasses with Mater on the lawn. She knew he must be doing these things – there was ample evidence now if she chose only to look – but she could not do it. She could not imagine him rocking a baby to sleep with his foot on the cradle he had made, singing softly to her until her long lashes made shadows on her cheeks. Michaela could only see a man who could barely read and write and whose life revolved around potatoes and straight lines in a field.

A Coloured man. All right – a Coloured man.

The Whiteheads had always prided themselves on being colourblind in a country which by tradition and by law had laid ground rules for making colour the first and sometimes the only issue that mattered. The Whiteheads weren't like that. Each of them in his or her own way had been campaigners against apartheid in the dark old days, and against repression of any kind ever since. Harriet and David were testimony to that, having been persecuted by Nationalist government authorities, officially and unofficially, for most of their adult lives for speaking out against discrimination and acting out their beliefs. Josh Whitehead was a hero of the oppressed majority. Even Blanche had had her hand in protest theatre when she was younger. Michaela was sure that the ugly word Hotnot which had slipped so unpleasantly from her mouth this evening had never passed her lips until that very moment. It was so raw Blanche was obviously severely in shock.

And Michaela? Michaela had grown up in that tradition too. She had no prejudices. Black, white, Coloured – none of that mattered to her. Then why would the fact of Frans's colour not slink away out of the shadows in her mind? Why did it suddenly matter? She was alarmed at the thought that everyone else was feeling the same way. How deep did apartheid go, for Christ's sake?

Nobody was concentrating on Blanche. She sat on a barstool in a pool of Frank's clever lighting and sang, and her songs washed over them and drifted out to the harbour while Antony sat deep in thought and Janus fidgeted with his wineglass and regretted bringing Chloë.

Janus could tell Michaela was angry. She was staring fixedly at her mother and frowning, and he knew she wasn't even seeing Blanche, let alone listening to her sing. Michaela's mind was alternately at Stillwaters and bashing Antony's brains in for the lissome and aloof Nancy. Michaela's approval was important to Janus and he had almost apologised to her for Chloë. That approval was something he had acknowledged long ago, and it didn't really bother him any more. When he had been in therapy a while back, he had explored all of that stuff with his therapist and accepted the whole absent mother surrogate thing, not that he really believed it in his heart of hearts. Michaela was too powerful a force in her own right to have merely replaced his mother. Michaela didn't replace anybody; she would have had none of that. And besides, he didn't need to replace Blanche. Blanche was a working mother. And mostly when she worked, she worked out of town and Janus was at school with other members of his family. He didn't feel he had missed out particularly, not when he compared the family life of some of his school contemporaries. His own had been a relatively happy, normal childhood, give or take a hitch or two here and there. He had had Michaela, who was close to him, his uncle David and Harriet. And Mater, of course.

Their father had left when Janus was born and had gone to live in Bermuda, the farthest place he could think of, Blanche told them years later, and he never communicated with his family after that. Blanche had cut his face out of all the photographs in their albums in a fit of spite and then hadn't had the heart to throw them away. Janus had found them in an empty Band-aid box when he was seven, twenty small faces cut off the shiny suits his father had liked to wear. He'd stuck them in an exercise book and drawn trees round them, the only thing he could draw with any remote resemblance to reality. Michaela had come across the book one day beneath Janus's mattress when she was looking for his pocket money. Apple faces in wax crayon leaves. Bemused, she had shown the pictures to Blanche who had dumped the whole book in a bin in the park.

One of Janus's most vivid memories of Mater was

playing cricket on the lawn at Stillwaters one summer, he and Antony and Mater. Mater was wickie, with her legs far apart and her skirt hitched into her pants, her long skinny legs, blotched with sunspots and some ridged veins at the backs of her knees. With her hair blowing out from beneath a straw hat – her poet's hat – going white even then. Where had Frans been that summer? Out in the potato field, no doubt, perched on the tractor like a malevolent scarecrow, always in the background, deferential – 'Hullo, Master Janus. Back from school?' – like the servant he was. Frans had made him a cricket bat once, but Janus hadn't liked the finish, it wasn't like his friends' at school, and he had left it behind in a cupboard. It wasn't there when he looked for it next holiday and he never asked for it.

Blanche had finished her last number. She was bowing low, standing beside the barstool with her legs together, very good legs in shiny black stockings. She was smiling out at them, a professional, bright smile, just as she would smile out across the audience when the club opened officially and the place was full. Blanche was good. There was a sheen of perspiration on her neck and shoulders. She had worked hard for Pauline. She walked off the stage to the side, down the couple of steps to the floor and disappeared into the makeshift dressing room which Frank had only just finished rigging up for her this evening. There were a few touches still to be completed, and they were all aware of a small crash as Blanche tripped over something and exclaimed briefly and colourfully in the pause before the band swung into the 'Gravy Waltz'.

'She was great. Wasn't she great?' Janus leaned over to Antony.

'Terrific. Blanche should be nowhere near retirement. She could knock spots off anyone, really. Anyone. What do you say, Mick?'

Antony's hand was being held. 'We should go up there, Antony. You and me.'

'Where?'

'To Stillwaters. We must go back.' Michaela poured soda water into a glass and left it standing on the table. She glanced over at Nancy, who was staring at Ernest pecking on something in a vase on an adjoining table. 'We will have to go back to the farm ourselves and talk to her. It's no good discussing it here among ourselves. Someone has to *talk* to her, and to Frans if necessary. And it has to be us.'

Pauline, who had been talking to friends at a table nearby, hearing Michaela's raised voice, came across with a pot of coffee. 'You haven't eaten anything,' she said.

'I'm sorry, Pauline. I can't get anything down. Don't take it personally.'

'Did I hear you saying you were going back to Stillwaters?'

'Don't you agree it's the only thing we can do? Not all of us, not a domestic confrontation. Just me and Antony, together.'

Pauline poured coffee and stood holding the pot like a waiter.

'Mater will certainly be expecting some sort of reaction,' said Harriet. 'And we're leaving town shortly. To be honest, Pauline, I don't think I'd know what to say. I've got so out of touch with Mater these past years.'

Michaela brushed Harriet's feeble cop-out aside. She could feel a steel rod of determination pushing up inside her, inflating her like a balloon. David was asleep.

If everyone was going to fall apart and sidestep the problem, or simply exhale a lot of hot air like Blanche was doing, Michaela wasn't going to join in. But she was damned if Antony was going to get away with not helping her.

'You'll have to excuse me if I borrow him,' she said to Nancy with her sweetest smile and using an expression straight out of one of her fiction entries (Joy Beamish had used it twice in a story called *Husbands Galore*).

'What, tonight?' Nancy looked at Antony, startled. He took his hand away.

'Well, not immediately,' said Michaela with regret. 'Tomorrow probably. I'll have to check my schedule.'

Antony looked marginally annoyed. He had a schedule too and he said so. 'But I'll check on it,' he added. It wasn't a good idea to cross Michaela at this time of night. She had dark patches beneath her eyes and had run her hands through her hair during Blanche's performance until it stood wildly around her head like a bush.

The boys from Greenbacks were moving into another soft instrumental number, a moody, bluesy sound on the keyboards that forced them all to quieten down for a moment.

Then, 'Come,' Helena beckoned to her husband. 'Dance with me.' She manoeuvred her wheelchair out from the table and weaved through the chairs to the small dancefloor. Michael followed her. He still had his napkin tucked in his shirt and a tender, soft expression on his face. Helena was a tireless dancer. She had danced in her youth and had hoped at one time to make ballet a career. Now, of course, that was a nostalgic dream, but multiple sclerosis wasn't going to stop her moving to the music she loved best, and fusion jazz was calling her. The wheelchair made hardly any sound on the floor as she swung and swirled and held out her hands to Michael. They filled up the dancing space in a wink of legs and flashing spokes beneath the ball of light Frank had centred above them. The tips of Helena's long fingers touched Michael's as she spun round and round, with her head back and her eyes laughing. Everyone's eyes were on them.

'Oh, God,' Pauline murmured. 'I'm such a fuck up.'

'You're not that bad,' Antony said, reaching for her hand. 'We've had a skop before, you and I.'

'I don't mean on the dancefloor, idiot,' Pauline said, but before she could explain, Tertius was there beside her, breaking the spell and taking her by the elbow. He led her off to the kitchen.

'Shall I go after them?' David said anxiously. Harriet was looking tensely at the swinging kitchen doors. They were parents waiting for their daughter's family to tell them what to do.

'Sit it out,' Michaela said calmly. 'Pauline's good with pots and pans. She's on her own turf in there.'

It was no longer a secret since Harriet had had a long and frank discussion with Mater about Pauline and her brutal lover. All the same, it wasn't their place now to interfere although the instinct was there.

'He'll be asking her to come home about now,' Janus said. 'That's the pattern.' If anyone was familiar with the pattern, Janus was, but he was looking anxious nevertheless.

'Will she go?' Harriet asked.

'I don't think so this time. She took her suitcase when she left my place this evening, but she said she was going to Michaela's.' He looked at his sister.

'Yes,' Michaela said tersely. 'Pauline will be coming home with us tonight.'

Susan came walking through from the dressing room, followed by Blanche in tight turquoise ruched dress. Susan had Ernest on her shoulder and a mighty grin on her face. 'Isn't he *glorious*?' she said. 'He's been singing something military to us while Blanche changed.'

'"The March of the Toreadors," I think,' Blanche said. 'What on earth is that noise in the kitchen?'

'Pauline is making coffee for Tertius,' Michaela said.

'Pauline's making coffee *on* Tertius,' said Susan. 'God.'

While they sat frozen in their seats, and the band played, Tertius came flying through the swing doors again, went straight past their table with a scowling face and rushed out into the night. They stared after him.

'Dance with me,' Michaela said suddenly, but she was too late. Nancy had Antony by the hand and was leading him onto the dancefloor and Janus had Chloë already on her feet.

'Now that those two are out of the way,' said Blanche, putting a restraining hand on Michaela's arm, 'can we talk family business at last? How was I?'

'Wonderful,' Michaela told her. 'We all thought you were wonderful. I'm sorry, Mother, if we seemed unappreciative, but you know where our minds are tonight.'

'Well, I've decided what we ought to do,' Blanche said. 'We —'

'You and Antony ought to go back up to Stillwaters and talk to Mater. Don't argue, Michaela. You've always been her favourite and I think if anyone can talk some sense into her you can. Take Antony for stability.'

'Take Antony with you. I don't like you going to the shops on your own.'

Janus watches from the top of the fig tree as Michaela and Antony take the path through the trees to the corner shop. He adjusts his telescope until he has them bobbing in his sights. He sees them go round the corner and he shoves the telescope in his pocket and climbs down, hurriedly, almost losing his footing. They walk round the corner, close together, their shoulders jostling against each other. Michaela takes Antony's hand and swings it up in front of them. They are laughing, but he is too far behind to hear what they're saying. They are almost exactly the same height now and they take the same size shoes. People are surprised that it is not they who are brother and sister, and always comment on the likeness between them. Janus doesn't look anything like Michaela. He is short and thin and his elbows are bony as a cat's. His hair is sandy coloured and very fine, nothing like Michaela's thick, tawny bush. Sometimes Janus feels very overlooked.

He stands at the corner and watches as they go into the shop together. Tommy the pinball wizard is slouching outside. He has no shoes on and his feet are grey with filth. He is holding the butt of a squashed cigarette between the thumb and forefinger of his right hand. Janus trains the telescope on him. Tommy has slitty eyes and they are dark and bright and darting. They flash from side to side from beneath the rim of his cap. He is leaning against the door of the shop with one foot up behind him. He drags on the cigarette and the end glows softly. Janus shivers. He knows he is afraid of Tommy without knowing why.

Michaela and Antony are coming out of the shop. They have a white packet with bread in it and orange juice. Antony is unwrapping a Rolo. They stop, their heads together. Then Michaela turns and gives something to Tommy – he can't see what it is – and Tommy slips inside the shop like a wraith. Michaela must have given him 50c. He is going in to play pinball.

Janus puts his hands in his pockets and steps into the road to meet them.

When their car crested the hill for the last downward run to the Stilfontein turn-off, Michaela was almost talking to Antony again, and by the time the farmstall board was legible she put a hand out to the steering wheel.

'Slow down,' she said. 'There's a message.'

The letters were in pale blue chalk and neatly printed in Frans's hand: *Conscience makes egotists of us all*,' Michaela read aloud.

'Wilde,' said Antony.

'Crazy,' Michaela agreed, 'but I guess that's directed purely at us. Prepare for a tough negotiation.'

'To be fair, Michaela, I don't think this is about negotiation and to be honest I think it's a bit rich the two of us coming up here as if we were reprimanding a wayward schoolgirl who's strayed from the straight and narrow. This is our grandmother and we've no business preaching to her.'

'We're not going to preach to her. We're just going to find out what's going on.'

'But we know what's going on.'

'Blanche isn't sure of that. Not entirely. And our brief is to be able to assure ourselves and the others that there's no funny business.'

'You're sounding too much like Blanche. I will take a bet with you that there's no funny business. We're going to come away looking and feeling foolish.'

It was early evening and they drove with the windows rolled down and the tang from the fynbos filling the car. The ribbon of river appeared suddenly, a brash burnished copper in the setting sun, with hardly a ripple visible from up here on the hillside. On the far bank they could see Stillwaters' roof in amongst the trees.

'I wonder whether Frans has moved in,' Michaela said apprehensively. 'I hope not. I'm not sure that I can talk to Mater properly if he's around. I'll keep thinking I'm expected to *pay* him or something.'

Antony changed gear as the road dropped steeply towards the bridge. 'Did you see the paper this morning?' he asked.

'No, why?'

'There was something about Bricknell Court.'

Michaela, curiously, hadn't given much thought to Bricknell Court lately. Mater had taken care of that. When it wasn't being thrust in her face she found she could almost get completely away from it.

'What about it?' she asked Antony. Bricknell Court was small beer.

'There's Frans — down by the river.' Antony pointed. 'With a potato bucket.'

'What about Bricknell Court?'

'I think it was a reporter trying to fill a space. Something about still no definite leads regarding identity of the skeleton, but that the police were busy following up some new information.'

'Oh?'

'They always say that,' Antony said encouragingly. 'Just to jog people into remembering. And to keep the case in the public eye. I don't suppose they really have any idea.'

'No, I suppose they don't.' Michaela bit her lip. 'You don't think they're closing in on us even as we speak?'

Antony laughed. 'Oh, for heaven's sake, Mick. Closing in on us. Can you hear yourself?'

Michaela was silent, watching Frans turn to look at the car. 'He brought it on himself, you know,' she said. 'He asked for trouble from the start. We all felt the same way about him in the end. It wasn't only me.'

Antony turned into the lane, slowing to a crawl and bumping along on the verge. The narrow lane was pitted with potholes along this first section. The candlestakes were still there.

'Here comes Frans,' Michaela murmured. 'He's coming this way.'

Frans was making his way across the field to open the farm gate, as he had done many times before. Only this time it seemed like there was a hidden agenda. He tramped steadily through the green plants, cutting a swathe as he went, carrying the metal bucket in one hand.

'What do we *say*?' said Michaela, looking desperately to Antony for help. Frans had taken off his hat and was smoothing his hair. Michaela imagined a jauntiness in his stride that hadn't been there before. (Did he and Mater sleep together?)

Frans lifted the catch on the gate and swung it open, standing at the side of the road out of the dust as they passed through. Antony greeted him through the open car window. Michaela smiled weakly. '*Middag*, Frans,' she said.

'Hullo, Miss Michaela,' Frans replied. Was there a

trace of irony there, or would she for evermore detect mockery in that brown face whether it was there or not?

'What's he doing?' she whispered, without moving her lips.

Antony looked in the rearview mirror. 'Closing the gate, Michaela,' he said dryly. 'What do you think he's doing? Nipping across the field to make sure we don't get to Mater before him? Let's try to be sensible here.'

Mater was trimming a hedge at the side of the property with a pair of garden clippers. She was wearing wide white shorts which accentuated her thin brown legs. Juanita was lying on her back on a blanket on the grass nearby. 'Well, here you are,' Mater said, smiling broadly at them. 'The deputation.'

Later that evening, much later, after Mater had gone to bed and Juanita had been given her last bottle, Antony and Michaela lay sprawled on the blanket on the front lawn with a bottle of wine and plastic picnic mugs.

'I don't feel very proud of myself,' said Michaela. 'You were right. We shouldn't have come.'

In fact, whatever it was they had attempted to achieve had been left by the wayside in the face of Mater's radiance and her innate dignity. Words of reproach and incomprehension had died on their lips and when Frans had brought homemade onion soup in fat bowls out to them on the grass and had sliced thick wedges of the bread they had both so greedily and disloyally dipped and eaten, the moment for questioning of wisdom withered away. Frans had eaten with them, sitting perhaps slightly to one side, but by no means the servant at the smaller fire. Mater had talked to him in Afrikaans about a problem with the tractor and he had brought Juanita's warmed bottle out to her and tested it on his own wrist. Michaela and Antony drank their soup in silence and watched the sun go down.

And then Frans had left them, making his way back across the field and down the track by the river towards Stilfontein village. He whistled as he went and the tune came back to them on the breeze and hung in the air like a substitute for the man so that they couldn't say a word about him.

'I know why you're here, of course,' Mater said gently then. 'And I've been trying to persuade myself it's out of concern. Perhaps by now you are both regretting having come. But don't worry —' she went on as Michaela tried to say something '— I do understand. Our news must have been a big shock to you, to the family, and I should have expected an extreme reaction, especially from Blanche.'

'Mater, we —'

Mater stopped her with a glance. 'It's all right,' she said. 'I can see why you had to come in person, and I'm glad it was the two of you. But don't you see, I have made up my mind? I am not a person to make hasty judgements or decisions, you should both know that. However, once made up, I am not inclined to go backwards, I never have been. Frans Swartbooi and I are to be married by Easter. I hope you will respect this. Oh, those Barberton girls, they're ski-ing mad. I don't expect you to be overjoyed. I do expect surprise, but once that surprise has worn off a little, I hope you will be happy for me.'

The noise of the hotel motorboat rose to a roar. Michaela couldn't find any words to say. Antony was picking at a grass shoot with what could only be described as a wry expression. Mater was stroking Juanita's back and humming to herself.

'OK, I give up,' said Antony suddenly, sitting up and laughing. 'We had to come. We had to come to see whether this made any sense at all, Mater. Blanche doesn't think so, Harriet is simply stunned, and the rest of us, well – we needed to see for ourselves that you were sure about what you were doing.'

'I'm sure,' said Mater, smiling back at him. 'Oh, I'm sure.'

'How long,' Michaela asked, clearing her throat. 'How long has this –'

'Been going on?' Mater's eyes danced. 'Well, let me see now . . .'

Michaela blushed. She could feel her cheeks reddening. She was mortified, wishing earnestly to be somewhere else, to be someone else.

'It's my bedtime,' Mater said. She got up and collected the soup bowls on a tray. 'I'll wash these up and put Juanita down. No – stay out here and watch the stars come out. It'll do you both good. One can never get blasé about stars in the country.'

They lay on their backs on the blanket, doing what they were told. The sky grew dark quickly and the stars were bold splashes, white above their heads. They lay without talking for a long time.

'Antony,' Michaela said, her voice very low. 'Look, there's a firefly.' A bead of light wove about in front of them and they held their breath and watched, enchanted, as another and then another joined the circle and the fireflies spiralled and spun against the backdrop of the black river and the night sky.

'This was a dreadful mistake, you know,' said Michaela. 'And I can't help feeling suddenly that my life has been a series of dreadful mistakes. There are so many things I wish I had done differently. Bricknell Court and that sickening boiler room. Danny. And now this. Things are getting too big for me.'

'Come over here.' Antony put out a hand and pulled her closer to him. Above them Mater had left a lamp in the window and it threw a golden net across their legs and feet.

Antony held onto her hand and gently massaged her fingers. His own fingers were cool and dry. Michaela could feel a pulse beating in her throat.

'We're going to make love tonight,' Antony said to the sky. 'Right here, beneath the stars. And we're going to forget about everything else, all the many things that are getting too big for us. Just for tonight, don't you agree?'

Michaela didn't trust herself to answer but she moved against the warmth of his body all the same and closed her eyes.

· 10 ·

Pauline had made American-style fudge brownies and she and Susan and The Dog sat down to eat them and watch *Horror Express* on television. Remembering a vague promise to her mother, Susan was trying to sew egg-yolk yellow name tags onto her school socks at the same time – she was the only person in the school with yellow name tags – but after she'd sewn the neck of one sock closed so tightly that no human hand would ever get it undone again, she gave up and she sat transfixed before the small screen with The Dog in a vice-like grip on her lap.

Pauline sat back with her plate and a sigh of pleasure. She always felt content at Michaela's house, finding that she slotted very comfortably into a domestic routine there. She made beds, cooked up little treats for Susan to take in her school lunches and washed sinkfuls of dishes in sky-blue rubber gloves while listening to the competitions on the radio. Sometimes she thought that of housemaid was her true calling in life, although she would never have admitted to this in front of anybody, least of all Michaela, whose idea of housework was plumping up the cushions on the sofa once a fortnight.

Pauline had cleaned all the windows this morning,

then fetched Susan and Florida from school and taken them down to the Waterfront for the afternoon. She and Frank had drunk a bottle of wine and cleaned up last night's débris, and one of the boys from Greenbacks had dropped by to fetch some equipment and stayed for two hours, playing his flute in the sunny doorway. Then they'd all taken a stroll round the harbour before locking up and fed the seagulls on leftover bread rolls. They'd watched a tug guide a listing Taiwanese tanker to its berth.

Pauline always suspected that the feeling of elation she experienced on pristine days like this one was somehow too good to be true, and especially too good for the likes of her. She had a fanciful notion now and then that the men in her life had been wished on her as a sort of divine admonishment, as if she had no choice in the selection of her partners. It wasn't permitted for her to feel at peace with her life for too long. When things were going especially well, like now with the club taking shape and the sparkling environment she was privileged to work in, she couldn't help taking Tertius's treatment of her as a sign that she was not to get too complacent. Tertius was her counterweight, her handbrake on the good side of things. She had tried to explain this feeling to Michaela once, when she was rationalising a return home after a particularly colourful beating which had left her with double vision for a month, but Michaela had got impatient with her and wouldn't listen. But then Michaela didn't understand about balance and ebb and flow. Michaela made things go her way as much of the time as she could, and when they didn't she went out and fixed them so that they were in her favour again. That was why the Bricknell Court business and the untimely skeleton was so very vexing for Michaela. It was a problem which was beyond her control to sort out because sorting it out would mean placing all of them, and Michaela in particular, in a less than favourable position. And of course that was to be avoided at all costs.

Curiously, it had been Frank who had been extraordinarily understanding. Sitting in the sunshine on chairs outside the club's front door with the flute's pure notes all about them, she had found herself, unprompted, trying to explain to him something about Tertius. She felt she owed him after Tertius's petulant entrance and exit the night before. Although Frank had never commented when her arm was in its sling and the bruising on her face was unavoidable, she had felt something like a bond developing between them as Frank had gone way beyond his brief, helping shift the heavy things and hefting and packing crates in the storeroom for a week. He had done a hundred other things to save her from the humiliation of having to ask for help without saying a word or asking any questions. Sitting outside with the salty smell of fish from the boats' fresh catches of the day and the hoarse calling of the gulls as they competed for pickings, Pauline told Frank how she knew it sounded odd but she felt she deserved Tertius and how she felt sorry for him because he couldn't help the way he was. There had been a time, believe it or not, she told him, when they had experienced something that could have passed for happiness. Tertius had once draped an I Love Pauline banner over a bridge spanning the highway for Valentine's Day. It had fallen down in a bad wind and draped a traffic cop in its folds on his motorcycle and nearly caused an accident. It was to his credit that Frank didn't ask why she stayed with Tertius. She hadn't realised electricians could be so sensitive.

Ernest was perched on an iron bollard with the wind ruffling his neck feathers. Frank had a loose leash around one of his legs, explaining sheepishly how he thought that once out in the sea breeze Ernest might revert to his ancestral pirate genes and take off for the crow's nest of one of the dubious Asiatic vessels that lurched into port every couple of days.

'I don't think they have crow's nests any more,' Pauline said consideringly, 'but whatever the modern equivalent is, I'm sure you're right. Ernest might feel the call.' Susan and Florida fed him sunflower seeds and sat tanning their legs with their school skirts hiked up to their thighs.

They decided on fudge brownies and apple juice as a sensible supper because Pauline had been thinking about real food all day and was tired of it, and Susan thought she ought perhaps to do her homework rather than cook the hamburgers Michaela had left for them.

'If you go with the maths quickly,' Pauline told her, 'there's a quite ghastly movie on TV we just don't want to miss. There's a manic Prussian in it played by Telly Savalas.'

'Who?' said Susan.

There they sat, brownie crumbs on their faces, attention riveted, when the telephone rang.

'It's probably your mother, reporting in,' said Pauline. 'You get it.'

'I can't. I can't *move*. The Dog's got her claws in my leg,' Susan replied. 'Please, Pauline.'

'Oh, all right. But Michaela had better keep it short. I've already dealt with Blanche on the phone today.'

Pauline wasn't gone long enough for it to have been Michaela and when she came back into the living room she had a strange expression on her face. Susan looked at her curiously. 'Anything wrong?' she asked. 'Was it Mum?'

'No,' said Pauline. She shook her head. 'No, it wasn't anyone really. I guess it was a wrong number, or a crank or someone.'

Susan turned back to the television. 'Oh, well,' she said. 'It could have been one of Mum's admirers. Sometimes they sound like cranks. Probably Simon.'

It hadn't been Simon and it hadn't been a crank. Or not the sort who dialled a number at random and made lewd noises. This crank had been rather more focused. For one thing he had assumed it was Michaela at the other end, because he had used her name.

'Michaela,' the man said, drawing it out. 'Michaela.'

'What? Who is this?'

'Michaela. We know each other very well, but you don't know who I am. I want to do you a favour. I want to save you from disaster.'

'I beg your pardon,' said Pauline, ever polite. 'Actually, this isn't —'

'You remember Bricknell Court.'

Pauline's heart gave a painful lurch.

'You know who it is, don't you?'

'I —'

'And what's more, you aren't the only person who knows. You think you've kept it in the family, don't you, but you're so wrong. You can identify those poor old bones, can't you? Can't you now?'

There was a click and then silence and Pauline remained stuck to the telephone making Hullo, Hullo noises and feeling a cold trickle of fear at the back of her neck.

191

When Michaela entered the kitchen she found Mater sitting at the table with a mug of hot milk in front of her. She was in her dressing gown and her silver hair was combed behind her ears. The light from the paraffin lamp turned down as low as it could go without going out threw huge shadows into the corners of the room. Michaela was cold in Antony's cotton T-shirt. She had forgotten to bring anything to sleep in.

Mater smiled at her. 'Can't you sleep either?' she said.

Michaela shook her head. It was two in the morning. 'I hope I didn't wake you?'

'No, but I saw the light.'

'I find warm milk with a banana mashed up in it does wonders for insomnia.'

Michaela looked at the mug. 'Is that what you're drinking?' she asked.

'With a splash of whisky,' Mater confessed. 'The banana doesn't quite do the trick on its own.'

Outside an owl hooted. The sound echoed down the chimney, sounding loud and hollow in the house. 'That will be the giant eagle owl,' Mater said. 'He's been here a lot lately. Some people would call it an omen.'

'A good omen or bad?'

'I never asked. Good, I hope, though I've no doubt your mother would call it bad. Why is Blanche so against my marriage, do you think? Is it merely because she perceives it as unseemly, or does she have a problem with Frans personally?'

'Both,' Michaela said flatly. She yawned. 'May I try some of that remedy of yours?' Blanche wasn't alone in thinking that, but she was the most vocal about it.

'There's the pot.' Mater pushed the bottle of milk over to her. 'The Scotch is on top of that dresser.'

Michaela peeled and absentmindedly ate the banana

while she waited for the milk to heat, then poured a dash of whisky into the pot just before it frothed.

'What do *you* think?' Mater asked. She sounded a little weary.

Michaela pondered. 'The truth?' she said. 'It's so unexpected. You never gave us any warning signals, or none as far as any of us was aware. I think we all feel a bit cheated and left out.'

'It had to be a surprise,' said Mater. 'And unseemly?'

'Unseemly – that depends.'

'On what?'

'What you're doing it for perhaps?'

'It's sex, isn't it?'

Michaela flushed and burnt her fingers on the handle of the pot. She cursed softly. 'You're doing it for —?'

Mater laughed. 'It's unseemly for a seventy year old to be thinking about sex, that's what's worrying all of you the most, isn't it?'

It wasn't. It was the fact that Frans was a barely literate Coloured man that had them gasping, but sex was almost a safer topic. Michaela was conscious for the first time in her life of feeling uncomfortable around Mater. Right from when she was a child she had been able to talk to her grandmother about absolutely anything. They had discussed sex quite openly when she was sixteen when she wanted to go on the Pill and Blanche was unapproachable on the subject, but that was her sexuality that was in contention, not Mater's.

Mater decided to let her off. She began ticking things off on her fingers. 'Friendship,' she said. 'Companionship. Things shared. Common concerns about the land. The love of a child – Frans and I hope to adopt Juanita officially. A fondness that comes of years of close contact. Isn't that enough, child?'

'But —'

'Before you go on,' said Mater. 'I want you to cast your mind back. Back a few years, about thirteen. To a young girl with the world at her feet, a university education and a choice of any number of careers. Travel overseas, a whole wealth of experiences waiting for her. Enter a penniless dropout who's good with his hands. A suitable match? I think not, and if I remember rightly, there weren't many noises of approval from the young girl's family.'

Michaela looked away. 'That was different,' she mumbled. 'But I guess I know what you're saying.'

'Thank you,' said Mater. 'And now I think I'll try to sleep a little. Juanita's still an early riser.'

In spite of the warm milk and the whisky, Michaela was a long way from sleep. She took the lamp through to the front room, then blew it out and sat in the darkness looking out to the river. It was a clear, starfilled night, with a yellow moon riding low in the sky. She sat for half an hour or so trying to make sense of Mater's decision, and then walked quietly into the room where Antony lay sleeping on his stomach with his arms around his pillow. She knelt down on the bare floor beside the bed and knocked on his head with her knuckles, a brisk tattoo designed to gain immediate entry.

'Antony,' she whispered sternly.

Antony didn't stir. He was a heavy sleeper.

Michaela relented. She brushed his cheek with her lips and leant her head for a minute against the roughness of his face. Talk about unsuitable liaisons, she thought. Danny was one thing, she and Antony were quite another. She was a fine one to preach to Mater. She thought of the long list of instructions

Blanche had given her, all the questions she was supposed to ask, the things they were to have said to Frans when the opportunity arose. Blanche had even suggested that they offer him money as a last resort. None of that had come up. Now they would have to go back and explain that not only had they failed in their mission, which was to get this unsuitable wedding cancelled at all costs, but that they had hardly discussed it at all. Blanche wouldn't understand, but neither would she come up here herself and talk to her mother. Michaela thought about climbing into bed with Antony for warmth, but it was a narrow single bed and she liked her comfort. She shivered and went back to her room, falling almost immediately into a deep, dreamless sleep.

The air is stale and bad smelling. It is hot as a furnace in here and there is a strange humming sound coming from somewhere. The cement is warm on his bare feet. His eyes are straining to become accustomed to the blackness and his heart is bumping loudly in his chest. He stands dead still, disorientated. There are muffled sounds coming from the other side of the door and the low murmur of voices. He cannot identify them, they mingle into one another and he cannot discern words, only sounds all garbled and distorted. He stands patiently, waiting. He scratches himself, feeling dirty prickles up the length of his spine. Then he leans against the wall and waits some more. He can still hear voices. It sounds as if someone might be stifling a laugh.

Then there is silence.

As soon as Michaela put down her bag and switched

off the porch light, she could sense something was wrong. Pauline was out of her chair in the lounge and grabbing at her hands.

'What's the matter, Pauline? You look peculiar. Has something happened? Is Suze all right?' Michaela took off her denim jacket and hung it on a peg behind the front door. 'I'm sorry I didn't call last night. It got late and we were talking —'

'They know,' said Pauline. 'Someone knows.'

'What are you talking about?' Michaela had a nauseous feeling deep down in her stomach.

'Bricknell Court.'

'Oh shit. What do you mean?' Michaela felt her hands tightening on Pauline's. 'Who knows what?'

Pauline told her about the call. Michaela felt unsteady on her feet and she moved through to the living room and sat on the edge of a sofa. 'Did you recognise the voice?' she asked tightly. Suddenly she felt achingly tired. The drive back with Antony had been difficult, facing Blanche was going to be difficult, and now this.

'No,' said Pauline. 'I was too shocked by what he was saying to concentrate on anything else.'

'Do you think I would have recognised it?' Michaela asked illogically.

'Well, how would —' Pauline's voice was becoming shrill. She had waited by the window for hours, watching for Michaela's car and hoping that the phone wouldn't ring again.

'Whoever it is, what do you think he wants?'

'To put you in jail?'

'Thanks. I mean, did he say anything? Indicate anything? Like whether he wanted money or just wanted to frighten me?' Michaela already looked frightened.

'I don't know,' Pauline replied miserably. 'He said

he was doing you a favour, something about saving you from disaster.'

'Jesus. Pauline, do you think he's for real? I mean, do you think he really knows about —'

'I tried to call Janus,' Pauline said. 'To help me think. But there was no reply, so I just sat up thinking and trying to remember. Trying to remember who could possibly have known.'

'Janus,' said Michaela. 'I'm going to get Janus for this. Him and his silly ass voices. It was Janus playing the fool.'

Pauline looked doubtful. 'But Janus knew you were at Stillwaters,' she said. 'And besides, he wouldn't have done that. It's too serious, even for Janus, Michaela.'

Michaela looked crestfallen. 'Oh,' she said. 'I suppose you're right. It wouldn't have been Jay. He'd know I'd kill him.'

'I've got to go to the club,' said Pauline. 'I was waiting for you, but I promised Frank I'd be there before lunch. We've got a meeting with the manager of the boys from Greenbacks. Blanche is going to be there too.' She went into the kitchen to pick up her basket and put on her hat. 'How did things go with Mater, by the way?' she asked. 'Did you sort it all out?'

Michaela looked at her and felt depressed. With her jaunty mustard coloured felt hat dipping over one eye, Pauline was visibly cheering up. She'd passed on the message and now it was out of her hands. Michaela could deal with the freaks on the phone. She could handle dead bodies in boiler rooms. Michaela had no doubt cleared up Mater too. 'In a manner of speaking,' she said. 'In a manner of speaking.'

'So what's the outcome?' Pauline adjusted the brim in front of the mirror. 'Blanche is bound to ask.'

Michaela held the door open for her. 'The outcome,' she replied, 'is that Mater is getting married to Frans.'

Michaela was reluctant to call Antony again, but she couldn't think who else to confide in. Before she did, she unpacked her bag and took a hot shower. Then she phoned the office and talked to Roz. There were a few messages, but nothing that couldn't wait till morning. A few more entries for the competition had come in and they were on her desk. Another batch of stories from Joy Beamish too. Michaela had a lot of catching up to do. She didn't want to be distracted by criminal charges at this point in time, nor by threatening phonecalls. She racked her mind for clues. There was nothing, no one that sprang into her head. She would phone Antony and they would meet and they would talk, and they would talk round and round in circles and get nowhere. There was nowhere to go with this. There was no getting away from it: Michaela was responsible for a dead person, long forgotten, long put out of the mind. But now it was time to pay.

Instead of calling Antony, Michaela put on dark glasses and a peaked cap. She tied her hair up and pushed it all into the crown of the cap and secured it with hairclips. As an afterthought she smeared dark red lipstick on her lips and changed into shorts. Then she took Susan's bicycle from the garage and set off down the road, moving swiftly in the bicycle lanes, out of the range of the traffic. She took a left, then a right and another right and then she was climbing hills, puffing a bit and zigzagging this way and that along the lower slopes of the mountain. She passed the old corner shop, still there but incorporated now into a shopping mall with designer clothing stores and two jewellery shops. The spot where Tommy the pinball wizard used to squat was paved over and there were benches outside and trees with little white fences around them. It was a designer walkway now, called Bricknell Mall, part of the previous phase of upgrading the area. No more pinball machines in that neck of the woods. It had been here that the yellow police vans would swerve and park and men in uniform would walk over to Tommy and pull at his elbow, meeting bewilderment and occasional resistance. And then Tommy would not be seen again, sometimes for weeks. Tommy disappearing was not unusual. Harriet would ask about him now and again, and once or twice she made inquiries at the local station, but Harriet and David preferred to keep as low a profile with the custodians of the law as they could in those days, so it was never pursued with any vigour and Tommy always showed up again in any event.

Michaela cycled up two more hills and then turned into the Bricknell Court road, the back entrance leading to the orchard. There were hoardings all round now and the earthmoving equipment was in action. Some walls had already come down on the east side, the side away from the boiler room wing. She got off the bicycle, feeling sharp pains in her buttocks. She read a notice in front of her. ALL VISITORS MUST REPORT TO THE SITE OFFICE. This, she supposed, was the corrugated iron lean-to to which the notice was attached. She watched men in hard hats come and go from the shed. They were ruddy-faced and wore ties with white shirts. One of them went in and came out again to stare at her with narrowed eyes. He had a fan of papers in his hand. She stood with her hand on the saddle of the bicycle, looking in past the cranes and front-end loaders to the orchard, which looked small and threatened and full of brown dust. There were chestnuts on the chestnut trees, she could see the spiny brown conkers from here. She remembered as a child collecting chestnuts every year at this time, the feel of the conkers held lightly in the hand so as not to incur the painful sting of the prickles. Then dropping them onto the ground and standing skilfully on the sides with both feet, easy in rubber soled slipslops, and easing the dark russet chestnuts from their pale green, silk-lined nests. Into Pauline's basket they went until a reasonable weight on Harriet's kitchen scale was decided on, and then it was down to the corner shop to haggle over remuneration. Who was collecting the things now, she wondered; probably the men on site. They could go home to their wives in the evening with pockets bulging and have chestnut stuffing on Sundays. Pauline had tried baking chestnuts in the oven one holiday but they were pronounced emphatically inedible, floury tasting, like fine grey sand.

'Can I help you, lady?'

It was the man with the narrowed eyes. His eyes were still narrowed even close up, and Michaela realised as she took in the scribble of purple veins across the cheeks and the sun roughened skin that he looked like that permanently, probably from years on sites just like this one, squinting at precarious highrise platforms and measuring progress.

'I'm a journalist, from the *Times*,' said Michaela, completely surprising herself. (A journalist, in shorts, on a bicycle?) 'And I wondered if I could have a word with the site manager about the skeleton in the boiler room?'

The man gazed at her. His eyes took in the bicycle, the

absence of any camera, notebook or writing utensils. He was not a stupid person. He could spot a rubbernecker when he saw one. 'Would that be the *Cape* Times?' he asked.

No, the skeleton Times, you idiot. Michaela smiled broadly at him. 'Well, no,' she said conspiratorially. 'The London *Times* actually. I'm out here on holiday —' she gestured ruefully at her bare legs '— but I thought as I was in the area I could file a story on the scandal.'

'There's no scandal,' he told her bluntly. 'And there's no story. Talk to the police. They're the ones handling this thing. There's nothing for you here. No personnel allowed on site without the necessary authorisation.'

Michaela was irritable now. This man with his slit-eyed look and stupid white plastic hat was in her way. 'May I at least have a look at the boiler room?' she asked sourly. She knew there was no way she was going to get in legally.

'Absolutely not. That section is cordoned off and under police guard.'

Try winsome. One last try. 'I realise that, but if you could —'

'I could have you escorted off the property, lady. Please be on your way.'

Wild effort. 'I'm a friend of the site manager,' she said, looking him straight in the eye.

He smiled kindly. 'Lady,' he said, and she mouthed the words with him, 'I *am* the site manager.'

Michaela pedalled home and arrived out of breath and bad tempered. There was a message on her machine from Antony. 'Mick,' he said. 'I need to see you.'

Antony is holding her head between his hands. They smell of suntan lotion. He brings his face closer and

Michaela can feel him trembling. She is feeling confused and elated and her stomach is churning. Antony is going to kiss her and she isn't going to stop him. This moment has been coming all holiday. It is the first school holiday she has worn a bikini and they have been in the pool and the sun every day. She is tanned and her stomach is flat. She is getting quite a waist too. Over the last few days Antony has used up almost a whole bottle of Ambre Soleil on her back. They are sitting in the shade of a peach tree. Pauline has gone into the apartment to fetch cold drinks and biscuits as she usually does at teatime, when she brings Tommy a snack if he is around. This is when Harriet and David are nearly always out at some meeting or other and there are no questions asked. Harriet doesn't always approve of the generous handouts for Tommy, although she is sympathetic to a point. It is the grocery bill that is her concern. She has four children to feed all holidays and she spends more time at the supermarket than she wants to as it is. Janus is inside watching television. He got so sunburned the day before yesterday that his shoulders are covered in watery blisters. He won't even let Michaela near them, although she has heard him crying in the night.

Antony's lips are soft and dry. His kiss is gentle, accurate and no more than a brush of the lips. Michaela opens her eyes. 'Do that again,' she says. 'Harder this time.'

He does and she feels her body responding in a way she has never experienced before. She ponders the heady possibility of being in love with her cousin.

There is a sudden enormous whoop and a splash and they shrink back against the tree trunk, showered with water from the pool.

'Gotcha!' says Crispian Younghusband.

Antony was not as interested in the phonecall as he ought to have been. He was more concerned with seeing Michaela that night, with going out for calamari and a walk on the beach. Michaela could feel the tingling in her cheeks again. Even though she had probably successfully eliminated Nancy of the long legs, she was beginning to think that a tête-à-tête of the kind Antony perhaps had in mind was not an entirely good idea. For once she found she did not want to talk about herself and her feelings. She wanted to forget who she was. She told Antony she had stories to read and that Pauline was at the club so there was no one to stay with Susan.

'Take Janus,' she added thoughtlessly. 'He likes calamari.'

Antony ignored the remark. He knew when Michaela was upset and it was obvious she was unsettled by the crank call. Even he recognised, though, that this was clearly not a random shot in the dark. The man knew something. 'Nobody saw what happened,' he told her with more conviction than he felt.

'So we thought, Antony, but it is apparent that we were wrong.' Michaela could feel her throat closing up and she felt close to choking on a mouthful of tears. 'What does this person *want*?' she said, exasperated. 'And *why*?'

'You'll have to sit it out,' said Antony. 'If the movies I've seen are anything at all like real life, he'll call again and next time give away a little more. It's round about the third phonecall that the final demand is laid on the table.'

'Do you think it's about money?'

'No. Well — I don't know. As I said, we'll just

have to grit our teeth and sit it out. He'll call again.'

'And if he doesn't? What do I do if he doesn't? He's out there, somewhere, walking around knowing about —'

'We agreed, Michaela, not to do anything, don't you remember? There is nothing *to* do. We don't have a choice.'

'I'm going to call Roger Rendell.'

'What in heaven's name for?' Antony was lost. 'Why Roger the Lodger?'

'He can get me in to Bricknell Court.' Michaela told Antony about her unsuccessful bid to gain entrance.

'But why do you want to get in there?'

'I don't know. To look. To see if —' Michaela's voice caught.

'To see if the pink blanket had the name Whitehead embroidered on it?' Antony laughed. 'Forget it. There won't be anything to see. They will have taken every shred of evidence away by now, and you won't be able to get near. And why involve Roger? The fewer people who know about this whole thing the better.'

'Oh, I won't *tell* him,' Michaela said with a hint of impatience. 'I'm not entirely gormless. I'll think of something plausible.' Then she relented. 'Listen, I'm sorry about tonight. Why don't we get together tomorrow? I could get a sitter.'

'I'm busy on a story tomorrow night,' Antony replied. 'For the *Independent*. It's good bucks and I'm on a tight deadline.'

'Oh,' said Michaela. 'Who's doing the words?'

'I'm doing both. I'd ask you to come along, but it involves the seedier parts of town – the docks as opposed to the Waterfront – and you'd stick out. Could we meet later for coffee at Pauline's?'

Michaela agreed, then changed her mind. She really did have a lot of work to do and the mention of Antony's dedication to deadline reminded her of her own.

'My advice to you for this evening,' said Antony, 'is take the phone off the hook. You sound as if you could do with some rest.'

It was good advice. Michaela disconnected the telephone and spread out her competition stories on the dining room table. She put her glasses on and poured herself a glass of white wine. Then she gave herself a choice of *He loves Me. He loves Me Not: A Gay Story* or *Afterglow* by Pinkie Harms, whose name, she reflected, sounded rather like a five letter cryptic crossword clue. *Afterglow* was shorter so she chose that and fell asleep after three pages.

· 11 ·

'Harriet,' said Michaela. 'Come in. Roz is bringing us coffee with biscuits and good grace. Unusual for Roz on both scores so we must count ourselves lucky.'

The *Focus* offices had been graciously decorated throughout in Duane Labuschagne Interiors' rather startling blood red and grey, because the Lifestyle editor was sleeping with Duane's partner at the time, but Michaela, having met the partner and seen the swatches, had elected to do her office herself, and her chairs and sofa were midnight blue pinstripes while her floor-length curtains and carpet were the colour of shortbread. The desk and coffee table were plain and pale and of Scandinavian design, Janus's choice, bought for a fraction of the market price from a client of his in return for a favour. Facing the ocean and without the hum of air-conditioning, Michaela's office was light and airy and the curtains smelled of the sea. She kept her windows wide open all summer so that she could hear the gulls on the shore and feel the sea breeze. Only the roughest of south-easters would make her close them; even winter, when the rain dripped off the eaves of the building and the mountain was hidden in mist, meant only that they were opened a little less wide. Michaela loved the smells of the city as they mixed like spices with the salt-sea air – petrol fumes, the flower seller's confusion of buckets down below, strange blends of coffee from the Italian coffee shop in the foyer.

Michaela walked across to the window and drew one of the curtains so that there was less of the glare coming off her desk which was making Harriet screw up her eyes.

'This place needs more clutter,' Harriet observed. 'How can you work in such neatness? It would give David instant writer's block.' She examined Michaela closely while she took off her jacket and aimed it carelessly at the back of a chair. 'You look a little off colour,' she said. 'Aren't you feeling well? We could do this tomorrow, if you like.'

'I'm tired,' Michaela admitted. Understatement. She felt like she hadn't slept for a week and all night she had heard phones ringing in her dreams. 'It must be all this going back and forth to Stillwaters and having to confront Mater. I suppose I'm feeling the strain. Why Blanche seems to think that it's my sole responsibility to change the course of family history, I don't know.' She pulled a face. 'But I suppose I did volunteer in a way.'

Harriet looked shamefaced. 'It shouldn't be your responsibility,' she said. 'I said to David after you'd gone, we shouldn't have sat back and allowed you to do it on your own.'

'I had Antony,' Michaela reminded her. 'We went up together.'

'Yes, of course, but if I know Antony, he was the reluctant partner in this. Perhaps Antony is a fairer judge than the rest of us. I think we might have been a smidgeon rash galloping in like that straight away.

And it was downright cowardly of us to leave it to you. Do you think it will help clarify things if David and I tried having a word with Mater before we go home? Although I don't know how much good it will do.' She looked doubtful.

Michaela could see that Harriet wasn't comfortable with the idea. Harriet was, naturally, thinking of Frans. The trouble was, nobody could get past the bland fact of Frans's colour and social status and Harriet of all people certainly wasn't going to make that the issue. It went too much against her principles. And she couldn't have done it, not with her background.

The thing about it was, nobody could get to grips with the objections without revealing themselves in an unattractive light. They were all skirting round the relevant things, none of them willing to articulate them, except Blanche, whose outburst at the club had since been topped with a variety of equally surprising epithets. She took the simple basic and vulgar line about the Whitehead entry for unlikeliest match of the year — but they were all used to not taking Blanche's tirades seriously, and it would have looked unhealthy if they took her advice now.

Michaela went to the doorway and took a tray of coffee and small cups from Roz. Roz lingered for a minute, making smalltalk with Harriet. She was getting practised talking to visiting celebrities. She had compared plantar warts a couple of weeks back with a former Rumanian gymnast who'd had a baby at fifty-three, and she had been vociferous on the topic for days. She would toss Natasha's warts into any conversation, even over lunch.

'Frankly,' said Michaela, pouring coffee and smiling Roz away, 'I don't think you and David talking to Mater at this stage will do the least bit of good. In fact I think our own attempt at dissuasion was pathetic and premature and probably did more harm than good. When Mater makes up her mind she's mighty hard to sway and when someone tries to force her hand it only makes things worse. We've all experienced that in the past – remember the time she brought in the angoras and we all told her she was making a mistake? And they got that hoof business? It took months and I don't know how many dead animals before she changed her mind, didn't it? She might have got rid of them sooner if we hadn't all thrown in our tuppenceworth. For the moment, Mater's mind is made up over this marriage. And it took courage telling the family, I'm quite sure of that. And when she did, how did we react?' Michaela left the question poised between then. She pulled a cup towards her and crossed her legs.

Harriet sighed and nodded. 'It's Blanche who isn't taking this too well.'

Michaela rolled her eyes. 'Tell me about it,' she said. 'But then Blanche is always edgy when it comes to relationships. She doesn't have much faith in them. I suppose it's because her own marriage to our father was so fraught and came to such a bad end. She didn't even have the satisfaction of booting him out. He just drifted out, never to return. Blanche can't ever accept that some relationships actually work.'

'Hmm,' Harriet murmured. 'She blew a raspberry at our wedding during the vows. She didn't think I heard her but she was sitting directly behind me and my ears were finely tuned.'

'You're happy, though, aren't you?' said Michaela. 'You and David?'

'Oh, yes, I think so, by and large. David's vague

and annoying sometimes and he always spills my tea in the saucer, but then he was vague and annoying twenty years ago and he spilled it then too. I've become accustomed to him. I would probably miss the irritations if they weren't there.'

'And look at Michael and Helena,' Michaela pointed out. 'They couldn't be more suited, and their life together can't be too easy sometimes. Antony lets things slip every so often – when Helena's in pain they both despair.'

Harriet nodded. She had long feathered earrings that bumped against her neck as she talked. 'Yet we've been lucky. We've made happy choices in the long run.' She put a hand on Michaela's. 'And you – you made a happy choice in Danny, although you were not given many years together like we've had.'

Michaela smiled, but the smile felt forced. She had been thinking too much about Danny lately and it didn't do her any good. It made her forget to do things, like shopping for supper or picking up The Dog's liver from the butcher. Danny thoughts made her play soppy songs in her car and drive slower than the speed limit. Sometimes she would find herself meandering in and out of the fast lane in traffic with the sound turned way up and irate taxi drivers skidding past her with black looks.

'Shall we get on with the interview?' she said. She took a small tape recorder from her desk and put it on the coffee table between them. 'You don't mind?' she said, gesturing at it. 'It's so I don't get anything wrong.'

For years Michaela had wanted to run a profile on Harriet and they had been corresponding for the last six months, laying the groundwork for this interview. Harriet was the kind of woman *Focus* readers readily identified with: strong, courageous, forthright – a woman who stood up for what she believed in and had never been reticent when it came to saying what she thought needed to be said. Perhaps she might not have been the role model some women might have wanted for their children then, but now, in her fifties, Harriet was dignified and less strident about her views. She was sharp and alert and the humorous set to her mouth was testimony to the acerbic wit always simmering below the surface. By now, in a different South Africa, she might have held a senior post in the cabinet; instead she was still in exile, never having been given the chance to prove her inherent leadership qualities.

Michaela could no longer reasonably put off the last big issue which needed to be dealt with and which they had only touched on in their correspondence. It was a subject that made her ill at ease at the best of times, but now that Bricknell Court was forcibly so fresh in her memory, it had sprung into vivid life once again. The betrayal that had led to Harriet and David being forced to flee the country, literally only hours ahead of the Special Branch, had had its roots planted firmly years before. They had all been entangled in those roots: Michaela, Antony, Janus, Pauline. None of them could have known then how insidious was their growth, yet all of them had watered and nurtured the plant, and harboured it within the core of the family like an indigenous fungus.

Michaela took a breath. She switched the tape recorder on. 'How did it feel,' she asked, keeping her voice deliberately steady and one eye on the cassette to make sure it was turning, 'knowing that you had been under surveillance in so basic a fashion?'

Harriet considered. 'We were all under surveillance

in those days,' she said. 'There was no question that at one time or another our activities were being monitored. Many of us were hauled in for questioning, stopped at airports or taken off the street during marches. It was a time when you were looking over your shoulder constantly. And yet, there was almost a code among the protagonists. There was a way of doing things, a method. You expected your study to be ransacked, drawers to be flung about the room and papers gone through. You expected mess and chaos, and even violence. But the way it happened to us was so subtle and yet so obvious that we felt . . .'

'Tainted,' said Michaela. It was the word she herself felt applied most.

Harriet nodded. 'Yes,' she said, 'tainted. We felt as if everything in our domestic life had been tampered with. And of course I felt stupid too – who wouldn't have? You go for years covering your tracks, taking precautions about where you go and whom you talk to, only to find that having your car washed or your groceries carried up the back stairs to your door was a compromising act. That realisation can make you feel silly. It can make you realise, too, just how much of an amateur you really are.'

'He certainly was a pro,' said Michaela.

Harriet gave a rueful smile. 'It wasn't playing fair, that's all,' she said.

'And yet all's fair in love etcetera,' said Michaela. 'And many of your detractors would have called what you and David were doing all those years not playing fair.' She pushed the tape recorder closer to Harriet, whose voice had grown quieter. 'Wouldn't they have said that the underhand tactics of your betrayer were no worse than your own?'

'Underground,' said Harriet. 'We were underground, under cover, but never underhand in that sense.'

When Michaela had been planning this article and setting it all in context in her notebooks, Bricknell Court had still been an apartment block on the mountainside, with people living in it, just as it had been all those years before when David and Harriet had thought of it as their sanctuary. It was solid and contained and non-threatening. Now that it was coming down, it was as if Michaela's own defences were sliding into rubble too, imploding in a puff of silent dust, revealing the sanctum as rotten in its very heart. Unsteady and uncomfortable, she persevered.

'All those years of feeding information on your movements,' she said. 'And you never had any idea?'

'No,' said Harriet simply. 'We had no idea. We came to realise, of course, that there was something going on. There were signs. We went through every possible weak link we could think of and doubtless thought badly of some perfectly innocent comrades, but we never for one moment thought of him.' She took a sip from her coffee cup, grimaced and pulled the sugar bowl towards her. 'And of course he was never named until after we had already left.'

'Gregory Beukes,' Michaela murmured. 'Funny – he never looked like a Gregory to me. I still can't think of him by that name.'

'You have to hand it to him,' said Harriet. 'He was very good. We never suspected a thing.'

But *we* did, Michaela thought with a pang. *We did*. And we never talked about it. If we had only been old enough to examine those feelings deep in our guts, beyond the confusion of misplaced compassion, we would have smelt him out and not assisted in conspiring against them. If we had been able to interpret what we were witnessing, perhaps things wouldn't have turned out as they had. Perhaps Pauline would have had parents who were there for her. But by the time we knew what was going on, the damage had been done and it was too late to change the course that had been set.

'Telephone,' said Roz, sticking her head round the door and startling them both to attention. 'Are you taking calls?'

'Who is it?' They hadn't really got very far.

'Susan. She wants to know something about Goodwill Zwelithini – history project.'

'Well, tell her, Roz.' Roz looked shaken. 'Look him up somewhere. No, on second thoughts, I'll call her back. We'll take a break in a minute.' She turned back to Harriet as Roz closed the door. 'Who were we talking about?' she said.

'Tommy,' said Harriet. 'The wizard on the pinball machine.'

Michaela leaned forward and switched the tape recorder on again. She felt stiff across the shoulders, as if she had been awkwardly hunched over. 'Tommy,' she echoed.

'Of course,' said Harriet, 'Tommy disappeared that summer when you all spent a holiday at Bricknell Court – Blanche was away singing, I forget where; you will remember – so there was even less reason to suspect him. For so long he had disappeared and then reappeared, always getting picked up by the cops –' she laughed bitterly '– and we felt so sorry for him, being persecuted in that way. Just a vagrant kid with no command of language or any of life's refinements, or so we thought. Those black eyes and that wild woolly hair – I can see him now. The hunted expression and the cringing gratitude, hands cupped for handouts. God – David gave him a jersey once and he wore it all winter until it was so grimy it was shiny. To think that it was he who was steadily feeding information on us, watching us come and go, noting all the people who visited the apartment. It still makes me shudder.'

'And when he'd got what he wanted, he disappeared,' said Michaela, looking past Harriet and out of the window to where the British Airways flight was doing its sweep of the seafront before coming in to land.

'Yes,' said Harriet. 'I wonder where he went?'

Michaela was sweating. Her hands were clammy. She got up and pulled both curtains closed. It made the room shadowy but more intimate. 'It was a very good cover,' she said. She had to believe that.

'Oh, yes – and ironic,' Harriet agreed. 'The deaf, dumb and blind kid, when he was none of those things.'

'We took him food, you know – sometimes.'

'I know.' Harriet smiled at Michaela. 'I did know that. And I didn't altogether disapprove. I knew all about the sandwiches Pauline used to make for him.'

And the pink blanket, Michaela thought. Did you know about the blanket? And the pillow that disappeared from the linen closet? And the cigarettes? And the way he would look at our breasts, although God knows they were nothing to speak of in those days, although we might have believed they were.

'What I could never understand,' said Harriet after a moment's thought, 'was how he got so *much* information on us. I mean, there's a limit, surely, or so I would have thought, to how much you can observe about a person just coming and going from an apartment block. The information they had on us was so much more intimate. And there were documents that had gone missing from the apartment, personal items too, which we could never explain. Now, whether Tommy had somehow accessed those, who knows? Perhaps he managed to break in when we weren't there – but if he did he was even more skilful than I thought, or perhaps we were more careless. But there was never the least evidence that things had been disturbed.' She paused and sighed. 'Well, it's so many years ago now, it really no longer matters, but it's curious. And it's something that has always puzzled us.'

Michaela thought it was time they pressed on, moved beyond Tommy to the nuts and bolts of the escape, but Harriet was locked in the mystery.

'I wonder whatever *did* happen to Tommy in the end?' she said. 'I wonder if he's even alive?'

The smell of bacon and eggs fills the small kitchen. There are sausages, too, and tomato, grilled brown on top and red and plump underneath. Pauline has burnt the toast and the kitchen is grey with smoke. There are baked beans as well, drying up in a silver pot on the stove. Pauline is unscrewing a jar of peanut butter with the sink cloth.

Tommy sits at the table with his hands on his knees. His body odour is almost as sharp as the smell of the bacon. He waits, saying nothing, only his eyes moving to show he is aware at all of what is happening. His strange, truncated legs do not reach the floor. Even Janus is taller than Tommy.

Pauline's invitation to breakfast at three o'clock in the afternoon was accepted with merely a grunt and a hunch of the shoulders, but he turned up all the same, standing outside the kitchen door at three sharp, just after Harriet and David had left for their meeting. His clothes are filthy and he has stains all down the front of his shirt. There are silver lines of snot along his upper lip.

'What he really needs is a good bath,' says Janus behind his hand, 'not food.'

'*And* food,' says Pauline. 'You can see how thin he is.'

Michaela is grudgingly smearing black toast with a thick layer of peanut butter. She is not good at doing things for other people at the moment and she is sullen about this chore.

Because Tommy never replies or acknowledges anything they say, Pauline has taken to talking in front of him as if he were really deaf and dumb, in a motherly tone way beyond her years. Where she gets this from is a mystery to them, certainly not from her own mother. Harriet is brisk and businesslike in things domestic. But Tommy has become Pauline's cause and she has strong feelings about him. She doesn't think they should allow him to stay on in the boiler room and live on occasional sandwiches. If she could she would find him somewhere better to sleep and as she can't, she has decided that the least they can do is make him a decent meal. This they will do once a week, when Harriet and David are out of the apartment.

She scoops at the egg in the pan and flips it over with a wobbly expertise. It spits fat onto the stove. The plate is too hot. 'There,' she says, grabbing at a second slice of toast as it sails out of the toaster, and putting it nimbly onto the plate in front of a sour-faced Michaela. 'Please butter that one while Janus drains the bacon.'

Janus slouches forward, the picture of reluctance. He is not happy with Tommy being in the house with his aunt and uncle not there. He knows they won't approve.

He will be surprised if they don't smell him when they return after everything has been cleared away. Like cigarette smoke clinging to a curtain, Tommy's odour is pungent.

Michaela, too, feels very uneasy about all this. Harriet and David have been away an hour, leaving instructions not to make a mess of the flat while they're gone. She would rather they'd gone skateboarding on the big hill, a more pleasurable illicit pastime. Philanthropy is not her strong suit, nor is being directed by someone else. So far, all they have to show for their free afternoon is a sinkful of dirty dishes and a frying pan with a black, gritty layer that is going to take a lot of Janus's elbow grease to dislodge.

Antony will have no part in this new deception. He is reading in his room.

'Eat,' Pauline instructs, pushing a plate across to Tommy and looking anxiously at the kitchen clock. 'Eat quickly if you can.' She smiles apologetically at her cousins as the pinball wizard picks up a fork and smashes it into the yolk.

Antony sometimes thought he should have concentrated his photographic talents in the actuality arena rather than on the fashion front. He got a particular buzz from photo-journalism and lately had found that he was acquiring a reputation in this field and getting more and more assignments as a result. He reckoned that at the moment he was doing about half fashion and magazine work and half photo features for foreign journals. It was a reassuring feeling, knowing that he was versatile enough to command the kind of fees they were prepared to pay him.

He had about all the material he needed from Susan's

school now. Susan herself probably featured in too many of the pictures, but he was paring them down to a selection of fifty. Susan was a striking child, more mature looking than her age. She would doubtless be approached one of these days by a modelling agency. She had everything they looked for – height, shape, hair, eyes. But Susan was careless about her good looks, just like Michaela. Appearance had little bearing on how she ran her life and she would have grown impatient at the suggestion.

Antony parked his car at a well-lit, all night parking garage in the city centre, reckoning that it would be worth the long walk back from the docks. At least he would have a car to go back to. He wasn't taking any chances. Car theft was almost a matter of course in the shadowy dockland roads. The clubs he was planning to visit this evening were a far cry from Pauline's and the others along the trendy Waterfront, where tourists and up-country holidaymakers sat out the long summer evenings. He was looking for hookers, sailors, men in false eyelashes and high pointed breasts, and after months of research and hours spent gaining trust and credibility, tonight was to be the first time he would be allowed to commit images to film.

He walked quickly, ducking his head into the collar of his greatcoat. He had his camera and rolls of film deep in his pockets. He looked over his shoulder frequently, walking with long, swift strides. It was almost midnight. He passed kids in the doorways of shops and they looked up at him as he went by with listless, tired eyes, their hard-soled feet sticking out in front of them. As he walked he thought about Michaela and about Bricknell Court and tried to get a fix, without success, on whether they were all really in trouble or not. There were no streetlamps down here and there was a ripe smell of urine which clung thickly to the walls he passed.

The club he was aiming for was on the second floor of a warehouse behind the dry dock. Antony climbed the stairs slowly, looking up ahead of him, hoping to see Galahad, his contact and guide. He had believed for a long time that Galahad wasn't his real name, but gradually he had come to realise that it was, and in a way it suited him. Galahad had red hair and he shaved his shoulders. Bristles, pale ginger, stood out against the smoky light like nails on an Indian fakir's bed. He saw Galahad at the far side of the room behind a sheet of blue smoke, leaning against the bar counter. He raised an arm. He shaved his armpits too and he looked slim as a girl in the deep violet wet-look dress which came to just above his knees. Antony made his way over, and by the time he had shifted his elbow onto the counter beside his friend a brandy and Coke was waiting for him. He almost never drank brandy and Coke anywhere else but had grown to savour the sweetness of it.

'It's a quiet night,' said Galahad. 'You should have been here yesterday. Breathing room only.'

They drank together in silence. Galahad was smoking Gitanes and waving at people as they emerged from the steep stairwell like bizarre jack-in-the boxes, masculine heads first and broad shoulders, then sexy women's clothing, lace chokers and pearls.

In all his visits to this and other such clubs Antony had become accustomed to the atmosphere and the outrageous outfits. He no longer felt uncomfortable but it was only recently that he had begun to feel accepted. It was by now understood that it wasn't a peepshow he was after or a quick sequence of shocking photos for a local rag. He had had to work on it, and no doubt Galahad had had a lot to do with it too, but the fact that this community was allowing him to take pictures of them gave him a sense of their generosity, and he looked on the project as a serious responsibility. He took his camera out and put it on the bar counter, leaving it there for half an hour before he took the cap off the lens.

Some people were dancing. The music was very loud and seemed to have become trapped somewhere in seventies disco. There was even a strip of ultra-violet light that showed up white blouses, sequinned evening bags and a thousand cotton threads in Antony's greatcoat, giving the impression of an embarrassing dusting of dandruff. The dancers on the floor didn't appear to pay much attention to conventional steps. They moved and turned and jiggled their shoulders in individual concentration, sidestepping each other in intricate, nontouching patterns that fascinated Antony. It was as if they were performing, but performing for themselves, each of them locked into the music on his own. He took some pictures, catching the glitter and sparkle flung giddily around the room by the strobe lighting. He caught high heels and knees in black sheer silk. One man with elbow high white gloves danced with his eyes closed and wore a shimmering evening bag across his chest like a sash. Another, thin as a stick, swayed without moving his feet, his torso bending first one way and then the other, his face turned to the slowly revolving silver ball suspended about the floor like a flower towards the sun.

Antony moved very slowly around the room, taking pictures from the shadows. Nobody took much notice of him, although some people held their hands across their faces and shook their heads. It was while he was on his third circuit and he had already used up two rolls of film and downed three brandies and Cokes, that a movement in one of the darker corners of the room caught his eye and he sensed something familiar which he could not immediately place. He turned back, uncertain, wondering whether someone had called his name, the feeling was so strong. Not wanting to peer too closely into the darkness, where a few tables and some chairs had been set deep against the walls, he nevertheless searched the gloom with his eyes. He stopped, leaning against a square pillar with posters advertising a gay cabaret artiste's months-old show, and tried not to stare, trying to control the sudden thud of panic that he felt deep in his chest. It was indeed something familiar that had caught his attention. It was a profile. It was an eloquent gesture with a gloved hand. It was his cousin Janus.

Michaela put The Dog out of the kitchen door and watched her as she walked away down the garden, pausing to sniff at selected patches of grass, flatten herself down and wiggle her fluffy bottom for the pounce that never happened. Her tail was a silver plume in the night, her purr reaching back to where Michaela stood leaning against the doorframe as strong as a rope between them.

Michaela watched the first bubble pop gently to the surface of the milk in the pot on the stove. She scooped browning mashed banana from the chopping board and stirred it into the hot milk as she removed the pot from the heat. She wasn't sure that this drink of Mater's wasn't an acquired taste, but she would do anything to try to get to sleep. The last thing she needed in her state of mind was a bout of insomnia, but it seemed that this was what she was destined to suffer. It was beginning to turn into a vicious cycle. The more desperate she was to sleep, the more elusive sleep became. She poured the milk into one of a set of ugly soup mugs Roger had given her one anniversary, the second of only two such celebrations and possibly a deciding factor in there never being another, and sat down at the table with the story she was currently reading. This one was not at all bad. It was about a cryptic message in a gin bottle which a disenchanted wife had cast into the sea one drunken night and a child who fished it out and set his mind to interpreting it and tracking down its sender. It was an ambitious story, with many twists and turns, not all of which worked for Michaela, but so far it stood head and shoulders above anything else in the pile she'd read. She had got to the part where the wife was climbing into a second bottle of gin and the writing was getting dodgy when the telephone ringing made her sit up and look in sudden terror at the kitchen clock. It was one o'clock in the morning. She let the phone ring and ring, wanting to run to it and rip out the cord. Eventually it stopped. She heard Susan get up and go to the bathroom, then pad down the passage and put her head in at the kitchen door.

'Was that the phone?'

'No,' said Michaela. 'Go back to bed.'

'Why didn't you answer it?'

'Because,' said Michaela. 'It's probably Simon. We had a . . . a fight, sort of, and I don't feel like continuing it in the middle of the night. Simon gets longwinded in fights.'

'Well, take it off the hook then.' Susan yawned.

She walked into the kitchen and sniffed at the pot. 'Hey, The Dog.'

The Dog came strolling back into the room and Michaela got up to lock the door. She tidied her pages into a pile and touched at the surface of her mug with the tip of a teaspoon. A long drip of white skin came with it.

'Ooh, gross *out*,' said Susan. 'I'm going back to bed. Why don't you drink something alcoholic like a normal person?'

The phone rang again about ten minutes later. This time Michaela snatched it up on the third ring.

'Yes?' she said.

She knew immediately that it was the caller. She almost felt relieved. The tension of anticipation had been worse than hearing the actual voice. It was low and husky and a little hollow, as if it was coming at her down a pipe. She tried to concentrate. It was important that she attempt to recognise, to be able to identify, so that she could —

'Michaela. It's me again. Your conscience.'

'What do you want?' Michaela didn't think there was any point in explaining that it wasn't her who had picked up the first call.

'You know what I want. I want the same as you do – I want to be free.'

Michaela's hands were trembling. She clutched with both of them at the mouthpiece of the telephone. 'I told you last time. I was only trying to help you.'

'I don't know what you're talking about.'

'We both know you have a secret. You thought no one else knew about it, didn't you? Well, I told you before: you and I both know who got buried at Bricknell Court. You and I both know what the police are trying to find out. That skeleton has a name. You surely haven't forgotten that name, have you?'

'You've got the wrong person. All of this means nothing to me, I'm afraid.'

There was a silence, and then a slow, throaty chuckle.

'Who *is* this?' Michaela felt sick. 'Who the hell *is* this?'

'Go to the police, Michaela. Confess. And take your punishment.'

'I don't —' But Michaela was left with only a dialling tone in her ear and a tightness in her chest. She replaced the receiver slowly and stood looking at it, without moving.

Antony waited half an hour in a doorway opposite the entrance to the club, his hands sunk in his pockets, watching a thin mongrel dog push its way through a garbage bag which had split its seams. Soft rotting vegetables fell into the gutter, a fish head and a broken tomato sauce bottle. The dog stepped gingerly through its pickings, making small gruff noises.

Janus came down the stairs alone and stood for a minute on the pavement, looking first one way and then the other. He had a long black coat on and it was buttoned almost to the top. It made him look taller than he was, although the heels he wore gave him a couple of inches too. He set off, walking with slow, measured strides, not appearing to be in a hurry although it was past two in the morning and there was a stiff, chill wind. Janus looked around him constantly. It was a dicey neighbourhood and it was as well to be vigilant. He wouldn't be the first victim of a late hour mugger down here. Antony followed slowly, keeping to the walls and feeling like a sleazy detective. He saw Janus reach his car, parked at a petrol station, and tip an attendant in a metal booth. His own car was parked a fair distance away still and he quickened his pace. Janus did a U-turn and headed off in the direction of the highway and, presumably, home.

When he reached Janus's apartment, his car was parked in its bay and for a moment Antony wondered whether he had imagined the whole thing and Janus had been home all night, visiting Chloë, the girl with the serious face, or working on a presentation. The lights in the apartment were on. Not altogether sure that what he was doing was either wise or would in any way be appreciated, Antony walked to the foyer and rang the buzzer. Janus's voice was guarded.

'Antony? What are you doing here?'

'May I come up?'

Janus had the door open when Antony emerged from the lift. He was wearing a towelling dressing gown and had a cup of tea in his hand. 'What's going on?' he asked.

Antony had sometimes felt that the role of older brother was expected of him where Janus was concerned, especially when they were growing up and he was so much under Michaela's influence. Although it was never articulated, Blanche clearly approved when he and Janus did masculine things together. Occasionally they went to watch cricket at Newlands, or hiking up on the Pipetrack. For a brief spell they had taken up running together too, until Janus got serious shin splints and twinges in his knees. If he hadn't been so concerned about what he had seen this evening, Antony might have taken a moment to feel sheer amazement that something so unlikely had come out of a life so perfectly ordinary. He realised that the community of people he had grown to know over the past months was a close one and that only a few of them were gay. The others, in the daylight hours and most evenings in the week, looked just like what they were: accountants, fitters and turners, bus drivers, lawyers – Galahad was a quantity surveyor. And now, advertising men. Janus's firm had won a prestigious award for a campaign he had personally spearheaded for a vitamin-enriched soft drink which had involved some impressive and dangerous stunts, all of which had been Janus's brainchild. Why that should indicate Janus's core of masculinity, or that masculinity was even, in fact, in question at all, Antony knew was illogical, especially in the light of his nighttime research, but the image just seemed so incongruous. He remembered Janus dancing cheek to cheek with a pretty girlfriend named Valerie at an advertising ball where Antony was doing the pictures for a magazine back in the early days of his career. It was another image which didn't gel with what he had witnessed tonight. Janus had his feet on the ground, surely. He had always been impatient with deviance. He conformed to type – or so Antony had always believed. He had never had any reason to doubt it.

'I saw your lights on,' Antony said. 'Is that tea you're drinking?'

'Come on in,' Janus said, rather grudgingly. He had dark circles under his eyes and Antony was immediately ashamed at the thought that they were more likely make-up than fatigue induced. He looked past him to the sitting room.

'You aren't entertaining?' he said hopefully. 'I'm not interrupting anything?'

'No, no. I'm alone.'

Antony followed Janus into the kitchen, glancing

surreptitiously despite himself for evidence of an outfit flung carelessly on the floor, gloves on the arm of a sofa. The apartment was, however, excessively neat. It had an unused look to it. Even the folded newspaper on the coffee table looked as if it wasn't going to be read.

'You're up very late,' said Antony.

Janus looked at his fingers while he waited for the kettle to boil. 'So are you,' he countered. 'Have you been with Michaela?' He slipped Antony a smile which was so fleeting it was impossible to interpret. He was often with Michaela; there was no need to justify it if he had been. He felt uncomfortable nevertheless.

'I've been working on an assignment,' he said. Had Janus seen him? 'Downtown.'

'Oh.' Janus poured boiling water into a red teapot. He took a second red teacup from a shelf. Did everything match his precious car, Antony wondered. There was something about drinking out of a red cup that made him feel hot. 'Something interesting to keep you out so late?'

It was now or never. 'I was at Cheapskates,' he said softly. 'Taking pictures.'

Janus reacted in classic exaggerated fashion. He started, spilling his tea and clutching at the back of a chair. Then he gave Antony a crooked smile. 'Oh,' he said. 'You must have felt underdressed.'

So Janus had seen him then. 'I didn't . . .'

'What? Take my picture? Gosh, thanks,' said Janus. He walked away from Antony into the living room, leaving his cup on the table. He sat down in an easy chair and put his feet on the coffee table with his back to his cousin. 'Why did you come here?' he asked quietly.

Antony shrugged. He wandered through and sat

down opposite Janus. He pushed his cup across to him. 'To talk perhaps,' he said.

'To talk,' Janus repeated. 'To talk. What about?'

'Janus, I —' Suddenly Antony had no words. He was regretting having come, having blundered into a situation he didn't understand. Lately he had been sticking his nose into places where it didn't belong and this time he couldn't even blame Michaela. He wondered fleetingly what she would make of this situation. Janus could have told him to go away and to mind his own business and he would have been quite justified in doing so. But it was too late for that now; there would never be any ease between them again if they didn't deal with this at once. They were both aware of that.

'It's not what you think,' Janus said finally, when Antony's words dried on his lips. 'I'm not a faggot.' His mouth twisted in a wry smile.

'I know that,' Antony said. He touched his cousin on the shoulder. 'I know quite a lot about those people. I've been hanging out with Galahad.'

The name clearly did not mean much to Janus, but there was a glimmer of a smile round his mouth. 'Galahad?' he repeated.

'Tall, ginger hair, wears minis mostly.' Antony couldn't believe they were having this conversation. 'He sometimes wears a wig too,' he added unhappily.

Janus shook his head and frowned. They both felt on steadier ground for the moment discussing a third party. 'Can't say I know him.'

'Oh, he's at all the clubs,' Antony told him. 'He's been enormously helpful in getting me in.' He finished his tea. 'He's with Pointer and Pointer. Quantity surveyors.' Macho crowd.

'I don't do the clubs,' Janus said after a pause.

'I've only been once or twice, and only to 'Skates. I don't much care for the music.' He laughed, a sharp mildly hysterical yelp. His eyes filled suddenly.

'We don't have to talk about it,' Antony said, 'if you don't want to.' He wanted to get up and fetch Janus a handkerchief but was ridiculously afraid of what he might find in his cupboards. It had been too dark to see what Janus had been wearing at the club, but the prospect of uncovering lace and twill was wildly unattractive.

'Oh, it's all right,' said Janus, composing himself with difficulty. 'But there's nothing to talk about really. I . . . I like wearing women's clothes, Antony. I'm a cross-dresser. So what does that make me?'

'Well —'

'Fucking miserable, that's what,' Janus went on before Antony could find an answer. 'But I can't help it. *You've* been doing all the research on people like me. *You* tell me why I do it.'

'I've been taking pictures for an American journal,' Antony said, feeling at the same time that he was letting his cousin down, 'not doing anything too in depth. I'm afraid I'm not sure how to answer you. All I can say is you're not alone in feeling uncomfortable with it sometimes, but it's nothing to be ashamed of. There's nothing *wrong* with you. It's unusual . . . that's all . . . in our immediate circle, that is.'

'Oh, whew,' said Janus. 'I was worried.'

'Look,' said Antony. 'It's late. We'll talk about it another time, J. This isn't the right moment. I shouldn't have intruded.' He got up to leave and Janus, un-protesting, walked with him to the door. Before they reached it the telephone rang and Janus, looking at his watch in surprise, walked back to answer it.

'Michaela,' he mouthed as Antony waited.

From the one-sided responses, Antony was not surprised when Janus told him that Michaela, weeping, had called for yet another family crisis meeting.

'I'm going to jail,' she had told him dramatically. 'I'll have to give myself up.'

· 12 ·

It has been raining, the first rain of autumn, and the sky is a low ceiling of grey cloud. Only the lower slopes of the mountain can be seen. When it is like this there is no knowing how high the mountain is or what shape: it could be a hill, a volcano, flat on top or rough and uneven at the edges like teeth. When the solid misty greyness sweeps down to smother its flanks it is a mystery that transforms everything else. With not much imagination there could even be no mountain there at all, and with the lifting of the mist there might be a vast, flat line of distant horizon, a view of modest townhouses or tall buildings with windows blinking.

In the orchard all the trees are heavy with moisture. They droop towards the earth. Underfoot the leaves from the chestnut trees have turned pale yellow and greeny transparent gold, and the oak leaves look mouldy and grey-edged. All the leaves are streaked with mud and scooped together in untidy, mismatched piles. There was some talk of a bonfire but that was earlier, before the heavens opened, and now everything is sodden and stuck together and altogether less appealing. Also it is cold and it gets dark earlier these days, and the attraction of being outdoors in the sharp wind, trying to coax a pile of leaves to ignite has palled somewhat. That fires are forbidden anyway has not entered into the decision. Ever since Janus and the magnifying glass, Harriet and David have frowned upon what they call the cousins' pyromaniac phase. David is currently in jail and Harriet is away for the afternoon trying to get him out. He has been subpoenaed over an article on detainees which appeared in his newspaper and has refused to name the source of the information. Harriet has taken him chocolate, a few back issues of *Finance Week* and the crossword from the *Guardian*.

Pauline, who has been sitting on the wet fence, has a black line across the seat of her beige jacket. She pulls her gloves off with her teeth and spits out pieces of wool. Michaela's knuckles are red and raw and she puts her hands in her pockets, embarrassed to look at them. She has just turned thirteen – she and Antony together – and the memory of last summer's kiss has made her gruff with everybody. Also Antony has spots on his chin and his hair is too short. He has grown taller than Michaela now too and when he laughs his voice has a creaky sound to it. He is wearing a saggy black tracksuit with red borders round the pockets and collar, and dirty running shoes. He throws the matchbox to Michaela.

'It's too gusty for a bonfire anyway,' he says. 'We'd never get it lit.'

'My mother should be back soon,' says Pauline. 'She'd read the smoke and give us grief.' Pauline has learnt a whole pile of slang phrases at school this term and she likes to bring them out in a diffident way, although no one has shown the least sign yet of being impressed. 'My chinas,' she adds wistfully.

'Let's go in and watch TV,' says Janus. 'It's cold out here.'

'We've been watching TV all afternoon,' Michaela points out. 'We need fresh air.' Fresh air and lots of fruit get rid of zits, or that is the theory at least. And Antony's chin needs all the help it can get.

They walk on past the tennis courts and the poplar lane where the remains of last summer's clubhouse are still to be seen. They stop and study it.

'That was a good one,' Michaela says with satisfaction. 'It was the best camouflage we've done, wasn't it, Antony? Janus took days to find us. Maybe we should have a winter clubhouse, somewhere cosy and warm.'

'Where we could take a Thermos and cocoa,' Pauline says. 'And have picnics. That would be rad cool.'

'But where?' says Janus. 'The bicycle shed has rats. Big ones.'

'The boiler room?' Antony suggests. 'It's always warm in there.'

Michaela stops suddenly. She has gone white in the face.

'What's the matter?' Antony asks her. 'You're not thinking about last summer, are you, and our last encounter with the boiler room? That was yonks ago.'

'Yonks,' echoes Pauline. 'What's wrong, Michaela? Why are you looking like that?'

Michaela's lips are moving, but it looks like something is stuck in her throat because the words aren't coming. They crowd around her. The wind pulls at their clothes and they huddle, shivering, beside the poplar fence. Antony picks at one of her limp hands. She turns her eyes to him and they are dark with fear.

'Oh, Antony,' she whispers. 'I've only just remembered. I never . . . I didn't —'

They all stare at her. They know exactly what she is talking about.

'You didn't let him out,' Janus says slowly. 'Michaela, don't say you never went back to let him out?'

And suddenly they are all running, all of them, jogging in their thick clothing, bundling Michaela along in the middle of them. Her legs are a ragdoll's useless limbs, her knees barely able to support her weight; they bend but they won't straighten. They scramble up onto the wall and run along its broad back, jumping down onto the coalshed roof which is slippery and glistening silver-black from the rain. They drop to the ground and come up short at the boiler room door, panting, with clouds of cold white steam coming from their open mouths. Janus is there first. He turns round, puzzled. The door isn't there. It's vanished, just like in a mystery story.

'Antony?'

Antony goes forward. Michaela is leaning against the coalshed, breathing hard, her eyes wide and round, although there is a forlorn look of hope in them, as if just by chance she might have imagined the whole thing, even the very existence of the door, the boiler room itself.

Antony is walking up and down. He runs his hand against the wall and stares hard at it.

'Oh,' he says at last. 'I see.'

'What?' says Pauline. 'What? Where's the door gone?'

'They've bricked it up,' Antony tells them, turning round. He swallows a couple of times. 'They've bricked the door up. They can't be using the boiler room any more. See – the coalshed is empty too.'

They all glance vacantly at the swinging door of

the coalshed, barely taking in its filthy, gaping interior. Then they stare back at the obviously newish brickwork, plainly visible now that they are looking for it. It is a neat job. A very thorough, solid job.

'I presume they must have taken the door off,' Antony says after a while, 'before they bricked it up. They must have opened it, mustn't they?'

'But when?' Pauline asks matter of factly. 'When exactly? It could have been days, weeks, *months* —'

'OK, Pauline,' Janus says. 'We get the picture.' He goes over to Michaela, who is now sitting on the wet ground as if her legs are quite unable to support her any longer. He touches his sister's head feebly.

Nobody has anything further to say as the enormity of what has happened sinks slowly in. It is almost dark. Harriet will be home and concerned about them if they don't get back soon. There is a smell of damp cement and more rain in the air.

Then Antony speaks in a decisive voice. 'It's not your fault, Mick,' he says. 'We're all equally to blame. Maybe you did say you would go back and let him out, but we're all guilty. We all forgot. I know I did. I never gave him a second thought until just now.'

'*Did* you forget, Michaela?' Pauline asks, running the tips of her fingers over the bricks where the door used to be.

Michaela turns a furious face on her. 'No, idiot,' she says. 'I just left him in there on purpose. What the hell do you think?'

Pauline backs off. She looks as if she is going to cry or perhaps it is the cold making her eyes water. Then they hear Harriet's voice carrying to them on the air, calling each of their names in turn. Automatically, they begin to move off, Antony pulling Michaela to her feet. Janus picks up a stone and throws it at a lamp-post, overthrowing by about a yard.

'What do we do now?' Michaela turns to Antony who has fallen into step beside her, a little behind the other two.

'I don't know. Nothing, I guess.'

'But what if he's still in there?'

'He won't be.'

'How do you know.'

'I just know, OK?'

'But —'

Pauline turns around and regards them gravely. She walks backwards in front of them, maintaining her distance, wary of Michaela's mood.

'If he's still in there,' she says, 'by now he's dead as a dodo.'

Janus and Pauline arrived at Michaela's house together and found Michaela stalking round the house with a manic expression.

'Can you smell it?' she demanded as soon as they walked inside. 'Isn't it revolting?'

'What?' Janus turned in a small circle, head raised.

'That,' said Michaela. 'That godawful smell, for Christ's sake.'

Janus and Pauline glanced nervously at each other. Pauline frowned and gave an imperceptible shake of the head.

'Drains,' said Janus after a moment. 'Definitely drains. Just throw some crystals down or caustic soda, or whatever it is you're supposed to use.'

Michaela paused, sniffing the air unattractively. 'I don't know,' she said uncertainly. 'Do you really think that's what it is?'

'Here's Antony,' Pauline announced with relief. 'Ask him.'

Antony had Susan and Florida in tow. They had school bags and Cokes and they flopped heavily down on chairs at the kitchen table, complaining about projects and the unfairness of an unexpected maths test. 'They shouldn't spring these things on you,' Susan grumbled bitterly. 'Sprung tests are a poor reflection of the teacher's lesson preparation skills. Ratface went out last night, you could see by the extra mascara and the purple eyeshadow she uses to blot out the evidence. Whenever she has a roughie she springs a test on us so that she has time to collect herself. I wish she'd let us have a copy of her social calendar.'

'Can *you* smell it?' said Michaela.

'Yeah, it stinks,' Susan replied. 'I've seen her boyfriend.'

Michaela gave up. Susan and Florida trailed off to Susan's room and the four cousins went out to the garden and sat in the shade of a lemon tree. There were dozens of bees touching the branches above them, making wide circles and coming in again and again. Janus batted at them tetchily with a rolled up newspaper.

Michaela got down to business straight away. She seemed more in control than they had all expected to find her and apart from speaking through her nose, her voice was steady and calm.

'We've all got to think again,' she said. 'I know we've all probably been doing a lot of thinking; well, I have anyway, but we simply have to rack our brains and cast our minds back to that day. What we know are these three things: somebody saw us at the boiler room that day. Somebody has made the connection with the skeleton they've unearthed. Somebody means to do me harm.'

A sudden blast of Tchaikovsky came rocketing out of Susan's window. She always played Tchaikovsky when she was cross, Rachmaninov's piano concertos in mellower moods. Michaela accurately threw a lemon at the window and two faces appeared side by side. 'Down a bit,' she called. 'You'll scare The Dog.'

Michaela had her hair back off her face and pulled into a ponytail. It gave her a severe look, whether the effect was intentional or not. In any event her pallor and the set of her mouth would have left no one in any doubt as to the seriousness of her mood.

'I seem to remember a window,' Pauline said after a while. 'Up above the boiler room, a little to the left. It could have been a kitchen window. It's not impossible that somebody was looking out that day.'

'I know the one you mean,' said Antony. 'That was Crispian Younghusband's apartment. There was no one there that day. Crispian Younghusband spent the day hanging around with us because his parents were out, don't you remember?'

'Oh,' said Pauline. 'Oh, yes.'

'What we also need to establish once and for all before we decide if there's anything we can do about this frightful business,' said Michaela, sounding as if she were addressing an editorial meeting,' is whether we have a simple moral issue here or whether we're merely involved in an evasion of the law. I mean, *should* I give myself up, go to the police and tell them what happened? As a reasonably law-abiding citizen.'

'No,' said Antony.

'Maybe,' said Janus.

'Well —' said Pauline.

Michaela ignored them all. 'I've given it a great deal of thought,' she went on.

They waited.

'And I'll probably burn in hell, but evasion of the law gets my vote every time I think about it,' she went on in a rush. 'I mean, how can this . . . this *crank* prove that I had anything to do with it? If the stuff we left in that boiler room was still there and there was some means of identifying it as our property, surely by now somebody would have contacted one of us? What else was down there? *Think*!'

Pauline rolled up the sleeves of her shirt. Her cropped hair glistened in the sun. 'A plate,' she said, turning to Michaela. 'We used to use that plastic one – army green. That plate might have been there. With a few fossilised crumbs.' She gave a nervous smile.

'Blanket, pillow, jersey.' Antony ticked the items off on his fingers. 'Plate. Nothing else, Mick. I'm sure of it.'

Michaela regarded each of them contemplatively. 'There is one other thing,' she said slowly, 'that none of you have thought of. One thing which was uniquely his. And there is a chance, a slim one, that it could lead to his identification.'

'What's that?' Antony looked at her and frowned. 'Will it link him to us?'

Michaela shook her head. 'No,' she said, 'fortunately.'

Janus was leaning back with his eyes closed, conducting the music with one finger. He opened an eye and squinted at his sister. Antony and Pauline were waiting.

Michaela was stringing them along. 'What was the one thing,' she said, 'that you could associate him with? The one thing that he was never without?'

They all looked at each other. Antony shrugged.

'Oh, God!' Pauline sat up straight and a hand flew to her mouth. 'I know!'

Michaela nodded at her.

'What?' Antony asked. 'What, for God's sake?'

'The cricket ball! The one with all the names on it. You're dead right, Michaela. He always had it with him.'

'Crispian Younghusband and his bloody cricket ball,' Antony said slowly.

'I was thinking about that ball last night, after the phonecall,' Michaela went on. 'I'm surprised there's been no mention of it. They probably found it clutched in his bony claw like a Larson cartoon.' She gave a snort of unhappy laughter. 'Oh, fuck. It's not really funny, is it?'

'Well, thank goodness,' Pauline said, settling back in her chair again, 'thank goodness it didn't have *your* name inscribed on it forever, Michaela. At least I hope it didn't. Remember when we found him carving your initials into the poplars?'

For a moment Michaela looked uncertain.

'I still say we do nothing,' Antony said. He had a lemon in his hands and was tossing it up and down in a way that made Pauline pull a face at him. He stopped. 'And I still say it's nothing like evasion of the law. No law has been broken.'

'It's really a moral issue,' Michaela said dully, 'isn't it?'

'Probably.' Antony shrugged.

'What about his parents?' Pauline said. 'They would have notified the police, surely. Filed a missing persons thing. They wouldn't have overlooked the cricket ball. Maybe the police still have it on file. His parents must have been searching for him all these years. Don't you think they'll be rushing over to look at his bones?'

'They probably went back to England after he disappeared,' said Michaela. 'All those transit people were out here on contract, remember. He was one of those. They won't be around here any longer.'

Pauline looked thoughtful. 'I don't know,' she said. 'Perhaps we ought to give them a clue or something. It doesn't really seem right that we know it's Crispian Younghusband and no one else does.'

'Someone else clearly does,' Michaela put in gloomily. 'That's the problem.'

'And if that person truly had Crispian Younghusband's interests at heart, he would have already told the police who it is so that he can be buried in peace and his family informed. That just proves that whoever it is is after something else.' Pauline looked almost pleased with herself. 'Blackmail,' she said triumphantly.

'It's quite possible,' Antony said. 'We'll have to wait and see.'

'I can't wait!' Michaela burst out. 'This is torture. Who the hell can it *be*?'

They all lapsed into silence, thinking, racking their brains. No one had the answer. No one had broken the pact made nearly twenty years before never to speak of Crispian Younghusband and the Bricknell Court boiler room. This was the first time they had discussed it and the subject was rusty and came awkwardly. Pauline was the most pragmatic, and the most puzzled.

'I can't believe we didn't hear anything about him disappearing,' she said thoughtfully. 'I mean, wouldn't his parents have made a fuss? I wonder why we didn't hear?'

'We went back to school the very next day,' said Michaela. 'It was the last day of the holidays. What would we have heard? We didn't buy newspapers or anything. We were schoolchildren.'

'I'm surprised Harriet and David didn't say anything to us,' Antony said. 'Surely they would have known, being right there, at Bricknell Court.'

Pauline unwrapped the cellophane off a box of Quality Street she took out of her basket. 'They were busy,' she said shortly. 'They went straight off to a conference. David was giving a paper.'

Michaela had lost weight. She sat with her hands beneath her legs and her shoulders hunched. Last night she had resorted to a sleeping tablet and was still feeling groggy. In the early hours she had had another nightmare. Thin brown bones with name tags around the grasping knuckles rising up to clutch and scrape at her throat. And the words: the ultimate fun. This is the ultimate fun.

They had never called him anything other than Crispian Younghusband, to his face or even among themselves. He was never Cris or even Crispian. Always Crispian Younghusband. It was probably another way of excluding him, of leaving him in no doubt that he was and always would be, an outsider, that they were never actually planning to welcome him into their games, but might just deign to use him if they were short of a player or someone to field when they played cricket or rounders in the clearing in the orchard. Looking back on it, it was astonishing that he had continued to seek them out when it was made so plain that he was never more than barely tolerated. It never occurred to Michaela that he might be lonely. She knew he was new in the country and didn't have any friends. School hadn't yet started and his family was in the transit apartment anyway, which meant that they wouldn't be staying there long. Any socialising he did was going to be short term in any event. Would it have killed them to be friendly?

All that long summer holiday Crispian Younghusband would appear, like a small black cloud on the horizon, usually just when they were getting involved in one of their complicated games, when Michaela had already allocated parts to everyone. He would scuff about on the sidelines in his sandals and socks, offering unwanted advice in that flat, adenoidal voice of his, while they ignored him until Michaela whispered to Janus and Janus would tell him to shove off.

Crispian wasn't used to outdoor life. He had soft white skin and a belly that hung over the Boy Scout belt of his shorts. He couldn't climb trees, he was scared of flying insects and he got out of breath when he ran. On the odd occasions when they allowed him to play K-I-N-G Spells King, he would run as if his life depended on it, puffing out his cheeks while his chest made alarming whistling noises. Sometimes he would have to sit down and wait to get his breath back. Antony said he was probaby asthmatic – there was a boy at his school who went an interesting shade of blue during physical exercise – but Crispian Younghusband never said anything, only scrambled back to his feet and panted after them, wheezing slightly. But no matter how horrible Michaela was to him, he would only blink at her from behind his glasses until she'd finished, and then try to distract them all with his useless nuggets of general knowledge. These he kept deep in the pockets of his shorts, or so it seemed, for he would push and pull with his fists at the inner lining and then out would come a peace offering, a 'Did you know –?' which was instantly dismissed or scornfully rejected.

Many of Crispian Younghusband's comments would be prefaced with '*My* dad says –' and they would mimic him and giggle behind their hands. '*My* dad says if you don't wear a hat in the midday sun the blood in your brain gets thinner and you pass out,' he pronounced one hot day when the cousins were teasing him halfheartedly by spinning his blue towelling hat from one to another out of his reach.

'My dad says, my dad says,' Michaela echoed, cruelly throwing the hat at his face and knocking his glasses sideways. 'Shut up about your dad, Crispian *Young*husband. Your dad's really boring and so are you.'

Like Janus, Crispian Younghusband was crazy about cricket and he carried his treasured cricket ball with him wherever he went. He had the signatures on it of the English XI who had just won the World Cup and it never left his body. When he was busy doing something with his hands, like fending off the sting of berries in a berry fight, the cricket ball was a bulge in his pocket. When he was standing beside the chestnut tree, hoping to be invited to play while Michaela took her time thinking about it, he would toss it up in the air and catch it in his fat white hands with studied nonchalance. Once, only once, Janus had jumped at him and caught it and streaked away across the orchard waving it above his head. Crispian Younghusband had become hysterical and blue in the face and Janus, taking fright, had thrown the ball into a hedge. It was Pauline who took pity on Crispian and had helped him find it. She had scratches all down her arms from the thorns and he hadn't even said thank you. Just run away home, blubbing like a baby. But no one had taken the cricket ball away after that and Michaela had soon declared that cricket was an intensely boring game and anyone who spent so much time thinking about cricket obviously hadn't been wearing his sun hat enough.

'Crispian Younghusband,' Antony murmured. He had peeled the lemon. It was small and shrivelled inside, with no juice at all. He smelled its skin. 'What a sad little sack he was.'

'A lot sadder now,' said Pauline without thinking. She looked nervously at Michaela.

'It's a moral issue,' Michaela said with finality, staring in front of her. 'I am a person devoid of morality.'

Janus had been silent for a long time. He was sitting with his hands pressed between his knees and his back curved inside his Hilton Weiner suit. He was twenty-eight years old but somehow he did not look very different from the eight year old kid he had been all those years ago: defiant and a little bit sulky, and suddenly afraid. Skin may fill out or sag with the years, but expressions don't alter much and secretive eyes will always remain guarded.

'Janus?' Michaela looked at him curiously, sensing something amiss.

'You're wrong about the cricket ball, Michaela,' Janus said, still gazing down at his hands. 'They won't have found it with the skeleton. Crispian Younghusband didn't have his ball with him that day.'

'Read to me, Roz, read to me. Give it the first line test.'
'It doesn't pass, I assure you.'
'Go on anyway. My head aches.'
Michaela lay on the sofa in her office with a bag of

ice to her temple. Someone moving floors in the building had backed into her with a filing cabinet, connecting painfully with the side of her head as she was coming out of the lift. Roz, being resourceful, had taken the whole icetray from the fridge in the boardroom and wrapped it in a cushion cover and made Michaela lie down and raise her ankles. Roz had done a first aid course but it had been a while since she'd looked at her notes.

'All right. Here goes.'

Michaela winced when she lifted her head. She lay down again.

'"Winthrop had legs like telephone poles and thoughts that buzzed around his brain like ants in a antheap."'

'You got my attention,' said Michaela drily. 'Don't stop. Please.'

'"Whenever he was on a trip he felt heavy in the knees and the noise between his ears was a message that he was about to flip out. He sniffed at the line of white powder and suddenly sneezed. 'Bless you,' said Harry —"'

'Next,' called Michaela.

'OK, how about *A Summer Swallow?*'

'Naah – what else we got?'

'*Flowers for Frieda*? *Yesterday's Lovers*?'

'Oh, God. This hurts and you're not helping. How about a cup of tea?'

The competition entries were still coming in, attracted by the prize of a fairly large sum of money and, probably better still, the prospect of immortality through the publishing house which was co-sponsoring the project. There was nothing so far that had a hope in hell as far as Michaela was concerned. The message in the bottle had deteriorated badly after the second bottle of gin, with the boy tracking the woman becoming a man with her the very same day in the sand dunes, with jubilant waves crashing all about them.

There were five different entrances leading to the apartments and each apartment was unlike the next. They differed in size and design, which sounded haphazard but which worked well in practice. Harriet and David's apartment had been one of the top ones in the west wing. They had their own entrance, two flights of blue slate steps and a beautiful balcony running the whole length of the sitting room and study windows, which looked out towards the hazy purple mountains in the distance. The rooms were all large and the ceilings high and wooden and painted white. Pauline's room looked out onto the orchard. This was to the back where the swimming pool and the tennis court were situated, and it looked as dense as a forest as you approached it.

Michaela, walking a pace or two behind Roger, tried to recognise the building. There was very little of Bricknell Court still standing. The west wing was completely demolished already and the section around the forecourt was a shell, a doll's house with the front cut off. They skirted a pile of oregon pine floorboards and some lead-paned windows lying shattered beside a sweep of steps which led nowhere. There was a pall of white, choking dust in the air and the roar of a pneumatic drill somewhere close by. They walked past men in hard hats and a gang of black workers in industrial overalls who glanced at them without curiosity. They had already paid their respects to the site manager who had looked hard at Michaela for a few moments and passed a hand over his perspiring face.

She could feel him staring after them, but she resisted a strong temptation to turn round and wink at him. He wasn't sure that he recognised her in her office suit and swinging mane of hair. She'd brought a clipboard and a notepad with her for effect, but had left it in the car in case Roger inquired.

Roger Rendell had a heavy stomach and his breath smelled of the garlic he'd had on his lunchtime chicken. He walked with his feet slightly splayed out as overweight people sometimes do in order to help balance the load. Michaela kept glancing surreptitiously at his profile. He hadn't had those jowls when they'd been dating, she was sure of it, nor the paunch. This was a man who'd gone to seed since his marriage to the pharmacist with the gap in her teeth he'd chosen shortly after Michaela had dumped him. It gave her a small feeling of satisfaction when her ex-lovers grew unattractive.

'There's nothing to see, you know,' Roger said, turning to her.

She trotted a little to keep up with him. 'I don't expect so,' she said demurely.

'I didn't even see the remains myself,' he went on. 'They took them away very quickly.'

'Oh.' That was disappointing. She had been hoping Roger would have been able to describe the arrangement of bones. How would he have been − foetal, spreadeagled beside the few breaths of fresh air seeping in beneath the door? With his metatarsals clutching at the boiler for warmth maybe? Michaela couldn't help but dwell on it. She had given up trying not to and let her imagination conjure up scenario after scenario until she was becoming quite numb. This morning in the weekly editorial meeting Crispian Younghusband had appeared in the middle of the table, his skin coming off in curling pink slivers like the shavings of a pencil, dancing like a dervish in between sentences while Michaela sat hopelessly and watched. She was mesmerised by the enormity of things.

'And you can't actually go in,' Roger continued. 'The police have put tape around the entrance to seal it off from intruders.'

'People like me,' Michaela interrupted apologetically. She was doing her best to charm Roger, she didn't know why. There was plainly nothing he could give her.

'Well . . .' Roger laughed and glanced at her. 'You're different.' He sounded wistful.

Michaela gave a little skip and put her arm through his. 'I really appreciate this all the same,' she told him. 'I can't explain why it's important to me. I grew up here in a way and . . . when I heard about the – skeleton, a whole rush of memories came back to me. I could picture the orchard and the apartments, and even the old boiler room itself. It was all so clear and so tragic. I just had to come back.' Lately she was beginning to hate herself.

Roger looked bemused. 'Yes,' he said, 'I see.' Roger was breathing hard. Michaela could see his buttons straining across his paunch. Crispian Younghusband would have had a paunch like that now if he'd been alive. He would have had thick treestump legs and a double chin.

They walked slowly through the orchard. The chestnut trees were a thick bright green, although they, too, had not been immune to the layering of dust thrown up by the excavations. Smuts's bench was still untouched. It was a wooden bench with a brass plaque on its back and it was set into the massive trunk of an oak tree.

Its planks were shiny and worn smooth. There was a mossy patch beneath it, smooth velvet green, and some mushrooms on stubby cream coloured stalks. Michaela saw them with a sudden pang, thinking of the time they'd tried to feed them to Crispian Younghusband, not knowing for sure whether they were poisonous or not. The mushrooms always came up on that patch, every year when it rained a bit.

'Well, here we are,' said Roger cheerfully. He led the way as if she might not know where she was, and it was true she found herself hanging back. 'The boiler room's down there,' he told her.

Michaela's heart was hammering in her chest. She felt lightheaded all of a sudden, no longer coquettish and in control. She took her sunglasses off and slipped them into her bag.

The boiler room had largely been left untouched by the bulldozers. There was no door, of course, and the bricks had been pushed in, but the steps leading down into it, chipped and marked, were still there. Six stone steps, an iron guard rail, the boiler itself, smooth and rounded and looking somehow cold, lifeless. The concrete floor was cracked and there was some rubble piled in the corner where Tommy had had his makeshift bed. Michaela was struck by how small and cramped the place was. She remembered it as cavernous and mysterious. And the smell. She remembered the hot smell of stale air. There was nothing of that now. Only dust motes wriggling in a ray of light from the coal shute.

'Apparently,' said Roger, taking off his hard hat and ruffling the few strands of hair on his head, 'apparently the child was found close to the boiler itself, round the back side of it, probably curled up there for the warmth.' He clicked his tongue and shook his head. 'Poor creature.'

'Mmm,' Michaela murmured. She folded her arms tightly, feeling the chill from the empty space. For warmth – she'd known it. 'And they still don't know . . .' She left the words hanging, vaguely.

'There were clothes,' Roger said. 'They were hoping that the clothes would have helped in identification, but as far as I know, they've had no luck so far.'

'Oh,' said Michaela. 'Nothing else?'

'What do you mean?'

'I mean, was there nothing else in here – besides the . . . skeleton and . . . and his clobber.'

Roger was no help at all. 'I don't know,' he said.

The boiler room was cordoned off effectively with white tape tied across the entrance in a confused and thorough criss-cross arrangement. Michaela went closer, leaving Roger standing where he was.

'Michaela –' he called out nervously, but she took no notice of him. She stopped at the tape. Dust and concrete filled her nostrils. And some other smell that she couldn't identify. Something cold. Cold metal? The boiler was dark brown and squat and it stood on the concrete floor back almost against the far wall. Michaela stood, with her hands at her sides, and looked at the room which now filled her thoughts night and day. As a child, in fact, she had seldom been into the boiler room herself. Pauline was the one who came here with food for Tommy. Michaela and the others had mostly stayed away. Once or twice, before Crispian Younghusband, they had come in here in winter, where it had been warm and dark and scary. There was no light, only a faint glimmer at the end of the coal chute, and their hands and feet had been black from the soot on the floor. Once they had played cops and robbers and had used the soot to make passable crooks' fingerprints. Michaela had a sudden vision of pressing Janus's thumbs down on a white piece of paper and examining the intricate swirls through a magnifying glass.

Suddenly, she slipped beneath the white tape and went down the steps into the room itself.

'Oh my,' said Roger quaintly. He stepped forward and looked about, obviously nervous. 'I don't think . . . there's supposed to be a chap on guard here and if he . . . Michaela, please.'

Michaela put the flat of her hand on the boiler. It was smooth and felt as cold and as heavy as a bullet. She pulled that hand back and massaged it with the other. She walked round the small expanse of floor, her eyes moving quickly this way and that. Her heart was beating in her throat. There was nothing to see, nothing. As she moved a piece of the floor gave way beneath her weight and she stumbled, almost crying out. Everything was giving way. Everything crumbling about her in a dreadful parody of her life. She wished it was Antony she had with her and not pompous Roger Rendell. Antony would have forced her to see some humour in the situation, black though it might be. And with Roger she had to pretend only passing and not morbid interest.

'There's a funny smell down here,' she called out to him.

Roger was looking desperate. His mouth worked comically. 'Please come back,' he said.

'What do you think it is?' she asked conversationally. She wondered why her olfactory organs were so acutely tuned of late. She was smelling corpses all over the place.

'I don't know,' Roger replied, edging closer. 'I don't think it's what you're thinking, if that's what you're thinking. I don't imagine that a skeleton has a smell, actually.'

'Was the skeleton *complete*?' Michaela asked, leaning with her bottom casually against the boiler. 'I mean — were all the bits together, as it were?'

'I believe so,' said Roger. 'I believe they were.'

'What else was there, Roger? There must have been other stuff surely.'

'Just the clothing, that was all, as far as I know.' Roger ran a finger round the inside edge of his collar. 'Michaela, please come out of there now. The guard —'

Michaela ambled back to the tape, lifted it and strolled out. 'It's all right, Roger,' she said. 'I wasn't doing any harm, just curious.' She gave him a pat on the shoulder. 'This place was as familiar to me once as my skin. I wanted to feel it again. Just curiosity, that's all.'

'I have to get back to the office,' Roger told her stiffly. They had been here half an hour and he was annoyed with himself for allowing himself to be manipulated. He had been manipulated by Michaela before and it always made him uncomfortable when he realised it too late.

'May I stay here a little longer?' Michaela looked up at him. 'If I promise to keep away from the dreaded boiler room?' She held up a hand. 'Promise.'

Roger looked unhappy. 'Well . . .' he said. 'I don't know.'

'I'll even remember to hand in my hard hat,' Michaela said solemnly. 'The site manager can't object. I won't be anywhere near where they're working. I just want to walk round the old orchard for a few minutes. It's the chestnut trees. They're practically the only chestnut trees in Cape Town, you know, and they need to be appreciated once in a while. For all you know, your grasping company might be about to bulldoze them to the ground if the stay of execution is lifted and the petitions fail. Think of it as an act of compassion. I won't stay long, truly.'

Michaela watched Roger walk away reluctantly. She felt limp with exhaustion. She could even feel her cheeks sagging as the muscles in her forced smile relaxed. Her back felt stiff. She walked up the path beside the row of poplar trees to the part of the orchard where the fruit and chestnut trees grew. It was cool in there amongst them. There were dead heads on the rings of hydrangea bushes which clustered round the boles of the oak trees. They had been a favourite hiding place that summer. They had hidden there from Crispian Younghusband and had shot orange berries at his shins as he walked past looking for them, throwing his cricket ball up and down.

Michaela looked for Smuts's bench. She sat down on it and stretched her legs out in front of her. She slipped a foot out of her sandal and ran a toe across the velvety surface of the green moss pads which sprouted up from the damp, dark soil. Just to the right of her, beneath the spread of branches, was where they had scored out their hopscotch pattern many years before. Antony had used a piece of stiff wire to gouge out the circles and squares. Each holiday all they had to do was sweep over it and run over the lines again with a sharp stone and the hopscotch would come up again, good as new. The earth was brown and smooth now and littered with chestnut conkers.

Michaela tried to empty her mind of thoughts of the past and focus it on the present. She cast her mind back to the telephone conversation and tried to concentrate on the voice at the other end. She was certain that the man had been disguising his voice anyway with some tried and tested method – even a handkerchief over the mouthpiece would have given it that muffled, slurring tone. So if the voice wasn't going to give her a clue, something else had to. Some piece of the puzzle that would come to her if she sat here long enough and imbibed a bit of the Bricknell Court atmosphere. A squirrel ran down the branch above her and paused, seeing her, frozen in mid-stride, its tail a quivering loop across its back. Then it leapt for a branch across her head and fled into the leaf cover at the top of the tree.

Suddenly Michaela sat up straight, staring out in front of her. 'Oh, Jesus,' she breathed. 'Of course. How blind could we be?' She got up slowly, put on her sandal and picked up the hard hat beside her on the bench. She turned to gaze in the direction of the boiler room and shook her head as if to clear it. 'Of course,' she said out loud. 'Of *course*.'

'Where have you *been*?' Roz demanded. 'Couldn't you have told someone where you were going? I thought you'd caught amnesia from the filing cabinet.' She followed Michaela into her office. 'You've got some black stuff on your forehead. Is it Ash Wednesday? Have you been to church?'

Sometimes Roz could get on her nerves. She would think about having a word with personnel and seeing if Desmond couldn't be recalled earlier than his three-month paternity stint allowed. She had a sudden strong need to experience his quiet efficiency and neatly marked correspondence files again. The way he closed her office door gently and discreetly at only a look.

'I had to go out for a brief while,' Michaela told Roz, who was standing in her Turkish pants with her hands on her hips. Given a turban she would have made a good Aladdin, so imperious was her pose. 'I wasn't gone long.'

'Yes, well, Food was looking for you. They wanted your cousin's number. I couldn't find it on your desk.'

Michaela felt mild annoyance flush her cheeks. She didn't like the idea of Roz padding about her office in her absence in her turned up slippers.

'For the autumn herbs promotion. They want him to do the pics.'

'I'll give it to you. Just give me a minute. I want to have a word with Antony myself.' Michaela waited. 'In private.'

Clearly disgruntled, Roz closed the door behind her and Michaela heard her turn her portable radio on to the afternoon talk show. The editor was due to be on today, talking about the effect the new budget would have on the country's women. They asked for her comments every year and every year they grew more gloomy.

There was no reply on Antony's number and he had neglected to leave his answerphone on. Frustrated, Michaela hung up and tried to call Janus. He was in a concept meeting and couldn't be disturbed. Michaela bit at a corner of her thumbnail and stared out of the window. Pauline. She would try and track Pauline down. There was no reply at home and she found she didn't have a number for the club. Pauline was bound to be down at the Waterfront. Unable to sit still and with her revelation burning a hole in her chest, Michaela took her handbag and walked round her desk.

Roz looked up at her and her mouth fell open. 'And now?' she said.

'Here's Antony's number.' Michaela put a piece of paper in front of her. 'I have to go out again.' She smiled. 'Take messages, Roz.' She hurried down the passage thinking how oddly satisfying it could be to irritate one's secretary.

The electrician was standing in the doorway to Pauline's with his parrot on his shoulder. He was smoking a handrolled cigarette and the strong smell caught at Michaela's throat. Pauline was not there, Frank told her. She had gone into town for light fittings again; the incorrect size had been supplied. But Michaela's mother was inside, rehearsing with the boys. Michaela could hear Blanche singing 'Some Kind of Wonderful' and for a moment she could not bear the thought of being sidetracked. She hesitated. Then she pulled out one of the outside plastic chairs and sat down on it. Frank smiled at her. 'Busy day?' he said pleasantly. He looked as if stress was not a word he was acquainted with at all. Michaela was aware of her dishevelled appearance and a tremor in her fingers. She thought a cigarette might not be a bad idea. It seemed to work for Franco.

'Is that birdshit on your shoulder?' she asked, squinting into the sun.

Frank laughed. He tapped ash onto the ground at his feet. He laughed again. He had black eyes and quaintly arched eyebrows. Michaela could see him on a postcard, as a gondolier with wide black pants.

'Pauline should be back any minute,' he said, grinding the butt out with the toe of his black patent leather shoes (about four hundred bucks a throw – electricians made good money, it seemed). 'I'll bring you out a nice cold drink. Talk to Ernest while I'm gone.'

Before she could protest Michaela found herself face to face with a sharp black beak and a calculating eye which opened and closed and blinked at her crazily. Frank took his time. She kept looking away and then back again at the apparition with fluffy pale grey feathers puffed up at the shoulders. They considered each other in silence, neither one looking happy about the situation.

'Just don't sing,' Michaela said grumpily. 'One songbird at a time is enough, thank you.'

Ernest put his head on one side and closed his eye.

'And you might as well know I have a cat,' Michaela said. 'Who would probably eat you for breakfast, horrible claws and all.'

Ernest opened his beak and made a strangled sound. He shifted sideways along the table and lowered his head to inspect Michaela's car keys.

'Now that we're talking,' Michaela said, moving them out of his reach, 'and seeing that no one else is interested, I'll let you in on something: I've discovered who it is who's plaguing my life on the telephone.'

Blanche was humming along to the first bars of 'Summertime'. Her voice was sure and true but the drummer was having a little difficulty with the tempo.

'It's Tommy,' Michaela said out loud. 'The pinball wizard.' She put her elbows on the table and stared at the bristle of masts in the yacht basin. The parrot hopped onto the back of a chair and moved his head from side to side in apparent time to the music. 'After all,' Michaela went on, 'subterfuge and deceit are his stock in trade, aren't they? Spying on people, bugging them, interfering in their personal lives – these are all things that come naturally to him. No one has laid eyes on him in years but he knew us all intimately. Uncomfortably intimately. He was around that summer, lurking around in the shadows, taking handouts, sleeping in the *boiler* room, eating our food and wearing our clothes. It has to be him. It makes perfect sense. It has to have been him watching us that day. Tommy was the only one who could have seen what happened. Now that he knows what's come to light, he's put two and two together and is probably working on a little blackmail game. Once his cover was blown with David and Harriet, they say he left the police. He's probably destitute or something and thinking about scoring with the Whitehead money.'

The parrot swivelled its neck around in a complete circle. It opened its black beak and Michaela could have sworn she heard the words 'fish're jumpiiiing' but it was over so quickly she fancied it was probably Blanche going slightly off key.

'Well, that's what I think anyway,' she went on. 'And if Pauline, Antony or Janus would be kind enough to turn up when I need them, it's a theory I'd like to share with something that has more than just a birdbrain.'

She heard a noise behind her but before she could turn Frank was there, with a hint of a smile and a tall glass of lime juice on a tray. 'I find talking to Ernest very soothing,' he said, putting the tray on the table. 'They say watching tropical fish is good too.'

The glass was filled with crushed ice and its sides were slippery and very cold. Michaela took hold of it gratefully.

'I told Blanche you were here,' said Frank. He gestured with his head. 'Why don't you go in?'

Michaela did as she was told. She took her drink

inside with her and waved at her mother. When her eyes had adjusted properly to the gloom, she gasped. Blanche was wearing fishnet stockings and a silver miniskirt with tassles all around the hem. Her top was a plunging strip of black clingfilm, or that was what it looked like. The bones of her chest stood out and her shoulders were as knobbly as knuckles. Her red hair was clutched to the crown of her head in a topknot, streaky tendrils hanging down into the nape of her neck. She leaned over the keyboard player like a hooker and the twenty year old on bass had his eyes on the backs of her legs and a slow grin spreading. Michaela felt tears start to her eyes and a blush of mortification on her mother's behalf colour her face. There was nothing wrong with Blanche's voice, though, and Michaela could see the cords in her neck stand out as she surged through 'Summertime' for the second time. Frank sat in the doorway with Ernest on his shoulder and he was smiling too, but less offensively. When they came to the end of the number Blanche shook a cigarette out of the box on the piano and waited until one of the boys strolled over with a light. Then she inhaled deeply and walked to the front of the stage.

'That felt good,' said Blanche. Her voice sounded scratchy and she cleared her throat. 'How did it sound?'

Michaela nodded and gave her a thumbs up. She didn't trust herself to speak. Blanche's skirt only just cleared her bottom. She came down from the stage, stepping with care on high heels, and sat down beside Michaela. 'I'm having so much fun,' she told her. 'What would you say if I told you I was thinking of coming out of retirement?'

Close up, her mother's face was lined and damp with perspiration. Michaela could see her pores through the thick makeup and the dark grey showing through at her temples.

'It wouldn't surprise me,' she answered.

'Do you like my outfit?'

Michaela had been hoping not to have to answer that question. 'What there is of it,' she said, 'is very nice, but —'

'I went shopping I felt so inspired,' Blanche interrupted. 'I also fell in love with a pair of leather pants and a leopardskin leotard so I bought them too. If you stick around for a little while, I'm going to do a costume change.' She smiled happily and drew deeply on her cigarette. 'This keyboard player has such intuitive hands,' she continued before Michaela could say anything. 'He must make a wonderful lover for some woman.'

'Or man,' Michaela said, looking over at him talking to the bass player.

'It was nice of you to drop by,' Blanche said. 'I was getting tired of singing to that Italian fellow – what's his name again?'

'Frank,' said Michaela. She took a sip from her glass. 'Pauline says he's from Pisa. There's not much call for electricians in Pisa.'

'Nor builders,' said Blanche.

'Well,' Michaela said, standing up. 'I can't wait any longer for Pauline. I'd appreciate it if you told her I was here. Perhaps she could call me at home.' She kissed her mother's cheek. It was clammy and she smelt strongly of perfume. The smell followed her to the door like a plea. Michaela was beginning to feel haunted by her extra-sensitive sense of smell. It was a relief to be out in the fresh air and she hurried to her car, anxious at last to get back to work.

· 13 ·

The ornaments on the dressing table had all been dusted and rearranged into conversations. The glass owl with the pincushion between its ears and the squirrel without a tail were squaring up to each other, while the cats had been put into a close, conspiratorial circle. The two Siamese were together, and the pink china cat with the sneer sprawled in the middle in a pose of reluctant submission. The stuffed toys, too, had been neatly laid out on the bed, two bears and a possum side by side. Pauline stood and looked but could scarcely imagine these things in Tertius' big hands.

She walked across to the bed. Her animals were all old now and had lost their softness. The bears were rough and patchy and full of tumours. None of the creatures had eyes. She sat down on the edge of the bed and took the possum onto her lap. Her suitcase remained where she had put it down, beside the closed wardrobe door. She sat for a minute or two and savoured the silence in the house. She could hear the steady tick of the clock on the bedside table. It was almost five o'clock. Tertius would probably be in soon. She thought fleetingly that it was not too late to leave again. She could walk down the passage to the front door, smoothing the bed's cover behind her, and never return again. She could take the blender on her way, and the Magi-Mix. Tertius would never miss them and they would be useful at the club. She didn't have nearly enough labour-saving gadgets yet.

Why had she come home? Pauline was always painfully conscious of that question every time she found herself in this position. She thought when she could answer it with something approaching honesty she would have reached a significant milestone, but the answer always eluded her, sneaking away out of sight just when she thought she might have caught a glimpse of it.

This was the third time in the last twelve months that she had left Tertius, but she had always known the moment she climbed the stepladder to heave the suitcase down from the top of the built-in cupboard that, sooner or later, she would be back. There had never been a plan further advanced than a spell at Michaela's or an extended stay with Janus. There had been one particularly debilitating occasion which had run too close to an earlier time with Michaela when she had checked into a hotel in Mouille Point, too ashamed to turn up again so soon on her cousin's doorstep. She had nursed her bruised ribs herself, binding them tightly with a pair of Extra Large longjohns she'd had with her (it was winter) because she suspected the toe of one of Tertius' imported Irish shoes to have caused a cracked bone or two in her left side. She had sat in misery at the window, taking shallow breaths and looking at the children on the brown rocks and shingle of the beach down below, wrapped up in jerseys and woollen caps, sent down to the beach with nannies every afternoon. At night she had lain awake feeling the heavy damp of the fog seep under the wooden window frames and listening to the dreary blare of the foghorn warning passing tankers of the shoreline's jagged treachery.

It was a residential hotel and there was a dining room with dark furniture and lumpy asparagus soup in the evenings, and the only other guests were an Indian woman and her two dark-eyed children who sat solemnly and in silence with an air of waiting at a table in the corner. After a day or two she and the woman began to nod cautiously to each other. Then an old man made an appearance in the dining room. He tucked his napkin into his collar and drank his soup furtively, never raising his head. Pauline wondered how she had so unerringly found her way to this place for damaged people. It was not a restful time. There was a feeling of anxiety about the place, an atmosphere of impending disaster. Sometimes she had crazy visions of partners bursting through the doors at mealtimes – an Indian man tall as a house with an axe in his fist; a woman in curlers and a jaw like desperate Dan. Tertius.

After five days of sitting at the window and living out of her suitcase, Pauline found she could inhale without the shooting pains and the nausea, and she had climbed in her car, gripping the steering wheel with white knuckles, and driven in one go up to Stillwaters where Mater asked no questions and Frans cooked mealies for her on the coals in their silky green cases.

It was at Stillwaters that the idea of the club had first come to her and she had found in Mater a sensitive and receptive sounding board. She was not looking for a financial contribution from Mater, and indeed had scarcely begun to formulate the idea, but Mater had taken to it with enthusiasm and personal interest and she had been persuasive in the end. Pauline would get the money anyway when she was dead, she argued, so why not take it now and put it into something that could give them both pleasure. Mater had laughed with the excitement of it, delighting in the prospect of being a sleeping partner. She used the phrase over and over again, and talked energetically about possible localities and even decor. They had both been drawn to the idea of the Waterfront for all the obvious reasons of tourists and trends. But they had also both been attracted to the proximity of the sea and the harbour and the fishing boats. And the gulls that swept across the grey sky as they did here at Stillwaters. Watching her longjohns dancing, captive, on the washing line, Pauline knew instinctively, as she had never known anything else in her life, that the club was going to become a reality and that it was a step towards something as yet unspoken but already in her heart.

Pauline had deliberately not yet taken on anyone else to help at the club, apart from soliciting the services of the students who were on call to be waiters and waitresses. She wasn't sure why this was. Perhaps it was the desire to prove she could do something grown up, something entirely on her own. There was probably still a part of her, too, that hoped Tertius would show an interest in lending a hand in the evenings, although she realised by now that this was unlikely to happen. Then there was Frank. To all intents and purposes, the wiring and the sound system were in perfect working order and Frank's job was really finished. But so far Frank showed little sign of moving on. He was always down at the club, tinkering at the back of the stage or in the kitchen, or sitting proprietorially in overalls in the sunshine outside, rolling cigarettes and passing the time of day with anyone who looked in the mood to talk a minute. He was acting like a manager, Pauline had realised suddenly one morning, and with that the germ of an idea was born and she had rushed off to buy something for Frank to install and to give her more time to think things through. She needn't have worried. Frank took his time and fiddled in the ceiling and chatted to Pauline about Ernest's moulting problem.

Time was passing. Pauline sat the possum upright on a chair and stood up and looked at herself in the mirror. She had to duck her head to get all of herself in and still she was not happy with what she saw. For the first time she thought her short hair made her face look too fat, and the earrings she had put on that morning were the wrong shade and shape for her man's shirt. The skirt was too long and the vertical stripes didn't help one bit with the hips. Instead of the sleek effect she had been hoping for, she looked like a canvas awning. No wonder, she thought, no wonder. She picked up the suitcase and opened it on the bed. If she unpacked quickly, she could put dinner on for both of them and they could share a meal together, sitting down. That would start things off well. And she would not go to the club this evening. Frank would lock up.

The late afternoon sun streamed in at the window. Pauline thought about Mater and how the river would be all spangles and light at this time of the day. She had not been in touch with her since the news and she felt particularly remiss. It was all very well to allow Michaela to take up the burden of finding out whether there was anything sinister going on in this talk of marriage, or whether Mater had gone ever so slightly off the rails out of loneliness, but she too had a responsibility towards her grandmother, and Mater knew it. Besides, Michaela was very stressed at the moment with Crispian Younghusband haunting her. Pauline thought perhaps they should all make the time to go up to Stillwaters again and talk to Mater and Frans together, to show Frans that they were a family to be reckoned with.

Pauline pushed the empty suitcase under the bed, then took it out again and stowed it in the cupboard where it belonged. It would do her no good to start out on the wrong foot with Tertius. Better not to remind him that she had been away at all. He always liked to take up the reins again without having to contend with blatant reminders of defection.

He came home and kissed her on the cheek in the kitchen. He lifted the lid on the pot on the stove and sniffed with appreciation. He lit candles with long matches and set out the mats and knives and forks. When the telephone rang just as they were sitting down to eat, he reached across and pulled the cord from the socket with a strong flick of the wrist and said, 'Let's eat undisturbed, what do you say?' and Pauline dished cinnamon pumpkin onto his plate without a word. She had changed into comfortable pants and a woollen jumper, one that Tertius had brought back for her from a country trip. It made the back of her neck itch but she decided it might be worth the discomfort tonight. The jumper always pleased Tertius and she did not wear it often enough. It was yellow, slashed with pink. She thought it made her breasts look like a pair of grapefruit.

'Mater is getting married,' Pauline said into a patch of silence, wondering immediately why she was risking this. She put dishes on the warming tray and watched Tertius out of the corner of her eye. She really did not want to anger him.

'Married?' said Tertius. He paused to take a sip from his wineglass. 'Since when?'

'She announced it after her party,' Pauline told him. 'It came as quite a surprise.' She smiled nervously.

'Who to?' Tertius asked the inevitable question.

Pauline cast around desperately for something plausible to say. Tertius was not big on mixed race marriages. She settled for something vague, something not entirely a lie. 'No one you know,' she said. Tertius, after all, did not know Frans very well.

'One of the old geezers from up the river, I suppose?'

'Well, no. From the village.' Pauline pushed at the food on her plate. She watched Tertius from beneath her eyelids.

'Big splash?'

'Oh. No, I don't think so. It will be a quiet affair, I'm sure. Round about Easter, I believe.'

Tertius's eyes gleamed unpleasantly. 'Well, you can be sure he's after her money,' he said. 'And the farm. River frontage. The place is worth a packet, even if the house is practically falling down.' He seemed to take particular satisfaction in the thought. He stretched across the table for the wine bottle, looked at Pauline's still full glass and topped up his own. He wiped a piece of bread across his plate and put it in his mouth. He had lost interest in Pauline's relations and she felt herself relax just a fraction.

'So why aren't you at the club tonight?' Tertius asked casually, glancing at Pauline's plate.

Pauline smiled at him. 'I've been working so hard down there,' she said. 'A night off won't do me or the club any harm.'

'Or us,' said Tertius. He put his big hand over hers for a minute and squeezed it. Pauline looked away.

She could feel an itch smarting under her collar. She had quite lost her appetite all of a sudden. Unbidden, she saw Frank waiting for her down at the Waterfront, with a glass of wine and a hand-rolled cigarette and the sun going down, washing the mountain with shades of gold.

After supper Pauline did the dishes by herself. Tertius didn't often help in the kitchen and tonight she was glad that he hadn't offered as he occasionally did following one of her desertions. He seemed subdued himself, as if his mind were elsewhere. Pauline was still not sure she had come home to stay this time. Tertius seemed strange to her and she was for once disinclined to meet him halfway. Looking around the kitchen she began to count the things that were hers, those items she had brought along to Tertius's house so cheerfully a couple of years ago. What could she have been thinking of? Having got over Angus, she had rented a cottage with chimneys and a fireplace in every room right on the perimeter of the botanical gardens. There had been silver trees and proteas outside the windows. Occasionally she had seen buck grazing on her front lawn. There were no fences and no tamed flowerbeds and in summer the sunbirds would hover and flash their brilliance in the bushes by the gate. She had given that up for Tertius and a suburban house with a brick wall and a hen-coop letterbox. But when she contemplated packing up and wrapping her plates in tissue paper and finding boxes to stack everything in, her energy whittled away to nothing. Pauline liked her things around her. They were her comfort and her security. When Harriet and David had left home so abruptly, they had naturally left behind everything that was theirs and Pauline had had no choice but to take it over. From cushions and table linen to toothbrush holders and bookends, most of Pauline's possessions had been with her since childhood. She had not resented this; she liked to have them with her. But sometimes she felt trapped by mementos and wished she could be like Michaela, who had no such attachments. Things were there for convenience, nothing more, to Michaela. She could have walked out of her front door without a minute's hesitation if she had to. She could probably never have even done an accurate inventory, whereas Pauline sometimes woke in a sweat in the night, having dreamed about a sudden fire and finding herself unable to leave the house because she couldn't make up her mind what to take.

When she was finished in the kitchen, it was getting on for ten o'clock and she found Tertius in his socks and underpants reading the newspaper on their bed. He smiled up at her in a fatherly way and watched as she put on a dressing gown and ran a bath. She resisted an impulse to lock the bathroom door, and when she was done she found Tertius swathed in a sheet and, mercifully, fast asleep.

Michaela was writing a letter to Joy Beamish. Beside her on the table lay a collection of poems on scented notepaper and a couple of coupons (twenty per cent off) for extra-sheer pantihose with gusset that Joy had seen fit to enclose. 'Dear Joy,' was as far as she'd got. She stared vaguely at the top of Simon's head. Simon was watching a documentary on Alaska on television with the sound turned down. Rather than go out, she had turned his invitation to dinner into coming over for coffee on the pretext of having work to catch up on. He seemed content just to be there, with his feet stretched out in front of him and the remote control held slackly in his hand. If she married Simon, as she suspected might be in his mind, they would probably have many evenings like this to look forward to. Simon looked very at home in front of her TV with his heels comfortably on a footstool. He probably watched motor racing on Saturday afternoons.

Reluctantly, Michaela cast an eye over a poem called 'In Sorrow and in Strife' which was almost, but not quite, a limerick in rhythm but a dirge in tone. 'Dear Joy,' she sighed, half out loud. 'Thank you for your four poems. Sadly, we do not appear to have space for any of them in the magazine at the present time. I did like "Unhappily Yours", but twelve verses does rather challenge our ever-present problem of space and it seems a pity to cut it down . . .' Michaela worried occasionally about her rejections. She had lost count of the number of letters she had had to send to Joy Beamish, who never seemed deterred or discouraged by their contents. She wondered what Joy did with them or how they appeared to her when she read them. Would she never understand that she just couldn't write? That it was unlikely that anything that came off the nib of her fountain pen would find a home in book or magazine? What drove her to write so frequently and so fiercely – what compulsion? Sometimes she had to admire her tenacity and determination, inappropriate though it was.

Michaela was finding concentration difficult. She felt as tightly sprung as a piece of coiled wire. Her life was so filled with confused, unfinished business. Preoccupied as she was with Crispian Younghusband's bones, she had not given too much thought to Mater and her marriage and Blanche's call earlier in the evening –

which had sent her flying to the phone with heart pounding – saying that she was now formulating Plan B, had unsettled her. She was sure that whatever Blanche had in mind would involve Michaela again in some way, and would doubtless be as unpleasant and unsatisfying as the last attempt. Blanche was determined that the marriage would not go ahead and she was going to work towards that end with a single-mindedness that Michaela had experienced with her mother in the past and which baffled her to a stupor. Blanche felt convinced that she knew better than anybody what would be best for Mater.

'"Bushman, Bushman, whither, pray?" was an intriguing piece of verse but, again, not quite right for our readers, I'm afraid. Do keep working – I hope we will manage to place one of your stories or verses soon.'

That should do it. Michaela sat back and ran her eyes over the lines she'd written. She felt a hypocrite. Why not simply say Your poems stink and no one in their right mind would ever use them, not even in the most experimental of journals. Why don't you go for another career, lady? But she couldn't do it to Joy Beamish; they had a longstanding relationship and she felt responsible for her. Another responsibility. Michaela felt dwarfed by responsibilities.

Everything on the television was white. Alaska in the grip of winter had no other colours at all. Even the bark on the trees looked white. Simon's eyes were drooping. She could legitimately send him home now, and then go to bed herself. She did not want to sleep with him tonight, not when she was so jumpy and Antony hadn't called.

Simon opened his eyes owlishly when the telephone

rang. He looked at Michaela sitting with her pen in her hand, not moving.

'Do you want me to get that?' he asked, sitting up straight, yawning.

'Er, no – thank you,' Michaela said.

'Well –' Simon looked puzzled. 'What about ... aren't you going to answer it?'

'I think not,' Michaela replied, sliding the top onto her pen.

Simon stared at her. The phone continued to ring.

'I'm tired of the telephone,' Michaela said carelessly. 'The blessed thing's been ringing all day. I need a break.'

'But,' Simon said, half rising, 'what if it's someone important? It might be your mother, or Mater.'

Or Antony, Michaela thought. Or Tommy. But she simply couldn't have had a mad conversation with either her cousin or the pinball wizard with Simon and Alaska in the background.

'Please leave it,' she said firmly. She folded up her papers calmly, as if the house weren't reverberating to the instrument's persistent call.

'Will someone answer the bloody telephone!' came from Susan's room just as the ringing stopped.

There followed a peaceful silence and Michaela smiled. 'There you are, see,' she said. 'It couldn't have been anything important.'

Simon ran a hand over his head. 'Time to go,' he said, standing up. 'I have a breakfast meeting first thing in the morning.' He smiled reluctantly at Michaela, still looking faintly puzzled. 'Sorry I can't stay.'

'I'm tired too,' Michaela said. She sidled over and turned the television off before he changed his mind.

Then she escorted him to the door, herding him along like a dog with a sheep. 'Thanks for coming over. We'll have dinner . . . soon.'

He had hardly gone down the path when the phone began again. Michaela leaned with her back against the front door, shivering.

'Mum!' Susan's voice was plaintive. 'For God's sake!'

Michaela walked heavily over to the table in the hall. She picked up the receiver, willing it to be Antony, or anyone else, even Blanche.

'I thought you were out.' Tommy. *Was* it Tommy?

'I'm here,' she said carefully. Try to keep him talking. Wasn't that what they did in the movies? (But to what end, in this instance?)

'You didn't forget about me, did you?'

'What do you want?'

'You didn't take my advice.'

Michaela's mouth had gone dry. 'I don't know what you're talking about,' she said. Straining her ears for some intonation, some clue to confirm her belief, all she could hear was a distracting roaring sound in her ears like the sound of the sea. She knew she should hang up but something was preventing her. It was the way to deal with crank callers. Just hang up every time you hear their voice.

'Don't play games, Michaela. The time for playing games is over.' The voice was not much more than a hoarse whisper. If Michaela hadn't been so afraid, she would have caught a sense of the absurdity, the drama, the unreality of such a situation being put upon her, Michaela Whitehead. She waited, saying nothing, afraid to speak yet afraid to put down the phone.

'It's time,' said Tommy.

'Time for what?'

'Time to pay. There comes a time when you have to pay for your sins.'

'This is ridiculous,' Michaela said abruptly. 'I don't have to —'

'Go to the police and tell them what you know.' Tommy was relentless.

Michaela made one last, lame attempt. 'But I don't even know what you're talking about,' she said.

'Oh, you do, Michaela, you do. Think back.'

Michaela didn't have to think back. She knew she was cornered and she felt the flutter of panic deep inside her.

'Why are you doing this?' she said softly. 'What is this all about?'

Tommy was quick, and self-righteous. 'About justice, of course.'

'Justice, what justice! You're just a crank, you're just – I don't believe you know —'

'Does the name Crispian Younghusband mean anything to you, Michaela?'

Michaela fought to control her voice. 'Tommy!' she blurted out. 'You lousy little shit! Tommy!'

But the line was dead. There was no one there.

It was nearly midnight. Michaela sat in a chair, hugging her arms and rocking, trying to get herself under control. Eventually, unable to prevent herself, she called Antony. Recognising real panic, Antony came over right away. He held Michaela in his arms, trying to comfort her and to get coherent sentences. Michaela was distraught with anger and fear.

'It's Tommy,' she said finally. 'Jesus Christ, Antony, if I could get to him, I'd *kill* him. I swear to God I'd slit his slimy throat.'

'Tommy?' said Antony. '*Tommy*? Are you sure?'

Michaela nodded vehemently. 'It all fits,' she told him. 'Only I don't know what the payoff is. That delight is still to come.'

Then Susan appeared in the lounge, tousled from bed and confused by Michaela's violent voice.

'Your mum's overworked,' was all Antony could think of on the spur of the moment. Michaela was gulping into a tissue and staring wildly past her daughter to the hallway. 'There's been a bit of trouble at the office.'

'Don't lie to me,' Susan said coolly. 'Who phoned? That's what's upset her, Antony, nothing to do with work.' She was sleepy, but scornful. Nobody knew her mother better than she did.

Michaela made a visible effort and took Susan back to bed. They walked slowly along the passage, arms about each other, while Michaela gave her a watered down version of anonymous callers in a general sort of overview and how upsetting they could be.

'Pretty upsetting if you had to get Antony over,' Susan said. 'Couldn't you just have hung up or something?' She crawled back into bed, eyes already half closed, pushing The Dog off her pillow. Michaela sat for a minute or two on the end of the bed, thinking about Tommy with anger and loathing. A double betrayal. First Harriet and David had been forced to completely alter their lives and leave behind their only daughter because of Tommy, and now he was doing it again, threatening to turn her own world inside out. And she couldn't get to him. There seemed to be nothing she could do. *What did he want?*

'There are cardigans and there are cardies,' Blanche said, sailing into Michaela's office and sitting down in the chair opposite her desk, 'and your secretary wears the latter. I've noticed it more than once. Besides that unfortunate habit of dressing, she is usually quite nicely turned out. But that skirt and top today need a jacket, not a beige cardie. You should tell her, Michaela, give her some tips. After all, this is a women's magazine and your staff should look the part.'

Roz wouldn't react positively to the suggestion that her outfits were a contradictory fashion statement. Michaela hoped she wasn't listening outside the door as she knew she liked to do, and Blanche never bothered to lower her voice when imparting confidences. Blanche herself looked as if she was getting serious about revamping her wardrobe. She was wearing charcoal stretch pants and a red and white diagonally striped top halfway down to the knees. Her legs looked like broomstick handles. Her lipstick was very red and her eye makeup heavier than she usually wore it. She was smoking heavily, ignoring the notice on Michaela's desk asking her not to do it at all.

Michaela removed her glasses and put them on top of the story she was reading. 'This is early for you, Mother,' she said. 'Is this just a social call?' She knew it wasn't – Blanche had a gleam in her eye.

'Of course not,' she said impatiently. 'I have another plan for Mater.'

Michaela sighed. 'Haven't you got enough on your plate?' she asked. 'The club opens next week and you're supposed to be busy with rehearsing. Why don't you just let Mater be?'

Blanche looked astounded. 'Let her be?' she echoed. 'Don't be ridiculous. Time is passing and we can't let the grass grow under our noses. We have an obligation to act swiftly.'

Michaela wasn't sure they didn't have an obligation to mind their own business, but there was no stopping Blanche once she had the bit between her teeth.

'What now?' she said.

'I talked to Mater last night,' said Blanche. 'And I suggested she come into town for a couple of days.'

'What for?' Michaela asked. 'Mater hates coming into town.'

Blanche tapped a cigarette on the back of her silver case and put it between her lips. 'Haven't you got an ashtray in here?' she asked. Michaela took her teacup off its saucer and shoved the saucer over to her. 'No,' she said.

'I suggested that she come into town for the opening of the club,' Blanche went on. 'It makes sense all round. She's a partner in the whole venture, after all, and Pauline would be absolutely thrilled if she were there.'

'What's this got to do with your plan?' Michaela asked warily.

'Well.' Blanche looked pleased with herself. She picked at a piece of tobacco on her lower lip. 'She'll come down a couple of days early, spend the weekend with me and do a bit of shopping. I told her she would need an outfit for the wedding and that she couldn't possibly buy something from the Stilfontein Modes again, not after the apricot slax suit they pressed on her last time.' She smiled innocently at Michaela and made an eloquent gesture with her hands. 'And she agreed,' she said.

Michaela frowned. 'I don't get it,' she said. 'You're bent on seeing that this wedding doesn't take place at all, yet you suggest that Mater come into town to buy an outfit.'

'Buying an outfit anyway won't do any harm,' Blanche replied. 'Mater could do with some new clothes. And when the marriage is called off, she'll at least have something nice to console herself with.'

Michaela's sceptical face was lost on her mother. 'Oh, it will be called off,' Blanche said, blowing smoke through her nose. 'And that's where you kids come in.'

'I see. I was wondering where we came in.'

'While Mater is in town you lot will go up to Stillwaters and have a heart to heart with the groom.'

'Who?'

'The bridegroom – Frans, of course.'

'Oh now come, Mother.' Michaela laughed without enjoyment. 'You can't be serious.'

'Oh, but I am,' said Blanche. 'I'm deadly serious. With Mater out of the way, you can show a bit of family solidarity and have a serious talk to the man. Make him see that this whole affair is quite ludicrous and appeal to the sensible side of him – I'm sure he has one. When Mater isn't there to prop him up, I've no doubt Frans will come to his senses. It will also be easier to make him an offer if he gets sticky.'

Michaela stared at her mother. Blanche blew smoke rings at the ceiling. Her lipstick was cracking in the corners. She threw a glance at Michaela. 'You look peaky,' she added accusingly.

'Mater will guess,' Michaela told her. 'She'll guess what you're up to.'

'No, she won't. Why should she? It's a perfectly legitimate reason to be here. She doesn't have to know you're up there, not right away, perhaps not at all. And you'll all be back for the supper club opening anyway. It's a good plan, darling, it is.'

Michaela marvelled at the way it was obvious that

Blanche had no doubt in her mind that they would all fall in with her plan. She had gone ahead and made the arrangement without even beginning to consult them. She compared this with the democratic way they had all been trying to solve the Bricknell Court problem. Democracy had never been Blanche's way at all.

'I'll have to talk to the others,' she said. 'I'm not agreeing to anything until I've discussed it with them.'

'They'll go along with it,' Mater said, 'as long as you persuade them. They always listen to you, Michaela, and you must see that it's a practical plan. We went about it all wrong the first time, you and Antony having a gentle word with Mater. We need a bit more oomph here and it's Frans we need to talk to, alone.'

'We?' said Michaela helplessly.

When Blanche had gone Michaela crossed to the window and flapped the curtains about to get the smoke moving out of the room. She didn't know why she allowed her mother to smoke in here; nobody else was permitted to. In fact she didn't know why she allowed her mother to get away with half the outrageous things she did. She would have to talk to her about the way she was dressing. God knew what sort of get up Mater would end up with if Blanche had anything to do with it in her current frame of mind. A virginal miniskirt and thigh high boots.

'This came.' Roz came into the room behind her bearing a plant in a tall pot. 'It's a fuchsia and it needs water.'

'Where did it come from?' Michaela asked, eyeing it. She didn't much care for pot plants. They always died on her. Pauline was the one with the green fingers in the family.

'Beamish. She's determined to win the competition.'

'Oh Christ. Can't you send it back?'

'Well, it didn't exactly come in the post, Michaela. She had it delivered.'

'Was there a note?'

'No. The delivery man had it in his book, that's all. It's from her garden.'

'You keep it,' Michaela said. 'I get hayfever from pollen.'

'I don't think fuchsias have pollen,' Roz told her. 'I'll just stick it here in the corner for the day. If you don't get along I'll take it home with me on the train.'

Michaela could just picture Roz in her cardie and flat shoes with the fuchsia in her arms, tramping loyally down to the station. Sometimes she did show willing, she'd give her that. 'Aren't you hot in that cardigan?' she asked her. 'You have such an attractive shirt on, it seems a pity to cover it up.'

'It's the colour.' Roz looked down uneasily. 'You don't think I look good in beige.'

'No, no,' Michaela protested feebly. 'Not at all. You look fine in beige. Really. I just thought . . .'

Roz was examining her image in the mirror. 'I look pasty,' she said dully. 'Definitely pasty. You're right.' She went out of the room with her shoulders slumping.

Michaela wearily picked up her glasses and prepared to do battle with the remainder of the stories. She was getting to the end and had a rather uninspired shortlist. Joy Beamish's *Love on a Wine-dark Sea* wasn't one of them.

'Roz,' she called after her suddenly. 'Do you think I look peaky?'

But Roz was out of earshot. Michaela let out a heavy sigh. Pasty and peaky. Music hall comedy duo.

She hadn't had much sleep the night before, nor the night before that and this pattern was beginning to take its toll. She'd noticed this morning that her skin had a slack, washed out look to it and her eyes were dull. It was all Crispian Younghusband's doing. That boy had been a nuisance from the day he'd walked into their lives. And Tommy. While not impinging on their lives in any meaningful way, he had always been an uncomfortable presence. He had had an aura about him, an aura of mystery and unfathomable secrets. Of course they had been too young to identify this as menace and power. It was they who had held the power, or so they had imagined, the power of the cohesive group able to dispense favours as they pleased, while Tommy loitered on the perimeter, ungracious recipient of intermittent largesse. But how cunningly he had manipulated them all, all those years ago, and he was doing it still, twenty years later. Michaela could not work it out. They had all tried to help Tommy, had given him things, fed him when he looked hungry. He had done odd jobs for Harriet, washed her car for her at the weekend. What motivated him to repay kindness with such devious treachery?

Michaela had a whole vocabulary of words for Tommy, that rotated around her head like a drumbeat. Unscrupulous, conniving, self-seeking. Some of those words rather fitted her, she had told Antony miserably, although Antony tried to stop her becoming maudlin as she was wont to do at the moment. Michaela wanted to throw her words at Tommy's head like rocks. Horrible – bonk. Diabolical – thwack. Scheming – doink. Instead she had stood with her hands at her sides while Antony had tried to push some spirit back up her veins.

Michaela pushed her glasses up on top of her head

and stared out of the window past the mountain towards the sea. It was a baking hot day, unseasonal to be quite this hot as the Cape moved towards the first of autumn's cool grey days. There was a breathlessness, a stillness in the air, a feeling of waiting. Or that was how it felt to Michaela. She felt as if she was holding her breath all the time.

Antony was another problem area. Michaela could not decide what it was that she and Antony were doing to each other. It was important to her, and had always been so, that the people she had around her were in one way or another intimately involved in her life. Janus was as much a part of her as one of her own limbs. So was Pauline in a more detached sense. Mater was her touchstone, her support in all things whether articulated or not. Blanche was her mother and the older Michaela got the more responsible she felt for her. Whether that was something common to most daughters, as she suspected it might be, it was a heavy feeling sometimes nevertheless. But Antony. Antony was different. Antony was family. He was as close to her as anyone ever could be. They had confided in each other since they could talk. He had a sensitive nature and a kindness and thoughtfulness that she had never come across in another man, not even in Danny. It was as if Antony could anticipate her every feeling and tune in to it and say the right thing at the right time. Well, most of the time anyway. Michaela still smarted when she remembered Antony's lecture in the sand dunes and Simon nodding off in his baggies in the shade. But of course as she knew now and knew then too, Antony had been right to remonstrate. She was being a bitch in no uncertain terms.

She and Antony had slept together for the first time

when they were fifteen, and it had been at Harriet and David's one Sunday afternoon. It had not been a big success and they had giggled with nerves quite a lot of the time. And then their aunt and uncle had come home prematurely and caused a panic, both of them grabbing at their jeans and fleeing into different rooms to dress. Then there had been the awful moment when they discovered in their rush they had picked up each other's jeans by mistake and they had both looked ridiculous all through supper. She had had to turn up the bottoms and tie a belt round her waist, while Antony's long sweatshirt had fortunately covered the buttons that wouldn't close. Janus had noticed. Janus had sat watching them over a pile of dark green broccoli, not saying anything, just watching with a shocked face.

Michaela's feelings for Antony had confused her then and they still did. She needed him, she knew that much, but in what capacity she was never very sure for too long at a time. Michaela had never lacked for admirers and there were long periods of involvement for both of them with other people where they both seemed to cope and enjoy and feel contentment. Antony and Danny had become good friends in the end. As long as she and Antony touched base every now and then, it was usually enough, but lately, it appeared, they both wanted more and it disturbed her. She knew she simply did not have energy for complications of the heart. She had tried to talk to Antony about this after the phonecall, but it had been the wrong time and the wrong emotion and he had gone away with his hands in his pockets and a frown on his face that would have had her worried if she hadn't felt so wretched. There were an awful lot of men in her life at the moment, dead and alive, and they were all giving her trouble.

And Pauline had gone blithely back to Tertius.

Michaela sat watching the gulls wheeling in the sky and thinking about Antony. We are too close, perhaps, she told herself. It's not good to get this close to people. She did not know quite where she fitted into Antony's consciousness, but she knew she was somewhere near its core. She nestled there, aware of it, like a splinter in his flesh.

With Antony gone reluctantly home, Michaela had tried to do some deep breathing exercises in the bath that the health and beauty editor had been explaining to them over papaw chunks that morning. She sat in the bath with her arms resting on her knees and breathed in slowly to the count of ten, trying to think of a beautiful colour. All she could manage was a kind of dark red paisley pattern and she couldn't even get past five without Tommy's hoarse whisper breaking through her concentration. Justice, he'd said. Justice. Why? Since when was he so interested in justice? And what had he cared about Crispian Younghusband anyway? He should have been the last person to care about him.

'Phew – what a pong!' Crispian Younghusband is holding his nose and grinning round at everybody. His socks are fat bunches round his ankles and his bare legs are covered in mosquito bites, livid pink weals that have been scratched raw.

'Well, I *like* the smell of rotting peaches,' Pauline says, looking up to the top of the peach tree. 'I think it's a *nice* smell, Crispian Younghusband.'

'I don't mean the peaches,' he says. 'I mean *him*.' The sun is glinting off his glasses as he stretches back his head. Tommy's feet are dangling just above them.

He is sitting on one of the lower branches, reaching through the leaves to the small green and orange fruit. These ones in the shade don't seem to be ripening as well as the ones in view of the sun right at the top, the ones that the birds have ripped open and strewn upon the ground. All around them lie squashed bits of fruit. Crispian Younghusband's sandal has soft green stuff all around the heel. Tommy's feet are black and sweaty and they scramble for purchase on the next branch up. The leaves rustle and bend and a hand comes through with three small peaches in its grasp.

'I wouldn't touch those,' Crispian Younghusband says loudly. 'You could get a disease. My dad says you can get a deadly disease from touching someone's germs just with your fingers. And that klonkie has a lot of germs.'

It is not clear whether Tommy has heard him, but Michaela has. Her eyes are silver slits and she steps up to Crispian Younghusband until she is almost touching him. 'What did you call him?' she says very softly.

Pauline pauses in her sorting out of peaches. She has had a notion to try and make peach marmalade from this batch. She looks apprehensive. Crispian Younghusband is proud of his new word, his grasp of the local lingo.

'Klonkie,' he says clearly. 'Goffel. My dad calls them goffels. It's —'

'Disgusting,' Michaela breaks in, and her voice is even lower. 'Obscene, like you, Crispian Younghusband. Don't think you can come to this country and parcel people up with neat little racist labels that you can post back to England with your pen-friend letters. Don't think you have a right to talk about people in revolting language just because you have a fat white skin. And *don't* think just because the person you are talking about hasn't jumped out of this tree and split you in two with his bare hands, which is what you deserve – *don't* think he can't hear you.'

Pauline starts juggling desperately with three small green peaches. She can't bear to look at Crispian Younghusband's face. There is a flurry in the tree above them and Tommy springs to the ground. He puts a handful of peaches in her basket and then he walks away, slowly, stopping a little way off to look back with a long, strange stare. Crispian Younghusband is polishing his cricket ball on his shorts. Michaela has not moved. It looks as if she is preparing to butt Crispian Younghusband between the eyes with her forehead.

For once he is trying to stand up to Michaela. Crispian's dad is a powerfully invigorating force when his racial stereotypes are brought into play. 'He's rubbish, anyway,' he says, swallowing. 'He steals hubcaps and sells them down the road, I've seen him.'

'I gave them to him,' Michaela says haughtily, Michaela who doesn't know what a hubcap is exactly. 'I gave him *all* my hubcaps to sell.'

· 14 ·

They decided to travel up to Stillwaters in three cars. Michaela, Susan and Janus squeezed into Janus's sports car, with The Dog taking up most of the space in her round and cumbersome basket. Michaela always worried about The Dog on longish trips with her brother. She had visions of her being blown out like a packet on the wind as it tore through their hair when Janus put his foot flat and drove with the hood down. Antony, who hadn't approved of this trip from the beginning, threw excuses at them until Michaela got stern. He was busy developing pictures for his overseas assignment but he undertook to catch them up, although with Janus's driving, this was unlikely. And Pauline had phoned Michaela in a strangled voice and told her that Tertius knew all and despite her admittedly feeble protestations, was insisting on coming up with them too. He was so appalled by the whole business that he felt only a strong posse of men had any hope of succeeding with Frans. Clearly, he didn't feel that Janus and Antony made up a good enough posse on their own. Pauline planned to try to calm him down with music and apple muffins on the way there.

It was a clear, sun-filled morning, with birdsong

and a strong hint of autumn in the trees they passed, and Michaela tried to concentrate on the fresh breeze on her face and ignore the feelings of misgiving which she hadn't been able to shake off since Blanche had set this whole dubious expedition in motion. And it was undeniably exhilarating, sitting up front in Janus's fast car with the roar of the engine mixing with the wind in her ears and Tommy's rasping voice receding into the distance with every mile they put between them.

'How can you be sure it was Tommy?' Janus had raised an eyebrow when she finally got to tell him. 'How on earth did you manage to recognise his voice?'

'What do you mean?'

'Well,' Janus pointed out, 'how often did you have a conversation with him back then, I mean a real conversation with whole sentences and things? When you think about it? Tommy never *talked* to anyone.'

Janus was right, of course. Tommy had communicated using a guttural series of grunts and gestures. These, they believed later, had all been part of his cover and very convincing too. But it was true: none of them had ever had anything like a meaningful two-way discussion with the pinball wizard. Still, having decided, Michaela was stubbornly sure it was him. Aside from the voice and the personal information, it was the only logical conclusion and Michaela needed some logic in this crazy situation. At this stage in the cat and mouse game, if that was what it was, Michaela hadn't worked out whether it would be a good or a bad move to call his bluff, to let him know she knew who he was. That last time, when she had blurted out his name, she had immediately regretted it, feeling instinctively that it might be wiser to at least have one card to play in case of a real emergency. She hoped the cousins would have an opportunity to discuss the situation again over the weekend, although Tertius being there now might be a bit of a stumbling block. They had all agreed it would be a good idea to get Michaela out of town and regroup, as it were. And Stillwaters always had a calming effect on even the most troubled soul.

In the end they had told Mater they were going. It was Antony who had put his foot down. 'We cannot go to Stillwaters behind Mater's back,' he told Blanche with such an air of decision that even she had backed down. 'I won't go along with it under those conditions. I wouldn't go along with it anyway except that —'

'Except that you know our intentions are sound, and that we are only thinking of Mater,' Blanche interrupted. 'Antony, darling, you know as well as I do that this is an ill-starred affair and that Mater simply isn't thinking rationally. She's seventy years old and at seventy your perspective on life begins to blur at the edges.'

Privately Antony was of the opinion that Mater's perspective had never been sharper and that Blanche's had always been conspicuously fuzzy, but he had to admit, deep down, that he was not yet quite comfortable with Mater's marriage plans. For that reason, he had agreed to go along, that and the fact that Tertius's imminent involvement needed urgent monitoring.

Mater said she was sorry she was going to miss them. She would leave everything open for them and Frans would be there, of course, to keep an eye on things. 'Of course,' Blanche said, catching Michaela's eye and pulling a face. They were all in Michaela's kitchen, drinking boxed wine and eating spaghetti. Each one of the cousins had drawn the line at calling Mater themselves. Sometimes Blanche herself had to follow through. Michaela was glad to have everyone there, filling her house. She lived in fear of the knock at the door and the sight of plainclothes detectives waving a piece of Crispian Younghusband beneath her nose. This way she could at least get Janus to answer the door.

Mater had been cautiously receptive to the idea of a wedding outfit and touched at Blanche's unexpected thoughtfulness. She had been planning to ask Jannie Brand's wife to run her up something, but hadn't yet got round to telling the Brands her news.

'Whatever could be stopping her?' Janus murmured.

Jannie Brand was one of the last remaining loyal members of the Afrikaner Broederbond and he held late-night meetings once a month with like-minded recruits in a private room at the hotel. It was a safe bet that Frans wouldn't be invited to join the circle.

Blanche was getting carried away, completely losing sight at the prospect of a shopping spree of her true intentions. 'We'll do the designer stores,' she told Mater with enthusiasm. 'Berthe Raymond has an end of summer sale on and she caters especially for the older woman – or so I believe. We'll start with Berthe.'

Michaela had a creeping bad feeling about this. She was uneasy about the deception. She could see Mater in ice-lemon silk or cool crisp linen, looking at herself in full-length mirrors, turning this way and that and thinking of Frans. It had disaster potential written all over it. If she hadn't been feeling so feeble lately, she and Antony would have banded together and refused to be a part of it. They could have stood up to Blanche. On the other hand, she did not really believe, in her heart of hearts, that the four of them would now succeed where she and Antony had failed. She did not think that Frans would be amenable to persuasion. Mater might yet get to wear her wedding outfit.

Susan was tucked into the small back seat of Janus's car, surrounded by bags and books and a basket of streaky red apples. She fed small pieces of apple to The Dog through the wooden mesh door of her basket. The Dog's pointed teeth made small grating sounds against the flesh of the fruit in between pathetic mews of terrible captivity. The Dog hated the basket. She paused in between nibbles to lift her chin and cry pitifully in elongated wails of desolation and to thrust her nose against the strap, earnestly trying to get her teeth to the leather fastening.

'Don't worry, The Dog,' Susan tried to soothe her. 'We've not far to go now.'

They were up and over the pass, leaving the hazy spread of the city far behind them. They stopped at the mini-market on the crest to buy rolls of dried apricot and the special sachets of camomile tea Michaela liked. Their dusty scent filled the car until they got going again, when it fled away on the warmth of the wind.

'Look, there's the bus.' Michaela pointed. 'That's the bus Mater will most likely be on. There's only one a weekend.'

'Will she see us? Should I slow down?' Janus asked.

'We'll wave, in case,' Michalea answered. 'And you could slow down anyway, J. We're not trying to break any records here. I'm not in a hurry to get there.'

'I want to arrive before Tertius,' Janus replied grimly, but he lifted his foot off the accelerator all the same.

The big luxury bus whizzed past them down the hill. They all craned their necks but couldn't be sure that they saw Mater among the passengers, although

Susan thought she had caught a glimpse of wings of white hair.

'If Mater knows what we're up to,' Michaela said softly to Janus, feeling a sudden qualm, 'there'll be a message on the farmstall board, you watch.'

'Do you think she does?'

Michaela shrugged. 'She's not a fool. And she should know Blanche doesn't give up easily.'

'Then why did she agree to go into town and leave us to it?'

'We'll soon discover. My guess is because she and Frans are so set on this idea that she's confident we won't be able to influence him.'

'That's what Antony thinks too,' Janus said moodily. 'I don't know what I think.'

'Or it could be that she trusts us,' Michaela added. She looked out at the countryside flashing by. Janus shifted his hands on the leather covered steering wheel and changed gear in silence as they climbed the next hill.

Alongside them ran the railway line, a pair of dull straight lines which gleamed and shivered like two furrows of water when the rails caught the sun. In the distance they could see a goods train, a long row of open-topped carriages, small as a toy set, headed by an electric locomotive. As they drew closer and came parallel with the engine, they could see the driver looking out of the window. He was wearing a green shirt. Michaela waved with both hands and Susan waved her apple in the air. After a moment the man lifted a hand slightly but otherwise made no serious effort to acknowledge their greeting.

'Surly thing,' said Susan. 'You'd think he'd be pleased we said hello.'

'He's probably half asleep,' said Michaela. 'Trains do that to you.'

'He's going at a hell of a speed,' Janus commented, looking at his speedometer. 'We're barely keeping pace.'

'Oh, we'll pass him before the bridge,' Michaela said. 'He has to wind round the koppie and then negotiate that narrow part alongside the river, don't forget. No wishes for us today.'

'Why don't we stop before the bridge and stretch our legs and watch the train go by?' Susan suggested. 'I think The Dog needs to pee.'

The Dog was turning round and round in her basket, uttering desperate staccato cries of anguish. Michaela turned and poked a finger through the basket and tried to scratch her chest. Her fur was as feathery as a bird's and made her think for a moment of the electrician's parrot with its thick grey down. 'Pauline and Tertius are probably not far behind us,' she said. 'We could have our Thermos of coffee and wait for them. Then we'll all arrive together. Antony too. We can keep an eye out.'

Janus slowed down a little while Michaela shifted the bags at her feet and started pulling out items of sustenance. A fruitcake, already sliced, and some thick plastic mugs. 'There's a picnic place just down here, beside the river.'

There was mottled sunshine and big trees and a clearing with concrete benches and a table. The grass around the table was long. Nobody stopped to picnic on the roadside much these days. The country was full of bandit stories, kids with AK-47s who stepped out of the foliage and took all your belongings and sometimes killed you. Michaela refused to bow to such pressure, she told Janus briskly when he looked dubious, but she allowed him to keep the engine running for a few minutes while they looked around. It was utterly silent down here, and very still, out of the wind and the traffic. The river ran past them, dark brown and full of round white pebbles. Susan immediately got out of the car and took The Dog across the road and down the gravelly slope. 'Let's look for tadpoles,' she said. 'Tadpoles for your tea.' The Dog was delirious with freedom and she jumped and trotted in Susan's wake, chirruping contentedly.

The railway line hugged the cutting on the other side of the river, winding tightly up against the mountain, carving a path through the granite rocks. The passage was very narrow here and everything echoed, even the teaspoons on the tabletop. They could hear the train coming in the distance, in a steady rhythm that shook the ground beneath their feet and made the Thermos flask rattle.

Michaela cupped her hands round her mouth. 'Bring The Dog back, Suze,' she called. 'She'll be terrified when that train comes round the bend.'

'I'll hold her,' Susan shouted back. 'She'll be OK.'

It was peculiar how it happened. Talking about it later, Michaela said how she had heard about how things that happened very quickly actually appeared to happen in slow motion at the time. Like terribly spectacular motor racing accidents that they slowed down on television, the better to show the viewer the dislodged wheel arcing through the sky and the ragdoll driver cartwheeling end over end. She had heard people who had witnessed accidents say how they had stood and watched it all unfold so slowly before them until there it lay, the debris of someone's life strewn in pieces of rubber and metal across a road.

So it was with the little goods train that came speeding into view, leaning into the mountain in a shimmer of distant heat. One minute it was bearing down on them with confidence and the next it seemed somehow to falter as they watched it, and then gradually, slowly, begin to bend. The engine turned as if to cross the river towards them and behind it two carriages stood up on their ends in a macabre dance of clashing, winking, screaming steel. Michaela didn't know whether it was she making the ghastly noise, or whether it was the mountainsides reverberating with the ripping sound of metal being torn apart, which was magnified a million times by the closeness of rock. But somehow Susan responded to her name and she shot back across the road and stood holding onto Janus, terrorstruck, as huge pieces of rolling stock skidded and twisted towards them, along the shallow trickle of water between the river's two banks.

'Jesus,' Janus said. 'Jesus *Christ*.'

Michaela was shaking. Her teeth were chattering in her head. She grabbed hold of Susan and they all clung fast to each other. The silence that followed suddenly seemed more deafening than the cacophony of what had gone before. The engine and the two carriages that had so inexplicably jumped the rails were lying in a huge distorted heap about two hundred yards up the river in the stony water. The rest of the carriages, looking small and sheepish, remained up above them on the track, as if waiting patiently for someone to come along and hook them up again and send them on their way. Cars were beginning to pull off the road and people were getting out and running across to have a look.

And then they saw the driver in his green shirt. It gave them quite a shock to see this sudden sign of life. The whole spectacle had been such a clanging together of pure steel and metal, like an enormous sculpture clashing its brutal way into existence, that they were startled by the sudden realisation that all this contortion of tangled shapes had been under the control of a human hand. The driver emerged from behind the engine. He was dragging one foot but otherwise seemed upright. He splashed through the river, walking without purpose or direction, and shaking his head as though to clear it of a ringing in his ears. Michaela noticed suddenly that one of the cars which had stopped was Tertius's and she caught a flash of Pauline running across the road and down the slope with a picnic blanket and a bottle of brandy. Pauline, it seemed, had a blanket for every occasion. She started to run then too, as the driver turned abruptly in their direction and appeared to be about to cross the road without looking to left nor right.

Pauline was there before her and she caught him in her blanket, like a mother grabbing and hugging a runaway child. By the time Michaela reached them, Pauline had the man sitting down on the verge where a crowd was gathering and he was rocking back and forth, crooning something in singsong Afrikaans. Other people were walking up and down in the river bed trying to peer inside the cab for any other sign of life.

'We saw the whole thing,' Michaela said, not addressing anyone in particular. 'One minute there it was chugging round the mountain, and the next —'

'Tertius is phoning for help,' Pauline told her. Tertius had a car phone. 'This man doesn't seem hurt, just in shock. But he doesn't seem able to hear me.' She patted the driver on the cheek but he didn't stop rocking. One of the men in the crowd propped him up while Pauline rather clumsily tipped a capful of Oudemeester between his teeth. Brown liquid ran down the lines in his chin. He was not a young man and his eyes stared.

'Is this the driver?' someone asked.

'I think so,' Janus replied. 'We saw the train from the road earlier on and we saw him at the window in the front cab. But there might have been a second man. I think there usually are two.'

'There is another man in the cab,' a woman said, coming across to them. 'He's unconscious. They can't get him out. His forehead is dented like an Easter egg.' She had on an ugly multi-coloured short-sleeved pullover, with short pieces of purple and red wool that stuck out all over it like a poisonous spiny fish. She had popping eyes too and a mole beside her mouth. 'This is the second accident we've stopped at today,' she added in what almost sounded like a pleased sort of voice. She would have plenty to talk about over the invoices on Monday.

There was quite a traffic jam now, with cars backed up right up the rise and beyond. Michaela was suddenly horrified at the sight of their Thermos and mugs and fruitcake standing brazenly on the table at the site of the disaster, as if they had settled callously down to watch the proceedings and have their elevenses. Susan seemed to have the same thought simultaneously and she sprinted back and began packing them away with fumbling haste. Meanwhile a second man had appeared who seemed to be attached to the train. He came running along the track from the back of the stationary carriages, slipping and sliding on the incline, in a black jacket and cap. 'Jikkel stikkel,' he said when he reached the group at the roadside. '*Kerneels.*' He was out of breath from running and had to take several sips from

Pauline's brandy before he was able to fill them in on details of the train's destination and passengers. There had just been the three of them, he in the back carriage and Kerneels the driver and his apprentice, the man still haplessly pinned in the engine.

Two traffic officers and a police van had suddenly materialised and they set about getting the cars moving and on the road again. The train driver and his colleague were helped to a traffic officer's car, Pauline discreetly but firmly tugging her blanket away before the door slammed. There was nothing more for them to do. The man in the black jacket had displayed marked reluctance to relinquish the brandy bottle and it seemed churlish to wrest it away from him somehow, so Pauline left it behind and walked with Michaela back to Janus's car.

'What a business,' she said. 'I didn't know trains could do that.'

Michaela was still shaking a little. Janus put an arm round her shoulders. 'Let's move on,' he suggested. 'Antony's bound to be stuck in all this traffic for a good while yet. Let's get going.'

'Are you OK to drive?' Pauline asked him.

'Fine.' Janus still didn't want Tertius to get there before them.

The cop waved them into the traffic and they drove on down the winding turns through the cuttings. Round the corner all was serene and the river undisturbed. The sun shone and the water murmured over the stones. And then they were climbing steeply again and turning away from the river onto the flat, wide highway where pale brown grass stretched away from them as far as the eye could see.

'Oh, Mum!' Susan clutched frantically at Michaela's

shoulder. 'The Dog! She's gone – we left The Dog behind!'

Janus heeled over to the side of the road and braked. They sat and stared, aghast, at one another. The empty cat basket was on the floor at Susan's feet. She remembered a sudden raking of claws on her arms and they all looked down at two long red stripes from elbow to wrist. They were beginning to smart painfully and Susan's eyes filled with tears. 'I got a fright when the train started kind of folding up with all that noise,' Susan said. 'And The Dog just leapt out of my arms. I couldn't hold her. Oh, Mum!'

'We'll go back,' Michaela said. 'Janus, turn around.'

Janus didn't even attempt to argue. He knew probably better than anyone what The Dog meant to Michaela and Susan. The Dog was no ordinary cat.

It took them an hour. First they had to explain The Dog to the sceptical policeman whose English wasn't too proficient, and then ask the traffic cop if they could park their car in the clearing. They talked to everybody still hanging around. They walked up and down the river near the train calling. 'The Dog! The Dog!' Susan cried, tears starting from her eyes. 'Come, kitty!' There was no sign, no answering chirrup. No fat, fluffy ball bounding from the bushes into their arms. The Dog was gone.

It was a sombre little group that drove slowly up the rise towards the farmstall. Susan was still crying copiously into a pile of paper napkins. Michaela sat bolt upright, staring straight ahead and thinking of Danny and a kitten with one eye, soft as chamois leather.

They hardly noticed the farmstall board until Janus braked hard and pointed. The quote was from Plutarch's *Lives* and it said 'It is circumstance and proper timing that give an action its character and make it either good or bad.' POTATOES SOLD HERE. JACARANDA CANDLE HOLDERS – WONDERFUL GIFT.

'Oho,' said Janus, putting his foot down again, 'Plutarch, eh? We have been warned.'

When they drove into the gate Tertius's Mercedes was parked in the shady spot beside the fence and he and Pauline were pacing about on the front lawn.

'What kept you?' Pauline asked anxiously. 'We didn't expect to be here so long before you.'

'The Dog's gone,' Susan said dully, before breaking into fresh spasms of hiccuping tears.

'Oh, no,' Pauline said. 'And Frans isn't here either. He's gone into the village with Juanita. And where the hell is Antony? Nothing's going right, Michaela.'

Shaken already by the train smash and The Dog's disappearance, the afternoon wore wearily on, with Tertius's attitude of dark anticipation casting a definite pall over all of them. Michaela, who wanted mostly to talk about Tommy and Crispian Younghusband, felt frustrated with Tertius around. It wouldn't have done to have him feeling he was part of that intrigue. One family skeleton was enough. From so many years of repressing the Crispian Younghusband incident, Michaela now found to her dismay that she wanted compulsively to bring his name into every aspect of conversation, as if by doing so she could in some way neutralise the poisonous effect he was having on her system.

To kill time, they all went for a walk along the riverbank at low tide, continually scanning the road for signs of Antony as they went. Now laid bare, the flat brown rocks were slippery and the water lapping at their base was cold and oily. Michaela pulled her jeans up to her knees and walked along in the shallows, enjoying the rough, icy grit on the soles of her feet, preferring the solid feel of it to the deceptive shiny slabs which were treacherous as ice. She had experienced many a sudden and ignominious descent onto her rear end after a misplaced step. The rocks were an ugly brown and slimy as seaweed.

'Where does Frans stay in the village?' Tertius asked suddenly, stopping to skim sharp corners of flint across the water.

'Um —' Pauline said nervously, looking at Michaela.

'The streets don't have names,' Michaela stalled. 'It's a case of down this one, across the next and the third house on the right after the clump of fynbos and the Valentine family's goats.'

Tertius looked sceptical. 'There must be a number or something,' he said.

'Probably,' Janus said unhelpfully. 'But we don't know it.'

'Why do you ask?' Pauline said. She had her long skirt tucked into her pants and was sticking her big toe into the sand bubbles that appeared in the wake of the outgoing tide.

'What is the good of waiting around here?' Tertius replied impatiently. 'It seems to me we're losing time. How do we know that the man is going to put in an appearance tomorrow anyway? You know how it is when the madam's away.' He was perfectly serious.

'The Barberton sisters are really into their skiing, aren't they?' Pauline said, as a motor boat took off from the opposite bank. They could all see the Kerry blue sitting in front with a long pink strip of tongue waving out of the corner of its mouth like a tape measure.

'And Saturday night is their night,' Tertius went on

undistracted. 'He'll have a *babbelas* tomorrow and be resting up somewhere in the shade. We'll get no sense out of him if we leave it till then.'

Where was Antony? Michaela turned and shaded her eyes. All they could see on the road was a farm bakkie loaded with vegetables and a boy with a boogie board, trudging home.

'I don't think Frans is much of a drinker, Tertius,' Janus said. 'And he goes to church first thing on Sunday morning.'

'He'll be over after that, Mater said,' Pauline added, with more assurance than she felt, although she knew she had to reinforce what Janus was saying, despite the risk to life and limb. Tertius's tone was making her uneasy. She was finely attuned to every nuance of Tertius's speech patterns and she could tell he was growing irritable. He had not come to Stillwaters to paddle and throw stones. Or not at the river, at any rate.

The motor boat splashed past them in a riot of spray, heading out towards the river mouth, one Barberton sister holding on grimly behind in a black wetsuit, bathing cap and goggles. She looked like Amelia Earhardt out of context. The Kerry blue gave a yelp and a scamper when Janus threw a branch into the water, causing the boat to rock wildly.

'Don't tease,' Michaela reprimanded him. 'You could cause a painful accident. The Barberton sisters are no spring chickens.'

They turned to go back to the house and as they did Janus said, 'There he is now – about time,' and Antony's car came into view across the bridge.

Pauline, who had sharper eyes than Michaela without her glasses, could see immediately that Antony was not alone. The passenger window was wound down and a slim brown arm rested along its sill. She looked at Michaela with a sinking heart, but Michaela was gazing eagerly towards the bridge. Things were looking up now that Antony had arrived. A deteriorating weekend might yet be salvaged.

'Who's the floozie this time?' said Tertius, but no one was listening.

The sun was beginning to sink behind the hills and long shadows turned the blue of the river into a moody grey. They reached the house just as Antony emerged from the side door and took the steps to the lawn two at a time. 'There was a train derailed a way back,' he told them. 'Sorry we're late, but I had to stop and take some pictures, it was too much to resist. It was right deep down in the cuttings, almost carved into the granite and the riverbed. Amazing. Amazing images. We stayed for ages.'

Michaela stopped where she was. 'We?' she said blankly.

'I brought Emma,' Antony said casually. 'Emma's back in town.'

Antony had had one truly serious girlfriend in his life. Her name was Emma Posthumous-Meijes, a sallow girl with poise and blue-black hair. She was someone important in the cosmetics industry and had flown off to Holland a couple of years back, leaving Antony closeted in his darkroom with a wistful look that had clung to him for months.

'Emma,' Michaela repeated in a dejected voice. Emma was no Nancy, no leggy model to be dismissed whenever she decided it was time. Emma meant that Antony took the steps two at a time and didn't focus his eyes directly on her.

'Emma!' Janus said heartily. 'Well, that's a surprise. Emma – good.'

Antony smiled at all of them. 'She's putting some camomile tea in a pot,' he confided. 'She found a box in the kitchen. Emma's big on herbal stuff.'

Michaela felt as if her smile was stuck on her face with glue. She simply couldn't get it off. Antony wasn't even doing this to be bloody minded after the last time she had told him to forget for once and for all a relationship with her. Antony looked heartbreakingly happy.

It was difficult to dislike Emma and nobody did. They found her curled in a chair, petite and neat as a doll. A tray with several cups and a pot with a tea cosy on it were on the table in the front room. She unfurled her delicate legs as they trooped into the room, Michaela feeling enormous and clumsy and ungracious at the aroma of camomile flowers which greeted them.

'Emma,' she said, sticking out a hand. 'How are you? Welcome back.'

Antony smiled and smiled. Then, 'Where's Frans?' he said suddenly, collecting himself. 'Have we missed the fun and games?'

'Be serious,' Michaela answered crossly.

'We saw him only briefly,' Pauline said. 'Tertius and I got here first and Tertius was about to ... Frans was on his way to the village with Juanita. It wasn't really the right moment ...' She looked awkwardly at Emma.

'I've filled Emma in,' Antony told her, 'on the salient aspects of this unfortunate business. She –'

'I've no doubt Emma has some useful insights to share with us,' said Michaela roughly. 'But we haven't had the best day so far. We watched that whole train accident happen right before our eyes, Antony, you know, and then The Dog ran away in the commotion and we haven't been able to find her. It's probably just as well Frans wasn't here. I don't think any of us would have been truly capable of handling the situation with any finesse.'

'Finesse isn't the word I would have ...' Janus murmured, sliding a look at Tertius, who stood peering suspiciously into the china cup Emma had handed him.

Susan came heavily into the room. She had lagged behind down at the river, reluctant to show Antony her tears. But when she saw him, they filled her eyes all over again and he moved across to her swiftly. 'Oh, Suze,' he said. 'The Dog. I'm so sorry.'

'If she was younger,' Susan gulped, 'perhaps she would have found her way home, like in the *Incredible Journey*, but she's not. She's an old lady. She's got arthritis in her back paws, for fuck's sake.'

'Susan,' Michaela said halfheartedly. She'd been thinking about arthritic paws too, but now she was thinking about Emma and how Emma wouldn't ever say anything vulgar or crude. Nor would Emma have been responsible for mouldy metatarsals in a boiler room. She also had perfect teeth, two even rows as small as a child's.

'So you saw the train happen,' Antony said, pulling Susan on to his lap. 'Was anyone hurt?'

'No,' Michaela answered him. 'Not badly anyway.'

'Except for the apprentice trapped in the cab, remember,' Pauline said. 'The dented head and the breastbone impaled on steel.'

'Oh, yes,' said Michaela. 'Who wants some fruitcake?' She went off to the kitchen and Janus followed her.

'What's she doing here?' she hissed as soon as

they were out of earshot. 'Why does Antony keep doing this, J?'

'To annoy you?' Janus said drily. 'Come on, Mick. Antony's always been partial to Emma.'

'Well, I don't see how she thinks she can just come swanning back into his life and expect to pick up where she left off,' Michaela said. 'It's not fair.'

Not fair to whom, Janus wondered, watching his sister hack the sliced cake into smaller pieces and pile them untidily onto a rose-bordered plate which was losing the gilt round the edges. He looked at her fondly and sighed. Michaela almost sounded back to normal. He didn't like it when she was anxious and uncertain as she had been too often of late. Michaela always needed something to be mildly annoyed about. It gave an edge to her tongue.

They went back into the front room. 'Where's Tertius?' Michaela immediately asked.

'He went for a drive,' Pauline replied. She put a hand to her mouth 'Oh. Oh, hell.'

'Pauline!' Michaela was exasperated. She put the plate down and went to stare out of the door. 'Oh, well, he'll never find the place at dusk. The goats will be safely inside by now and so will Frans if he hears Tertius coming.' News of a white Mercedes in a cloud of dust would have reached Frans's ears long before Tertius located the right street, if he ever did, relying as he would have to do on the expected dumb headshakes of the kids he asked for directions. But if nothing else had alerted Frans to their intentions, he would be well prepared for them by the morning.

Nobody said anything when Tertius finally came back with a bag of wood and charcoal for the fire. They sat out on the boathouse roof with beers and

Pauline's famous cheese twists and listened to the nightbirds calling, while Janus and Antony turned pieces of chicken slowly over the coals.

'Hi.' Susan watched Frans back the small green tractor out of the shed and turn it, rattling and squeaking, on the rutted road. 'Can I have a ride?'

'Jump up.' Frans put out a brown hand and Susan held onto it as she lifted a leg. It was as steady and solid as a branch.

'This is so cool,' she said. 'I love Stillwaters before the sun is up, don't you? I love the smell of the grass and the way everything is so icy wet. Oh, and the giant kingfisher was on the end of the jetty just now. His call woke me up.'

'Kek-kek-kek-kek.' Frans' imitation was perfect and Susan clapped her hands.

Susan looked at the river lying silky smooth alongside them. 'It's almost as if the river hasn't woken up yet, isn't it?' she said. 'When it's still in shadow like that. It needs the sun to warm it before it can begin to move. It's like it's waiting for a sign.'

Frans pushed his hat back off his forehead. 'It's always like this when the change of the seasons is coming on us,' he said. 'Living things slowing down for the turn.'

'I can't wait for the wedding,' said Susan. 'I've never been a bridesmaid before so Mater had better not stop me now. I've given up on my mum wanting to get married again and it will be such fun to be bridesmaid for my *great-grandmother* – imagine!' She laughed. 'It's outrageous fun. Florida wants to be a bridesmaid too. We've been planning what to wear.'

Frans looked down at her and smiled slightly. The

tractor took a sudden dip into a rut and struggled out again.

'Flowers, lots of flowers. I think weddings should have millions of flowers. But not the stiff kind you get in shops that look as if they're made of icing. I want wild flowers from up on the hills and we're going to braid them into each other's hair. And Mater's, if she'll let us. And we're going to pick arum lilies from the marshy bit over by Mr Brand's place and put them in pots all over the house. Mater loves arums. They're so dignified, she says. Are you getting married in the Stilfontein chapel, because if you are that organ was broken the last time Mum and I were in it. It just wheezed dust when they tried it out. I think you should ask the priest about it in good time because you have to have music. I'm not so good at hymns, though, you and Mater will have to choose those. Do you think Mater will wear a long dress? I hope so.'

Frans looked at Susan's eager face. He sighed gently. 'The ceremony will be very quiet,' he told her in a soft voice. 'There will be no fuss. No fuss at all.' He slowed the tractor for a turn into a field. Susan jumped down and opened the gate for him. 'There's Antony,' she said. 'I'd better go in for breakfast.'

They had rusks and muesli and some more camomile tea and when the sun was climbing in the sky Antony suggested that Susan take Emma out on the river in *Christmas Present*. Emma wore a big white hat and Factor 30 sunblock across her nose and cheeks. Susan put on her costume and took a flask of orange juice and a fishing net. She loved to scoop through small shoals of silver fish and watch them twist and jump before she let them go.

'I can't talk to Frans surrounded by potatoes,' said

Michaela. 'Or lucerne for that matter. Antony, if we have to do this, for pity's sake go and invite him up to the house for coffee or something.'

'I wonder why he hasn't gone to church,' Pauline said, watching the tractor. They could hear the peal of bells coming clearly from beyond the hill which hid Stilfontein village from their view.

'He must know what's coming,' said Tertius with an unpleasant laugh.

'And what's that?' said Michaela, turning quickly. She was growing to dislike Tertius more and more with each encounter. She almost felt like calling the whole confrontation off just because she knew it would irk him. She could see how much he was looking forward to it. He dunked his rusk right up to his fingers and put the whole thing in his mouth. Michaela turned away. 'Go on, Antony,' she said. 'You go.' Had he slept with Emma last night? They had shared a room with two single beds in it. Emma had emerged this morning with her hair in a towel and a white cotton dress that brushed her ankles. Her arms were softly tanned. She had no need for makeup, and Michaela wondered in passing why she had chosen a career in cosmetics when she herself was so flawlessly unadorned. Emma had yawned behind a small brown hand and smiled artlessly at Michaela. 'Goodness me,' she'd said, 'one sleeps so well in the country.'

The swallows were gathering. They swooped in crazy spirals about Antony's head as he walked down to the lucerne field with his hands in his pockets. Lined up in an anxious row, a pace back from the window, the others waited like a chorus line with their cups. They saw Frans climb down from the tractor seat and shake Antony's hand. They saw them converse briefly and

Frans gesture eloquently at the waving green plants all about them. Then they turned and began to walk up towards the house. Instinctively they all took a step backwards, all except Tertius, who put down his cup and rubbed his hands together. He all but licked his lips. Pauline was very pale. Suddenly she turned and gathered the crockery onto the tray. 'I'll put a pot of coffee on,' she said. 'But I can't ... I –' and she vanished into the shadows of the house.

Frans took off his hat as he ducked through the door. He was taller than he seemed out in the fields, taller inside the house at any rate, and very slightly stooped. His black hair was thick and wavy and it looked almost polished.

'*Ja, meneer*,' Tertius greeted him gruffly.

'Miss Michaela.' Frans inclined his head and gave Janus a small smile. 'Beautiful day.'

'Yes,' Michaela murmured. 'Sit down, Frans. Please.'

They sat on the edges of chairs. Tertius remained by the window, leaning against the frame. Michaela asked after Frans's mother, his sister, Juanita and the potatoes. They were all in good health. She almost asked after the tractor and would have if Antony hadn't decided to come to the point because he could see that Tertius was about to.

'We wanted to have a word about this marriage business,' he began, with a hint of apology which made Tertius frown and shift his position. 'We are a little concerned about it.'

Frans looked up at him with an open smiling face. He said nothing.

'It seems to us,' Michaela said, 'that it is a little late in life for Mater to be thinking about marriage again.'

'Some of us are blessed,' Frans replied. He smiled at her.

'Our grandmother is a wealthy woman,' Janus said, looking past his head. 'You are surely aware of this.'

'She is rich in many ways,' said Frans. 'She is fortunate.'

'You mean *you* are fortunate,' Tertius broke in, moving away from the window. 'Getting your dirty hands on —'

Frans turned mild eyes on him. 'Sir?' he said. There was an edge to the word that made Tertius go redder in the face.

'We need to put our minds at rest,' Antony said in a calm, authoritative voice. 'About your reasons for going into this marriage. You are a lot younger than our grandmother and you stand to benefit in many ways. When she dies you will be wealthy. You will have this farm. You will not, I think, have the support and admiration of most of your neighbours along this stretch of river. We need to know that you have thought all of this through clearly. We want to help you see clearly what you are about to undertake.'

'I think I can make him see clearly,' said Tertius with that laugh again. Antony was being far too polite for his liking or understanding of the situation. 'How would a fat smack help you think, *meneer*?'

'Tertius,' said Michaela, looking round for Pauline. 'I don't think —' She turned and glared at him. Pauline was nowhere to be seen.

Frans's smile was beginning to falter. He looked confused. There was a long thread unravelling in the band of his hat.

'We think Mater might be making a mistake,' Michaela said gently, putting a hand on Frans's arm.

'But it's not too late to fix it,' Janus put in quickly. 'It will probably be a better idea if you were to forget about this marriage, Frans, altogether. Mater is too old to go making such decisions on her own.'

Frans looked at each of them in turn. He began to get to his feet. 'Winter and summer,' he said, turning his hat round in his hands. 'Winter and summer we are here, when you are away in the city doing city things —'

'And when our backs are turned you take a lonely old woman and worm your way into her affections,' Tertius butted in. *'Dis 'n skande*, a scandal.'

Frans looked at Michaela. 'It was I who was the lonely one,' he said.

Tertius made an impatient noise. It looked as if Frans was getting away. 'Listen,' he said brusquely. 'Listen, my friend. *Dis witmense se goed in hierdie huis. Wat soek jy hier? Daar's niks vir jou hier nie. Jy behoort anderkant, anderkant die bult. Moenie dink dat jy hier kan kom inpas nie.*'

Tertius stood with his chin thrust out and his hands making fists at his sides. Belligerent as a boxer, he waited for Frans to crumple. Michaela put her face in her hands. Pauline slipped in, put a pot of coffee on the table and slipped out again. Nobody moved a muscle. Slowly Frans turned and looked Tertius up and down.

'I know where I belong,' he said in a low voice. 'I know on which side of the hill I fit in. And I know what colour I am. I also know when to hold my tongue and when to keep my nose out of my neighbour's business. You are not family, *meneer*. This is not your affair.'

'Frans —' Michaela started forward.

'It's all right, Miss Michaela. I know you mean no harm, but here's the thing. Your grandmother does not make decisions on her own. She has not done so for many years. She has me. We make decisions together — the two of us.'

Michaela felt ashamed. Suddenly she could not bear to be here, in the same room with this man and his unravelling hatband and his dignity. She saw them all as he must see them, interfering, grasping, threatening, deceitful. If ever they had imagined they could slip up here to Stillwaters and clear this matter up in a matter of a few brisk sentences, how terribly stupid they had all been. It was no good blaming Blanche. Quite simply, they should all have known better.

Frans was putting on his hat. 'Thank Miss Pauline for the coffee,' he said, and he walked to the door and down the steps, striding back to his tractor like a man half his age.

When Frans had gone and after Antony had had to restrain Tertius from going out after him, Janus went through to the kitchen and found Pauline eating yoghurt, leaning with her back against the sink.

'Don't tell me,' she said. 'I got the gist.'

Janus groaned. 'Talk about a fuck up,' he said. 'Never again.'

Pauline looked at him. 'You know I've never been very good at facing up to things,' she said. 'I wouldn't have been any good in there. Not when Tertius started —'

'I know. It's all right. You couldn't have made any difference.'

Pauline rinsed her spoon and dried it with the dishtowel. 'You want to hear something strange?' she said.

'I don't know.'

'Something strange happened while you were all in

there making fools of yourselves. Something happened to me.'

'What?' Janus looked around. The kitchen seemed in perfect order.

'I was standing here eating a piece of fruitcake and watching the wagtails on the grass over there and hearing Tertius's voice, and ... It wasn't even what he was saying, just the *sound*, the *tone*. And I thought to myself: I don't want to listen to that voice any more, that sound, that tone. And what's more I don't have to. I'm going to leave Tertius, Janus. For good. I'm going to leave him today.'

Pauline didn't mind that Tertius believed it was the way he had treated Frans that had made her angry and peremptory in a way he'd never seen her before. If that was what he wanted to believe it was all right with her. She packed her overnight bag and put it into Janus's car and suggested that Tertius drive home on his own. Everyone else had backed off and he had packed up and left, leaving a half drunk cup of coffee on the table. Then Emma and Susan had come in and forced everyone into the river for a swim. They floated on their backs, bobbing effortlessly towards the bridge on the incoming tide. The water was quite warm but the wind when they climbed out onto the rocks brought goosebumps up on their arms. Antony dried Emma with a beach towel and held her hand when they walked back to the house.

Michaela and Susan had no option but to go back to town in Antony's car. Janus was taking Pauline straight home to pack some suitcases before she changed her mind. All the way back Susan hung out of the window, her eyes raking the bushes and gullies for any sign of

The Dog, while Michaela tried not to take part in the conversation Emma kept trying to draw her into, and failed not to notice how a small brown hand touched Antony's every now and then for emphasis. By the time they were home she had forgotten Pauline's bravery and was in as bad a mood as she could be. Never again would she interfere in a relationship, not Mater's and not Antony's. They could all sink or swim without her help.

Susan went straight to bed after calling round the garden for The Dog until she was hoarse. Michaela sat a while in the study with the phone off the hook. Neither Blanche nor Tommy were welcome this evening. She glanced at her letter to Joy Beamish and it struck her as sickly sweet and utterly hypocritical. The poems had been quite unpublishable. It was hopeless of her to give the woman even the most meagre crumb of encouragement. She tore up the letter and began a clean page. 'Dear Joy,' she wrote, 'there is not a line in any of these so-called verses of yours that hasn't been cribbed from somewhere else, and rather badly at that. I suggest that you attempt to do something a little more original in future. Or give up poetry altogether. It is a difficult medium at the best of times, and frankly, you are bad at it.'

She put the letter in an envelope and sealed it, writing Joy's name and address with an emphatic flourish on the front.

· 15 ·

Janus took Pauline and Mater to see Harriet and David off at the airport. Their leaving was more subdued than their homecoming, and they all clung to each other outside the departure lounge. Mater, who had been shopping all morning with Blanche, looked tired and a little confused by the crowds and the hustle and bustle of people coming and going with suitcases and backpacks and trolleys clashing. She leaned on a walking stick, the first time any of them had seen something like an admission from Mater of advancing years.

David had five jars of his favourite brand of anchovy paste in his hand luggage and two of Mrs Ball's chutney. Pauline could not afford to be tearful with the opening of the club only hours away. Janus was taking her past the house on the way back to pick up more clothes and she couldn't waver, not now. Tertius had not tried to contact her and his car was not there when they had driven past earlier in the first of a series of recces.

'That's our flight,' said Harriet, listening. She looked stricken.

'It's gone so quickly,' David said, puzzled. He

stretched, as if waking from a long nap. 'We haven't seen or done or said half the things we intended to. Where did the time go?'

'We'll write,' Harriet said forlornly. 'We'll try to be better correspondents.'

Pauline held out her arms to her mother and they stood in a silent embrace. 'Take care,' she said gruffly, drawing away. 'Call, sometimes, if you like.'

David stooped and gathered Mater up in his long arms. She almost disappeared inside his jersey. 'We'll be thinking of you,' he told her, giving her a little shake by the arms.

They stood, a sad little group, and watched David and Harriet walk away. At the last moment, Harriet turned and gave a salute, a bunched fist in the air. Whether this was directed at them or at the country in general wasn't readily apparent but Janus, Pauline and Mater smiled at each other. Pauline wiped at the corners of her eyes with the end of her scarf.

'Well,' she sighed, 'there they go. Australia is home now, I guess.'

'Let's go.' Janus led the way.

Mater walked slowly, leaning on her stick more than seemed necessary. She was wearing a new pale green skirt and blouse and she had a deeper green Alice band keeping back her silver hair. It had sequins on it, dark red and gold. She looked about her with an air of being somewhere else. The car park smelled of aeroplane fuel and they had to wait in the exit queue for fifteen minutes. Pauline sat silently in the back of the car, feeling her cheeks damp with tears. She wasn't sure why she was crying, whether it was for her parents, soon to be settling back in their seats with in-flight magazines and many hours of dislocation ahead of them, or whether it was because she herself was feeling dislocated.

'Janus,' she said, as they hit the highway. 'Let's go straight back to Michaela's, if you don't mind. I can get clothes another day.'

Janus cast her a surprised glance. 'Are you sure?' he asked. 'It's no trouble.'

'I'm sure.' Pauline sank lower in her seat. She wished she were on her way to Australia too, all of a sudden. There was no Tertius in Australia, with his big flat hands. She was afraid of him coming after her, dragging her back to make him dinner.

'What made you decide?' Mater asked her gently.

'To leave? I ... I don't know exactly,' Pauline replied, flickering a look at Janus, who was concentrating on the traffic. 'I suppose it's something I've been subconsciously trying to do for a long time now and yesterday, at Stillwaters, I suddenly knew the time had come to make a break for it.'

'Did you see Frans yesterday?' Mater asked in a flat voice.

'Yes,' said Janus, hesitating a fraction too long. 'We saw Frans.'

Mater sighed. 'So you talked to him,' she said.

Janus shifted uncomfortably. Pauline said nothing.

'Ah.' Mater looked out of the window. Cars swept by them on both sides as Janus weaved in and out. He drove skilfully but very fast. Mater had one hand on her stick, the other gripping the seat beside her legs. 'I thought you might,' she said, smiling sadly. 'And how did it go?'

'It was Tertius. Tertius was abominable,' Pauline said before Janus could respond, suddenly blaming everything on him. 'Tertius tried to strong-arm Frans.'

Janus was silent. He thought Pauline had not heard any of the goings on from her retreat in the kitchen.

'You don't mean . . .?' Mater turned round to look at Pauline.

Pauline hung her head. 'No, nothing like that,' she said. 'He was . . . shall we say . . . direct.'

'Janus?'

Janus swallowed. 'We wanted to discuss the marriage with Frans,' he said. 'To make sure . . . To find out . . . Well, Blanche —'

'Go on,' Mater said frostily.

Janus lifted his hands off the steering wheel. 'It's not going to be an easy ride for him, Mater. You know that you both run the risk of being shunned by all your friends up and down the river. We wanted to make Frans aware of that and to make sure he was as committed to this marriage as you seem to be.'

Mater said nothing, but her lips were a straight, stubborn line in her face. She looked all of a sudden old and shrunken, sitting back against the passenger door, away from Janus and Pauline. She put both hands on her walking stick, smoothing up and down its polished length.

'You are treating us like children,' she said at last in a voice full of weary disappointment. 'And I would ask you to cease immediately. How often do I interfere in your lives? When you make decisions that I might think are not very wise, how often have I come to you and asked you to reconsider before you act?'

Pauline shifted uncomfortably. She was thinking of the club and how Mater had encouraged and supported her, never using any of the arguments others had heaped at her feet.

'You're right,' Janus said feebly. 'It was none of our business.'

'Yes,' said Pauline. 'We had no right to go up there and talk to Frans. We all know that now. We're sorry, Mater. Antony and Michaela are too. They said right from the start —'

'I trust Frans put you right?' Mater permitted herself a small smile and a glance at Janus's profile.

'Oh, he did,' Janus told her, glaring ahead. His neck had gone quite pink. 'Quite right.'

Mater smiled again and looked back out of the window. 'Mind that motorbike,' she told him.

There were faint stars over the harbour and a new moon, a fragile silver crescent in the fading blue-grey of the evening sky. A tug guiding a Taiwanese fishing vessel to a berth outside Greenbacks was causing a slap of oily water against the dockside. Gulls screamed in its wake and a smattering of the crew, in sleeveless vests, rested their tattooed arms on the rails and watched the strolling crowds on the waterfront below. Over everything hung the sharp smell of fish.

There was a queue outside Pauline's, a straggling snake of people, moving restlessly about, talking, sitting down and standing up, strolling across the dockside to the edge of the water and back again. The carefully engineered publicity campaign had reached its target with accuracy. First there had been the teaser campaign run by Janus's agency over a fortnight in the press: 'Pauline's – the hottest lady in town', 'Do yourself a flavour – visit Pauline's'. Then there were the posters plastered all over the Waterfront and beyond since the beginning of last week. 'The legend lives on', they announced, beneath Antony's famous picture of Blanche in profile, head bowed, sitting on a barstool with a microphone in her hands in her lap. That picture, one of a series Antony had done for a concert for returning exiles in 1991, had won him an international award. The original, a poster-sized print, hung in the front room at Stillwaters.

And finally, invitations to the entertainment media and the city's ten best known food critics had been hand-delivered a week ago by Frank and Ernest personally. They had all replied with alacrity and only two of them had pleaded prior engagements.

Pauline's first partner, in a sudden burst of energy and remorse at not having involved himself earlier, had all of a sudden descended on Pauline and found it imperative to persuade her to change the menu three times in as many days. He now sat nervously at a corner table between rushes to the kitchen, drinking tapwater and listening with an air of anticipation to the noise of the swelling crowd outside the doors. It would be standing room only by the time the club opened at nine o'clock, and judgement by his peers would be keenly begun. The delicate spicy aroma coming from the open kitchen door set his taste buds smarting.

At eight-thirty Frank, in midnight blue velvet jacket and with Ernest digging his talons deep into his shoulder pads, appeared outside the club with trays of complimentary cider, with which he passed ponderously among the throng, bowing ostentatiously and murmuring softly in Italian while Ernest held grimly with his curved beak to a corner of his bowtie. It was becoming increasingly apparent that Ernest was not comfortable in crowds. He croaked and groaned and every now and then whimpered like a puppy, pushing the crown of his head beneath Frank's jaw. Women in the queue held out their fingers to him and smiled. Every second person was the plumber come to fix the pipes.

A stiff breeze whipped around the harbour and the awning above Greenbacks flapped and cracked and strained at its supports. Greenbacks was closed tonight – the boys were setting up inside and their manager, in an effort at appeasement, had a good table near the front. Blanche had not yet arrived. She wasn't due to sing before ten o'clock and Blanche knew all about making an entrance.

Inside Pauline was talking things through for a final time with the student waiters, and Janus and Mater topped up the bowls of nuts Ernest had been making free with all afternoon. Frank had constructed a platform for the parrot high up above the stage. He had a bowl of water up there and some sunflower seeds. It seemed that Ernest was all set to become something of a fixture. When Janus had queried this with Pauline, she had just smiled and shrugged and told him that Frank still had some odds and ends to finish off and had agreed to stick around until the end of the month.

'Are you paying him?' Janus asked.

'Oh, yes, I think so,' Pauline said vaguely. She suddenly couldn't recall paying Frank anything so far. Perhaps he was keeping a tally.

Invited guests were arriving and moving to the reserved tables. Mater went across to the one Michaela had taken for them. She was without her stick and had changed into another new outfit and Alice band. Ramrod straight, with her sweep of white hair, she sat with her hands in front of her on the table and looked expectantly at the stage. Some of the food critics had notebooks with them and they nodded to each other and collectively shuddered at the band. The boys were starting up, kicking off with some light, fast background jazz. Pauline, for a moment sitting dreamily at the front entrance watching people come in as if she couldn't quite believe they were real, was startled by Michaela's face at the kitchen door.

'Is this sauce really supposed to be this green?' she hissed into Pauline's ear. 'You asked me to watch it for a minute while you disappeared and it's turning into a witch's brew before my eyes.' Janus was in the kitchen too, with Chloë, who was also watching the sauce with amazement. Her glasses had steamed up with anxiety. Pauline laughed gaily. She was ebullient, carefree, confident in her green sauce. 'It's quite all right,' she told them all. 'Leave it to me. Go on out – don't let Mater sit out there all on her own.'

'She's got Simon,' Michaela told her. 'Shall we keep a seat for you?'

'Oh no.' Pauline waved them away and as they went reluctantly through the kitchen doors, Frank opened the door at the front and a breath of air gushed into the club, and the place began to vibrate with noise and colour.

Michaela slipped into her seat beside Simon. He beamed at her and poured white wine into a frosted glass for her. Mater took her hand and squeezed it hard. 'Is Pauline all right?' she asked. Michaela nodded. Simon was popping nuts into his mouth in a disconcerting rhythm. She looked at the tufts of hair on the backs of his fingers and wondered if it was fair to continue to have him around. There had been a time when she had thought she was getting fond of him, when he had made her laugh and there had been a sense of pleasure in his company. But somehow that time seemed to have been so long ago. So much had happened over the past weeks that she could not share with him, she felt as if she had been away, cocooned in a vacuum all on her own like some sort of experiment in isolation. It was probably unfair to blame him for her continued feeling of anxiety, but where was one to start? You couldn't just throw a child corpse and betrayal and blackmail into a conversation during interval at the movies. This was something one had to work up to over years. How could she share Tommy with him, and Crispian Younghusband, not to mention the quirkiness of a self-righteous grandmother embarking on a marriage no one was able to digest. It was as if everything of importance that had taken place lately was pushing Michaela further and further into herself, like nails in a coffin, and she was struggling to breathe. It was a strain making conversation with an outsider, and Simon was an outsider.

Michaela picked up her glass and touched it to Mater's. 'To Pauline's,' she said, and smiled. Mater smiled back at her and nodded her head. 'To Pauline,' she said.

Michaela had expected Emma but when Antony arrived he was alone. She had kept him a seat but he declined it and walked around the back reaches of the club with his camera, standing near a pillar at the back for most of the time. At ten minutes after ten Michaela began to feel anxious. She had expected Blanche to keep them waiting but suddenly she felt unsure and nervous for her mother. Mater, too, was looking strained. There was such an atmosphere of expectation and excitement that she wondered fleetingly whether Blanche had decided she wasn't able to live up to it. She was also wondering what Blanche was going to wear.

Frank had put up a black velvet curtain on the small stage. Now he came onto the stage from the back, pushing the curtain aside with a flourish. He put Blanche's trademark barstool beneath the yellow spotlight and breathed throatily into the microphone. 'Ladies and gentlemen,' he said with an Italian accent none of the cousins had heard so far, 'I give you – the one and only – the legendary – Blanche Whitehead.'

Michaela and Mater gasped. Scarlet lycra from ankle to bottom and not a stitch of underwear. Admittedly, Blanche was skinny as a scarecrow and there was not so much as a bulge of the stomach to spoil the lines, but such a blatantly sexy outfit was nevertheless still hard to take in. The sequinned top shivered under the lights and Blanche's arms and shoulders were as white as milk. Her auburn hair was caught up at the back with a sequinned headband.

Blanche snatched at the microphone with long painted fingernails and, legs astride, launched straight into 'Nutbush City Limits' while Michaela reached addictively for her glass. After a little while she pulled her eyes away from her mother and Janus's transfixed face and ventured a look around. Every eye, every face was focused on Blanche. There wasn't a sound in the club beside the pulse of the music and the deep resonance of Blanche's show-stopping voice. The lycra did nothing to detract from the quality and range that sent shivers up the arms and had earned her the rapt attention she now once more commanded as she had done for years. Blanche Whitehead's coming out of retirement was going to be a triumph.

Michaela doubted that she would ever retire again.

Antony moved about slowly, taking roll after roll of film, never settling, prowling like an animal. And

Pauline came and went silently too, padding back and forth on her ballet shoes, smiling all the time. The drink flowed and the plates went back empty to the kitchen. Nobody went home.

When Blanche finished her last set with 'Tears in Heaven', accompanied only by an acoustic guitar, Michaela looked across at Mater. She was still sitting up very straight but her eyes were moist and her lips slightly parted. When Blanche vanished abruptly behind the black curtain with a dramatic wave of one white hand, Mater led the applause, standing impulsively and at first alone in the centre of the room. Soon everyone was on their feet, shouting for more. Blanche's encore was without question a demand that had to be met. Michaela knew she had planned a four-minute wait and a new outfit to end off the evening. She waited in trepidation. It surely couldn't be more surprising than the lycra.

Blanche stood behind the curtain, breathing heavily, the sweat run down her neck. She could feel her heart hammering loudly. From down the passage in the small makeshift dressing room she could hear the murmur of the voices of the boys from Greenbacks as they waited for the encore call. On stage, Finney on guitar was running once more through Clapton's bittersweet melody line. Blanche walked softly down the narrow passage towards her friends, a feeling of pure elation moving her feet along.

'We're on, guys,' she heard one of the boys say and sounds of movement, the scuff of shoes and the clink of bottles, swept along the confined space towards her.

'Yup,' said someone – Jeff, keyboards? – 'here goes mutton.'

'Mutton dressed as lamb,' came the instant, practised rejoinder, to a burst of laughter, quickly hushed. It was not a new joke.

Blanche stopped dead. She pressed against the side of the passage and felt a cold tingling beginning at the base of her spine and spreading across her shoulder blades. She caught a glimpse of her own reflection in the glass door of the dressing room before it opened. Her shoulders sagged.

'Oh, the old girl's not so bad,' she heard the bass player say. 'There's nothing wrong with her voice, hey.' He was the kid with the nimble fingers and the waxed dreadlocks. 'I think her bod's in good shape really.' His name was Ricky.

'Yeah – but it's the hands and the neck that are the dead giveaway.' That was the drummer, the boy she liked the most. 'Like an old turkey – shame.'

There was a side door leading onto the alley beside the club and Blanche found her hand on the handle. Grabbing an offcut of the black stage curtain in the other, she leaned on it and it yielded. Quickly she slipped outside and stood in the cold wind, shaking, with the curtain round her shoulders. She rubbed at her arms with her hands.

Inside the crowd had stopped calling for her and were beginning a slow clap. The boys from Greenbacks must be reassembling, she could hear the instruments. Someone played a bar from You Got a Friend.

Waiting at their table, Janus leaned across Chloë and tapped Michaela on the arm. 'Where is she?' he whispered.

'You know Mother,' Michaela whispered back. 'She likes to string it out.' She glanced at Mater, who was dozing with her head back and eyes closed.

After ten minutes and a couple of instrumental numbers, the audience had stopped clapping and were looking round inquiringly for stray waiters. Pauline appeared in the kitchen doorway and stared hard at the stage with her hands on her hips. She had a huge white apron on over her dress. Antony moved across to her and said something. Then Michaela got up and slid over.

'Where's Blanche?' she said. 'Isn't she doing her encore?'

'I'll go and check.' Antony gave his camera to Michaela and went quickly through the curtains on the stage. The boys were faltering. Antony was back within minutes. He frowned at Michaela. 'I can't find her,' he muttered. 'She's not in the dressing room. And the side door is wide open.'

'Oh, for God's sake,' said Michaela. 'What's going on? Pauline, do something.'

Pauline was taking off her apron. She handed it to Chloë on her way past their table, who took it and folded it neatly onto her lap like an item of laundry. Pauline stepped up onto the stage and took the microphone in her hands. She was wearing a deep purple dress with golden threads running through it. She glimmered under the lights and her copper hair shone. Everyone hushed expectantly, waiting for an explanation of the star attraction's sudden non-appearance. Instead, Pauline leaned across and said something to the bass player in a low voice and, slowly at first, in a soft, husky voice, Pauline herself began to sing. Nerves made her tremble slightly and shift the microphone from hand to hand, but Pauline had been blessed with perfect pitch and the notes were pure and true. Usually too shy to sing before anyone other than her cousins and mostly restricting herself to family rounds at Christmas time on the river at Stillwaters, or to singing old folk songs at home with an awkwardly played guitar, Pauline's voice grew steadily stronger as she edged forward on the stage. Nobody stirred. The club was electric with attention. Only Antony, standing in the shadows, was busy with his camera.

Then suddenly, as Pauline moved to the last verse of the song, Frank was there with her on stage with his blue velvet jacket catching the yellow spot. He put a hand on her shoulder and bent his head in to the microphone. They sang the last verse together as if they had been doing this for years, with Frank's light tenor harmonies blending in perfect timing with Pauline's strong melody line. At the end of the song the audience were on their feet as one and yelling for more. After a quick consultation with the band they sang again and again, grinning hopelessly at each other as if they had been waiting for this moment all their lives.

As the last song faded, Michaela got up quickly and slipped out of the front door. She stood outside for a moment, looking around. There were a few people wandering about, but it was close on midnight and most of the other Waterfront activity was on the other side of the dry dock. Then her eyes fell on what she was looking for: like the French lieutenant's woman, Blanche, swathed in a black cloak, was standing on the end of the pier, looking pointedly out to sea.

Michaela walked quietly up to her and leaned beside her on the wooden railing. Beneath their feet, foamy white water churned and twisted.

'You were wonderful,' she told her.

'Yeah,' Blanche said heavily, pulling on a cigarette. 'I know.'

'You wait for the reports in the paper tomorrow.'

'Sure.'

'You'll get better notices than you ever got before.'

Blanche sighed. 'I'm old, Michaela. Before I'm ready, I'm old. There's no escaping the clutch of time. It hits you in the stomach and leaves you gasping for air.'

Michaela put an arm through her mother's. 'Come on,' she said. 'It's time to go home.'

Blanche held back. 'I feel I've let Pauline down,' she said, 'but I couldn't go back. I couldn't go on again. I can't explain . . .'

'Oh, it turned out all right,' Michaela told her, smiling. 'Better than you'd have thought.' She plucked at the material her mother was draped in. 'And what is this?' she said. 'Berthe's androgynous line?'

Blanche rolled her eyes. 'More like Frank's,' she replied. 'Or Ernest's, if you count the bird droppings on the hem.'

Blanche waited at the car while Michaela collected Simon and Mater from inside the club. Simon held her jacket for her. 'What's this?' she said, pulling a piece of white paper, folded, out of her pocket. It was a note and it was addressed to her in upright pencilled letters, all of them capitals.

'YOU ARE BEING WATCHED,' the note said. 'I WATCH YOUR EVERY MOVE.'

'Michaela?' Mater looked at her curiously.

Michaela felt the beat of the music thrum right through her and out the other side. She felt as if she were floating outside of herself, watching unseen rhythms batter at her ribs. Her body felt bruised and tampered with.

'What is it, child?' Mater leaned across to her and touched her hand.

'I —' Michaela's eyes filled with hot, embarrassed tears and she grabbed for her bag. 'Let's get out of here,' she said. As they went, stopping to embrace Pauline on the way out, Michaela could not lift her eyes, nor look around her. She could not have borne it if she had looked into those dead, black eyes that were Tommy's best disguise. She walked stiffly to the door, feeling dirty and defiled, as if someone had been sick down her back.

Michaela had volunteered to drive her grandmother home to Stillwaters the following day. Mater had a pile of clothes in carrier bags on the back seat. 'When Mater comes to town she goes to town,' Blanche had sighed happily, bearing shoeboxes and suits on coathangers out to the car. She seemed jauntier this morning, though tired. And she had picked up a few little numbers herself. For the first time ever, Michaela thought her grandmother was looking frail. She wore cream pants and an aquamarine shirt with small pearl buttons and a high collar, but inside the new clothes, she looked pale and uncertain. At Stillwaters Mater was so much in command, wearing her wide shorts and patched shirts and sandals. Winter and summer she moved around with definition and confidence. Here, in the city, she seemed to lose a sense of identity. She knew she didn't belong here and it showed. She slung a new lambswool jersey across her shoulders although it was a warm day, and she seemed almost to curl back inside it, as if she sought protection.

They had three hours in the car together and Michaela was again grateful for the opportunity to get away. She had felt like a fugitive lately, a criminal on the run, but at least there was some purpose in today, some legitimate reason to be on the move. Blanche had had some notion of trying to persuade Mater to spend more time in town – after all she and Josh still had their house there. The house stood empty above the beach for most of the year, except in the summer season when Mater let it out to a Hungarian couple in their sixties who travelled every year to the warm southern sun. They were due to move out shortly and Blanche, assuming that the cousins would be successfully working on Frans at one end, had attempted to make Mater see the advantage at the other of spending more time closer to the rest of the family. She suggested spending a few days a month at Stillwaters and the rest of the time – what with winter coming on – in town. She was sure Mater would benefit from a different environment.

Blanche was all innocence and persuasion. Mater was sardonic. 'Frans doesn't care much for the city,' she told Blanche flatly.

'Yes, well . . .' Blanche's eyes had grown vague with dissatisfaction. She hadn't been going to mention Frans at all. Whether she imagined that once Mater was away from Stillwaters, Frans would simply slip from her mind like a stranger in a dream was neither clear to herself nor to Mater, but to Blanche Frans was not a reality. Mater would realise it herself, sooner or later. Once she had Mater with her, Blanche had scarcely mentioned the wedding. The wedding outfit had quickly been absorbed into 'a few little things that will make you feel better about yourself', as if leather belts and shoulder pads were what Mater needed to bolster the flagging sense of self-esteem that had occasioned the misguided idea of allowing herself to sink to labourer level.

Blanche knew she had not succeeded and she watched Mater climb into Michaela's car with a vexed expression. All those city clothes going back to the river.

As soon as they were on the highway a subtle change began to take place in Mater which manifested itself in interesting body language. She sat up a little straighter. She opened the window an inch or two. By the time they had hit the top of the pass she had discarded the lambswool and was taking deep satisfying breaths and requesting music on the radio. The light was returning to her eyes.

'Did Blanche make you spend all your money?' Michaela asked with a smile.

'She enjoyed herself,' Mater said. 'That was important.'

'And did you get something for the wedding? Susan will want to know.'

'I think so,' Mater said, frowning. 'I would have liked blue, it's Frans's favourite colour, but your mother . . .'

Michaela couldn't imagine Frans having a favourite colour or that Mater and he would ever have discussed something so odd. When did they play those childlike getting to know you games? What's your lucky number? That's funny, that's mine too! What's your star sign – how compatible are we? What would you like to be when you grow up? How did they link into those common threads, she wondered.

They did not stop anywhere on the way. Michaela drove at a steady speed. She was planning to be there and back in time to pick Susan up after school. She leaned forward and tuned in to a regional news broadcast.

'– Bricknell Court,' they heard, and Michaela started.

'What's that about Bricknell Court?' said Mater, leaning forward.

'There has been a further stay of execution over the historic orchard at Cape Town's Bricknell Court,' they heard. 'Local petitions having gathered over a thousand signatures protesting the intentions of Grosvenor Life to turn the property into landscaped gardens in Phase 5 of its development programme, the city council has decided to put a hold on plans to go ahead for the immediate time being. There is a move to declare the orchard a national monument and until the national monuments council has reviewed the situation, the orchard remains untouched.'

'Well, thank God,' said Michaela brightly.

'There have been no further developments in the case of the mystery skeleton turned up during building excavations.'

Michaela turned the radio off. She wound up her window and frowned at the winding road ahead.

'Michaela,' said Mater. 'Why do I get the impression that there is something troubling you about Bricknell Court? Something other than the fact of it being demolished.'

Michaela turned her face to her grandmother, then looked back at the road. Her palms were sweating.

'There is something troubling you, isn't there?' Mater coaxed. 'I'll listen if it will help.'

Michaela felt a miserable, ill-timed tear well up and drop down her cheek in an abysmally sudden display of self-pity. She brushed it away, annoyed, but it came back again and then was followed by another and another until Mater made a wry comment about windscreen wipers and she had to pull to the side of the road and blow her nose. Then, without really meaning to and without paying much heed to the logic or the flow or chronology of the story, she found herself telling Mater everything. About Bricknell Court and the boiler room, and Crispian Younghusband with his cricket ball and fat knees. About Tommy and the pink blanket and now the midnight phonecalls. And finally, about the note last night at the club and the new, unwelcome feeling of being stalked. How the only place she felt safe was right there in the car like an astronaut in a space capsule, far from the pull of reality and accountability. And how heavy all of this had suddenly become. She must have carried this baggage around with her for years and never before been aware of the excess weight.

Mater undid a couple of buttons on her aquamarine shirt and rolled up her sleeves. She patted Michaela on the shoulder and stroked at the back of her hair. 'Well,' she said. 'That's quite a tale. And on top of all that I've gone and sprung an unsuitable marriage on you too. No wonder the bloom in your cheeks has all but drained away.'

'But what should I do?' Michaela said wretchedly. 'Where am I to go with all this?' Her voice was a little steadier now. 'Mater — tell me what to do.'

Mater sighed. 'I can't do that,' she said.

'What do you mean? You've always —'

'You can't transfer this to me, child. It's time to take responsibility. Responsibility is not only an adult issue and you've carried that knowledge with you in your heart ever since you ran away from that boiler room door. And much as you might not like the feeling right now, and you may be all grown up, that responsibility has not rubbed away with the years. It is as sharp and as urgent as it ever was.'

Michaela felt conscious, almost, of pouting. 'It's my problem, is that what you're saying?' she said.

'Sometimes we are called on to make difficult choices. Sometimes it isn't even very clear what those choices are, especially when the issues are so emotive and murky. But for you to find peace with this thing, you have to dig deep down inside yourself and find an action that best fits the problem. You don't need to look any further than that.'

'It feels so *unfair*. It was so long ago. My life has a pattern to it now. I don't want to – I can't —'.

Mater regarded her steadily. Her eyes were a smoky grey-blue. 'There is nothing that I or anyone else can do to help you, Michaela. You must find a solution – because there is a solution to any problem, be it an unpleasant one or an easy one – within yourself. Take that guilt out from where you've hidden it. You might have to probe and sift because there are years and many layers to uncover, but once you've released it, it will not be so very powerful. It is only powerful because you have not tried to look it in the eye.'

'But what about Tommy? Should I go to the police with what we know?'

'Examine your motivation without Tommy and his threats. Bullies seldom follow through.'

'Is that all you think he is, a bully? You don't think he really means to hurt me? We never realised just how dangerous he was all those years ago, but it was proved with Harriet and David, wasn't it? He could really do some damage, he's capable of it, and completely ruthless.'

'Not if you deflate him.'

'How? By going to the police? Wouldn't that be playing into his hands?'

Mater shrugged. 'Listen to your inner voice, that's

all the advice I can give you,' she said. 'And never be afraid to trust your instincts.'

If Michaela had been hoping for something more concrete and more palatable from Mater, it was apparent that she wasn't going to get it. And all her instincts at the moment screamed at her to run and hide. Had she really spent all of her adult life so far harbouring a secret in her gut like a maggot, feeding on her and growing until it threatened to take over her life? How much longer could she ignore it, Tommy or no Tommy?

He has been with them all day long. They have allowed him to be pig in the middle until he is red in the face and his feet no longer leave the ground when he attempts to catch the ball. Janus and Michaela swing it high over his head, back and forth. They are lethargic about it. There is no fun in hearing him grunt with effort.

They have tried running away from him and hiding. They have held him under the water in the swimming pool until he has popped out of their grasp like an inflatable ball. Crispian Younghusband is not a good swimmer. He swims along the surface with his face out of the water, turning his head from side to side, swimming almost upright. All the cousins are expert swimmers and they cruise up and down, in and around him, swimming lengths underwater and pinching at his ankles. But the fun has gone out of tormenting him today. They are tired of hearing his voice.

'My dad says you can get water on the brain if you dive too deep. Also your ears fill up and you can lose your balance for ever. They've done tests. In America.'

'What gunk your dad talks. I think your *dad*'s got water on the brain.' Michaela is scathing. She is bored and restless. Also she has got water in her own ears and there is a rushing sound that is making her feel uncomfortable. She wants to hop on one leg and get the water out but she won't give Crispian Younghusband the satisfaction of seeing her in any discomfort whatsoever so that he can offer his little pellets of unwanted advice.

'I'm cold.' Crispian Younghusband has a shrill whine in his voice. 'Let's play French cricket to warm up. I'll teach you. It's easy.'

'We don't want to play French cricket, Crispian Younghusband. When are you going to get that through your head?'

'The sun's going down. It'll be behind the mountain in ten minutes.'

'And I suppose your *dad* says that you'll get a little chill if you stay in your wet costume?' Michaela is really in a bad mood.

Janus and Pauline have put their T-shirts on over their costumes. Janus flicks at Crispian's legs with the end of his towel.

'I know,' says Michaela brightly. 'Let's go and warm up in the boiler room. It's always warm in there.'

Crispian Younghusband looks doubtful. 'That's a spooky place,' he says.

'No, it's not,' says Antony.

'You're afraid to go in there,' says Michaela, grinning slowly.

'No, I'm not.'

'Then I dare you. I dare you to go into the boiler room and shut the door. Come on.' And Michaela is off, streaking ahead of the others in her black school costume, her long legs flying and her heels kicking up the dust. Things are looking up. There is yet some fun to be got out of this boring day.

'What about . . . you know —?' Pauline slows down as they get close to the boiler room. She pulls on Antony's T-shirt.

'Tommy?' he says in a low voice. 'I haven't seen Tommy for days. They said at the café that he's been picked up again.'

'Oh.' Pauline stops. She expects that Crispian Younghusband has fallen so far behind that he has sloped off home. But, no, he is panting, red-faced, after them, his heavy stomach flopping over the line of his costume. His skin is pale, untanned.

'I've seen . . . I've seen . . . the wizard go in here,' Crispian pants. 'The boiler room is his . . . den.'

'Oh, rubbish.' Michaela is scornful again. 'There's no one in there. Take a look.'

'I have seen him, I swear. He brings his loot in here after he's been out stealing. He's got light fingers, Tommy has.'

The cousins feel compelled to defend him, even though Janus saw the pick-up van last week with his own eyes. 'Tommy comes and goes,' Janus says defiantly. 'He's his own man.'

'Go on then. Go inside and have a look,' says Michaela.

Antony and Pauline look at each other. Michaela steps forward and squeezes the bolt out of its hole. She heaves the door wide. 'Go on, Crispian Younghusband, I dare you.'

Crispian Younghusband turns his eyes on her. He hasn't had this much attention from Michaela since the day he came into their lives. He wants urgently to keep it. Also he is shivering with cold and a warm gust of stale air surges out at them from the dark, hot-smelling room.

'What are you waiting for?' Michaela taunts. 'Scared?'

As Crispian Younghusband steps tentatively inside the boiler room, the cousins stand in a row and watch him go. Janus has his arms folded across his chest. Antony is looking at Michaela. Pauline takes a step as if she intends to go in after him, but Michaela stays her with a swift, fierce gesture. 'Wait,' she hisses. The minute he is inside the gloom she leaps forward and slams the door closed. In a second she has worked the bolt home and she whirls around and smiles at the others, her eyes shining with fun.

'Hey! Wait! Michaela?' Crispian's voice is already muffled.

'Ssh.' Michaela puts a finger to her lips and whispers, 'He'll think we've gone.'

Crispian Younghusband bangs on the door. 'Hey!' he calls again. 'It's pitch dark in here, you know. Open up.'

They stand in silence, grinning at each other.

'Come on. It's not funny. I can't see a thing. There are spiders in here. I can hear rats.'

Janus stifles a giggle. He cups a hand over his mouth.

'Michaela —' Antony starts forward. 'That's enough.'

'Wait!' Michaela puts a hand up again. 'Stay where you are.'

Crispian Younghusband is banging at the door again. 'Is there anyone there? Michaela? Pauline? Come on, you guys!'

Suddenly Michaela turns away and begins to trot back up to the orchard. The others watch her go and look at each other, nonplussed. Then Antony breaks into a run and after a minute, so do Pauline and Janus. They catch her up at the hopscotch. Michaela is flying over the circles and squares, her long hair bouncing round her shoulders. The sun has disappeared behind the mountain and most of the orchard is in shadow.

'Michaela,' Antony says. 'What are you doing? We can't just *leave* him in there. He'll suffocate.'

'No, he won't. Air gets in through the holes in those bricks up there.'

'But —' Janus's mouth is a round circle.

'Oh, grow up,' Michaela jeers. 'We won't *leave* him in there, idiots. I'll let him out. We'll just let him sweat a little. It won't do him any harm and he's annoying me anyway. If I hear him talk once more about French cricket I'll throw up.'

Antony is feeling responsible. 'You're going too far this time,' he says. 'I don't think it's right to do this. Even if it is only Crispian Younghusband.'

'Exactly.' Michaela throws a flat stone and takes a huge leap over two circles. She is determined now to see the game through the way she has suddenly planned it. 'It's suppertime,' she says. 'We'd better go in before Harriet gets cross. Look –' She stops on one leg, balancing '– I'll go back after supper and let him out. I promise.'

They are all uncertain, but Michaela in this mood is dangerous. No one likes to cross her, not even Antony.

'No longer than supper,' Antony says. 'Not a minute longer than supper or I'll tell David.'

'OK, OK!'

'Let's not fight,' says Pauline, the peacemaker, as they hear their aunt begin to call. 'It's our last night of holidays. It's pissy old school again tomorrow.'

· 16 ·

The forest floor was damp from the rain that had fallen intermittently throughout the day. Although serious autumn was still some time off, already there was a dense carpet of assorted leaves showing autumn colours, pale gold, tawny brown and burnt orange. The chestnut trees and the oaks were beginning to lose their leaves and fallen conkers and acorns crunched and crackled underfoot with a muffled sound. Alongside the footpath, high up here on the slopes of the mountain, away from the noise of the city and the traffic on the road below, grew a hedge of wild almonds over three hundred years old. It was heavy with fruit, bowed towards the ground, twisted and knotted and wet with raindrops. Thrushes picked silently along the ground among the trees, stabbing and thrusting beneath layers of soggy leaves. A couple of dogs, adrift from their owners, wandered blissfully from the path, following scents unknown. Occasionally a call or a whistle would be heard, and a child's voice, shouting.

Michaela came walking up here in the forest as often as she could. Before women on their own started to get accosted and sometimes attacked, she would frequently come to walk alone and allow the silence and the pine-filled air to restore within her that sense of wholeness which living and working in the city whittled away through the week. Sometimes she would persuade Janus to come with her, but he was not a happy walker and never had the right shoes or attitude. He had followed complaining in her wake from an early age and it seemed to be a pattern out of which he was destined never to grow. Antony was a far more appreciative companion and he loved the forest as she did. It had been some time since they had been among the trees together. It seemed that nothing of her routine lately was quite intact.

The forest was one of the tests to which Michaela subjected any new relationship, usually at an early stage. There were certain things in life, she knew, which needed to be shared and if they were the very important ones, as the forest was to her, passing the test was crucial. Simon had loved the forest from the beginning. In fact, he turned out to know paths which Michaela herself had not been aware of and he walked with an easy, comfortable swinging of the arms which spoke of pure relaxed enjoyment. It probably wasn't fair of her to spoil the forest for him.

Michaela knew she had to do it. Going with her instincts was how Mater had put it, and if Simon hadn't exactly been the issue she had been talking about, it was still something Michaela knew had to be addressed and the sooner the better. Simon had arrived in hiking boots and a faded varsity sweater. He had also brought Michaela the paperback of an Anne Tyler book she had been wanting for some time. Knowing what she was about to do, she felt reluctant to take it, like a child being offered sweets by a stranger. Still, it seemed churlish to refuse when he was so obviously pleased with the result of what had been a chance remark on her part. Michaela fanned the pages with a mixture of dread and anticipation. She had a vision of Simon going eagerly to a bookshop, pestering assistants, even perhaps going so far as to fill in a special order form, waiting impatiently for the book to arrive and hoping she hadn't got it out of the library in the meantime. And now here it was, with its muted cover and the price sticker removed. And she would have to take it and read it and think of Simon and Anne Tyler, haphazard relatives, for ever more joined together in her mind.

'How much do I owe you?' she asked him in an unhappy attempt to even things up.

Simon smiled broadly and shifted his feet. Michaela was so independent. 'Nothing, of course,' he told her. 'It's a gift, my pleasure. I know you're a fan.'

They left their car at the forester's house in a clearing beneath the trees. The forester was on his stoep and he waved to them. 'Watch the mist,' he called. 'It's coming down. Don't go too far.' He had shorts on and no shoes and legs white as paper up to his knees where his socks usually were.

They set off along the path, almost immediately plunging into pine and sodden leaves. There was no noise, only the dull rhythmic thud of their shoes and the sound of rushing water up ahead. There was a point up here, Michaela knew, where you could see the roofs of Bricknell Court. Well, no longer, probably – that part of the building had already been pulled down. Michaela allowed Simon to set the pace, it was the least she could do, and she fell behind him where the path narrowed to the width of one person. His boots came up to his ankles and they were new, a dull mustard colour, the colour of some river clays, with the logo of the shop where he'd bought them, Hill 'n Dale, on the side. They looked as if they had been fashioned from clay, Michaela thought, as she stared at them tramping steadily before her, sort of pinched together and moulded round the toes.

Just off the path and down a slope the chestnuts were thick on the ground. Large areas were covered in brown spiny conkers. They saw a bergie, one of the many ragged people who lived up here on the mountain all year round, hitting at the conkers still on the trees with a length of pole and ducking suddenly sideways as an avalanche of nuts fell down about his shoulders. Susan loved to collect chestnuts in the forest at this time of the year. She always came back with pockets bulging. She kept them in her room until they turned wrinkled and mouldy and Michaela had to throw them out. Occasionally they had brought The Dog for a walk here. She had stalked the squirrels and the small grey birds that hopped in and out of the underbrush and progress had been frustrating and slow. Susan was inconsolable over The Dog. She put cat pellets out in the garden every night and still called at suppertime, just in case an incredible journey might be taking place just around the corner and The Dog was wandering the suburban streets on bleeding paws, mewing for home. Michaela, too, missed the warmth at her back when she went to bed, and the heavy jungle purring in her ear at six o'clock in the morning, more consistent than any alarm clock.

Simon had picked up a large, crooked stick and he ran it along the almond hedge, sending showers of raindrops onto the ground. Michaela hurried a little to walk abreast with him. She was getting out of breath, more with nerves than anything else. 'Simon,' she said,

'I have to talk to you.'

Simon slowed down. He smiled at her, waiting. His eyes were dark brown, just the colour of the chestnuts, and they gleamed at her fondly. He was growing a moustache. The man was impossibly hairy.

Michaela picked a couple of almonds from the old hedge and rubbed them between her fingers. 'It's like this,' she said, looking down at her feet.

'What?' Simon was puzzled at her tone of voice.

'I'm going through a bit of a personal crisis at the moment, Simon. Nothing that should concern you, really, or anyone else for that matter. It's just that . . . well, until I know where I'm going with it, how I'm going to get through it, I think I need . . . you know —'

Simon knew exactly. 'A friend,' he said decisively. 'You've got one.' He stopped and tried to take Michaela's hand, but she pulled away, broke open an almond and studied the uninspiring contents closely.

'Well, thank you,' she muttered, 'but that's not quite what I . . . Actually I —'

A family of brisk, short-sleeved hikers broke through the cover of the trees and strode towards them. Red-cheeked and healthy, they chorused good evening and swept by, leaving a scent of Deep Heat and perspiration in their wake.

Michaela looked enviously after them. 'I think we should stop seeing each other,' she said as they rounded the bend and disappeared out of sight. 'At least for the moment.'

Simon looked immediately crushed. He was a man who showed his emotions openly. Here he was, expecting to be given a key role to play in the management of Michaela's personal crisis, and she was giving him his marching orders. He had thought there would be more for him to do than fade obediently away into the shadows.

'Surely,' he began, clearing his throat. 'Surely . . .'

'I don't know how to explain to you,' Michaela went on, 'that this isn't a personal thing, that it doesn't have anything to do with you or with our relationship. It's just that there are some things I have to work out in my head by myself and until I can get them straightened out, I can't give anything of myself to you – or anyone. I know it sounds pretentious and it probably is, and this isn't coming out like I intended it to, but oh, I don't know, Simon – I just haven't got *room* for you at the moment. Or anyone else,' she added when she saw a look of distant doubt beginning to cloud Simon's face. He was going to say it. He was going to say it anyway. They always did.

'Is this a convoluted way of breaking up with me?' he asked, his voice hardening. 'Is there somebody else?'

A sudden flash. Antony, smiling sardonically in the back of her head. Antony in the sand dunes, among tumescent succulents and searing heat, telling her to lighten up on Simon. Michaela shook her head vigorously. 'No,' she said. 'Nothing like that, I promise. I'm telling you the truth. I'm sorry if it sounds mysterious and pathetic. It isn't really.' (It was both.) 'I don't mean it to be. I just need to be on my own for a while. And being with you, concentrating on you, trying to think of your needs as well as my own – all of that is twisting my head around and I can't think straight. It's not fair to either of us.' Michaela was painfully conscious of how trite the words sounded but she didn't have any others.

Simon had a guileless face. His expression had

moved from crushed through to suspicious and then perplexed in about three minutes. Now it remained stuck on perplexed, his eyebrows drawn together in a frown. He rubbed his head. He had some dirt on his hands from his stick and it gave his frown a comical intensity that made him look more confused still.

'I wish I could say I understand,' he said.

'I'm sorry.' Michaela really was sorry. She hadn't expected to feel so bad about doing this. 'Let's walk back,' she said. It would be excruciating to continue walking.

They walked in silence, Simon banging away at clumps of leaves to either side of the path with his stick. Michaela kept wanting to apologise again but she couldn't think of what to say to take the harshness out of her decision. Nor did she want Simon to leap into an opportunity of trying to talk her out of it. It was safer to trudge along and take huge gulps of forest air into her lungs and pretend she didn't feel like crying, that it was only the chill that was making her nose run. When they reached the car Simon leaned against the door and folded his arms. 'And when you've got through this, er, personal crisis,' he said, his voice stiff now with hurt dignity, 'can we . . . I mean, will we be able to go back to seeing each other again?'

Michaela was thinking hopelessly of Anne Tyler, the roses, the many other small, sentimental offerings over the past few months that seemed to have risen to a toppling pyramid, that Simon was probably feeling foolish about and which were making his voice gruff. She felt mean and heartless. Still she struggled through. Go with the instincts. Make the right choices. 'I don't know, Simon,' she said, looking up at him. 'I don't know.' Where would she be anyhow – in jail? Would his devotion send him off to Pollsmoor Prison to visit her in her grey prison shift and bring her sustaining literature to keep her brain from stagnating? Gazes of intensity through double glazing? A file in a fruitcake?

Simon sighed deeply. He opened the door for her, courteous to the last. 'What is it anyway,' he asked bravely when they were on the road and heading home, 'this crisis of yours? You have seemed a little on edge lately.'

'Oh,' Michaela looked purposely vague. 'Family business mostly – things I have to come to terms with in my own mind. It's a long story.'

'And one which wouldn't be helped by sharing,' he said flatly. He was still trying and she couldn't blame him. The whole thing sounded fabricated and suddenly stupid. They had been getting on perfectly well until the weekend at Stillwaters when he'd tried to come too close to her. It wasn't his fault after all that her life was in such a mess. She just knew, after her talk with Mater, that she had to shed things, to pare away at the outer layers before she could hope to get near the core. And Simon was the first layer she had come to. This was probably the first honest thing she had done in a long while and ironically he thought she was conning him.

'I have to work this one out on my own,' she told him ruefully, laying a quick hand lightly on his knee and as quickly removing it. 'I'm sorry, Simon, truly I am. I hope in the end we can still be friends, but I honestly can't offer you anything more than that at the moment.'

'Can I call you now and then – a sort of crisis check-in?'

Michaela hesitated. She smiled at his dejected profile, reflecting that the moustache would probably suit him.

She thought it best to make things as final as possible.

'I'll call *you*,' she said lamely.

When she got home Susan told her Antony had called. Michaela resisted the temptation to call him back. She could not now begin to justify her treatment of Simon to Antony's sceptical voice. Antony was another layer she would have to take a closer look at too.

Susan was drawing an undulating earthworm in her biology book and Michaela was steaming baby marrows for their supper when the front door opened and Pauline staggered in, laden with baggage. She had a suitcase in each hand which she immediately dropped in the hallway. She was also wearing a large amount of clothing: three coats that Michaela could see and beneath them a colourful array of jackets and jerseys. On the lower half of her body two skirts and a pair of navy blue tracksuit pants were readily apparent. Her face was bright red.

'Good grief,' said Susan.

Michaela studied her. Pauline was an iridescent lesson in layers. 'Did you run out of suitcases?' she asked her.

'I've been home,' Pauline puffed. 'And Tertius was there in spite of the drive past Frank and I did first. I don't know where he could have left his car.'

'Are you all right?'

Pauline grimaced. 'We had words,' she said. Her voice was breathless. Susan came to the rescue with a fistful of coathangers and she stood, fascinated, as Pauline began peeling items of clothing from her arms. 'Thanks, Suze,' she said. 'I feel like the abominable snowman.'

'More like the Michelin man.' Susan laughed. 'You look too hot for snow.'

'Words?' demanded Michaela. 'How many? What sort?'

'Oh, the usual,' Pauline admitted. 'But I didn't fall for any of it this time. You would have been proud of me. I packed my things and I left.'

'He didn't —?'

'No, but he made a grab at me when he heard Frank revving outside the gate.' Pauline looked annoyed. 'My top jacket came away in his hands. I had to leave it. The maroon one — my favourite.'

'Isn't there an animal that does that as a defence mechanism?' Susan asked solemnly. 'I think it leaves whole chunks of its body in the enemy's jaws.' She looked enquiringly at her mother.

'Lizards,' Michaela agreed. 'Or geckos. One of that lot. I think they ditch their tails.' She looked at Pauline half out of her third jacket, an emerald green one with black braiding. 'But Pauline looks more like a chameleon that sat on a rainbow and couldn't make up its mind,' she added. Pauline was down to the tracksuit pants. Susan waited like a valet with her arm out. Then she went off to the guest room laden with coathangers and wearing Pauline's scarlet and silver fez on her head.

'What have you done with Simon?' Pauline asked Michaela, looking round.

'Dumped him,' Michaela replied, after a moment.

'Oh, why?' Pauline showed surprise. 'I really liked him. I thought you did too.'

'I just can't deal with him and everything else,' Michaela said shortly. 'I like him well enough, I guess, but it just wasn't working.'

At once Susan put her head out of the door of the guest room. 'Did I hear *right*?' she asked. 'Have you broken up with Simon?'

'Don't look so pleased,' Michaela said drily.

'I'm only pleased if you're pleased.' Susan's expression was demure and innocent. 'And frankly you look like hell.'

Michaela flapped a hand at her. 'Go check on the marrows,' she said. 'Pauline will finish your earthworm.'

Later on, when Susan had gone to bed, Michaela and Pauline sat out in the garden with a bottle of wine. Overhead an army helicopter clattered past, quite low in the sky. It was moving towards the township on the outskirts of town.

'You know,' said Michaela. 'I feel so self-absorbed. I haven't read a newspaper for days. I hear there's been some bad stuff going on.'

A military leader had been gunned down by mistake in a police ambush. The man was a people's hero. There had been red faces all round and the funeral and the rioting that followed accounted for fourteen more deaths and the looting of several shops in the city centre.

'Harriet and Helena went to the protest vigil outside the City Hall,' Pauline told her. 'I think Harriet got quite nostalgic. It perked her up no end, though, raising the fist and shouting the odds again. I think she misses all of that in Australia. There's nothing much to get involved in, or not the kind of drama Harriet was used to.'

'It's depressing to think that she's less out of touch than I am,' Michaela brooded. 'They were talking about this military man at the magazine this week and do you know, I couldn't even conjure up a picture of him in my mind. I can't even remember a point where I switched off politics. It used to be such a preoccupation. I read everything, I followed the negotiation talks. I even helped with the run up to the elections, but now – I don't know. We have the new government we've been expecting and working for for so long, and I haven't got the energy to care. All I can think about is myself and the small selfish world I inhabit. People are dying out there in the townships and my whole life is focused on a crumbling old building and a kid who once got up my nose.'

'It's understandable,' Pauline soothed her. 'And threats like the ones you've been getting do have a way of focusing the mind.'

'Tommy.' Michaela sighed. She glanced instinctively round the garden. It was well lit by an outside light up until the agapanthus beds. They swayed on their tall stems in the night wind, bending their dark round heads in Michaela's direction, as if they were eavesdropping. 'I feel watched,' she said. 'Even out here in my own garden, I feel watched.'

'It's natural to feel that way about Tommy.' Pauline leaned over and filled Michaela's glass. 'I hope you don't mind, but I read the proofs of your article on Harriet – they were lying on your desk. I've been thinking about that rat most of the day. That was how it always was with him – watching, lurking around. He was always watching us. We knew it back then, but we didn't recognise it as a menace. Or if we did, we were too young and naive to understand and interpret it. To us, back then, he was just unsociable, unknowable.' She paused a minute, thoughtful. 'But there was something compelling about him too,' she went on. 'Almost attractive. I still can't lay a finger on what that something was.'

'And we were so schooled in caring for the underdog,' Michaela said. 'We saw Tommy as a candidate ripe for our philanthropic attentions. And at the same time we raised him to the level of equality where we thought he belonged. Remember that summer, the Crispian Younghusband summer, when we spent so much time defending him because Crispian was so disparaging about him?'

'It's ironic, isn't it?'

'I *hate* the thought of Crispian Younghusband being right about Tommy, even now,' Michaela said as vehemently as if she were twelve years old again.

'But he was only right about him being a low-life,' Pauline pointed out. 'Not about anything else.'

'Yes, but we should have been sharper,' Michaela told her. 'We should have been the ones to pick up on him.'

Pauline stretched her legs out in front of her. She was wearing navy blue ankle socks with pink cherubs on them. 'We were kids, Michaela,' she said wearily. 'You're being too hard on us, on yourself especially.'

Michaela was clearly bothered by the memory of Tommy and in trying to come to terms with him as they had known him then, she was also trying to get into perspective the predicament she was now facing as a result of his unwanted attentions.

'When Tommy was gathering information on Harriet and David,' she said, laying back and talking to the sky, 'he must have been acutely devious. It wasn't just observing how they came and went and who came to visit them. And it wasn't just a short period of observation either. He was around for years. It's so appallingly intimate when you think about it. It's like having someone living in your home and then finding out years later that he's been stealing your recipes and selling them off to the opposition.'

'Oh, nice analogy,' said Pauline. 'You've been with the magazine too long.'

Michaela ignored her. She crossed her arms beneath her head. 'He must have found a way to get into the apartment too,' she said. 'That's what really galls, because the only way he could have done that was through us. We let him in. But as far as I can recall with any accuracy, we only let him in a couple of times when we gave him meals in the kitchen. And at least two of us were with him all the time, cooking and fussing round him – Christ! when I think of the flapjacks, the baked beans on fucking toast! When did he find a moment to lay his hands on anything of importance is what I can't understand. Harriet thinks he may have broken in through one of the smaller windows because she and David were never very security conscious and careful about locking things up. But we were usually around, at least in the holidays. Why didn't we notice?'

Pauline leaned on an elbow. She brushed at some midges dancing in front of her eyes. 'I don't know, Michaela,' she muttered. 'I don't know.'

Michaela was getting into her stride. It was as if she couldn't contain all the words that suddenly came spilling out. As if talking honestly to Simon had at last unleashed her conscience. It was as if she didn't care whether Pauline was there or not, or whether she was really listening. As long as she made an interjection now and then to show she wasn't actually asleep, that was all the audience she needed.

'And Crispian Younghusband,' she said. 'You know, knowing what I now know, thinking of him dying in there as a small, frightened boy, I still can't dredge up any great feelings of remorse. I don't know why. He was so damn *offensive*, so horribly unlikeable.'

'We were mean to him,' Pauline said sleepily.

'He didn't have to stick around,' Michaela retorted. 'We certainly didn't invite him to.'

'We certainly didn't.' Pauline had her eyes closed. She was having a night off from the club. Sundays the keyboard player from the boys would keep guests entertained and Frank and the student waiters did everything else. It was a quiet night and Frank had displayed a talent for fettucine.

'Do you remember the berry fights?' Michaela said after a pause. She sounded wistful.

'Uh huh.' Pauline opened one eye and looked at her. There was a trace of a smile playing around Michaela's mouth.

'I can still feel their sting, the handfuls we ripped from the bushes. The war cries.'

'Janus got hit on the eyelid and it swelled up like a bee sting,' Pauline said. 'And then my father forbade us to desecrate the bushes after that.'

'And making Crispian Younghusband do push-ups until he got that white ring round his mouth and sat gasping like a fish.'

'And insisting that he climb the tree with the help of the long ladder and then taking it away so he couldn't get down.'

'That was Janus's idea,' Michaela reminded her.

Pauline sat up. She smoothed her skirt. 'We were cruel,' she told Michaela. 'Inexcusably cruel.'

'All kids are cruel,' Michaela replied. 'We weren't abnormal.'

They both fell suddenly silent. The boiler room loomed large and putrid in front of them. Michaela picked up a twig beside her on the ground.

'Let's go inside,' she said abruptly. 'I'm getting cold.'

Pauline is running a bath. The bathroom window is closed tight and the steam from the hot water has fogged up all the mirrors. She stands beside the tub with her sleeves rolled up. She leans forward and tests the temperature, adjusting the cold tap slightly. Then she takes some of Harriet's Island Temptation bath crystals and scatters them carefully into the water beneath the gushing tap. She picks up a towel from the floor and folds it slowly, smoothing down the corners. She puts it on a chair. She feels like a mother, fussing with the soap in the dish, straightening the bathmat. She puts a fish-shaped sponge beside the bath on a small stool. It is red and has a large eye stencilled in black and flaking white on one side. Someone has broken off the tail and it has a ragged, bitten look to it, as if some larger predatory fish had taken a fancy to it.

There is a knock on the bathroom window and she looks up to see a shadow pass by and slide towards the back door. Quickly she turns off the taps. She hurries to let him in and Tommy slips inside and stands with his hands behind his back in the dim light of the hallway.

'Everyone's out,' she says as she always does, smiling shyly. 'They won't be back till this evening. I've laid everything out for you.'

She leads the way down the passage. There is a picture of Harriet and Walter Sisulu on the wall outside the bathroom, and another of a younger Harriet and David on a platform in a hall. David is at the podium in a turtleneck sweater and Harriet is sitting on a folding chair with her feet neatly together. Her hair is long, in a plait down one shoulder. Tommy stops and looks at the pictures without expression. Pauline hovers behind him. She looks down and sees that she has a cake of soap in her hand. It is damp and has made a slimy stickiness of her palm.

'There you are,' she says, gesturing. 'I've put everything ready for you.' She is repeating herself but Tommy's brooding silence always makes her talk more than she means to.

Tommy's bath has become this summer holiday's ritual. She hasn't really meant it to. On Wednesday afternoons, when Harriet and David are at their committee meeting, Michaela and Janus have been enrolled in a school tennis clinic. Antony goes along to hit balls against a wall and wait for them to finish. Pauline is no good with a racket and she makes excuses to stay behind. Later she catches the bus to the courts, taking cold drinks and carrot cake which they share beneath the trees. That is after she has taken a scrubbing brush and thick white layers of Vim to the bathtub's black rings. She lets Tommy look at magazines in David's study while she labours. Once she went off to catch the bus and left him to let himself out. Tommy seems to like the magazines, although whether he just looks at the pictures she's not sure.

Tommy gives her a small smile, or what she imagines is a smile – it is no more than a twitch of the lips. She takes a step backwards. Aromatic bath crystals have filled the passageway and she makes a mental note to open the front and back doors while he is bathing.

'There's a sandwich for you in the kitchen when you've finished,' she tells him. 'I've put it under a cover so the flies don't . . .' Her voice trails away. She feels uncertain when Tommy looks at her so directly.

'*Dankie*,' Tommy says, without any facial movement

whatsoever. Thank you is almost all he ever says. His hand is on the door handle. Pauline smiles again and ducks her head anxiously. 'Um, could you hurry a bit,' she says. Last time there were large pools of water to dry and she had had to run to catch the bus.

Janus stood at the open door of his cupboard in front of the full-length mirror. He wore a brocade jacket over a long black pleated skirt and he turned sideways, feeling the soft material brush against his legs. He frowned and turned the other way. Then he sighed. He faced his image and gave a painful laugh. 'Well, hell, J,' he said in perfect imitation of his sister's voice, 'that jacket fits so snugly over the hips I wish I'd beaten you to it at the summer sales.'

'Not a chance, Mick,' he said sternly to his reflection. 'And you should have seen the evening wear. I picked up a marvellous backless number with underwiring in a salmon pink that Pauline would have killed for.'

'Well, I do have a salmon pink pillbox hat,' he said in Pauline's soft breathy voice. 'Maybe we could share the ensemble?'

'And maybe I could kill myself.' He slammed the cupboard shut and slumped down in a chair in the corner of the room. Earlier this evening he had taken Chloë to a movie and had felt like an adolescent all the way through, not knowing whether holding hands was all right any more or if it was something she was expecting him to know. Or even if it was what he wanted to do. She had sat with her hands in her lap anyway and he had looked at them at intervals throughout the film. They lay there like a pair of empty gloves, slim, white and lifeless. Chloë, he noticed, bit her nails, and her ears stuck through the thin curtain of her hair. When she laughed she gave a little hiccup that he found endearing.

How could he subject Chloë to someone like him? He could never explain. She would stare at him through her glasses and never understand. In the end he would have to move away, start up again in another anonymous apartment block and forget about ever having a normal relationship, one that might bear scrutiny.

What would Michaela say if she could see him? How would she react to knowing that her brother had a wardrobe of women's clothing? It went beyond all comprehension.

Janus had always liked the substance of material, of cloth. There had been a time, long ago, when he had thought it meant he might take up fashion design as a career. Sometimes, when they were children, he and Michaela had played at dressing up. They had used Blanche's stage clothes, clinging gold lamé and sequinned bodyshirts. Michaela also liked to try her makeup skills on him and Janus would stand, compliant in high heels and feather boas, while she scored his lips in hard harlot red and rubbed dark grey shadows onto his eyelids. 'There you go,' she would say. 'Look in the mirror. Don't you look bootiful. Bootiful boy.' Then she would twirl in satin ballet slippers and make him dance with her. She had long expressive arms to coax him with and coltish, dangerous legs. His bright, alarming sister would move and direct him into submission until in the end, uneasy and fretful, he would beg for a game of leggy or races on roller skates.

The downstairs buzzer sounded suddenly, breaking his reverie. It was Antony's voice. Janus pressed the button at the front door. He stood in thought for a moment. Then he turned the catch to leave the door unlatched and walked into the living room. When

Antony strode in, festooned with cameras, he found Janus watching a township demonstration on television and adjusting his shoulder pads.

'Oh,' said Antony. 'Well, hello, J. What's happening in Langa?'

· 17 ·

Antony's portrait of Harriet was an interesting one. It had been taken one late afternoon at Stillwaters, on the boathouse roof, with the river and a bristle of reeds in the background. She was leaning on her arms looking out over the water, barely aware of him, unselfconscious, as if a long way off in thought. He had chosen to do the picture in black and white to maximise the effect of the shadows and light on the river, which appeared, charcoal grey and grainy, arrested in motion, and gave the picture a surreal atmosphere that was at once poignant and strong. Antony took so many pictures of everybody at every conceivable time of the day, Harriet had in actual fact not given him a second glance and she was surprised at the power of the pictures when he had shown her the results. '"The exile, dreaming of home",' he had said, laying a row of prints down in front of her like playing cards. 'Or some such caption.'

Actually, Harriet confessed, she had been waiting on the boathouse roof for David to bring her his corduroys to mend and had been wondering whether she had enough brown thread with her to go the distance, but that was not necessarily something that needed to be shared with the *Focus* readers. They would probably relate better to the exile angle.

Michaela agreed. She and Roz had the photographs on her desk and were trying to decide which to use with the article.

'I like the one with the more pronounced laughter lines,' Roz decided.

'How about this one?' said Michaela, holding it up. 'I'm happier with the lighting here.'

'Suit yourself,' said Roz. 'They're all good. Your cousin has a special feel for portraits. He's very talented. You should have seen his rosemary.'

'Who?'

'The herbs promotion. Stunning work.' Roz had discovered accessories. She had orange beads down to her navel and fruit bowl earring clusters. Her nail polish was a matt gold and she picked up the pictures with the tips of her fingers as if her nails were wet.

Michaela put a yellow sticker onto the top photograph and clipped it to the proofs of her article. She handed them to Roz. 'That's that taken care of,' she said. 'Will you send it down?'

Roz slipped them inside a grey folder. 'I've had a couple of late entries for the competition,' she told Michaela. 'Do you want them now?'

'Titles?' Michaela flipped through her messages. Simon hadn't called even once and she felt a small twinge.

'Let me think. The first is called *Burning Barricades*. I glanced through it – lots of necklacing and petrol bombs and, um, a rape, I think.'

'By whom?'

'The rape? Er —'

'No, the story, Roz. Male or female? Female, I guess.

Ex-Rhodesian, cropped hair, sleeveless cotton frock. Brown leather sandals with the loop over the big toe.'

Roz looked at her, awed. 'You saw her come in,' she said.

'No, I didn't. Promise. I'm pretty close though, aren't I?'

'You got the sandals and the dress. I haven't looked at her personal details.'

'And the other one?'

'*Surprise for September*. You don't wanna know.'

Michaela laughed. 'Why? What's the surprise?'

'September.'

Michaela looked confused.

'September is the gardener,' Roz explained. 'His madam throws a party for him and invites all the maids up and down the street. It's her bit for the new South Africa.'

'I won't even begin to guess.' Michaela closed her eyes. 'I think I'll pass for the moment. I have an editorial meeting in five minutes. You give them the thumbs down, Roz. You know which pile is which.' She waved a hand at her desk.

Michaela was halfway out of the door when she turned back to the ring of the phone. 'Who is it?' she asked Roz.

Roz shrugged. 'He won't say,' she said, holding out the receiver.

Then Michaela knew, even before she raised the instrument to her ear, that it was the call she had been dreading. She had expected it at midnight, and at home. Now, with the sun streaming through the curtains and lighting up the picture of Susan in its frame on her desk, it seemed that even this space was about to be defiled. It had been days since the last call and she had begun to hope, to pray that Tommy had decided he'd scared her enough and had tired of his game. Antony had even managed to persuade her that the note in her pocket at Pauline's could have been from anyone in the club, someone trying to attract her attention in a facetious manner. 'You are being watched'. If you gave it another kind of slant, it could even be amusing, a smooth operator whose next move would have been to send her a drink and raise his glass to her from a table in the corner. Only Michaela had hurried out of the club with her head down and her shoulders hunched. The poor guy must have been surprised and disappointed. Michaela was coming round to believing this fiction. She had looked at the note again, and it did seem to be hastily scrawled, as if on impulse.

This time, though, there was no mistaking the caller. The same muffled sound, the husky, rasping distortion on the voice. She strained her ears for a giveaway intonation. She sat down slowly in her chair and swivelled it round so that she was facing the window and looking out at the blue-grey flanks of the mountain. She could see a flock of gulls circling, reduced to thin slices of silver as they turned and spread out. She followed them, unseeing, with her eyes.

'Who is this?' she said tersely. She was determined not to give way this time to panic. She tried to concentrate her mind on Mater and how she had turned to face her in the car and told her how bullies seldom followed through. She felt like Pauline with her affirmation statements. *Bullies seldom follow through. Bullies seldom* . . . She waited, listening.

'Michaela.' It was rough and faint.

'I've had about enough of you,' Michaela said, surprising herself, and suddenly deciding to persevere while she had a handful of courage. 'I've had about all I need to hear about this business. I have nothing to say to the police and nothing to say to you. I don't need to listen to you interfering in my life and making threats. Your threats are nothing more than hot air and I won't be pushed and goaded and *put upon* like this any more.' She paused for a breath and then rushed on, feeling all at once strong and in control. *Bullies seldom follow through*. She would show Tommy. She was not going to be shoved around by a scumbag spy with the morals of a louse. 'And what's more, you have no proof of any of your crazy allegations. You're a chancer and a liar and —'

'I have proof.' The voice was lazy, unperturbed, and Michaela felt the start of a slow burning pain deep in her chest, as if she were being squeezed by the ribs.

'I don't believe you.' What proof – a blanket, a plastic plate, a —

'Your silver locket,' said Tommy softly. 'Your silver locket, on a silver chain. Is that proof enough?'

Michaela went flying back in time. She felt hot and cold and completely unable to respond. She had had a silver locket once, when she was a child. Blanche had given it to her on her eighth birthday. It opened on a delicate hinge and inside she had put a picture of a pink sugar mouse which she had cut off a children's birthday cake in a magazine. Michaela had cherished that locket and had been heartbroken when it had got lost one summer holiday.

'What?' she said and her voice came out just above a whisper. A rock pigeon landed with a thud on her windowsill. It looked in at her with its head cocked on one side. 'What did you say?'

'The locket was found in the boiler room. With the skeleton.'

Roz put her head in at the door. She looked fiercely at Michaela and pointed to her watch. The meeting in the boardroom was about to start. They would all be waiting for her. She had to report on the short story competition. She shook her head at Roz and frowned.

'I don't know what you're talking about,' she said brusquely. 'I don't own a silver locket.'

Tommy chuckled softly. 'It has your name on it,' he said. 'And your date of birth.'

It flashed into her head. Tommy had stolen the locket. He could have picked it up anywhere. He could have lifted it from the apartment. Her mind raced in frantic circles. She wished Antony was there, to pick up the other phone and help her out of this.

'So you see,' Tommy went on, 'it's only a matter of time before they trace it to you. It would be better for you if you were to own up now. Before they have to come to you. It would look better for you.'

Michaela found difficulty speaking. Her throat had gone dry. 'I don't believe you,' she said finally. 'You're lying. How do you know so much?' How did Tommy know so much? Because he was a police spy, that was how, and if anyone had police connections and access to classified or private information, it was Tommy. Now that she thought of it, she considered, as her brain darted around the possibilities, it wasn't impossible that Tommy was part of the whole investigation. He could just be playing with her, mocking her, waiting for her to break cover and run. Or he could be guessing. Or he could be trying to frame her. He might have stolen that locket and kept it all these years for just this sort of moment.

He could also be bluffing.

'I make it my business to know,' Tommy said. 'Like I am making it my business to see that justice is done.' His voice had hardened and was closer to her ear, a penetrating whisper.

'Why are you doing this?' Michaela cried out desperately. She felt close to cracking. 'What do you want from me? I don't buy this justice shit. What do you want!'

There was silence. Michaela thought he had rung off. She had broken out in a sweat and she could hardly keep her hand around the phone. Then, just as she was about to put it down, shaking violently, he was there again, as intimate as a lover in her ear. 'A trade,' he said softly. 'I'm offering you a trade. A trade for the locket and my silence.'

Michaela knew that this was a crucial moment and she saw the trap with certain clarity. The pigeon on her windowsill had been joined by a mate and they sat darkening the frame, side by side, staring in with bossy red eyes. Shuffling a little, they settled. One of them began to preen its tail feathers. Then Roz came into her office, not even knocking. She had a sheaf of papers held against her chest and she stood, sternly, waiting at the front of the desk for Michaela to finish her call. It was Roz's responsibility to take notes at this meeting. She had organised tea, everyone had a set of the last editorial minutes, and pencils with sharpened points. All that was missing was Michaela.

'Just a minute.' Michaela put her hand over the mouthpiece. 'Roz,' she said. 'Start without me. Take them through the last minutes, see who's actioned what. I . . . this is an important call. I'll be through in just a moment.'

She waited, white knuckles clamped over the mouthpiece until Roz had closed the door behind her. She hoped she wasn't thinking of listening on the extension. Slowly she put the phone up to her ear again, hoping somehow, that Tommy might have hung up.

'Michaela Whitehead.' He was there immediately. 'Such a busy person. Meetings here, meetings there. You have such a full and interesting life. A little too full right now perhaps.'

'I have to go. I am going to terminate this conversation right now. I am not going to horsetrade with the likes of you.' Still she couldn't bring herself to hang up the phone.

Tommy had the effect of reducing her to a child-like status, stripping off the years like bark off a tree. Any minute now she would find herself pouting, refusing to play. She was not strong enough to put the phone down and Tommy knew it. She had to wait and see what he would do next, so that she could try to counter it with something else. This was playing his game and probably playing into his hands, but she couldn't help herself. And in spite of everything, she still felt a sense of unreality. Real things like this didn't happen to her, Michaela. She might be afraid but a part of her was also curious, curious to see out this charade, to find where it was leading. In her airy office, with its blonde Scandinavian furniture and her coloured paperclips and Russell Flints on the wall, she still felt a measure of inviolability. Surely nothing could wrest her away from this?

'I know you want the locket,' Tommy said. 'And I might be prepared to give it to you.'

Michaela waited. She did not say anything.

'You have a powerful position there, at your magazine. You have influence and words at your disposal.'

'What are you getting at?' Michaela was guarded. She looked at her watch. Even her wrist was trembling. It looked damp.

'I want you to tell my story.'

'What?'

'In your magazine. I want you to tell my story, to the nation. To the world.'

Michaela thought at once of Harriet, a woman of courage and determination, who had suffered and been ostracised for her beliefs, persecuted and finally run out of the country – by this man. Was he asking her to let him use *Focus* as a vehicle for putting forward his own justification for the work he did? Tommy and Harriet in the same magazine? Betrayal and steadfastness. It was ludicrous, preposterous. She'd never do it.

'That's my trade.'

For a minute she thought he meant betrayal was his business and she was about to react in anger when she checked herself. Tommy was not yet aware that she knew who he was – or was he?

'What's your story? What do you mean?' she said.

Tommy chuckled, a low gurgling that made the line buzz. 'Ah, no, Michaela,' he said. 'Not yet. Do we have a deal?'

Michaela straightened and swivelled her chair around to face her desk again. She dug deep into her reserves. 'I don't make deals,' she said. 'With anybody. You're lying. I don't believe in your so-called proof. I don't believe in your silver locket, and I'm not interested in your story. In fact, I know your story. I know what you are.'

There was a pregnant silence on the line. Michaela was not at all confident that she had done the right thing. She felt the hairs on the back of her neck stand up and gooseflesh prickle her arms.

'All right,' Tommy said quietly. 'But you will be sorry. The locket will be used as evidence in due course. For the moment it is in my possession.'

'I don't own a locket,' Michaela said again, despising the desperation in her voice.

'I will give it to you,' Tommy went on calmly, 'but only in person. And only if we have a deal.' He paused. 'This is your last chance.'

Then, 'Where?' Michaela said, hating herself even more, feeling despair run down her back like a streak of fire. She had lost it. She had lost the advantage, thrown it out of the window at Tommy's feet. She was as good as doomed.

Tommy was ready. 'In the orchard at Bricknell Court. Tomorrow night. Midnight. You will have your locket.'

Michaela felt as if she had sold her soul. This wasn't facing up to her responsibilities. This wasn't the course Mater would have advised. This was the coward's way, not the Whitehead way. Protecting her back, ducking the issue. Fear and guilt were a powerful combination and she did not feel equal to the fight. She felt her throat squeeze closed and tears threaten behind her eyelids.

'I don't – I can't —'

'And make sure, Michaela, that you come alone. Don't think of bringing anyone with you.'

Someone was tapping on her office door. Michaela made one last attempt to extricate herself from the web. 'I'll think about it,' she said. 'I'll think about it – Tommy.'

She put the phone down lightly and sat back limply in her swivel chair.

Blanche had toned down her outfits. She sat on her barstool, all in black, with the light above her head shining onto her piled red hair. She wore little makeup except for the coal black lines around her eyes, and her face looked thinner and somehow more at peace. She sang country songs, 'Blue Bayou' and 'Comin' Home', with a bittersweet flavour that had the full house at the club leaning forward in their chairs and forgetting all about the food that was cooling on their plates. The melancholy notes reached in and pulled something out of them that few of them had even known was there. On the last number of the first set Pauline came and harmonised with her, sitting on the edge of the stage at Blanche's feet, while Ernest sent showers of sunflower husks raining down on their heads from his platform above.

Michaela and Antony sat outside, with the black harbour water lapping at the boats tied to their moorings. There was a yacht from the Phillippines in the harbour just here, smooth and ivory white in the darkness. There were people sitting on the deck just out of sight and they could hear the sound of glasses and chat, and occasionally a high pitched laugh from a woman. Frank came out with a bottle of wine in an ice bucket and some calamari rings on two plates. 'Compliments of the owner,' he told them.

'This has gone quite far enough,' Antony told Michaela. 'You simply can't involve yourself in Tommy's manipulative games. He has spent half his life turning your family upside down, you can't let him get away with tormenting you in this way.'

'What do you suggest I do?' Michaela asked fretfully. She didn't need rhetoric. She needed help.

'Perhaps it's time we went to the police.'

Michaela stared at her cousin. 'Oh, Antony,' she said. 'I can't. I can't do that *now*. We've been through that. And you know I've thought about it until I can't think clearly any more. I still haven't got the courage. I can't do it.' She stopped. 'And besides, Tommy has my locket.'

'You don't trust Tommy, surely?' Antony said. 'Blackmailers never stop at the first demand. And we don't know for sure that he has the locket at all. And if he has, and if he gives it to you, what then? Another phonecall, another demand. It won't stop there, I guarantee it.'

'But —'

'And what about this story crap? What are you going to do – sit down with a tape recorder and ask him sensitive questions about the methods he used to shop your aunt? Try to put across a sympathetic record of – what? You can't do it, Michaela. The magazine would never buy it in the first place, and even if they did, how would you explain it? And why? You'd have a hard time trying to convince them that you truly thought this was a good idea. What if they just said no, refused to carry the story – what then? You've got to think this through, you know. Blackmail is a serious offence. You know who it is trying to blackmail you, and I think you have a strong case going to the police with it.'

Michaela looked out to sea. The wind blew her hair across her face and she pulled Antony's jacket across her chest. 'I suppose it would almost be better than this,' she said. 'Confessing. Owning up. At least it would get it out in the open. Maybe Mater was right.'

'You haven't been listening,' Antony said. 'You don't

have to give them the whole story. I've been thinking about that. You could tell them that we knew Crispian Younghusband when we were children and there's a possibility that he —'

'I'm going to the orchard, Antony. I have to get that locket.'

Antony made an impatient noise. 'If he has it at all. I'm unconvinced,' he said. 'My guess is that Tommy planted that locket. Or else he's chancing it. We don't know that it was found with the skeleton at all. We only have his word, and we all know what that's worth. I am willing to bet that Tommy stole it from the apartment and is using it now just to spook you. How would he have had access to it if it had been found in the boiler room? It's evidence, surely? He wouldn't be allowed to take it away. That in itself is an offence.'

'Unless he's involved in investigating the case,' Michaela pointed out.

'Then he's in even worse trouble, trying to blackmail you with it,' Antony said. He put a whole calamari ring in his mouth and pushed the plate across the table. 'Here's Janus now,' he said.

Between them they filled Janus in on the latest developments. Antony did most of the talking while Michaela toyed with a piece of calamari on the end of a fork and drank more than her normal quota of wine. Janus seemed almost as shaken as Michaela. He pulled up another chair and put his feet on it, looking pale and drawn. His hair was growing longer and it curled over his collar as he hunched his head into his shoulders.

'This has gone beyond a joke,' Janus said, echoing Antony's earlier sentiments.

'I never found it funny,' Michaela replied. She gave a reckless laugh.

'So what's the plan?' Janus looked at Antony, who was sitting with his chin in his hands. 'You're not really going to meet this maniac in the orchard? At midnight?' He sounded incredulous. 'Who was it said something about Enid Blyton?'

'Shut up, J.' Michaela looked at her brother. 'This is something I have to do, a chance I'm going to take. I need to get that locket. I can't think about anything else.'

'The locket. Oh, yes.' Janus looked down at his hands.

'I lost it that summer,' Michaela reminded him. 'Don't you remember, Janus? I cried about it for at least a day. I used to take it off when we went swimming and I thought I had lost it that way. How it got into the boiler room with Crispian Younghusband I don't know.'

'If it did,' Antony interrupted, straightening up. 'I never thought you would be this gullible. But since you're so set on going through with this extraordinary move, there's no way that you're going alone.'

'What do you mean?' Michaela said, staring at him. 'I have to go alone, Antony. He made that clear. He'll never hand over the wretched thing if I have a crowd of wellwishers dragging along with me. Especially you lot.'

'Yes, well, I have a plan,' Antony told her. He held up a hand. 'Hear me out before you jump in. We were all in this together from the beginning and there is no question of you handling it alone. Don't you agree, Janus?'

'Oh,' said Janus. 'Of course.' He ran a finger round his collar and looked down at his hands again, spreading his fingers and examining his nails. There was louder laughter coming from the deck of the yacht and Blanche was singing again, more bluesy now, and more strident.

The drummer was lagging a beat behind. The door of the club opened, letting out a breath of hot air and a burst of song, and Pauline plumped down beside Michaela. 'How are you feeling?' she asked. 'Are you really going through with this?'

Then Antony told them his plan. It was complicated, but simple at the same time. All it required was good timing, coordination and cooperation. It may have sounded like something out of a bad farce or a crib from *Cyrano de Bergerac*, but there was no reason why it shouldn't work if they all played the parts he allocated to them.

'To start with,' he told them, 'without trying to alarm you, I think Tommy may be dangerous. We already know how devious he is and how untrustworthy. There's no reason to suppose he's entirely on the level with this scheme of his. So you need to be protected, Mick, and there's just no arguing with that.'

Michaela looked at him patiently. 'Go on,' she said. She was still determined to do this on her own.

'I,' Antony announced, 'will be you. And Janus will be your voice.'

'*What*?'

'It's easy.' Antony went on quickly. 'It will be dark, there are no lights in the orchard. I am assuming Tommy means to meet you at the hopscotch tree and Smuts's bench, in the clearing where we always used to congregate. You and I are not too far off in height and looks and at that time of night shapes and things are deceptive.'

'You're a boy, Antony. I'm a girl.'

Antony waved her sarcasm away with a hand.

'Janus will hide in the hydrangea bushes and mimic

your voice,' he went on. 'You know as well as I do that he's flawless.' Janus took in a deep, audible breath and let it out slowly. 'So I will stand at a safe distance, Janus will do the talking and together we will retrieve the locket and make him promises we've no intention of keeping. You, Michaela, won't be anywhere near the place.'

'The hell I won't,' said Michaela. 'This is madness. I won't let you do it. You're outrageous, Antony.' But even as she spoke, a tremulous smile began to break through. Pauline, at first wide eyed with concentration, grinned round at them. She slapped Antony on the shoulder.

'I think the idea has brilliance,' she said. 'And Janus does do you perfectly, Mick.'

Michaela was beginning to waver. 'He'll see immediately it's not me,' she said doubtfully. 'Unless you wear . . .'

'A wig and a dress,' Antony replied promptly. 'We'll do this properly, of course. Won't we, J?'

'A wig and a dress,' Michaela protested. 'From where? Nothing of mine will get past your shoulders.'

Antony's eyes flickered over to Janus, who took his feet off the chair and pulled the bottle of wine out of the ice bucket by the neck, not looking at anyone. 'Oh,' Antony said, 'that will be the easiest part.'

'So what do you say, Michaela?' said Pauline. 'Janus – will you do it?'

'If it will mean an end to all this, I suppose so,' said Janus in a startlingly good imitation of his sister's voice.

'Mick?' Antony raised his eyebrows.

'Well,' said Michaela. 'I still think it's ridiculous and unnecessary, but it's very generous.' She looked fragile for a minute and then defiant. She pulled her hair back and twined it round her fingers. 'And I'll go along with it – but only on one condition.'

'What's that?' said Antony. He was smiling at her, pleased with himself.

'I'm going too.'

'Oh, now wait,' said Antony

'Yes.' Michaela would have no opposition. 'We'll go early and I'll climb the chestnut tree. Nobody will see me – I know exactly where to sit. But that's final. If you're going to risk this for me, then I'm coming too.'

'Christ, Michaela,' said Janus. 'When last did you climb a tree?'

Michaela looked at him. 'That's why we're going early.'

Pauline laughed. 'And don't think for a moment,' she said, 'that I am going to be left behind. That settles it. After all, someone has to bring sustenance.'

They all went back inside the club. Frank took away their glasses and brought back fresh ones and a bottle of Meerendal Shiraz. Antony raised his glass and looked at Michaela. 'To the end of the affair,' he said softly and he touched his glass to hers.

Helena and Michael were at the club tonight and they pushed their tables together. Helena had made friends with Ernest. He was using the back of her wheelchair as an alternative perch and allowing her to scratch the top of his head with a swizzle stick. When Blanche had finished her final set she came across to join them.

'Mater's told Jannie Brand,' she told them. 'Now nobody's talking to her except the Barberton sisters, bless them, who want to host the reception.'

'I hope you didn't say I told you so,' Helena said,

knowing that Blanche probably had. 'We had expected Coventry.'

'The minister has been to see them,' Blanche went on gloomily. 'From the Coloured holy-roller church. She expects us all to be there, of course, to clap and hallelujah.'

'Well, of course,' Pauline said. 'We have to be there, no matter what.'

'Yes,' Blanche sighed. 'No matter what.' She looked around at the four cousins. 'Cheer up,' she told them. 'I don't know how much, but things could be worse.'

Janus is watching Crispian Younghusband throwing his cricket ball up in the air and catching it. He gives little jumps where both feet leave the ground and then bump down heavily, his legs creasing at the knees. He grunts when he catches it. The ball slaps his palm with a satisfying sound.

'Wanna play?' Crispian Younghusband slides a sly glance over to Janus sitting on the fence and throws the ball straight up over his head. The sun is in his eyes and he has to dive for it. He trips and falls. 'Ouch,' he says. He rubs at his knees. Janus picks up the ball and tosses it to him, underhand. The ball is hot and heavy. Janus sits back on the fence again. 'Naah,' he says. Michaela has told him to ignore Crispian Younghusband's overtures. He looks over his shoulder. There is no sign of his sister. She and Pauline were washing their hair this morning and making each other tiny plaits all over their heads, sitting in the sun by the pool. 'Well, OK,' he says. 'Throw here, then.'

He holds the ball for a moment in his hand. He turns it over, looking at the scribble of famous names in indelible ink. He feels a flush of pure envy come over his face. He has never coveted anything like he covets Crispian Younghusband's cricket ball. He throws it back and Crispian Younghusband scrambles for it, reaching out with a fat arm, the skin at his elbow deeply studded with dimples. He throws it back and Janus catches it easily, feeling the sting in his hand connect with the tug in his breast. If he could . . . Just till the end of the holidays. Just for a couple of days . . .

'Hey,' he says, walking over. 'Can I – would you let me borrow your ball, just for . . .

Crispian Younghusband is smiling, a stupid slow smile, and already shaking his head. He backs away a step or two, holding out both hands for the ball.

'I'll swop you,' Janus says suddenly.

'For what?' Crispian Younghusband moves forward again, his small black eyes cautiously curious. He is wary of the cousins.

Janus is digging deep in his pocket. He brings out a handkerchief, a Chappies chewing gum coming out of its wrapper, some jacks – a silver locket on a chain.

'It's Michaela's,' he says in a low voice, not meeting Crispian Younghusband's eyes. 'It's even got her name on it.'

Michaela and Antony had once decided, with all the sexual experience of sixteen year olds, that they were good together in bed, and Michaela reflected that they had certainly been on the right track. Each time they did this, and admittedly it wasn't very often, and before she regretted it and determined that it would not happen again, she remembered those first experimental days and felt a warmth and a closeness that she seldom felt with any other lover.

She had not yet told Antony about Simon and

she did not ask him what his plans were for Emma. There was an unspoken code of privacy between them when it came to other relationships. Their encounters were precious in their isolation. They always remained pockets of painful pleasure to be cherished and protected.

Michaela drove home in the early hours, hanging onto the wheel, feeling the day's events take over her limbs with fatigue, and avoiding the guilty eyes of fellow clandestine travellers on the road. She had had enough of guilt. She felt achingly tired, bemused and satiated all at the same time, and as if she had won Antony back after a titanic struggle. She felt exhilarated, too, as if on the brink of something sobering and momentous, as she supposed she was.

· 18 ·

The construction site at Bricknell Court was eerily empty of people. High wire perimeter fencing topped with giant silver coils of razor wire effectively sealed the area off from all possible intruders. There was one official point of entry, illuminated by powerful spotlights – two tall gates where the trucks and labourers passed in and out, and these were locked up at night by a security guard who sat, now, on a red plastic chair reading what appeared to be a Bible in the site office just inside the open door. He was clothed in a black uniform and had a flat black hat pushed to the back of his head. Michaela could see him quite clearly through her binoculars from where she sat concealed by a ring of hydrangea bushes beneath a tree. She had seen him come on duty at five o'clock. Now he turned his attention to a doorstopper sandwich, hunching over it, holding it with both hands. A curl of steam rose off the surface of a mug at his elbow.

Michaela had slipped into the orchard in the early afternoon. Despite Antony's protests she had insisted on coming in alone. She didn't trust Tommy. He might have said midnight, but what if he came earlier? What if he intended to be waiting for her when she arrived?

Their whole plan would have fallen apart. At least if he did pitch up and catch her unawares she would be alone, as he had stipulated, and then she would try to busk her way through. But by now Michaela was satisfied that Tommy wasn't here yet. She had been over the whole orchard, checking out all the old hiding places and some new ones as well. Then she had come back to the clearing and Smuts's bench, where she had tucked herself in amongst the hydrangea bushes with a clear view of the narrow path which led directly into the clearing – the direction from which she was almost sure Tommy would come – and a view through the bushes to the site office and the path which led down to it, the only other way through to this place.

Quite why Michaela had seen fit to bring the binoculars she didn't know, but it had seemed somehow appropriate as she had gathered her things together for the evening's showdown. She herself wore what could have passed for camouflage uniform: Susan's dark green school tracksuit and the floppy brown hat Simon watched cricket in and which he'd left behind on the hall stand. She had felt tempted to smear streaks of makeup on her cheeks like you saw in Vietnam movies but Susan was asking too many questions as it was and anyway her makeup drawer didn't run to olive eyeshadow.

Despite the security there was still a way of getting into the orchard without being detected if you knew what it was. So far the orchard itself had been largely left untouched and the cousins were all confident of making their way to the clearing without any difficulty. West of Bricknell Court was a school playing field which was separated from the orchard by a splitpole fence. The fence hadn't been in good shape when the cousins were children and it was not much better now. There were gaps where rotten planks had been removed and never replaced and which could be negotiated with a little care and some squeezing. All that remained was a rockery and some spiky plants to be stepped through and then the path was right there, leading straight down to Smuts's bench in the mossy clearing.

Michaela kept one eye on the path and one on the site office as daylight began to fade. She chewed nervously at her fingernails. She looked frequently at her watch. And then she saw Pauline. She was coming round the bend in the path on the way down from the fence, swinging her basket, resplendent in voluminous lilac parachute trousers, a long white shirt and a purple bowtie. Since she had left Tertius Pauline had displayed a flamboyance and gaiety in her outfits that was disarmingly infectious. She was a riot of colour and cheerfulness, but tonight Michaela closed her eyes in despair. When she opened them to look again she raised her binoculars, then put them down with an exclamation of impatience. She stepped out of the bushes and waited as Pauline came nearer. She grinned when she saw Michaela and waved.

'Jesus Christ!' Michaela hissed at her when she was within earshot. 'Jesus Christ, Pauline, what do you think you're doing? This isn't a game. And what is that creature doing here?'

Pauline's smile faded. 'Ernest?' she said, and the parrot on her shoulder blinked and gnawed at the leash tied loosely around his leg. 'Well,' she looked at Michaela doubtfully, 'it's just that Frank's been too busy at the club to take him out much, and as I'm not going to be there this evening to help, I offered to take him off his hands for a while. He won't be a nuisance,

I promise. He only ever says anything when Frank's around.'

Michaela's eyes were checking the path behind her. 'How can you be sure?' she asked icily. 'What if he chooses tonight to reel off eighteen verses from the *Mikado*?'

'He won't,' Pauline said confidently, turning to look where Michaela was looking. 'I've brought dozens of snack things to keep him happy.' She lifted the wicker basket, smiling again. 'See?'

Michaela grunted. 'You'd better get out of sight,' she grumbled, pulling at Pauline's arm. 'With a couple of fairy lights you could look like a Christmas tree.'

Pauline looked down at her clothes. 'Oh,' she said, 'I'm sorry. I didn't think —'

'That's your problem,' Michaela said roughly, guiding her through to her hiding place.

Pauline looked crestfallen and Michaela immediately felt sorry. 'Look,' she said softly, 'I'm scared, Pauline. I've been watching for Tommy all afternoon and the later it gets the more nervous I'm becoming. I need you to take it seriously, that's all. It may seem ridiculous but I don't really know what Tommy's up to and we need to be one jump ahead of him if we're going to pull this thing off.'

Subdued, Pauline moved backwards into the cover of the hydrangeas, pulling her basket in after her. Michaela put her binoculars to her eyes and scanned the fence. 'Where are the others,' she murmured uneasily. 'I told them to be early.'

'Which way do you think Tommy will come in?' Pauline asked in a whisper.

'Well, he has a choice of two,' Michaela replied. 'It depends, I suppose. If he's involved in police work, he'll be allowed in any way he chooses. If it's cloak and dagger we're dealing with, he'll find his way in through the school, like we did.'

'Either way we'll be able to see him coming,' Pauline said with a note of encouragement in her voice.

Michaela was bristling with tension. 'As long as we're vigilant,' she said without turning. 'As long as we don't let our concentration slip.'

Pauline settled back and leaned against her basket. 'Tommy also makes me nervous,' she admitted. 'He always did slip in and out like a wraith. One minute he was there and the next he wasn't. It was uncanny.'

'I know.' Michaela came and sat beside her. She shivered and rubbed at her arms. It was a warm night but she was suddenly cold inside the heavy tracksuit. Her legs were longer than Susan's and the bottoms allowed two inches of ankle to show. She pulled at her thick brown socks to cover them.

'Just look at all the chestnuts,' Pauline murmured, stretching out a hand and picking one up. 'Nobody's been collecting them. Remember how we used to and how we'd take them to the café and get them weighed and try to haggle over the price with George?'

Michaela scuffed at a dense pile of conkers. She was glad she'd worn running shoes. 'I never liked chestnuts actually,' she said, looking back to the path again, almost in darkness except for a section near the fence which was lit up by a light on the school field. 'I just liked collecting them, I think. Susan does too.'

'Probably hereditary.'

Michaela clutched at her knees. It was growing very dark now and the leaves on the trees all around them were shades of grey and black. Branches shook suddenly near the top of the tree above their heads as if something heavy were up there. Ernest, peering through the leaves from Pauline's shoulder, cocked his head and Michaela drew in a breath.

'Squirrels,' Pauline told her in a low, conspiratorial voice. 'Working on their winter stash.'

'Is this the right party?' It was Janus, stepping into the clearing and walking straight over to where Pauline's white shoes stuck out from the bushes. He was all in black and he looked nervous and jokey at the same time. He bent and parted the leaves. 'Isn't Antony here yet?'

Michaela and Pauline had grabbed at each other and shrunk back in fright, and they sat, frozen together, staring out at Janus. 'God!' said Michaela, letting out a breath, 'where did you come from?'

'Through the front,' Janus said. 'There's a side gate open just beside the main gates – for the security guard, I suppose. He didn't see me. He's patrolling down on the side, I could see his torch. I walked straight through.' He looked at his sister's face. 'Don't worry, Mick,' he told her. 'I was careful.'

'Yes, but we weren't,' Michaela said, getting up. 'Christ, if *you* can creep up on us easily, Tommy —'

'I gather he hasn't pitched yet,' Janus said. He looked at the parrot kneading Pauline's shoulder with his feet. 'What . . .?'

'Don't ask,' Michaela said darkly.

Michaela knew they would have to be more vigilant if they wanted to spot Tommy before he saw them. They would have to take turns keeping watch over the two entry points and they should all take up their positions well before midnight. She looked up into the waving branches of her tree with a sense of trepidation, unsure all at once about her agility. It had indeed been a long while since she'd climbed this tree, or any tree for that matter. Suddenly Michaela looked at her brother and cousin, Janus in his black cashmere sweater and shifting from one jittery foot to the other, and Pauline and her battered old picnic hamper, and she saw only the ludicrous side to this situation. What they were about to do was absurd. They would never get away with it. Tommy was not a kid they could hoodwink. Tommy was a thug, a dangerous animal, streetwise and clever. Espionage was what he did for a living. It was his stock in trade. How did they think he wouldn't cotton onto this facile attempt to outwit him? And what would he do when he discovered the deception? Michaela felt a cold rush of despair. She was about to speak, to cancel everything, to tell them to call the whole thing off, when they heard a swishing noise behind them and, caught unawares for the second time, Antony came sashaying through the trees.

'Oh, Antony!' Pauline cried out spontaneously, then clapped her hand over her mouth with a sidelong look at Michaela.

The others turned to study him more critically. Michaela stood with her arms folded and her feet apart and felt the grudging lift of hope. She and Antony had always looked alike, right from when they were babies, and right now they could have been twin sisters, although Antony's hair was darker and he was a head taller than her. With flat shoes, however, and a pink dress as deep as a blush midway down his calves, he could easily have passed for Michaela, even in daylight. The deciding factor was the hair, a tawny brown wig, shoulder length, which hung heavy and smooth on either side of his face.

Only Pauline was smiling. Janus was frowning, looking anxiously at Antony's scooped and slightly gaping neckline. Michaela was turning in small circles again, checking both pathways. She knew some comment was expected from her. 'Well,' she said when she was satisfied that both paths were clear for the moment, 'it's not exactly my colour, but . . .' and she gave a wry smile.

Antony kissed her on the cheek. 'It's going to be all right,' he told her. 'Take it easy, Mick. We'll get through this.'

'Keep your voice down,' Michaela pleaded. She pushed Janus and Antony over to the bench and Pauline came out from the hydrangeas, dusting her trousers. 'If we all sit over here,' Michaela said, 'I've checked it out – we can't be seen from either entrance, but we've got a pretty good view of the path from the fence and the site office and path down that way. I think we should all keep our mouths closed –' she looked at the parrot '– and our eyes open.'

'Should we get into position now?' Janus asked.

Michaela was growing less and less keen on the tree. She shook her head. 'Not yet,' she said. 'We'll sit it out a bit longer, I think.'

It was now completely dark and the orchard was a place of looming shapes and shadows. The trees seemed to press in on them from all sides and although the terrain was utterly familiar to each one of them, in darkness it seemed to take on another, less friendly dimension. The earth felt cold and unyielding and the broad trunks of the trees were solid as armour. None of them had thought to bring a torch and they were thankful for the faint light from the moon which trickled through the cover of the trees.

Pauline was silently busy with her basket which she had brought with her over to Smuts's bench. Out of its capacious depths she drew a couple of small candles in brass candle holders. 'I brought them from the club,' she explained apologetically, 'at the last minute. I thought they would give ambience . . .'

'Plenty of that here already.' Janus shuddered, peering through the bushes to the path.

Michaela shook her head decisively and Pauline dropped the candle holders back into the basket as if they were red hot. She smiled around tentatively. 'Well,' she said, 'anybody hungry?'

'No,' Michaela said firmly and she turned to face the path. Janus was watching the other direction but he sneaked a look into the wicker basket and raised his eyebrows at Antony. None of them had had supper.

'Pauline,' Michaela said, not turning. 'The *last* thing we need right now —'

'It's all right, Michaela,' Antony said quietly. 'We could all do with a little sustenance while we keep watch. What you got, Pauline?'

Without the muted glow of candles, one of Pauline's famous picnic meals took shadowy shape – cold pork pies and chippolata sausages on toothpicks; warm, fragrant wedges of quiche; marinated mushrooms with little silver forks; miniature porcelain bowls of ribbon noodles. Efficiently, concentrating while the others turned their backs and watched for signs of Tommy, Michaela's shoulders stiff with disapproval, Pauline handed out food on small black plastic plates, while Ernest sat on the back of the bench above her. When she'd finished she passed him a shallow dish of sunflower seeds, balancing it on the back of the bench. He stared at it dolefully, and fluffed out his neck feathers.

The cousins sat close together beside the bench, not

speaking, eating with their fingers. Michaela shook her head shortly and pushed her plate aside, but Antony appeared relaxed. He hitched his dress up over his knees and sat crosslegged, licking flakes of pastry from his fingers, unconcerned. Michaela glanced over at him. 'You're not wearing a bra,' she pointed out gruffly. 'Am I that flat chested?'

Antony wiped his mouth with the back of his hand and grinned at her. He kept his voice low, barely above a whisper. 'That's where I drew the line,' he told her. 'There had to be a line. Besides, I didn't think Tommy would notice an absence of breasts in the dark.'

Pauline and Janus were packing things back into the basket, deftly and silently like two figures in a mime show. Janus was barely visible in his black clothes. All that could be seen of him were pale fluttering hands and a luminously anxious face. He tapped Michaela on the shoulder. 'Oughtn't we to be rehearsing or something?' he whispered. 'Or am I to take all my cues from Tommy himself?'

He looked towards the hydrangea bushes round the bole of the tree. 'Is that where you want me, Antony?'

'Right there.' Antony nodded. 'I'll be here on the bench, or standing beside it. I won't wander further off.'

'What if Tommy goes somewhere else, in another direction?' Michaela asked abruptly. 'Then what? Janus isn't a ventriloquist.' This plan was suddenly as full of holes as a cheese grater.

'We'll have to take that chance,' Antony said. 'But I'll do my best not to move. We should try to say as little as possible, J. Let Tommy himself do the talking. And do our best to cut it short. We don't want to be hanging around here all night exchanging pleasantries. We've got business to conduct so let's try and keep it brisk and to the point. Isn't that what you would try to do, Michaela?'

Michaela nodded heavily. She found she had begun to shake, imperceptibly at first, but with a steady trembling that had begun somewhere round her knees. She got up and paced restlessly around the mossy clearing, hugging her arms. Antony looked at her for a minute. Then he got to his feet, smoothed his dress down and walked over to where she was running a toe over the place where the hopscotch squares used to be. He took her by the elbow and walked her a little way away, into the deep cover of the peach trees. When they could not see the others, he put his arms round her and pulled her head in to his chest. She could smell aftershave on his cheeks and feel the long sweep of his hair as it brushed against her neck. Michaela felt as if she were in a pantomime, she the principal boy dressed in pants with her hair concealed beneath a hat and Antony beautiful in drag with his high cheekbones and red lipstick. The whole fiasco was theatrical, unreal. It couldn't possibly work.

'This is a mistake,' she told him, looking up into his eyes. 'It's not too late, Antony. Please go home, and take the others with you. Let me do this on my own. It's madness to involve you. We'll never pull it off.'

'We won't if you panic,' Antony agreed.

'I'm not panicking,' Michaela said with some irritation because she was close to it. Antony was too calm, too controlled.

'Good,' said Antony. 'Then you'll go up your tree when the time comes and try to keep Pauline quiet, and you'll stay there until I give you the all clear.'

Michaela swallowed. 'This is all so fucking sinister,' she said. 'I can't —'

'In an hour it will all be over,' Antony said firmly, giving her shoulders a shake. 'And then we will meet back at your house as we agreed and have a well earned drink and put this whole business behind us.'

Michaela was not fooled. She could see the shadow in Antony's eyes, hear the doubt behind his confident words. He was as troubled and unsure as she was. They both knew that the chance of Tommy being on the level was slim and that Crispian Younghusband would remain a threat and an obstruction in their lives, locket or no locket. Until the issue was resolved, they would never reach a truly peaceful place, and Tommy was not the means to its resolution. They were playing games on the surface, dangerous cosmetic games, skating down a treacherous path of deception and compounding lies.

When the trembling had almost stopped and Michaela felt Antony's hand fold round her own they went back to join the others. Janus was keeping watch in both directions, which irony was lost on all of them, and Pauline was on her hands and knees, one hand cupped around a candle stub. 'I found it,' she said in a hoarse, triumphant whisper. 'I knew it would be here still — look.' It was the hopscotch, dimly discernible in the puddle of yellow light. They could just make out the faint, uneven squares and circles, still scored deeply into the ground. Pauline was so excited she looked as if she were about to start casting round for a stone.

Antony leaned over her and blew out the candle. 'It's getting late,' he said softly. 'I think it's time we took up our places.'

The moon gave some light on the mossy patch

and Smuts's bench as it filtered through the branches, washing the space in a buttery light. Pauline, subdued again and apprehensive, took her basket and pushed it out of sight into the thick of the hydrangea bushes. They were all looking round, eyes straining to the outer edge of the clearing. Antony sat down on the bench and crossed his legs. He smoothed back his hair. Nobody was talking. They moved silently, like actors on a stage at the moment before the curtain goes up, conscious of an audience just beyond the footlights. Pauline settled Ernest on her shoulder. Janus gave her a foot up and she scrambled up onto the lowest branch of the chestnut tree. It was wide and flat and she walked along it like a highwire artiste, one careful foot in front of another, looking for a handhold further up. She grunted as she stretched and the leaves rustled and swayed as she pulled herself up and then up again, until there was nothing left of her to be seen. Janus stood back and shaded his eyes. He walked around the tree and then walked backwards to the edge of the clearing and looked from there, but Pauline had effectively disappeared. He nodded to Antony.

'Now you, Mick,' Antony said.

Michaela looked hard at her cousin. 'Antony —' she began.

'Up you go,' he said lightly.

Michaela followed Pauline's route, allowing herself to be guided by Pauline's soft voice above her. She felt rough bark on her hands and recoiled at the touch of something pricking her face. 'Be careful of the conkers.' Pauline's low warning came too late. 'Keep your face down.'

This tree had been many things to Michaela. It had been a boat and a camel and a castle in countless exotic countries. Never, in any of the games of wild imagination and fantasy that they had played here as children, would they have dreamt of its branches serving such a purpose as this. Two grown women taking refuge in its foliage, waiting for a blackmail scene to play itself out below their feet. Michaela wondered for an uncomfortable moment what Mater would say if she could see her now. Mater's understated advice had been, in effect, to take the bull by the horns and live with the consequences, not hide away beneath ever more suffocating layers of deception and subterfuge. This evening's events could not have been farther removed from Mater's intentions and this, ultimately, was not Michaela's way. She was used to being in command of situations, of taking the lead. It was guilt, pungently laced with fear that had made her allow herself to be led in this direction, and she was finding it increasingly regrettable. She looked down, seeking Antony out and could discern the top of his head at the edge of the bench. He stretched an arm out along its length. He looked as relaxed as a socialite at a garden party.

Of Janus there was no sign and the ring of hydrangea bushes, the same bushes, perhaps, where they had played sardines a long lifetime ago, was completely still. They sat in silence, Pauline playing loosely with Ernest's leash. He sat serenely on the branch beside her with his eyes closed, as if he were meditating.

Just before midnight, Pauline touched Michaela softly on the arm and nodded with her head towards the edge of the clearing. Michaela felt her breathing quicken and perspiration break out in her armpits. A figure in what looked like a long dark army greatcoat was slowly making its way towards them. At first she almost hoped it was the security guard but she knew it couldn't be. She had just watched his flashlight way below near the site manager's office. He would have no reason to come up to the orchard. The most he would probably do would be to come as far as the old poplar fence. The only equipment this far up was the front end loader and it was unlikely that anyone would make off with that on a nocturnal joyride.

The figure was coming closer. Antony had seen him too. He stood up, slim and tall, hair shining in the moonlight. He moved back, closer to the trunk of the chestnut tree, and Michaela saw him make a sign with his fingers to alert Janus. A sudden gust of wind swept through the branches, making Michaela grab onto her branch and bite her lip as a cluster of conkers made sharp contact with her cheek.

Tommy had stopped a short way off. He stood facing Antony, with his hands in the pockets of his greatcoat. Antony was almost completely in shadow. Neither of them moved.

Michaela's eyes bored through the darkness, smarting with the strain of trying to see. Something was wrong. She didn't know what it was but there was something that didn't add up. Slowly, balancing by hooking her shoes under the branch just below her, she raised her binoculars to her eyes. It was difficult to find Tommy at first and Pauline had to hold her by the arm as she swayed forward, but then he slammed suddenly into focus and she felt nausea again, and the unpleasant taste of real fear. She sat almost motionless, balancing, trying to get an angle where his face was in the moonlight. He was wearing something on his head, pulled down low over his forehead, and the collar of his coat hid the rest of his face. And then, suddenly, she knew what it was. The legs. Tommy had short, truncated, almost deformed legs, and a disproportionately long torso. This man was altogether too tall and heavily built. He had long legs, in long dark trousers.

This man was much too tall to be Tommy.

Michaela wanted to shout and she nearly did. She let the binoculars fall and swing round her neck on their strap. She wanted to call out to Antony, to warn him so that he would be prepared. She wanted to grab Pauline and whisper into her ear. She did none of these things. Instead she sat on her branch, like a bird trapped in lime, and listened to the blood rushing through her head.

Antony cleared his throat softly.

'Well, here I am,' said Janus in a stiff, clear voice so accurately Michaela's that she could not prevent a stab of pride and emotion. She closed her eyes and the branch rocked a little as Pauline shifted her weight. 'Have you brought the locket?'

The man did not move. Then slowly he took one hand out of his pocket. He held something up between his thumb and forefinger. Michaela caught a flash in the moonlight, but if it was the locket she was too high up to see it. The man took a step forward. Antony stepped backwards.

'Throw it to me,' Janus said quickly. 'Stay where you are.'

The man faltered, then threw the locket down onto the moss. It landed at Antony's feet. Michaela was tempted to lift the binoculars again but she would see no pink sugar mouse from up there. She saw Antony stoop, bend his head to examine the locket. He looked at it closely, opening the clasp and shutting it. Then he closed his hand over it.

'That is my part of the bargain,' the man said, and his voice was as muffled as it had been on the phone.

Michaela couldn't help herself. She trained the binoculars on him once more. He appeared to have something like a scarf round the lower part of his face. For someone who wanted to spill the beans on his life story, she thought, he was being pretty cagey about his identity.

'Who are you?' Janus said, taking the initiative, 'and why are you doing this?' Could Janus see from behind the hydrangea leaves that it wasn't Tommy?

'Who I am is not important for the moment,' the man replied, 'but you know our agreement. My story needs to be told and your cooperation buys my silence.'

'And if I can't guarantee anything?' Janus said, as Michaela had coached him. Perhaps Janus was also thinking ahead. If this wasn't Tommy and it wasn't Tommy's story – his police activities, how he had stalked Harriet and David all those years, his life once his cover had been blown – they were dealing with, then what story was it they were talking about? And what was his connection with Crispian Younghusband? *And how did he know?*

'You can guarantee it. You're Michaela Whitehead, aren't you? You control what is published in your magazine.'

'That's not right. I don't. I have an editorial board, there are other people . . .' Antony was making all the right accompanying gestures. Michaela glanced over at Pauline, who was staring down through the leaves, her expression rapt. She had let go of Ernest's leash and the parrot had hopped two branches above them. Michaela looked up nervously and saw a dark shape and a head swathed in leaves.

'You will push it through. I have every confidence in you. If you don't . . .' The man lifted his big shoulders, took his hands from his pockets and eloquently spread his fingers.

'So where is this story?' Janus asked, a little too conversationally, Michaela thought. It was time to wrap this up. She could see the light of the security guard's torch playing through the poplars. It flashed across them momentarily and she blinked, shrinking back into the shadows. 'What guarantee have *I* got that you won't pursue this crazy notion of yours even if I do publish your story, whatever it is?'

Antony folded his arms, just like Michaela did. She gazed down at him.

'We have a deal,' the man said. 'That is your guarantee. I will be in touch with you. I do not intend to walk out of your life after one meeting, Michaela. I feel there is already a measure of trust between us, don't you? We have a relationship now. It does not end when we walk away from here. We are tied together, you and I.'

Michaela suddenly felt as if she might vomit. She had a pain in her chest and her eyes were blurring from the strain of staring down into darkness. Involuntarily she gave a small moan.

Immediately the man stopped speaking. His head jerked up, and he cast about, this way and that, like an animal trying to identity a scent on the wind. Antony stood very still, with his hands by his sides. The hand with the locket was a clenched fist.

'What was that?' the man said. 'Who's there with you? You didn't come alone?'

It was at that precise moment, as Michaela held her breath and fought to control a gust of dizziness, that

Ernest took flight. Spreading his wings, the undersides white as cream in the moonlight, and with the leash on his foot slapping against the branches of the tree as he went, he soared and then swooped towards the ground, singing 'On the goo-ood ship, Lollipop' over and over as he banked and turned and skimmed perilously close to the top of Antony's wig with claws outstretched.

'It's only my parrot,' Janus said in a voice a notch too high. 'Come here, Polly.' Antony made feeble gestures with his fingers, beckoning and clicking ineffectually. Ernest took no notice, alighting on the back of the bench and tucking comfortably into the sunflower seeds they had all forgotten to pack away.

But the man was nervous now. He took a step forward and made as if to look up into the tree. He swivelled his head to look at the parrot. He jiggled his hands in his pockets. 'You would be very foolish to have told anyone about this rendezvous,' he said. 'Very foolish.'

'I didn't tell anyone,' Janus said calmly. 'I came alone. As you can see.'

The man's neck was jerking. He was staring up into the tree, walking backwards and forwards, murmuring, 'Oh, Michaela, Michaela.'

Antony shuffled awkwardly. This was taking a tricky turn. Janus was momentarily silent. Then suddenly, like water gushing from a tap, the man began to talk. A rapid stream of words came out of his mouth. He sounded like a soap-box preacher gone off the rails, Jimmy Swaggart speaking in tongues. Antony stood helplessly with his hands at his sides and Pauline and Michaela leaned forward in astonishment. Michaela tightened her grip on Pauline's arm. 'What the fuck?' she mouthed, her eyes wide.

From their position in the tree, looking down on his head, it wasn't easy to hear all the words or to get any clear idea of what the man was trying to say. Snatches of sentences came up to them, strong, excited words. '. . . in my power . . . passionate heights . . . can never be broken . . . the dark side of the soul . . . your every waking moment . . . inside of you . . . all-consuming . . . Till death us do . . .'

Everything about Antony's body language spelled alarm. Janus, shaken into silence, must have been scrabbling for an appropriate response. The man was verbally out of control and he appeared to be getting more agitated by the minute. He began advancing on Antony. Antony stood his ground but moved sideways, aiming to get behind the tree if the necessity arose.

And then, distinctly, they all heard the tramp of heavy boots and the beam of a powerful torch swung high over the clearing. Michaela could see from her vantage point that it was the security guard, possibly alerted by Ernest's cracked warbling and the rising sound of the man's voice. Michaela was afraid. There was no predicting what he might do if the guard stumbled in on them. He was steadily, accurately, making his way in their direction. Again she had forcibly to prevent herself from calling out a warning.

The guard reached the edge of the clearing and shone his torch round, narrowly missing Antony in its light but catching the stranger, who put an arm up over his face and teetered backwards. Michaela felt the back of her tracksuit snag on a sharp piece of bark. Already leaning forward, she jerked it away, lost her balance and, shouting out in fright, found herself bouncing towards the ground, crashing through the leaves and swearing like a sailor.

'Oh, for fuck's sake!' said Janus loudly in his own voice, parting the leaves with his fingers. 'Wouldn't you just know it.'

The guard began to call out as Antony instinctively positioned himself to break Michaela's fall, while the man in the greatcoat stood frozen like a cornered beast, shielding his face from the light. Then he began to whirl around, looking for an escape route, churning up chestnut leaves and conkers and dust. In front, advancing on him, was the security guard, in uniform and night-stick and shouting in Xhosa. Then there was Antony, startled and disorientated, in his pink dress, Janus stepping wearily out of his hiding place and throwing up his arms in despair, and Michaela herself, still swearing and crying and getting up onto her knees.

'You set me up!' the man shouted, staring at Antony, and his voice was high and hysterical. 'You set me up, you bitch!'

In an instant they saw his hand go to his pocket and watched, stupidly, as he drew out a snub-nosed revolver which was almost enclosed in his big hand. The guard dropped to his stomach, there was a flash and a noise, a bloodcurdling screech from Ernest and dust and blinding light everywhere. And then they all watched in helpless amazement as with another loud report the man put the weapon to his head and pulled the trigger.

Janus got to him first, before the others. He pulled down the scarf and moved to feel for a pulse, then he stopped, sat back on his heels and stared. He looked up at Pauline, who had appeared, breathless, scraped and bleeding, at his elbow.

'Jesus,' he whispered. 'Do you see who it is? Where's Michaela?'

Michaela wasn't there. Janus looked around for her. The guard was shining his torch on the man's face and jabbering panicstricken half sentences, feeling for his two-way radio or his Bible with a shaking hand.

'Michaela? Antony?'

Michaela was sitting on the ground beneath the chestnut tree. She looked vacantly up at Janus and Pauline as they moved slowly across to her. She had Antony lying across her lap. The wig had come off and his dark hair flopped down over his forehead. His eyes were partly open and he stared past them. A black stain the size of a spread hand was creeping down his chest. Michaela looked down at Antony in her lap, and back up at her brother and cousin. 'I think,' she said with a half smile, shaking her head, puzzled. 'I think Antony's dead.'

It couldn't have been more than twenty minutes before the paramedics and the police arrived. The site manager, too, was summoned, and he came in hastily thrown on clothes and sheepskin slippers. While the paramedics worked on the man in the greatcoat Michela sat cradling Antony's head, stroking back his hair and touching his cheeks. Pauline and Janus huddled together, watching the men at work, Pauline crying silently in long streams of tears. Then the paramedics stood up, one by one, shaking their heads reluctantly at the motionless figure on the grass, packing equipment back into cases. They put the man on a stretcher, covering his face and the hole in his head with a grey blanket. Then they put Antony's body on a stretcher too and took him down the path to the ambulance waiting on the roadway below. Michaela stood numbly by and watched them go, making no attempt to follow. The pink dress stuck out from beneath the blanket like a private signal.

Janus drew his sister to one side. 'Listen,' he said, taking her hands. 'There's something you need to know.'

She looked at him dully.

'He's dead. Your blackmailer is dead. And the mystery is solved.'

Michaela frowned distractedly. 'It wasn't Tommy,' she said in a tired voice. 'I could see at once that it wasn't Tommy.'

'I know,' Janus told her. 'It was Crispian Younghusband.'

· **19** ·

Michaela had been thinking about the black egret and its unique method of catching its prey. She and Antony, on the way up to Stillwaters once, sharing a flask of coffee beside a small dam as the sun was going down, had watched the bird at work close to the water's edge. It would stride about, before stopping abruptly and bringing its jet black wings over its head like an old black raincoat, completely covering its body with this dark canopy. Underneath it would stir up the murky bottom with its yellow feet and stab at the fish or mud crabs below the surface of the water. She could not help feeling a sudden affinity with this strange bird. She found herself going about her day to day activities, doing the things that had to be done, like putting out the garbage, filling her car with petrol. Then she would stop suddenly, metaphorically, and put her arms over her head, making her own dark tent, shutting out the light and the world above. Beneath it she would dig and probe ruthlessly, gouging deep inside herself for something that might nourish and replenish the gaping void that was there. Antony had taken pictures of the black egret. In the pale mauve evening light they had had a weird, surreal quality. 'Oh, look,' had been

Susan's comment, 'someone left an umbrella out on the dam.'

Why Michaela was dwelling on this image she didn't truly understand, but somehow it suited her frame of mind. She had never felt the urge so strongly to creep away beyond the reach of outside scrutiny. The black egret became her private symbol. She was tempted to blow up Antony's picture of it and stick it over her front door like a biblical sign for a house with the plague. Throw out your dead. Some days she could have lain herself down in the street and waited for someone to take her away. She dreamed one night about doing that, and saw herself hovering over her bloated body lying in the gutter, watching as a horse-drawn cart turned the corner and moved relentlessly towards her. The hooded figure at the horse's head was none other than Crispian Younghusband, in open-toed sandals, with a raised whip in his hand.

Another night he appeared beside her bed wearing a salmon-pink dress, his neck weighed down with lockets as heavy as padlocks; still another, he was on stilts, a tall circus clown with painted boyish cheeks and a stiff-legged gait. She never saw him dead any more: he was always larger than life. All her dreams were of Crispian Younghusband.

There had been things to get through. Funeral arrangements, cleaning the fridge in Antony's apartment. Getting hold of Emma on her way back to Holland. Michaela had done very little but tag along, unable to bear being left out but powerless to contribute very much in practical terms. She did not want to be alone but at the same time she craved solitude. And all the time she felt she had cheated fate. Antony's death should have been hers. It should have been her with a bullet splintering her heart. She wished, over and over, that she had never agreed to Antony's plan. She wished it all undone, *undone*. She recognised a recurring pattern now, and it was uncomfortable and weighed heavily. Michaela in command, manipulating situations at minimum risk to herself, sidestepping responsibility, letting others do the dirty work for her and take the blame. All her cowardly life she had been doing this and she hadn't stopped yet, leaving wreckage in her wake, never being there when it could have mattered. And now it had caught up with her. This was her punishment. Never mind what her rational mind told her, it was as crude as that. Antony was dead and she was alive.

Explaining events to Helena and Michael had been appalling. She, Janus and Pauline had done it together, Janus doing most of the talking, in a monotonous voice, staring at his hands. Michael had stood like a statue behind Helena's wheelchair, holding onto her hands in a grasp reminiscent of the catcher in a pair of trapeze artistes. They had remained like that, not moving, throughout the increasingly bizarre-sounding story and Michaela had the miserable impression that they would hold the pose long after the three of them had gone away, frozen, gripping onto each other as if moulded together.

For days Susan had refused to believe that Antony was dead and would leave the room impatiently if anyone mentioned it. She had no real recollection of her own father's violent death, only hazy images which she seldom talked about. Between Antony and Janus, however, she had never lacked for a father figure and there was a closeness between the three of them that Michaela had encouraged and been grateful for through the years. Antony and Janus complemented each other in their personalities, which had meant that Susan, unknowing, was able to draw from them experiences that were all enriching in their different ways. Janus almost always represented unorthodox fun. He would arrive, usually unannounced, push aside her homework, and spirit Susan off for a drive round the mountain for halva ice cream and fish and chips at a trendy beach café on the way to the point. He would take off his flashy socks and shoes and sit on a rock beside the sea with his pants rolled up and ice cream at the corners of his mouth like a small boy, and give Susan the rundown on the latest gossip in the advertising world – who was sleeping with whom, which campaigns had been disasters and how the sweet looking model in the pantyhose ad had told everyone on the set to Fuck off and die the minute the cameras stopped rolling. Sometimes he would collect Susan on a Saturday morning and take her to the movies. They would sit right at the back and wear hats and sunglasses and hold hands and Janus would make comments below his breath that made her giggle.

Antony represented something else, no less important. With his more serious nature, his interest in his niece was somehow more thoughtful, more considering. His gifts to her were unusual but no less appealing: beautiful old-fashioned clothes, pearl buttons and lace, a set of children's classics for her birthday, a term's worth of riding lessons on Noordhoek beach. He watched her progress at school with quiet satisfaction and tried to share, whenever he could, the weekly burden of school lifts and homework supervision when Michaela was tied up in meetings or out of town. Antony was a solid anchor in Susan's life and without him, she drifted round the house, looking out at windows, waiting with a glazed expression for someone to tell her that it was all a mistake. Michaela half expected her to start calling out for Antony, plaintively, like she still did for The Dog every night, hoping by some desperate miracle that the sound of her voice would guide him home.

There was a desolation in the atmosphere at home, and a lethargy that hung about the two of them as heavily as any fog. Susan didn't go to school. It wasn't that she consciously decided that she couldn't face it; it was more as if she forgot to go, and Michaela didn't have the energy to mind. Susan wore the pale blue polo neck jersey Antony had given her for Christmas and ate the school sandwiches she continued to make sitting on the kitchen steps gazing out into the garden. She and Michaela didn't talk much, but they touched each other in passing.

For the first few days the house was full of other people. Blanche came and sat smoking at the kitchen table, listening with a sharp expression while Michaela went over the story again. Michaela knew it by heart, even the parts she was still only prepared to gloss over. She even used the same words each time, and identical intonations in repeating the chain of events: Bricknell Court, the skeleton, how Crispian Younghusband had got locked in there by mistake when they were children, how they all thought the skeleton was him and hadn't known quite what to do with the knowledge when an anonymous man they had thought was Tommy the pinball wizard had blackmailed Michaela with 'proof' of her locket being found with the body, and how she had been scared enough of his threats to take them seriously. The blackmail attempt. The orchard at midnight. Ernest giving the game away and unsettling everybody. And then the awesome discovery that it was Crispian Younghusband himself, clearly deranged and having lost none of his obsession with Michaela, who had thought to gain advantage by playing slippery games. Michaela was weary with the telling. Blanche had narrowed her eyes and drawn deeply on her cigarette, making few comments.

Pauline stayed long hours at the club, trying out new and ever more outrageous recipes until her clothes reeked of spices and she had Band-aids all over her fingers from distracted slicing and chopping. Frank cleaned and polished with a serious demeanour, and took the money in the bar every evening. The boys from Greenbacks did a late night set and one evening Blanche broke down on stage and had to be coaxed through two double Scotches before she could carry on.

The surprise to all of them was Janus. If Michaela had been in a mind to comment, she would have said that Janus had showed a strength of character she never would have believed he possessed. He was like a man with a mission. He took it upon himself to make himself available to Helena and Michael and he visited them every day. Sometimes he went shopping for them, coming in with plastic carriers crammed with everyday necessities – TV dinners, fresh bread and boxes of rainbow tissues. Helena, like Michaela, took little interest in anything. All of a sudden the wheelchair seemed too big for her and she sat in it with an old lady's rug across her knees as if she were permanently cold. Antony had been an only and much loved child and attentive to his mother as an adult, always concerned and available. His was a presence that was immediately missed. They all looked for pictures of him and when they pooled their findings were dismayed to discover that very few existed. Antony had lived much of his life through a lens, but it was never he who was the subject. So his father found himself looking at portraits on the walls of their home of any number of other people, family members, girlfriends, friends from Antony's schooldays, all bearing his hallmark and tracking his progress, but as a photographer, not a person. Other people's stories were their reminders of their son. 'This was taken when Antony was about twelve, your age,' Michael told Susan when she went over there to prowl morosely round their house. It was a picture of a guinea pig, paused in mid circuit on an exercise wheel and looking disdainfully at the camera. 'And this was taken during Antony's embarrassingly short sojourn with the Scouts.' Michael held up a group shot of youngsters in short pants and strange hats, none of whom was Antony, putting up a tent in a field of sunflowers. 'And this,' Michael chuckled, shaking his head, 'was Antony's first really good camera and the first thing to come out of his own darkroom.' It was Michaela and Mater, showing a leg for the camera, on the boathouse roof at Stillwaters, their arms linked like showgirls. A brief life through photographs, a personal photo essay, with the subject conspicuous by his absence.

Susan had her own photograph of Antony. She had taken it herself just the other day, with his own camera during one of the sessions at her school while Antony was busy with his project there. It was the most recent picture existing. She had seized the moment when Antony had put the camera down to help chase the school goat back into the grounds from the street outside, capturing quite by luck his look of comical concentration as, arms wide and eyes wider, Liquorice's stubby but potent horns bearing down on him, he attempted to guide the angry goat towards the gate. She hadn't even told Antony she'd taken it, leaving him to discover it for himself when he went back and developed the film. He had laughed and given it to her to keep, along with a shot of Susan and Florida with their arms loosely flung around each other and smiles from ear to ear. Susan carried Antony's picture around with her underneath her jersey, Antony and Liquorice, pressed against her heart.

Emma came to the funeral on her way to the airport. She wore a dark blue dress and flat black Italian shoes and she put her pale hands on Michaela's shoulders and kissed her on both cheeks. Janus had organised everything – a minister with a mop of curly yellow hair and a lisp, a coffin without any trimmings, even flowers and music for the organist to play. Not for Antony a mournful murmur of unidentifiable church music. Janus had chosen a selection from the Notting Hillbillies because he knew Antony had liked them. The rich, melancholy notes of 'Bewildered' and 'Blues Stay Away from Me' filled the church with sound, and had everyone swaying despite themselves in the pews and tapping their fingers on their hymnals. Neither Pauline nor Blanche could be persuaded this time to sing anything, and nobody pressed them.

Tertius had come to the funeral, unexpectedly, and he had stood at the back of the church with his head bowed and his hands folded respectfully in front of him. Afterwards he had shaken hands with all the family, formally, including Pauline, who skirted past him nervously with a quick, alarmed smile.

Simon had been there too, but he did not linger

and did not go back to Helena's and Michael's house afterwards for tea. It was enough that Michaela had seen him, that she knew he was around.

The papers had tried to run with a story that was confused and macabre, and Janus had had his work cut out for him trying to protect Michaela and Susan from reporters and other media people. They had two prominent names – Antony Whitehead the photographer, and Michaela Whitehead, magazine editor – neither of whom were strangers to the social pages, and although no one had yet got hold of the true story of the bizarre shooting in the Bricknell Court orchard, this hadn't prevented the press from speculating, distorting or simply guessing. Michaela had opted for a no comment approach, and the story they claimed to have got from Antony's parents was simply that Antony had been following a lead for a story which involved his cousin, and a case of mistaken identity had evolved. One paper had somehow latched onto Michaela as having the lead role in everything. By chance they had come reasonably close, having interviewed a loquacious porter at the hospital Antony had been taken to in his pink dress and taking a wild stab at putting two and two together. CITY PHOTOGRAPHER IN TRAGIC MISTAKEN IDENTITY SHOOTING was the headline, beneath which a press award picture of Antony draped in cameras and a picture of Michaela at a literary luncheon were shown as small insets. 'It is believed that the mystery gunman, whose name has not yet been released, who fatally wounded fashion photographer Antony Whitehead, had thought he was aiming his weapon at Whitehead's close cousin, well-known fiction editor of *Focus* magazine Michaela Whitehead. It is not clear why the photographer was posing as

Ms Whitehead, but the result was as tragic an event as could have been anticipated under the strange circumstances. Ms Whitehead could not be reached for comment today. Friends and family have reported that she is under sedation.'

'Mystery gunman.' Michaela sourly gave the paper back to Janus. Janus had just come off the phone from talking to Mater, who had called every day from Stillwaters, anxious to speak to Michaela, who had simply cried every time she tried to take up the phone. 'Jesus, I'm sick of mysteries.'

'What I want to know is,' Susan said suddenly, turning to look at her mother and Janus in turn, 'if it wasn't Crispian Whatsisname in the boiler room, then whose skeleton was it?'

Michaela had been thinking about that too.

'Well, it wasn't Tommy,' Janus said after a while. 'We know that much.' He sighed. 'Boy – were we ever on the wrong track.'

'I no longer care,' Michaela said stiffly. 'I've wasted enough anguish on that skeleton as it is. I wish to God it *had* been Crispian Younghusband. I wish it with all my heart, may he rot in hell forever.'

'Michaela —' Janus said uncertainly. 'Look, Pauline's been baking. Do you want a —'

'No, Janus, I don't want a damn cookie. I wish Pauline would let up. She made nine batches of shortbread before seven this morning. I can't stand it any more. This place looks like a florist and smells like a bakery.' Michaela curled her feet beneath her and stared grimly ahead of her.

For nearly twenty years Crispian Younghusband had been at the back of Michaela's head. How long had he been focusing his attention on her? It gave her the creeps to think about it. How long must he have been watching her, reading about her, tracking her down? And why? What was the story he wanted her to publish, if there even was one, if it wasn't a fabrication of his crazy mind? His useless fat life? What had he been doing all these years? Masturbating over a *Focus* article? Polishing up her silver locket, waiting for a chance to use it?

It was a week after the funeral that Michaela took a call from the detective who had been assigned to the case. She called Janus right after she put the phone down. 'He wants me to go to Crispian Younghusband's apartment,' she told him. 'He says it's relevant.'

'Relevant,' Janus repeated. 'Oh.'

'Will you come with me?'

'Of course.'

Crispian Younghusband had lived in a nastier part of town, in a block of flats with shiny black steps and lifts that carried the smell of boiled cabbage up and down with them locked inside their old wooden doors. There were the stalks of plants long dead in Ali Baba pots at the corners of the corridors and, when Michaela and Janus picked their way along, babies in vests, without nappies, playing outside kitchen doors. Their mothers followed Michaela with slitted eyes. She could feel them looking at her clothes as she passed.

The detective was waiting for them and the front door was open. He was leaning over the balcony, smoking, tapping his ash down to the floor below.

'Ms Whitehead,' he said, putting out a hand to shake and blowing smoke out of the corner of his mouth. 'Thank you for making the time. I thought you should take a look at a couple of things and see if you can help us make sense of them.'

Michaela didn't know what to expect.

'What things?' she said blankly. She stepped over the threshold, followed by Janus, who looked around with distaste.

The place was a slum. Crispian Younghusband was obviously as sloppy in his domestic habits as an adult as he had appeared to be heading all those years ago. There were dirty plates and mugs on a table pushed up against a wall, and a single bed grubbily unmade, against another. There was a smell of decaying plant matter in the stale air. But Michaela's first impression was of paper. There was paper everywhere. Papers spread out on the table and on the floor. Papers piled on small occasional tables dotted throughout the room. There were large loose white sheets and pads of notepaper. Michaela could see tightly scribbled black words, page after page after page, and an overflowing wastebasket beneath the table. There were cascades of paper sheets from one end of the room to the other.

'Good heavens,' said Janus. 'What a mess.' He stepped fastidiously over a pile of exercise books.

Michaela stared around without expression. 'What was it you wanted me to see?' she asked finally, her eyes coming to rest on the detective, who was leaning against the wall watching her take everything in. He led her over to the table and gestured to the wall above it. At first glance it appeared that the wall was papered with memos or notes. They were plastered all over, stuck on with Press-Stick. 'Take a look,' he invited. 'We hope you might be able to throw some light on these.'

Michaela went closer and as she did her heart began to beat a little faster. She fumbled in her handbag for her glasses and put them on. She leaned forward across the table. They were letters. Some of them were typed, some handwritten. Some were on *Focus* letterheads. And all of them bore her own distinctive signature. Michaela caught her breath.

All of the letters were addressed to Joy Beamish.

Janus, peering over Michaela's shoulder, stood back and looked at the detective, who was lighting another cigarette from the butt of the last and watching them through the smoke. 'I don't get it,' he said. 'Joy Beamish? I thought this was something to do with Crispian Younghusband?' He turned to Michaela. 'Isn't Joy Beamish the woman you always . . .?'

'Yes,' said Michaela, straightening up and pushing her glasses further up her nose. Her eyes moved rapidly around the room again, as if seeing it in a different light. Her heart was beating furiously. There was a box of breakfast cereal on a corner of the table with half of the back cut away. She picked up a pile of similar cardboard squares cut off cereal boxes. Send in five and win a pair of tiger striped shoelaces. No doubt they would have found their way onto her desk in due course with a fresh batch of purple prose. Also on the table was a small portable typewriter. It had a piece of paper in it and Michaela leaned forward and looked at it. The typeface and the style were all too familiar. 'Thousands of dainty stars peppered the midnight sky like birdshot as Portia lay waiting like a sacrificial lamb on the forest floor with bosom heaving and a prayer leaving her lips like the last train from the station . . .' Another story with nowhere to go.

'Michaela?' Janus still looked puzzled.

The detective strolled over to the table.

'I think they're one and the same person,' Michaela told her brother. She switched the typewriter on and then off again. 'Don't you see? Crispian Younghusband

and the illustrious Joy are – *were* – one and the same person.' She tried to remember some of the garbled sentences the man in the orchard had uttered. How they were closer than she suspected. How they already had a relationship. (Hadn't they just?) She remembered with a coldness in her stomach the last rejection letter she had sent to Joy, the vicious, unkind one which she had later regretted. She looked back to the papers on the wall and found it at once. There it was, handwritten on Michaela's own notepaper. It had been scored through the middle with a black pen. Was that the one that had had Crispian Younghusband loading up his gun?

'Let me get this right,' the detective said. 'This Beamish person was known to you as well?'

'Yes,' said Michaela. 'Only I don't think Joy Beamish is a real person, if you know what I mean. I believe that Crispian Younghusband was using the name Joy Beamish as a sort of pen name, the one he wrote stories and poems under. He submitted a number of stories to my magazine over a period of several months. Years, actually.'

'And you didn't know who the real author was?'

'Not until this moment,' Michaela told him.

'So Beamish Joy was a beamish boy,' Janus murmured. 'What a turn-up.'

The detective drew on his cigarette. 'Were his stories no good at all?' he asked suddenly.

'Not good enough to use in the magazine,' Michaela said. 'But he never gave up. He sent something in nearly every week. I sent them back.'

'Were they always addressed to you?'

'Always.'

'She used to send you things, didn't she, Michaela?'

'He,' Michaela corrected woodenly. 'Crispian Younghusband used to send me things.'

'What things?' the detective asked. He had a notebook out and he pushed aside some papers on the table so that he could have a surface to write on. He was going to make a list.

Michaela recited and he wrote slowly, in capital letters, as if it was important. A sachet of liquid soap, flowers, stockings. 'I don't remember everything,' Michaela said. She had left out the condoms.

'And you accepted these gifts?'

'Well.' Michaela bit her lip. 'It seemed a little churlish to refuse them, or to send them back. I thought of Joy Beamish as a lonely old woman whose only outlet was her stories and her writing, even if it wasn't any good. I thought she would have been hurt if I'd rejected her offerings. I rejected everything else.'

Janus gave a hollow laugh. 'Joy Beamish was hurt all right,' he said. 'Rejected enough to want to kill you.'

Michaela hadn't yet found a motive for Crispian Younghusband actually wanting to kill her. She found it hard to believe that an eleven year old child would have carried such hatred with him through the years as to reach such a drastic climax. Was it revenge for the boiler room or the extraordinarily subtle power of a standard rejection letter? Surely not. Surely Crispian (Joy) hadn't felt so strongly about his stories not making the grade? It wasn't as if she hadn't been civil to him over the years. Dismissive, yes. Cool, sometimes. And only the last time, when she had been in an uncharitable frame of mind, had she written to tell him that he lacked talent in the one medium in which he appeared to want to shine. But was that enough motivation to want to kill someone? And had he in fact gone to the orchard intending to kill her? These were all questions never to find answers.

The detective sighed. He put away his notebook and stubbed his cigarette out in an ashtray. He shook his head. 'An unfortunate business,' he said.

Michaela said nothing.

'Are we finished here?' Janus asked. 'Is there anything more we can help you with?'

'Not for the moment. I will stay in touch.'

'What are you going to do with all this stuff?' Michaela asked, gesturing at the table and the papers on the floor.

Janus was wandering round the room, poking at pieces of paper, flipping open notebooks.

'We have managed to contact his next of kin,' the detective told her. 'His father, who is flying out from England.'

'My dad,' Janus chipped in. 'My Dad Says.' He gave a wild hiccup of laughter from across the room. 'I'm sorry.'

Michaela's lips twitched. She looked as if she wasn't sure whether she wanted to laugh or cry.

'Sorry?' The detective looked from one to the other with his eyebrows raised.

Michaela couldn't allow herself to speak. Janus came back to the table. 'We're a little overwrought,' he said. 'This whole affair has been very traumatic for all of us. We have tragically lost our cousin, and this latest revelation isn't too digestible right now. If you don't mind, I think I'd better get my sister home.'

'Of course,' said the detective. 'You're free to go.'

'You'll get in touch if there's anything further?'

The detective nodded. He tapped a cigarette on the

back of its box and fumbled in his trouser pocket for a lighter.

In the car Michaela didn't feel much like laughing any more. She leaned her head against the window. 'Jesus,' she said. 'Joy Beamish.'

'Look on the bright side,' Janus said grimly. 'It's one less aspirant writer you'll have to deal with.'

Michaela didn't reply, nor could she raise a smile.

'It begins to make a kind of crazy sense,' Janus continued. 'Crispian Younghusband's obsession with you.' He turned the car into Michaela's driveway. 'And,' he went on, 'perhaps this will give us more clues.'

'What?' Michaela looked over at him.

'This.' Janus drew a hardbacked book out from beneath his jacket.

Michaela frowned, puzzled. Susan had appeared at the front of the house, flinging the door wide and staring at them anxiously. She didn't like to be left alone for long.

'I think it's a diary,' Janus said. 'Although I didn't get a good enough look while the cop's back was turned.'

'You took it out of the apartment?' Michaela asked. 'Don't you think that's a little risky? Tampering with evidence or something?' She also doubted she would want Crispian Younghusband's outpourings anywhere near her.

'Oh, they'll never notice,' Janus said confidently. 'There was so much junk in there, one notebook isn't going to be missed.'

Michaela got out of the car. She faced Janus across the roof. 'They've probably done an inventory,' she pointed out.

'Then we'll deny everything,' Janus said promptly. 'Let's see if Suzy's got the kettle on.'

Florida had come over with news from school and a bagful of homework for Susan. Susan picked through her maths book with a desultory hand.

'When are you coming back to school?' Florida asked her, her eyes flickering over to Michaela who was filling a kettle at the kitchen sink.

'Oh, tomorrow,' Susan said, sighing.

'That's Saturday.'

'Whatever.' Susan closed the book as if it were far too heavy. 'I'll get into this over the weekend, I guess,' she said. 'Thanks, Flor.'

'I brought videos,' Florida said suddenly, with false brightness. She rummaged in her school bag. 'In case you didn't feel like talking.'

Michaela appeared to be stuck to the tap. She stood with one hand on the top of it, the kettle hanging limply in the other. Susan looked across at her. She was holding her breath. Then Michaela turned the tap on with what looked like obvious effort and lifted the kettle and Susan exhaled, her shoulders sagging. 'So what you got?' she said, turning her attention to Florida. 'No ill-treated horses this time, please God.'

Michaela was carrying a tray into the living room when Pauline walked through the door. She put her basket down and kicked off her shoes. 'It's hot out,' she complained. 'This is summer's last fling.'

Janus told her about Joy Beamish and Pauline sat listening, drinking a Diet Coke. She had lost weight since she'd left Tertius. Her hair was getting longer too, and it gave her round face a softer, sweeter expression. She made no comment until Janus had finished. 'So how do you feel about all this, Michaela?' she asked then. 'You look a bit in shock.'

Michaela didn't know how she felt. There was a

numbness in her head as if there was a lump of stone where once her brain had been. It was an effort to think, an effort to move. Everything had slowed down almost to a halt. She picked up a teacup in both hands.

'How do I feel,' she said. 'Consumed.'

'Not with guilt?' Pauline said quickly. 'You shouldn't —'

'By life,' Michaela interrupted. 'I don't feel as if I have an adequate coping mechanism somehow. I'm defective there.'

'It's natural to feel that way, I'm sure,' Pauline told her, putting a hand lightly on her arm. 'As long as you're not flagellating yourself over Antony.'

At the mention of his name Michaela felt a flush come over her face and neck. Before she could stop herself, in her mind she saw Antony crumple to the ground, his face surprised and a little annoyed. Antony occupied all her waking dreams; Crispian Younghusband still held sway over the nights.

'It should have been me,' Michaela said simply. 'It's as straightforward as that. I was horrid to Crispian Younghusband as a child. I was horrid to him as an adult. He took it personally. What more can I say? I just wish I could feel sorry but I can't. He was an odious person.'

Pauline tried to elicit a smile. 'He's out of your life now, Mick,' she said gently.

'Yes,' Michaela said. She put her cup on the tray. 'And so is Antony.'

Janus had been paging through the thick black diary, stretched out on the sofa. Now he put the book down and reached for the teapot.

'Well?' said Michaela. 'What does the diary tell us?

What pitiful little secrets does Crispian Younghusband spew out?'

'It's all one sentence practically,' Janus said after a minute. 'Didn't Joy Beamish know anything about full stops?'

Michaela and Pauline waited, Michaela looking resigned, Pauline expectant and curious.

Janus sighed. 'I suppose this was it,' he said finally.

'What do you mean?' Michaela asked. She got up and crossed over to the window where she stood leaning her back against the sill. The late afternoon sun was a shaft cutting through a gorge in the mountain and it shone on her hair like a halo. Dust motes writhed in a beam beside her.

'The "story" which we thought Tommy wanted to tell through the magazine?' Janus said. 'And we all imagined it was his life story and his whole undercover business? Well,' he ran a hand through his hair, 'Crispian had a life story too – and it's mostly right here. In hardcover.'

Michaela closed her eyes.

'The boiler room?' Pauline ventured nervously. 'The boiler room's in there?'

Janus nodded. 'Fraid so.'

'Oh God.' Michaela groaned softly without opening her eyes. 'Do you think the police have read that? Do you think they know it was me?'

'Michaela.' Janus gave his sister a quizzical look. 'It wasn't Crispian Younghusband's skeleton in the boiler room. That much we've established. And unless you locked somebody else in there, you're in the clear, remember?'

'Oh.' Michaela gave a shudder that ran visibly through her body like a live wire. 'Oh, yes.' She opened her eyes and smiled sheepishly and Pauline gave a relieved laugh. 'I am, aren't I? I guess that's one mistake I don't have to pay for any more.'

Then Janus told them what was in the diary and it was a record remarkable for its pain and its detail. And Michaela was there on every page, from the golden-haired child with the long, quick legs, who laughed and scoffed and tormented, and who sometimes gave something, some small thing, that was cherished and cosseted and turned inside out until it became something other, a sign of encouragement and a sign of hope. It was a story of a boy with no friends who had stumbled into a charmed circle, a magic circle of gifted, confident children, who made the rules and bent and broke them at will and who never had to handle the consequences. The circle repelled and attracted at the same time. It drew the boy to its perimeter and it kept him there, always looking in, never able to step over the boundary. And in the centre was the golden-haired child, dancing, spinning, beckoning, and then whirling away to a place of shared and private jokes for which he would never have the code.

Then came the dark time, the terror. The silence. The blackness. Fingernails bleeding and tearing at the lining of a solid door. Shouting for help and hearing nothing but the echo of his own voice. Stumbling, tripping and finally crouching down beside a huge warm shape, exhausted and afraid, not knowing the hour or the day, not able to see the time on his own wristwatch or the fingers in front of his face. The only thing in his pocket a silver locket from the golden-haired child. How he had wished on that locket, prayed on it, held onto it in the blackness. And how, finally, there had been light, a faint whisper of light, and pain, and blood, hot, wet and bitter.

'What's he talking about?' Pauline asked. 'Who let him out?'

'I'm not sure,' Janus replied. 'But he must have been damaged in some way. Unless this is later. It's not clear. The whole thing is disjointed.'

'Somebody must have heard him eventually,' said Pauline, 'thank goodness.'

Michaela was scowling.

'Shall I go on?' Janus asked.

'Yes,' said Pauline.

'Suit yourself,' said Michaela. 'This story doesn't move me, I'm afraid.'

'There's a big gap,' Janus continued, 'but it seems that Crispian Younghusband was still at Bricknell Court the next holidays. Unless what follows is all made up or fantasy. But it seems that the boy – he always calls him "the boy". You, Michaela, go from golden-haired child to "M" round about now – well, the boy saw the enchanted children again, but he didn't venture near them. He watched them instead, from his window, from a distance, but that was all. He never showed himself again, never tried to become a part of their lives. Then come gaps again and bits of cranky poetry, Joy Beamish, no doubt, in pupa stage. And the beginnings of stories with golden-haired heroines who get kidnapped and tortured and then fall in love with their captors. Did Joy Beamish ever send in any stories like that?'

'All the time,' said Michaela, looking dejected again. 'One particularly memorable one with tarantulas and cobras in a pit. I thought she'd been reading Edgar Allen Poe.'

'And the hero is always pretty hot stuff?'

'Dream on,' said Michaela. 'Fat slob.'

'Is that all?' Pauline interrupted.

'Oh, no, there's much more,' Janus replied. 'But it's very muddled. Some of it seems to be in past tense, some in the present. It's hard to get a fix on where he's at. But Michaela runs through it like a trail of breadcrumbs.' He looked at his sister apologetically. 'He loved you. He hated you. He wanted you to suffer like he suffered, whatever that means. He wanted you to feel what it was like to be him. And instead you thrived. You flourished. He followed your every move. You found a man. You had a child. You went from strength to strength in your career. You couldn't put a foot wrong. It's uncanny how much he knew about you.'

Pauline shivered. She put her hand on the side of the teapot, then poured herself half a cup. 'You'd think Danny dying might have made him happy,' she said absentmindedly, as if she were talking to herself.

'He doesn't mention that, not specifically,' Janus said.

Michaela was looking pale but stubborn. Janus hesitated, then held the book out to her. 'Do you want to read any of it for yourself?' he asked.

Michaela shook her head. 'No,' she said. 'Throw it away.'

It is dark outside. There is a strong wind blowing, a south-easter which rattles the windows and moves the curtains slightly, although the windows are closed tight. Michaela can hear Pauline gargling with Disprin in the bathroom next door. She has a psychosomatic sore throat because they are going back to school tomorrow. She has some sort of ailment at the end of every holiday. Last summer it was water on the knee and stoic hobbling to see the cousins off. A tragic grimace and a brave wave of the hand.

Michaela takes off her T-shirt and her shorts. She folds them up neatly and puts them on top of her overnight bag. She opens the cupboard in the room she shares with Pauline and checks each shelf for left-behinds. Her aunt Harriet always sends on a parcel of left-behinds after every holiday no matter how carefully they check. Once Janus's left-behinds consisted of his entire school uniform, even his shoes.

Michaela looks around the room for her library book. She is reading *Anne of Green Gables* for the third time. She removes the bookmark, an I Love the Communist Party bumper sticker David passed on to her, and climbs into bed. She turns on her bedside light and plumps the pillows up behind her head. The wind sounds like it is reaching gale force proportions. It buffets the building so hard she almost fancies she can feel it swaying on its foundations. She gets up and looks out of the window, pressing her face against the glass and shielding her eyes. The trees in the orchard are a crowding, thrashing welter of bending branches. She hears a faint tinkle of glass and is aware of a sudden blackness in the vicinity of the coalshed and the boiler room where a light has blown out.

The boiler room.

Abruptly, with a lurch of the stomach, Michaela remembers Crispian Younghusband. She looks at the clock on the dresser. It is past nine. Janus is already asleep. Antony is talking to his uncle and aunt in the living room. Pauline is in her pyjamas. Michaela had undertaken to go back and let him out before it got dark. Hours have passed and it has completely slipped her mind. She looks at the clock again. Should she put on her clothes and try to sneak out without being detected? It is unlikely that she can pull this off and if caught, what excuse could she give? Not the truth. Never that.

After a long minute Michaela carefully closes the curtains. She gets back into bed. She opens her book, smoothing down the pages, and with a peaceful, attentive expression of deep concentration, she begins to read.

· 20 ·

Chloë was doing her exercises. 'I had a friend once,' she panted, lying back on Janus's exercise mat and lifting her legs, one at a time, pointing her toes, 'who was into cross-dressing.'

Janus froze. He cleared his throat and looked down at her, not wanting to make an inappropriate response. 'Ah —'

'Yes.' Chloë smiled grimly, her face contorted. 'At university. We were partners in zoo.'

'In what?'

'Zoology. We helped each other with our experiments and things. His name was Barnaby Rudge — can you believe that?' She laughed, wheezing. 'He was really great, Barnaby. He had a big barrelly laugh that came up from his toes and eyebrows that were naturally curly. He looked like a rugby prop, but he was the biggest softie going. Not gay, or anything —' she glanced at Janus '— just big-hearted and kind. He used to cover for me when I couldn't manage the squeamish bits. I was never any good at slicing things open. Even plants.' She sighed, sat up and rested her arms on her knees.

'And he was . . .?'

'Oh. Yes. Actually he was quite open about it, at least with me. It wasn't a big deal. He liked women's underwear mostly. It just gave him a buzz somehow. I went with him once to Woolworths and he made me help him pick out these huge silky bloomers, size forty-two or something. I'm sure the sales assistant thought they must have been for a brothel-keeping grandmother. We laughed about it a lot, but I think he was really serious.' She started doing slow sit-ups. The front of her leotard was wet with perspiration. 'It wasn't a big deal,' she said again.

Janus tidied Antony's prints into a pile and began putting them back in their box.

'He got married to a nurse with a lute,' Chloë added.

'Rich, huh?'

'The musical instrument.' Chloë sat up and threw a cushion at him. 'I remember she did a turn at her own wedding.'

Janus looked at Chloë in her lilac legwarmers and felt a spontaneous surge of affection. She had an artless, open face and childish freckles across the bridge of her nose. She was no longer shy with him. She chattered to him as if they had been friends for a long time, and sometimes he felt they had.

'What are you going to do with those?' Chloë asked, gesturing at the box of pictures.

'Well, the ... er ... transvestite pictures should be sent off to the States,' Janus told her, riffling nonchalantly through them, as if they were comfortably familiar. 'I managed to find a letter from the editor of the journal; I've already written to him.'

'Had your cousin finished the article?'

'I don't think so,' Janus said. 'At least I couldn't find it.' He had turned Antony's apartment upside down, scrutinised every flounce and frock in every picture. 'Perhaps it doesn't matter very much. The photographs are an essay in themselves.'

'Why don't you finish it?' Chloë asked, looking at him briefly and then looking away. She put one foot behind her neck.

Janus looked carefully at her profile, but she sat motionless, contorted and inscrutable, playing with the fringe on the edge of the carpet with her long fingers. She didn't look at him again. He wondered suddenly about Barnaby Rudge and his size forty-two silk bloomers, but Chloë was innocent, serene. She had two feet round her neck. Then slowly she unwound her legs and got up to sit on the sofa beside him. She leaned over to kiss him on the mouth. 'I bet you'd do a good job,' she said. 'You're good with words, aren't you?'

Janus had told Chloë about the orchard and the shooting and about Crispian Younghusband. He needed urgently to unburden himself as days and then weeks went by and Michaela closed in on herself and couldn't be roused. All of a sudden Michaela was inconsolable. From being stoic and brave and even quite jokey some of the time, she seemed to have gone into a steady decline, as if the realisation of Antony's death had finally seeped through her system like some slow-acting poison, gradually afflicting each of her limbs in turn. She had become heavy and slow and her skin had a pallid, uncared for look that she seemed neither to notice nor to care about. She was preoccupied most of the time, starting when anyone talked to her and giving vague, unsatisfactory answers. Not even Susan could light the spark that had always burned so brightly and steadily behind Michaela's eyes.

Mater had finally come through from Stillwaters,

travelling on the bus with Juanita on her lap, hoping that a new and vibrant life would jolt Michaela into recognition that she wasn't the one who'd died. Michaela had taken Juanita wordlessly into her arms and the baby had grown still and passive and lay staring up at her with black unfathomable eyes.

Janus was exhausted. Between Helena and Michael, and Blanche who was still trying halfheartedly to involve him in trying to at least get the wedding postponed, if not permanently called off, using Antony's death and Michaela's depression as strong enough reasons on their own, and Michaela herself turning hopeless eyes on him whenever he was round there, it was all he could do to get through a day. Then Chloë had presented herself at his door, having read the reports in two newspapers, and had left again only to change her clothes and water her plants every morning. It had been strangely comfortable having her with him, organising his life while he organised others'. He hadn't even minded when she re-catalogued his CDs and turned all the jars and cans on his pantry shelves so that their labels were facing out. Chloë had not been particularly shocked at the Crispian Younghusband story, had not been awed by the enormity of their crime. 'The things we do as children,' she'd said, placing slices of brinjal in perfect patterns in a casserole dish while Janus sat and watched her. 'There's a perfectly natural cruelty in all of us, isn't there?' she went on merrily. 'I remember tying my sister to a tree once and pouring honey on her feet, hoping that the red ants would come and eat her from the toes up. She was three, and when she screamed and called for our mother, I stuck sticking plaster across her mouth.' She threw back her head and laughed. 'I hated my sister.' She laid strips of bacon of exact length across the sliced brinjals. 'She's OK now, though.'

'How are her toes?' Janus asked.

Chloë slid a look across the table. 'Well, she never wears sandals,' she said.

Chloë's sister was still alive. They went on holiday together every year to the casino at the Wild Coast, where she gambled away her savings on the Dream Machine. She did not carry a gun nor compose feverish verse.

Chloë opened the door of the oven and a gust of heat swept out at them. She took up the heavy dish in two hands and pushed it onto the tray. She untied the apron she was wearing and hung it on a hook behind the kitchen door. 'I don't know how long it should stay in there,' she said. 'Long enough for —' She beamed at Janus and took his face in her hands. Her cheeks were flushed from the hot air in the small kitchen. Janus pulled her down onto his lap and held her tightly.

'What is it?' she asked. 'What's wrong?'

Janus smoothed her hair behind her ears. 'There's something I haven't told you,' he said.

Chloë looked at him, her arms round his neck. 'Oh?' she said.

Janus waited. The timer on the stove ticked loudly. He disengaged her arms, one at a time. Then he got up and walked round the kitchen. They could smell the onions in the casserole. Chloë waited, on the chair, her hands in her lap.

'The locket I told you about,' Janus said in a low voice, so low that she frowned and had to swivel on the chair to face him. 'Michaela's locket.'

'Yes?'

'I swopped it for Crispian Younghusband's cricket ball.' Janus looked wretched, almost, for a fleeting moment, as if he might cry.

Chloë regarded him levelly, waiting. If the information, so suddenly revealed, confused her, she gave no sign of it.

Janus gave a short laugh. 'I have the ball still,' he said. 'At the back of my cupboard, buried in a box. Sometimes when I'm lying in bed at night I imagine I can hear a kind of humming sound coming from behind the cupboard door. I dream about opening the door and seeing it glowing, like some sort of evil orb, humming and glowing and levitating among my shoes.'

Chloë smiled gravely. 'Perhaps,' she said after a while, 'it's time to get rid of it. Don't you think?'

They stood together on the balcony, looking out at the dark gardens down below. There was a stream running through the grounds of Janus's apartment block and on the other side of it the lower slopes of the mountain beyond the razor wire fence. Janus balanced the ball in his hand, transported backwards suddenly through the years, feeling again the roughness of the stitching and the smoothness of the ball's glossy red sides. The signatures were faint grey smudges.

He took a step backwards and swung his arm. Then together they watched as the ball looped high against the night sky, arcing across the stream shining silver in the moonlight. It hung for a moment at the top of its curve, then fell gracefully into the brushwood beyond the fence without a sound.

Perhaps because it was now permitted and she was still revelling in the unaccustomed pleasure of free passage, or perhaps it was nothing as conscious as that, but whatever the underlying emotion, Harriet had not hesitated. As soon as she got the news, she had taken the first flight out from Sydney and walked into Helena's house as if she had never left. She and her brother Michael had always been close and Antony had been unashamedly her favourite nephew. During the lonely years of exile, Antony had been a better correspondent than any of the rest of the family, sending long, intimate letters and family pictures across to Australia, undeterred by the erratic nature of Harriet's replies. She had kept all his letters and she brought them with her, in two duty free shopping bags, and put them on Helena's dressing table where they remained untouched for the duration of her stay. Everyone was offering Helena paltry snippets of her dead son, as if in doing so, something of his life could be retained and recreated.

'Read them one day when you feel up to it,' Harriet offered lamely. 'I hoped they might comfort you.'

Helena had smiled faintly and given an almost imperceptible sigh. She had spent the morning parked in front of the wardrobe in Antony's old room with her face buried in some clothes he still had hanging there. Harriet, walking in unexpectedly, had seen the tracks of tears on her cheeks, two parallel silver lines in the light from the window.

One morning Harriet and Pauline went across to Mater's townhouse which had just been vacated by the summer tenants.

'It's ideal.' Pauline was excited. 'Why didn't I think of it before?'

Mater had offered the townhouse to her as a place to stay while she got her own life back together. Pauline was reluctant to leave Michaela while Michaela was so low, but the prospect of her own space nevertheless gave her spirits a lift. Almost like the farmhouse at Stillwaters, the whole of the living room was dominated by huge windows giving onto the sweep of the ocean and the granite teeth of the Twelve Apostles towering above the beach. She sat out on the patio with her mother, rolling up her sleeves to catch the last of the late summer sun. 'Imagine,' she said. 'I can take walks on the beach early in the morning. I might even need to get a dog.'

Harriet had a copy of *Focus* with her which Roz had delivered that morning. Antony's picture of her was on the cover. 'My first cover,' Harriet said, holding it out at arm's length. 'I guess it's not *Vogue*, and I know no one will confuse me with Cindy Crawford, but you have to admit the lines on this face have *character*.'

'Antony was a brilliant photographer,' Pauline said. She turned her face to the sun. 'Have you read Michaela's article?'

Harriet had. 'She writes well,' she said. 'She should turn her hand to something more creative some time. I think she could do it.'

'Michaela reads so much *bad* writing,' Pauline said. 'I think it gets her down. She thinks it would affect her own attempts – I asked her about it once.'

'Hmm. Like . . . what was that name?'

'Joy Beamish,' Pauline said immediately. 'Alias Crispian Younghusband. I can't believe you don't remember him.'

'From Bricknell Court?' Harriet shook her head. 'I can't recall him. You never brought him upstairs, did you?'

'Christ, no. Michaela wouldn't have allowed it. She couldn't stand him.'

'Poor kid.'

Pauline looked at her mother, not knowing for a minute which kid she meant. 'I know,' she said. 'But—'

'Yes.' Harriet sighed. She squinted at her watch. It was getting on for lunchtime. 'Michaela never did know the strength of the attraction she exuded. It was like a smell, even as a child. People were drawn to Michaela. She was enchanting, beautiful, wily and passionate. It's no wonder . . .' Her voice trailed away.

'We were all to blame,' said Pauline firmly. 'We all went along with it.'

They sat looking out at the sea. The sun, still high in the sky, caused a glare off the water like sheet metal. It made Pauline's eyes water and she groped around her chair for her sunglasses. Down below a game of volleyball was in progress on the beach. Four young men in Speedos with chains round their necks grunted and lunged in the sun. A dog with seaweed hanging from its tail whimpered and pawed frantically at something buried in the sand. An ice cream seller, leaning listlessly against his cart, stared off into space, waiting for the end of school and children with pocket money.

'Who *was* it in the boiler room?' Harriet asked all of a sudden.

Pauline sat up and looked at her. Harriet was frowning. She shifted her chair further back into the shade and adjusted her wide-brimmed hat. Harriet always cringed away from the sun. Just being out on the balcony had made her forearms turn a pale, painful pink.

'The skeleton?'

'A male child, twenty years ago.' Harriet shook her head. 'No idea, huh? No one come forward?'

'We nearly did,' Pauline admitted. 'I think Antony was half inclined, but he was trying to protect Michaela, as always.'

Harriet looked doubtful. The volleyball players had fallen down on the sand. They were wiping their faces with towels. 'You know,' Harriet said slowly, staring out to sea, 'I think I know who might be able to cast some light on the mystery.'

'Who?'

'Mr Bones.'

'*Who?*' Pauline thought she was referring to the skeleton.

'There was an old caretaker at Bricknell Court round about that time, I remember. Mr Bones. He was an old man even then, well past pensionable age, so he might well be dead by now. If he's still alive, he might have some ideas. I wonder where in the world he would be?'

Pauline looked highly sceptical. 'Mr *Bones*?' she said. She wasn't altogether sure that she wanted to play girl detective. She, like the others, thought that the sooner Bricknell Court was no more, the better. She wouldn't have cared if the bulldozers had taken out the whole orchard, the chestnut trees and Smuts's bench included. They could flatten the fig trees, gouge out the moss, obliterate the hopscotch squares. Good memories would be forever overshadowed now by an ill-fated midnight tryst among the trees. She had gone over it in her mind, over and over. If only Crispian Younghusband hadn't been armed. People were so gun-happy in this country. Every lunatic could get a license. If only Crispian had stuck to words as his weapon.

If only.

Still, Harriet's suggestion stuck in her mind. That

evening, at the club, she talked it over with Janus, who talked it over with Chloë the following day. Janus confessed to a certain curiosity and felt perhaps if they could actually clear up the mystery, Michaela might come out of her gloom. He half thought Michaela still believed, in a strange kind of way, that it was Crispian Younghusband after all who had perished in there. Sometimes he wasn't absolutely convinced himself. It had been a conviction so strongly held that it was hard to prise their minds away from it.

Then Chloë had gone away and found Mr Bones for them before they had decided whether or not to take the suggestion any further.

'Twilight Grove,' she told Janus simply. 'Your Mr Bones has just turned ninety. They had a party for him, the matron told me, and he played the harmonica and did a tap dance for the other inmates.'

'That doesn't augur well,' Pauline commented when he told her. 'He's probably got slush-brain.'

Still, they went to see him, without telling Michaela, uncertain if what they were doing was wise and not wanting to be influenced either way.

Twilight Grove was out of town, laid out on a huge ranch-like piece of ground, with hedges and bushes trimmed into fanciful animal shapes along its perimeter. Astonished into slowing their steps, they identified Bambi in bay leaves and what appeared to be a cross between a swan and a giraffe as they approached the main entrance. 'Where is Antony with his camera?' Janus exclaimed. 'Hey, isn't that Dumbo?'

'Why is it,' Pauline said, 'that the very old and the very young are supposed to identify with cartoon animals? Would it embarrass you if I asked the matron?'

'Don't annoy anyone,' Janus advised. 'Matron probably leaps out here with the secateurs herself on moonlit nights. She probably calls everyone "We".'

'She didn't on the phone,' said Chloë. 'But she did refer to "our Mr Bones" in a protective kind of voice.'

Having instigated this expedition, Pauline was now looking thoroughly apprehensive. She eyed a couple of old men in jackets and ties sitting side by side on a bench before a fishpond.

'It's not a mental institution, Pauline,' Janus told her. 'They're just *old*, for heaven's sake, not dangerous.'

Mr Bones was in the frail care unit. The matron took them to him, walking at a spanking pace through a field of elderly women on an exercise circuit round the corridors with gleaming steel-framed walkers.

'It's gonna be a photo-finish,' Janus said out of the side of his mouth as he skirted two granite faced grannies with their chins thrust forward, and Chloë gave a sudden hoot of spontaneous laughter which rang about the passages, bouncing off the pale green walls.

Marshall Bones was well named. He had small wrists and big hands with soft, parchment-like skin stretched thin against the knobs of his arthritic fingers. The bones in his face, too, were prominent, thrusting through his skin, stretching it like fabric until it shone. His eyes swam luminously at them from behind thick glasses and he had a hearing aid behind each ear. The matron had primed him and they did not have to spend long on introductions. In fact he seemed pleased to have visitors, especially ones so young. He had a daughter, the matron told them, who came to take him out once or twice a year but she had transport trouble and a circulation problem which affected her legs, and her visits were difficult times when neither of them seemed at ease. Mr Bones always perked up once she had gone home. He appeared to prefer to boast about his daughter and grandchildren rather than see them hanging about in the flesh. That way he could lay claim to a tribe of gifted offspring who led busy and fascinating lives and were a credit to him.

Mr Bones remembered Bricknell Court. He even remembered Harriet and David – 'the Commies', he chuckled, wheezing into a cough while Pauline scowled at the wisps on the top of his head. And he remembered, though not by name, Crispian Younghusband.

'That boiler room,' he told them, 'was always a problem. Before we closed it up and even afterwards. Kids. Kids off the street. Runaways. They would find their way in there because it was warm, even once it ceased to function. Especially in the winter when life out on the streets was very hard. One time I found four or five of them living down there. It was warm, you see, next to the boiler. But they used to mess – *man*. I had to get the garden boys in to clean up. Food, filth, *dagga*. Plastic bottles with their glue. And there was no sanitation, no toilet.' He shook his head. He had big loose ears, like joke ears, which were red and almost transparent. Chloë stared at them until Janus bumped against her arm.

'How did they get in,' Janus asked, 'after you had the door bricked up?' (Or out, for that matter?)

Mr Bones laughed and something in his chest made an alarming whistling sound. 'Oh, they found their way in,' he said. 'Whatever we did, they always managed to get in there somehow. Those kids. They could force their way in anywhere if they put their minds to it.'

'Do you remember Tommy?' Janus asked. 'The kid who played pinball?'

Mr Bones smiled vaguely. Then he opened his eyes very wide. 'You mean the half-wit?' he said. He nodded. 'He used to sleep in there too.'

One of the kitchen staff, in an apron with red toadstools on it, came by with a tray of plastic tea things. She put it on a table beside them. 'Will you be mother?' she said to Pauline, who took it in her stride, reaching out valiantly for the teapot's toadstool lid.

Mr Bones appeared to have dropped off. Chloë was looking at him nervously, but when Janus touched him on the arm he opened his eyes straight away, blinking and staring about him in surprise.

'Matron told us you remembered a child getting locked up in the boiler room,' Janus said gently. 'Did you let him out?'

Pauline put a cup of tea beside Mr Bones's elbow. He glanced at it but made no move to take it in his knotted fingers. Pauline wondered for a minute whether she should offer to hold it for him, but then retreated, not wanting to presume.

'Mr Bones?' Janus prompted.

'A boy got locked inside the boiler room one day,' Mr Bones went on suddenly as if Janus had not even spoken. 'Not a street child, that one, but a child who was living at Bricknell Court. We didn't know how long he had been there at first — we didn't realise. His family were very upset. They thought he had run away. He was not a happy child. Two days, three days — it's a long time ago now, I forget how long he was in there. Nobody knew how he got locked in there in the first place, but when he came out —' He laughed again, wheezing. He seemed to have forgotten he'd been talking and he stared off into space, his eyes beginning to droop.

Swiftly Pauline leaned forward and pinched him on the inside of his arm. Janus looked at her with his mouth gaping. 'Go on,' Pauline hissed fiercely. 'Go on.'

'He didn't speak,' said Mr Bones.

'He didn't tell anyone?' said Janus. 'He didn't tell anyone what happened?'

'He didn't speak at all,' said Mr Bones. 'For six months that boy never uttered a sound. Doctors, specialists, head doctors – nothing.'

Pauline sat back in her chair, staring at Janus. Chloë handed Mr Bones his cup. He took it slowly, awkwardly, folding his fingers round its warm, smooth sides.

'Then what happened?' Janus prompted again. 'Did he remember how he had come to be in the boiler room? How did he get out?'

'Did *you* let him out?' asked Pauline.

'Oh, no,' said Mr Bones after a minute. 'There was a coal chute which was partially blocked. He managed to squeeze his way up the coal chute. He was black from head to toe and badly scraped. They had to do skin grafts on his back at the hospital.' He laughed ruefully. 'He was quite a large boy and that vent was narrow.'

'Jesus,' said Janus.

'The coal chute,' whispered Pauline. 'The *coal* chute.'

'The family moved away then,' Mr Bones continued. 'They were in the transit apartment.'

They could see the matron coming down the corridor in her brown lace-ups. She fixed a smile on them that had them all getting to their feet and putting down their cups. It was quickly apparent that their interview with Marshall Bones was to be wrapped up.

'Did Matron tell you about the skeleton they found in the boiler room the other day?' Pauline asked quickly, bending down to his ear with almost a furtive movement.

'I can still read a newspaper,' Mr Bones said indignantly, cocking his head on one side and winking an unexpectedly lewd wink. 'I still enjoy the back page of the *Sunday Times* too.'

Pauline stepped backwards, disconcerted. She half expected him to reach out and pat her on the bottom.

'I think our Mr Bones is tired,' Matron said as soon as she reached them. 'He's not used to such a crowd, however nice it is to have you here.'

Indeed he did appear to be dozing off once again, although his eyelids fluttered slightly as if he was pretending. As they walked away, murmuring thank yous and goodbyes, Mr Bones lifted his head. 'A runaway,' he called after them. 'A no hope street kid with his dreams in a plastic bottle of glue.'

They walked out three abreast. Once in the sunlight they spontaneously linked arms, walking in step. Chloë pulled a leaf off the Bambi hedge and crushed it in her fingers, letting the pieces whirl away on the wind.

Janus and Pauline took an edited version to Michaela. She was alone at home, having taken leave from the office and dispatched Susan with Blanche and Harriet to Stillwaters for the Easter school holidays. Florida had gone along too. Invited or not, she was determined not to miss out on Mater's wedding. She had packed her bridesmaid's shoes just in case. The wedding was to go ahead as planned on Easter Monday. Mater had thought carefully about it and had discussed it with Michaela on her brief visit to town.

Michaela was adamant. Mater should not hold up her plans for her sake, and she was convinced Antony would have wanted her to go ahead. Antony, after all, had been the only one in the family who had not voiced strong opposition to the marriage from the beginning. It would be ironic if it were now to be shelved on his account. And who knew what obstacles Blanche would be able to toss in the way to postpone the event indefinitely if Mater showed the whites of her eyes now. There was a glimmer of a smile on Michaela's face and she clung fiercely to Mater's calloused hands.

'Take your second chance,' she urged her grandmother. 'You deserve another shot at happiness.'

Mater looked into her eyes. 'So do you, child,' she said.

Michaela slipped her hands away and looked out of the window.

Janus and Pauline arrived at the same time as Roz. Roz had come into her own at the office, taking care of Michaela's mail and finalising the judging of the short fiction competition with something approaching efficiency. At the front door she startled Janus by confiding in a whisper that she had killed Joy Beamish's fuchsia, the ingratiating plant which had been sent to Michaela shortly before all was revealed.

'How very bloodthirsty,' Janus said helplessly. 'What did you do – hack the heads off?'

'Oh, no,' Roz replied, stepping out of the way so that Pauline could get a key to the door. 'I merely cut its water rations. It lingered for a few days, but —' She gave a shrug heavy with meaning.

Pauline rolled her eyes. Roz was becoming a Michaela clone, or trying to. She had taken to wearing her hair the same way and had on a pair of glasses with frames similar to Michaela's. She wore a nice black jacket, also like Michaela's, but the bobby socks and black school shoes somehow ruined the whole effect. She was a halfhearted imitation, with prim, self-righteous lips.

Michaela sat listlessly while Roz gave them all an animated rundown on the status of various projects at *Focus*. There were many messages for Michaela, of sympathy, offering help of any sort she might require, of courage and support. Cards had arrived at the office, and flowers which Michaela waved away impatiently. Roz also had with her the final shortlist for the competition.

'The other judges already have their copies,' she told Michaela. 'These are for you.'

Michaela cast an eye over them. 'When's the deadline?' she sighed.

Roz looked nervously at Janus and Pauline, who looked at her impassively. They were clearly waiting for her to leave. 'You have a couple of weeks,' she said. 'Why don't you take them up to Stillwaters with you? A change of scene . . .' Her voice died away and she got up slowly, leaving the file of stories on the edge of the coffee table.

Michaela suddenly made a sterling effort. 'OK, Roz,' she said briskly. 'Leave them with me. They'll get read, I promise. You take care of things now.' She shepherded her towards the front door and when Roz had gone she came back into the sitting room and shrugged. 'Roz,' she said. 'She tries.'

They told Michaela then about Mr Bones and Twilight Grove, working up to the relevant information through the pruned bushes in the garden and the elderly women and their walkers. They told her about Mr Bones's theory about the skeleton in the boiler room. They told her that he had confirmed that Crispian Younghusband had got out safely by sliding along the coal chute to fresh air and freedom. Then they sat back and watched her.

Michaela gave a small smile. 'I'm sure he's right about the skeleton,' she said. 'I'm sure the police will come to the same conclusion.'

'I'm sure they will,' said Janus. 'Some street kid OD-ing on something. It must be almost impossible to track down next of kin.'

'Especially after so many years,' Pauline agreed.

'And Crispian Younghusband got out.' Janus thought it was necessary to emphasise this seeing that Michaela had made no comment. 'Through the coal chute.'

Michaela lifted her eyes slowly to his. They were cold and hard. 'Careless of me,' she said. 'I should have blocked it up.'

Pauline looked stricken. 'Oh, Michaela . . .' she began.

Michaela turned away. Her shoulders were straight and stiff. Janus started to put out his hand but then withdrew it. Michaela had resisted contact over the last weeks. She didn't want to be held and stroked. Only Mater and Susan could get anywhere near her. She turned around again, sighing and rubbing her neck. 'I feel so tired,' she told them. 'I keep thinking I'm going to fall asleep on my feet. Like a cow.'

They were all silent for a while. Pauline looked as if she were struggling with something important.

'What?' said Janus.

Pauline hesitated. Then, 'I can't help thinking,' she began, 'that we made a mistake all those years ago.

When we made the vow never to mention Crispian Younghusband and the boiler room.' She paused. 'And I can't help thinking it would be a mistake now if we were to put Bricknell Court and what happened there out of our minds and never talk about it again. My own instinct is to do just that, cut it out and pretend these last weeks never happened. But it would not be doing justice to Antony's memory, to ignore what's been going on inside all of our heads. There have been a lot of things I think none of us has been able to face up to. And I think it's time we did.'

Janus looked uncomfortable. Pauline, post-Tertius, had begun to display an assertive side which they had never seen in her before. She had even thrown away her box of affirmation statements. 'I don't mean,' Pauline went on steadily, 'that we should sit round and hold hands and pour out everything that's been festering away inside us for years. I don't think that's necessary or even particularly useful. But I, for one, am trying to confront things – issues – from that time which, I now realise, I've been hiding away from all my life.'

They hadn't noticed but they saw now that Michaela was weeping, quietly, with her head bowed.

Pauline raised her shoulders and then let them fall. 'It feels better,' she said softly. 'That's all.'

Helena and Michael were not going up to Stillwaters to attend the wedding. Helena was not feeling strong enough, Michael told Mater, and he didn't want to put her through the journey by car. They would come up for a visit soon, when the aloes were in fiery bloom beside the boathouse and Mater and Frans had had time to adjust to their new status.

They had agreed to allow Michaela to take Antony's

ashes up to Stillwaters to scatter on the river. The man from the funeral home delivered them personally to Michaela's door. She had to sign a receipt and take the surprisingly heavy box in both hands. ANTONY JOHN WHITEHEAD, it was labelled, CREMAINS.

'Cremains,' said Michaela. 'Jesus God. *Cremains*.'

She put the box on the passenger seat beside her, beneath her sunhat and shaded by Susan's boogie board which Susan had left behind. It was a square, cardboard box, taped up along the sides, with the logo of the funeral home on top. Michaela tried to imagine it being someone's nine to five job to tape up people's 'cremains' all day long. She wondered about the job satisfaction level in a task like that. Who would voluntarily choose such a bizarre career? She had heard a story once – which she had believed at the time to be true and now hoped wasn't – about how they apportioned the ashes of bodies which had been cremated. She had heard that the ashes you thought you were getting of your own special loved one weren't in fact his or her ashes at all. They just scooped a whole lot of the stuff together and dished out representative amounts according to the person's mass. You never got your own dear departed one's ashes at all, but bits and pieces of everyone else who'd been done that day. She imagined a cosmopolitan Antony on the seat beside her, a random collection of other people's dust. She wondered if there was anything of him in there at all.

What did it matter in the end? She was trying to dispel the morbid tone which had crept into all her waking thoughts. Gloominess and self-pity were qualities Antony had never admired or shown any patience with. For his sake, Michaela straightened her shoulders, gave the box beside her a brisk pat and set off for the open road.

Michaela drove fast, feeling her senses respond as they always did to the smells and sounds that meant she had left the city behind. The wildness of the tough fynbos and the sour reek of the grass told her that she was approaching the part of the country where the clocks slowed down just a fraction, where the pace of people walking along the side of the road was measured but not leisurely. Where a man would stop and watch a car go by and raise a hand in greeting.

As she saw the brown snake of a train in the distance, approaching from the opposite direction, Michaela remembered the last time she had been up here: the accident, their clumsy, humiliating attempt to talk to Frans; Antony and Emma. It seemed like a lifetime ago.

It was automatic. As the train drew nearer, she found herself beginning to wind down her window. The wind tugged roughly at her hair and she held it back off her face with one hand, keeping the other on the steering wheel.

'This one's for you, coz,' she murmured and, pressing her hand on the hooter, she lifted an arm and waved it back and forth. The train was parallel, close to the road, and she could see the engine driver very clearly, even the expression of mild astonishment on his face. He raised a cautious hand after a minute and waved back at her, smiling in a pleased and rather puzzled kind of way, as she sped by, aiming for the connection at the bridge. A metallic blast from the train's hooter followed her, echoing through the cuttings, pushed along by the wind.

Michaela was going so fast that she almost missed

the message on the farmstall board just before the turn-off. The stall was open and she caught a glimpse of a small child sitting on a stool in the shade beside the ginger beer cooler, brown legs scuffing sand. The quote was oddly disturbing although she didn't know why. It was from T S Eliot and it said, 'For us, there is only the trying. The rest is not our business.'

· 21 ·

High up on top of the cliffs, where the wind whipped at the grasses until they stung the legs, the beach was a biscuit coloured stripe along the shoreline. It curved around the bay and was lost in the mist off the sea, a path leading nowhere. Two fishermen with rods and tackle boxes trod steadily along the sand, making for the dark outcrop of rocks which could be seen rising out of the spray. They wore black gumboots and they walked with their heads bent into the wind. Sandplovers skittered up and down in front of the waves, their black legs thin as needles, racing over the wet sand. A child appeared out of the mist and stood calling, hands cupped to his mouth, until the fishermen stopped and turned and then waited while he ran to them, with his own small tackle box and rod bouncing in his hands. One of the men put out a hand and ruffled his hair and the faint sound of voices drifted up like a gift on the back of the wind.

The sun was beginning to go down but Michaela sat on, filtering cool sand through her fingers and feeling the sharp edges of rock against the small of her back. She had made patterns in the sand at her feet with her toes, intricate swirls and fanciful curlicues. She had drawn hearts and diamonds with the pointed end of a sharp stick. Now the wind had caused a fresh layer of sand to blow across her artwork. It was as if a very fine veil were being drawn over it, gradually spiriting it away. Soon it would be as if it had never been and the sand would be smooth and untouched as it had been before. A slate wiped clean.

Michaela had been doing this idly all afternoon. First she had written Antony's name in the sand and watched the wind obliterate it. Then she had cleared a long space for Crispian Younghusband and the wind had made him disappear too. She had added her own name and Danny's and a crude drawing of a shark and the wind and the sand had taken them as well, slowly, gradually, so imperceptibly yet so decisively. There was nothing permanent up here, only the rocks and the sand and the wind, as relentless as the setting of the sun and impervious as time itself.

Michaela knew the family would soon be getting anxious about her. No one had been happy to see her go out walking on the cliffs by herself. A woman on her own out of sight of the village was no longer a wise idea, even in Stilfontein. There was a time when they were children when they had all run wild up here, running along the dirt paths and climbing hand over fist to get to the top. They had had picnics up here and sometimes made their way down the slippery, steep sides of the cliffs to the beach below, crashing into the welcome chill of the sea, with the salt stinging at the scratches on their legs and arms. Michaela remembered Antony, burned brown by the sun, stripping off his shirt and running into the waves as if to embrace them, with his arms outstretched and then turning with the sun behind his head, shaking his head like a dog and sending sprays of water splashing like sparks. They had stopped going so far afield when they were teenagers, preferring to suntan on the lawn at Stillwaters and fall into the river in front of the house. And then a woman from the village, out walking with her dog, had been attacked and raped and Stilfontein had reverberated for months with outrage and indignation. They were sure it must have been a stranger to the area; no Stilfontein resident could have done such a thing. And yet, after that, there hung about the village a suspicion and a fear that had affected everyone.

Michaela had seen no one on her walk. Apart from the goats grazing near the top of the cliffs and a small puffadder she had very nearly stepped on in her path, there were no visible signs of life and the only sound was the low hum of the wind over the grass and the occasional gull wheeling up above her head. She and Danny had come up here when Susan was a baby in a cloth sling against her stomach. They had walked for miles, until the path meandered inland, away from the sea and led to farmland and wire fences. Once they had stopped at a smallholding and asked for water and the farmer and his wife had engaged them in a conversation about Dr Verwoerd and his educational policy as if he was still alive and a force to be reckoned with. The farmer's wife had not a tooth in her head and she wore an old Voortrekker bonnet with ribbons beneath her chin. Afterwards they were convinced that they had either dreamt the whole bizarre episode or that the old couple were ghosts. In fact, so disturbed were they by the encounter that they had retraced their steps a few days later, but they couldn't find the little farm again. Danny was even more convinced that they had experienced a breath from the spirit world; Michaela was sure they had taken a wrong turning.

Michaela said Danny's name out loud. It sounded flat and strange on her tongue. There was no one there. No Danny. No Antony. Only Michaela, alone on a clifftop with an infinity of ocean spread out before her. It would be dark soon and Michaela knew she ought to be setting back. By now, she reflected wryly, Antony would have come looking for her. She would hear his voice calling first, then see the familiar set of his shoulders, the long stride. The camera in his hand. Always the camera. What had happened to Antony's cameras, she wondered suddenly. She hoped Janus had them safely somewhere, that he hadn't sold them or given them away. She would ask Helena if she could have one. She wanted to hold something that was smooth and worn from Antony's fingers. She knew she was getting morbid again and that there was a thin line between that feeling and sheer self-pity and that there would be months where she would find herself teetering along it, dwelling in the past. But she knew, too, that there would be a point, a corner, which she would turn before she was even aware of it, when she would find herself looking forward again and not back.

'If I can get over you, Danny,' she said out loud again, the wind snatching the words as they left her lips, 'I can get over anything.' It sounded trite and suspiciously like one of Pauline's affirmation statements. She was suddenly talking more to dead people than to living ones. Michaela wiped impatiently at the last of her doodlings and got to her feet. She began to jog along the path in the direction of the village.

When Michaela got back to Stillwaters, she found the rest of the wedding party had arrived. Janus was there with a carful of presents, all giftwrapped in ostentatious gold and silver paper. He had brought Chloë and they carried the gifts in together, smiling behind the piles. Pauline had Ernest with her, in a cage. He looked mutinous and resentful, hunched over, clucking to himself. She showed him to Juanita who regarded him shrewdly with her pitch black eyes.

'I hope it's OK,' Pauline was saying to Mater, 'but I asked Frank to come up. He's been working so hard at the club he needs some time off. The manager of the boys is taking over for the weekend. Greenbacks is closing down – did you hear, Michaela? – and it looks like the boys will move across to us permanently, not just on loan. And Blanche, bless her, is staying with the late night slot for another month – or two, or three –' she flashed a smile at Blanche, who was painting her toenails on the bed beside the windows in the front room '– so everything's going, well, wonderfully.' Pauline threw her arms wide and beamed round the room. 'I feel as if we're on the brink,' she said, 'of something big and happy and positive.'

'Wedding fever,' said Janus dryly. He gave Pauline a hug. They both looked over at Michaela. She smiled at them and held out a hand to Chloë who was standing back, waiting.

'Welcome to Stillwaters,' Mater said, coming forward and taking her other hand. 'We're glad you're here to share this weekend with us.'

The evening was warm and they took advantage of it, carrying a trestle table out onto the lawn and building a fire in the old half gallon drum Mater used for this purpose. Frans arrived with fish fresh from the sea and Pauline quickly took charge. Herbs were produced from the garden, and lemons from a basket on the kitchen window sill. Rings of onion and knobs of butter. Chloë helped her wrap the fish in silver foil and they cooked them over the coals. The flesh was soft and tender and came away gently from the bones. Frans filled their glasses with wine and sat beside Mater with Juanita sleeping on her stomach against his chest.

Nobody spoke much. Chloë held Janus's hand and stared transfixed at the phosphorescent lapping of the river against the bank while the nightbirds called and the frogs in the reeds competed with their cries. Susan and Florida were down at the water's edge with their jeans rolled up to their knees, splashing about in the water and sending ripples of vivid light sparkling and dancing about them. They shouted with pleasure, holding up their hands and shaking beads of light from the tips of their fingers. Michaela kept her eyes on her daughter. Susan was probably the same age as she had been when Crispian Younghusband had entered her life. Did Susan already have some burdensome secret that she would carry with her into adulthood, that would sink and surface and resurface over the years and reach into her dreams to trouble her sleep? Did she already harbour the seed that would push its way through her system like a noxious weed, winding its foetid tendrils round her heart and her stomach, crippling and choking her? Was she even aware of its presence? Michaela hoped with all her heart that Susan was as free as she had always seemed, a child involved in a child's concerns, unharmed, protected. Her laughter carried up to the lawn and it was infectious and unrestrained. Michaela reflected that she hadn't heard her laugh since Antony had died. She met Mater's eyes and they held each other's gaze for a long moment and Michaela felt that maybe, just maybe, there was a chance that she could move on again, beyond, where life might still have something to offer.

'Come,' said Mater after supper, when Frans had gone out to deal with the embers and Janus and Blanche were busy washing dishes. She took Michaela's hand and led her to the bedroom. 'I need a sensible opinion.' She opened the door of her wardrobe and drew out a hanger with a plastic cover over it.

'Your dress?'

Mater nodded. 'This was your mother's idea, remember? And I'm having grave doubts. I think Frans prefers me in gardening trousers and slip-slops to be honest, and personally I think I'd feel more comfortable going up the aisle in my old church dress.'

'Let me see,' said Michaela. 'Try it on, Mater. I'll close my eyes.'

'Oh, I don't know . . .'

'Go on. Please.' Michaela lay back on the bed and put a pillow over her face. She could hear sounds of Mater wrestling with plastic and the continuing shrieks of Florida from the front lawn where she and Susan were running round with a torch playing a game which involved espionage and interrogation.

'It definitely looked better in the shop,' Mater said forlornly.

Michaela opened her eyes. She regarded Mater at the foot of the bed, standing meekly with her arms by her sides and a large price tag swinging gently from the hem of a shimmering gold dress. Blanche's influence could be felt all over the room.

'Hmm,' said Michaela.

'Bad choice,' said Mater, watching her. 'Your mother talked me into it.'

'I can imagine,' Michaela said. She got up off the bed and walked round her grandmother, first one way and then the other. 'Do you want me to be honest?'

'I'm not sure.' Mater twisted and looked at her reflection in the full-length mirror in the wardrobe door.

'It's mostly the length,' Michaela said thoughtfully, looking at Mater's bony knees from behind her shoulder.

'*And* the colour,' Mater put in miserably. 'And the style and this unpleasant cling-film effect that's beginning to make me itch.' She sank down onto the bed. Michaela thought for a minute she was going to cry as she put her face in her hands. Then she realised that Mater was laughing, laughing until the tears ran down her face. 'I get it,' Mater said, gulping and feeling for a tissue from the box beside her bed. 'I get it. This is your mother's final attempt to sabotage me.'

Michaela suspected she probably wasn't far wrong. Either that or Blanche had one unscrupulous eye on the outfit for herself. Michaela had cast a discreet look at the price tag and she knew what Blanche's budget was like.

'Well, there we are,' Mater said, beginning to strip energetically from the shoulders down. 'Gardening trousers it is.'

'Wait,' Michaela said suddenly. 'I've got an idea.' She pushed Mater back down on the bed and then slipped out of the door. She was back in a minute with a plastic bag of her own. 'Something borrowed,' she told Mater, holding it up. 'Try this for size.'

It was Michaela's own wedding outfit, a pearl grey linen dress with loose matching jacket. It was elegant, understated, classic in its fine timeless lines. She held it out. Mater considered it. She frowned. 'Darling child —' she began.

Michaela gave the dress a little shake. 'Just try it on,' she said. 'To please me. It should fit you —' She put her head on one side '— although it could be a little too long.'

Mater held out a hand for the dress. She held it on her lap for a moment, looking at Michaela, her eyes suddenly brimming with unshed tears. 'You know,' she whispered, as if imparting an awful secret, 'I'm so damn happy. I'm sorry. I know it's inappropriate, but I can't seem to shake it off.'

The night before the wedding Mater retired early. When Michaela looked in on her she found her asleep, with Juanita resting on the pillow beside her. The baby lay on her stomach, her head turned sideways and her black eyes watching flickering shadows from the paraffin lamp dancing on the wall. When she saw Michaela she tried to struggle up onto her knees, whimpering softly. Michaela held out her arms. She took Juanita out to the front room where the others were talking and reading. Frank had arrived earlier and he and Pauline were playing billiards. He closed one eye when lining up his ball and guided Pauline's hands on her cue. Florida, Susan, Janus and Chloë were playing Monopoly. Florida had hotels on every property and she watched the board like a hawk, barely waiting for a turn to be finished before slapping her open palm and yelling, 'Pay up!'

Michaela sat down in the rocker and held Juanita in the crook of her arm. She was warm and solid and her wild black curls tickled Michaela's chin.

'Has Frans gone?' Michaela asked, looking round the room.

Harriet looked up from the Ndebele pattern she was painting on an Easter egg.

'Yes,' said Blanche before anyone else could respond. 'Frans has gone home for his last night on the other side of the tracks.'

'Mother —' said Janus, glancing at Chloë who was smugly helping herself to a windfall from the bank.

'I can't believe,' said Blanche, 'that we are all just sitting here on the eve of the most disastrous day in Mater's life and doing nothing about it.'

'There's nothing to be done,' said Michaela.

'We've been through all this,' said Pauline, lying almost flat along the billiard table. 'Haven't we?'

'The rest is not our business,' Michaela murmured into Juanita's hair. She turned to her mother. 'Mater has made up her mind,' she said. 'She doesn't appear to be uncertain or insecure with her decision. There's no pressure in any way from Frans. These are all things we've established over the past weeks. There is nothing more to be done except respect and support her decision.'

'Harriet?' Blanche glanced sharply at her sister.

Harriet put down her paintbrush. 'Frans is a good man,' she said quietly. 'I suspect we all panicked for nothing. They will make a good team.'

Blanche made an impatient noise and threw up her hands. Pauline stabbed and missed and made a noise of her own.

'You shouldn't have come, Mother, if you knew you couldn't cope with it,' Janus pointed out. 'Why did you?'

Blanche snorted again. 'And who else, may I ask,' she demanded, 'is going to play the organ?'

Carpenters from Stilfontein village had been called in and consulted about the organ's chronic wheeze and had managed to get it functioning after a fashion. Asthmatic notes swelled and died, the wedding guests filed into the small Stilfontein chapel and Blanche, in body-hugging gold lamé and a pincushion hat, pumped desperately at the pedals with her feet.

Mater did not lack for guests on her wedding day. It seemed that the entire community from the village had turned out for the occasion to wish her and Frans well. Frans was a man much respected in the community and was known for his generosity and commitment towards his friends and family. They had come from far and near, some clearly intending to make a day of it, settling on the stony ground around the church from early in the morning so as not to miss a minute of the proceedings.

Frans's aged mother, in the rustling black crêpe she wore on all worthy occasions, took silent charge of Juanita, who had been dressed up to her neck in shiny white satin and squirmed uncontrollably. Michaela had a sudden feeling of *déjà vu* when the old lady began her circling round the chapel, crooning and holding the baby in her arms, and she couldn't help turning round to look for Susan. Susan and Florida, beautiful in identical pink dresses and flowers in their hair, stood waiting for Mater to arrive, whispering at the back of the church and swinging their confetti baskets. They had spent all evening making confetti, using discarded but carefully hoarded Easter egg wrappers. Mater would be showered not with pastel pinks and yellows, but shimmering purple, silver, orange and scarlet rain smelling faintly of chocolate.

Michaela looked around the church, getting the measure of true friends and supporters. She was astonished to see Jannie Brand among the crowd, sitting stiffly beside his wife and staring straight ahead. The Barberton sisters were there too, in gloves and hats. They had baked Mater and Frans a wedding cake and had brought it with them to the church. It sat between them, three white tiers on fluted pillars, with miniature arrangements of everlasting flowers bunched around the sides. The deaf postmaster and his son sat beside the organ. They smiled and dipped their heads when they caught Michaela's eye.

Michaela shifted her gaze to Frans, sitting in his black suit and bare head beside his nephew in the front row. He sat up straight, facing forward, his hands between his knees. There was a swell in the murmur of voices from outside the door and the sound of a car on gravel. Blanche paused with her hands above the keys and the priest walked onto the altar and waited, smiling out over the congregation. Michaela could hear Mater's voice outside and her laugh and the laughter of the children out there who had been waiting for hours for a glimpse of the bride. At a signal from the priest, and pumping furiously at the ancient pedals, Blanche breathlessly launched the organ into Handel's Wedding March.

Peter Barrett's wedding gift to Mater and Frans, although it would cost him dearly probably, was a night and a champagne breakfast in his hotel. After the festivities of the day had died down Janus drove them across the river in his open car. Someone had tied a variety of sinkers to the back bumper with fishing line and Florida and Susan had brought balloons which they tied to the aerial. Multicoloured confetti flew about their heads like fairy dust in a children's movie as they set off and everyone gathered on the road at the back of the house to see them go. Mater's candlesticks still lined the driveway and Susan and Florida had lit them all and they flickered brightly in the darkening gloom.

There was a lot to clean up and Blanche, Harriet and Pauline were already hard at it when Michaela walked into the kitchen with a box beneath her arm. 'Well,' she announced. 'I'm going to do Antony.'

Harriet turned with a baking dish in her hands. 'Now?' she asked. 'It's dark out there.'

Blanche went over to where Michaela was standing in the doorway. 'Is he . . .?' she said in a hushed voice.

'Right here.' Michaela patted the box firmly. 'Janus has already put *Christmas Present* into the water for me.'

'Are you sure you want to do this on your own?' Pauline asked her. She looked concerned.

Michaela nodded. 'I'm fine with it. Really,' she said. 'I'll see you later.'

'Wait,' Pauline said as Michaela turned to go. 'I'll come down with you with a torch. We wouldn't want —'

'No,' Michaela agreed, clutching the box tightly. 'We wouldn't.'

Janus had pushed the boat out onto the river and secured its rope round a heavy stone on the bank. Michaela settled the box on the seat in the stern and pushed off, rolling her jeans up to her knees. The boat carved its way soundlessly through puddles of phosphorescence on the black water. Pauline stood for a while on the shore, watching. Then Michaela took up the oars, moving one of them gently and rhythmically until she was pointing in the direction she wanted to go. 'Don't go too far,' Pauline warned.

The oars splashed softly in the water. Michaela

made for the lights shining from the Barberton sisters' house on the other side of the river. When she was more or less in the centre she pulled in the oars and let the boat drift on the tide. The tide was still coming in and she floated up river, slowly, bobbing smoothly over the little waves. She could feel the spray on her face and smell the strong night-smell of the sea. When she had floated far enough, almost to the bridge, she threw down the anchor and sat with the box marked ANTONY JOHN WHITEHEAD neatly on her lap. The sky was white with stars. Michaela threw her head back and looked up at them, remembering another night with Antony, just the other day it seemed, when they had lain together at Stillwaters and looked up at the stars, the very same stars which now seemed so cold, so bright and impersonal. Slowly, breaking a nail on the cardboard, fumbling and beginning to shiver in the dark, Michaela began to break open the seals.

Michaela sat for an hour in the shelter of the bridge. For the first time in what felt like a long while she felt almost at peace. Small fish jumped out of the water around her and the movement of the boat rocking against the tide was a comfortable, dependable motion. When all the lights but one, the single paraffin lamp they had left burning for her in the window of the front room, had gone out, she put the oars back in the water, pulled up the anchor and turned *Christmas Present* for home.

Suddenly she felt bone-achingly tired, as if she had been doing strenuous physical exercise all day. Her legs felt unbearably heavy as she went up the steps to the front lawn. She sat down for a moment on the cold grass, looking out once more over the blackness of the river, hardly able to see it now, all the luminous phosphorescence mysteriously vanished.

As she sat and watched, a huge white moon rose slowly up over the crest of the dark hills beyond the river. It hung, flat as a coin, directly opposite her, unrolling a silver strip of carpet over the water towards her, and she gasped at its extravagant size and the closeness of it.

Suddenly she heard a movement in the aloes beside the boathouse roof. There was a rustling noise and something that sounded like a hoarse cough. Michaela strained her eyes in the darkness, curious but not alarmed, expecting a shrew or a fieldmouse. She saw the bushes move. Then she saw a large pale shape moving behind them. And then, as the moon bathed the lawn in silver light, she heard a chirrup and she stood up, heart pounding, as The Dog crawled out from the stems of the aloes and staggered weakly towards her across the damp grey grass.

*Also by Alison Lowry
and available from Mandarin Paperbacks*

Natural Rhythm

Fran Phillips' life revolves around her small daughter Sophie and her circle of female friends: loyal, humorous Jessica; Mary, whose whitewashed farmhouse has always been a retreat; and Cassandra, whose tennis parties provide a welcome burst of frivolity. The easy friendship they share has helped them deal with any crises in their lives.

But nothing has prepared them for the shock when Sophie is abducted and Fran's world falls apart. Gradually, hidden tensions and conflicts rise to the surface, disrupting the natural rhythm of their lives, as each of the women's emotional strengths are tested to the full.

Natural Rhythm is a powerful novel of the unique bonds of female friendship.

A Selected List of Fiction Available from Mandarin

While every effort is made to keep prices low, it is sometimes necessary to increase prices at short notice. Mandarin Paperbacks reserves the right to show new retail prices on covers which may differ from those previously advertised in the text or elsewhere.

The prices shown below were correct at the time of going to press.

☐ 7493 1352 8	The Queen and I	Sue Townsend	£4.99
☐ 7493 0540 1	The Liar	Stephen Fry	£4.99
☐ 7493 1132 0	Arrivals and Departures	Lesley Thomas	£4.99
☐ 7493 0381 6	Loves and Journeys of Revolving Jones	Leslie Thomas	£4.99
☐ 7493 0942 3	Silence of the Lambs	Thomas Hams	£4.99
☐ 7493 0946 6	The Goldfather	Mano Puzo	£4.99
☐ 7493 9605 9	Fear of Flying	Erica Jong	£4.99
☐ 7493 1221 1	The Power of One	Bryce Courtney	£4.99
☐ 7493 0576 2	Tandia	Bryce Courtney	£5.99
☐ 7493 0563 0	Kill the Lights	Simon Williams	£4.99
☐ 7493 1319 6	Air and Angels	Susan Hill	£4.99
☐ 7493 1477 X	The Name of the Rose	Umberto Eco	£4.99
☐ 7493 1931 3	The Ex-Wives	Deborah Moggach	£4.99
☐ 7493 0581 9	Daddy's Girls	Zoe Fairbairns	£4.99

All these books are available at your bookshop or newsagent, or can be ordered direct from the address below. Just tick the titles you want and fill in the form below.

Cash Sales Department, PO Box 5, Rushden, Northants NN10 6YX.
Fax: 0933 410321 : Phone 0933 410511.

Please send cheque, payable to 'Reed Book Services Ltd.', or postal order for purchase price quoted and allow the following for postage and packing:

£1.00 for the first book, 50p for the second; **FREE POSTAGE AND PACKING FOR THREE BOOKS OR MORE PER ORDER.**

NAME (Block letters) ....

ADDRESS ....

....

☐ I enclose my remittance for ....

☐ I wish to pay by Access/Visa Card Number

Expiry Date

Signature ....

Please quote our reference: MAND